The Northern Blockade

M C Smith

Note

HMS *Burscombe* and her sister ship HMS *Farecombe* are wholly fictitious. The concept of these powerful sixteen-gun light cruisers for the Royal Navy never made it past the testing stages in the 1930s and was dropped because of difficulties with the design. In reality the last two Town Class Cruisers, HMS *Belfast* and HMS *Edinburgh* were originally intended to be those ships. For the purposes of this novel I have launched my two new superior vessels and it is they that are going out to guarantee British supremacy in Home Waters during the 1939 economic blockade of Germany.

Finally, for their helpful comments and suggestions, I must thank naval veterans Edward Hill, John Lillywhite and Kevin Price; and army veteran Lee Harrison for his knowledge of post-traumatic stress disorder.

Chapter One

Captain Charles G. Dollimore, RN

He had once heard it said that a story could be best described as having a beginning, a muddle and an end. For a long time he had carried those words around as a useful way of summing up his life. His beginning had been fair; a nice life of respect, professionalism and satisfaction until the muddle had suddenly kicked in. That had come about through the dire experience of the first monumental event that he would call pivotal to everything he had become. He was sure that the same thing happened to all men and women that went through any such dark trial; that every aspect of the memory remained never to fade. It had been with him for twenty three years so there was no chance of hoping that it would leave him now.

He counted himself fortunate that he had not had to carry the burden alone all this time, but there was no escaping from the fact that it had been and always would be his. His wife had been wonderful and understanding – logical and grounded as much as anything else – but the experience did not live on in her mind. It lived on in his. Sometimes he wished that he could talk to the other men who had been with him but there was none of whom it was possible to broach the subject with. That would expose weakness.

Charles Dollimore had been a mature lieutenant at the time in question and was literally on the verge of being promoted further. For the whole month of May, 1916, he had been serving with the Home Fleet in one of the world's greatest new battleships, HMS *Warspite*, with her colossal 15-inch guns set in pairs in four immense turrets. It was an excellent posting for a career officer as the navy revolved around its battleships. They were the key to Britain's maritime supremacy of the world. He had been busy familiarising himself with the ship and the men, finding her to be a tough old girl and the boys a keen bunch. He felt that he was respected by them and believed he was putting in enough hard work to warrant that promotion. But more than that, he was becoming rather anxious to do his bit in this great war.

4

With his son Philip having just been born he felt it more than ever. Of course, he was full of good cheer at the news and had even got a chance to pop home and see the new addition to his family. So happy was he that he sent some cake to the men of his division and they toasted his happiness with their rum issue. But it did nothing to assuage the feeling that the British Army, the Royal Flying Corps and other parts of the navy outside the Home Fleet were making all the sacrifices. This birth in its turn had set him to thinking of his son getting older and asking, in all his innocence, 'Daddy, what did you do in the war?' Would he be able to offer up a suitable answer?

Late one evening at the end of the month, the *Warspite*, part of a semi-independent force of fast ships, was given orders to put to sea from her Scottish anchorage of Rosyth in the Firth of Forth. Was this the day he had been waiting for? Had the German High Sea Fleet finally crept cautiously from its hiding place in Wilhelmshaven? That elusive fleet was the reason why the British had been sitting here all this time largely inactive. Until the Germans came out for a scrap the issues could not be decided.

Dollimore looked out over the assembled ships with pride as they proceeded into the North Sea. Far ahead, well beyond the great Victorian Forth Bridge, were the huge battlecruisers, six of them led by HMS *Lion*. Following them were the four *Queen Elizabeth* battleships of the 5th Battle Squadron, which was where *Warspite* took her place. Around them were as many escorting cruisers and destroyers as a man could want, and the man that this collection of floating fortresses belonged to was Vice-Admiral Beatty, a popular, charismatic leader. There was immense firepower to be found here. Yet still, Dollimore marvelled, this was but a minor element of the British Grand Fleet as a whole. He knew that more than a hundred other ships would presently be setting out from Scapa Flow in the north. Was it excessive? No. The Germans had nearly as many ships in their High Sea Fleet and it must not be forgotten that they had been built as a direct challenge to the British Empire and were one of the reasons why Britain had gone to war in the first place.

As Beatty's force took to the open sea and the day turned to dusk it turned out there had been no particular evidence that the Germans were planning to do anything at all. The Admiralty was only reacting prudently to an increase in enemy radio traffic in sending out the fleet.

Therefore they steamed lazily and without incident throughout the night. On the following morning Dollimore, savouring the sunny warmth of what had turned into something of a pleasure cruise, actually found time to relax upon the weather deck. The sun burned away a light mist from the flat calm surface of the North Sea and a wispy black funnel of smoke swirled out of the stack far above his head. It would seem that he would have to wait longer still to do his bit.

They continued on their way, aiming for a set time that they would come onto a northerly course to rendezvous with the rest of the fleet and ultimate disappointment, but then Beatty's battlecruisers suddenly started deviating from the plan. As those ships unexpectedly turned onto a southerly course it was Ordinary Seaman Hacklett who disturbed Dollimore to make him aware of it. Hacklett, a ginger headed lad of eighteen, whose skin was so bad that shaving his babyish chin subjected him to a terrible rash daily, had something of a speech impediment which Dollimore believed was put on in order to be obstructive. So the boy said, in his South London accent, 'Ol' Bea's 'e'in o' in 'urry.'

'Sort out your consonants!' scolded Dollimore.

'Aye, sir,' the boy replied, looking sheepish, though he was probably laughing behind the mask.

But he was right, the battlecruisers and some of the escorts were truly steaming off into the distance at speed. If something was finally happening then why was the 5th Battle Squadron still cruising carefree on its original course and not following? Oh well, thought Dollimore, our own rear-admiral, Evan-Thomas, has better things to do with his time than discuss his plans with me, a mere lieutenant. It would strike him before too long how unquestioning he was of the senior officers. But had it not been drummed into him and his fellow officers to be wholly dependent upon and obedient to orders?

A few minutes later, Hacklett commented again, but this time on the fact that the 5th was now turning onto a course in order to head off after Beatty. Up ahead, HMS *Barham* and HMS *Valiant* were turning to starboard and pushing for full speed. *Warspite* dutifully followed suit with HMS *Malaya* conforming to bring up the rear. What was going on? Why had the two parts of the force put such a distance between themselves? Was it not the idea that they were all to go into action as one? If there was some sort of trouble waiting over the horizon then the 5th and its escorts were lagging behind quite terribly.

Chief Petty Officer Collins appeared and strenuously reminded Hacklett that he was supposed to be helping his mates to stow away blocks and tackles in the bosun's store. Then they took themselves away leaving Dollimore on the deck wondering at the squadrons' odd manoeuvres.

A whole hour was to pass before the reason for the new course presented itself. At that point, Captain Phillpotts, high up in the bridge somewhere, ordered *Warspite* brought to Action Stations as the lines of ships cut their way through the flat sea at about twenty four knots. Dollimore proceeded to the upper deck roughly amidships, putting himself in command of a section of the Maintop Damage Control.

CPO Collins already had everything under control with the equipment and men. Hoses were attached to the hydrants and run out in thick lines along the wooden decks and water was then allowed to run freely from them. Having the decks already soaked was part of the fight against fire should they get into action. The damage control lockers were also opened and tools made ready and then the team stood waiting patiently. Before long the captain spread the word that enemy ships had been sighted and huge White Ensigns were ordered hoisted up the masts to indicate their intention to do battle.

All the men about Dollimore cheered. He himself shared a grin with Collins. That was crucial for his own expectations for he knew that the chief had some considerable experience with the war at sea. He had been present throughout last year's abortive Dardanelles campaign and was now looking positively happy at the prospect of getting back at the enemy. Any apprehension that battle might be a frightening thing was dispelled by this veteran's optimism. If he was not worried, then how bad could it really be?

On a personal level his life would finally be complete. He had a family who always occupied a place in his mind no matter what was going on around him, and now he was going to be able to tell them that he had played his part in defending his country and their liberty. Looking out across the water he knew that he could not be in a better position from which to witness what was about to happen. Hundreds of men were locked inside their respective compartments down below, completely enclosed and blind in machinery spaces or gun turrets. He was glad he was not with them.

Then it began. Just above the full power roaring of the Warspite's own oil fired machinery there came a rumbling like distant thunder. He leaned over the portside rail and tried to look out ahead while the wind, which had been created by the rush of the ship, whipped across his face. Some of the other men were with him. What could they see? Not quite an empty horizon. There was black smoke billowing up into the sky and it was clear that it was not all being pumped from ships' uptakes. Beatty was in action – with his force divided.

'Sa'o' ge'n' 'andin',' said Hacklett.

Dollimore turned to face the arrogant seaman. 'Do go away if you're going to speak to me like that. Chief! Keep Hacklett away from me!'

'Hacklett!' Collins then shouted as he stared down his nose at the boy, 'If you keep on bothering the officer like that then I'm gonna bother you till your bloody head drops off!' Then he took him to the other side of the deck where he could not see anything of what was going on up ahead. Hacklett, of course, feigned ignorance.

The constant roar of the guns just a few miles away was growing in intensity and a couple of those smoke pillars were now touching the bright cloud base which was hanging over the battle at about a thousand feet. Gradually the silhouettes of the German ships were taking shape. They, too, were steaming in line on a southerly course and exchanging heavy fire with Beatty's battlecruisers.

He was so taken with the sight of the enemy that he was only dimly aware of the Warspite's gun turrets being trained to port. The distant line had been gained upon and the enemy was almost on the beam. It was only when Collins said to him, 'You might want to put your fingers in your ears, sir,' that he realised that the range had been decided upon and the guns were about to open fire. The men in Fire Control had obviously been observing their targets for some time from their superior position overhead, and the German armour was now about to be tested by the battleships with a total of thirty two of some of the most powerful guns and heaviest shells in existence.

Along with the other ships in the line, the Warspite's guns opened fire with a deafening roar. The decks shook violently and the very air was sucked from Dollimore's lungs. Thick black smoke which was mingled with the dirty, sulphurous smell of exploded cordite enveloped him, making his eyes water and throat constricted. From what he understood of gunnery he knew that they had opened fire at extreme range.

It was all too simple. Great plumes of water cascaded around the distant targets while *Warspite* continued unhindered. It was obvious that the main fight was still taking place further ahead but nobody from here could quite tell what was happening.

Dollimore was getting the feeling that the firing was becoming routine after a while and his biggest concern now was that his ears were beginning to hurt and the effect it was having on the surrounding atmosphere was wearying him. However, if this was to be the pinnacle of his career, then so be it. He was a happy man.

Suddenly, Collins shouted, 'Sir, take a look at this!'

Dollimore shifted his gaze onto a sight developing far off the port bow. Four battlecruisers heading in the opposite direction came up fast to pass them about a mile and a half away. They were British. They were Beatty's, except that there were only four of them instead of six, and three of them were pouring smoke due to significant battle damage. The flagship, HMS *Lion* herself, had a smouldering mess near the stern where her X-Turret should have been. What was left of her 13.5-inch guns in that area were pointing out at odd angles, smashed and useless.

'Tha's 'e Lio',' gasped Hacklett.

'Thank you for that,' said Dollimore sarcastically. Shielding his eyes from the light, he added, 'And she's flying a signal. Does anybody have a pair of binoculars?'

'Hacklett,' said Collins, 'You've got the best eyes. Do you know your signal flags?'

'Aye, Chie',' replied the ginger lad. 'O' Bea'y wa's us a fo'arim.'

'Beatty wants us to follow him,' Collins translated. Trying to look out ahead at the 5th's own column, he saw nothing but *Barham* and *Valiant* steaming straight on into the fight without any alteration to their course. 'But if he wants us to follow him, then why aren't we, sir?'

Dollimore said nothing. He was not about to start discussing higher decisions which even he did not understand, but a doubtful thought did form in his mind. It once again concerned the flexibility in the command structure. In the short time that he had been with the fleet he had been trained to know that subordinate admirals and captains attempting to think for themselves was not the done thing. There were to be so many ships involved that, for fear of cocking up an action, they must only wield the power of their squadrons according to the orders given by their superiors and in no other way. Power was fully centralised in the fleet of 1916.

Yes, here was Beatty flying a signal for the 5th to follow his northward turn but Rear-Admiral Evan-Thomas, up ahead in the *Barham*, did not do so. Dollimore now remembered an earlier specific instruction that orders were to be executed only at the moment the signal flags were *hauled down*. Time was passing. The flags stayed up and Beatty was getting away from them. Again. Our saintly Admiral Lord Nelson would never have allowed things to get this way, he thought.

Eventually, however, the battleships did begin turning hard to starboard. Evan-Thomas had obviously succumbed to his own doubts about the signal flags and belatedly tried to conform to Beatty. They wheeled round in turn, leaning over to a considerable angle as they sought to head back on to the opposite course. The guns continued to fire as they went and midway through the manoeuvre, Dollimore got a grandstand view of what lay in the south. Beyond a smoke-blotched sea filled with destroyers, cruisers and battlecruisers still slogging it out amongst copious amounts of wreckage, was a huge fleet of powerful German battleships. They were all heading for him.

'We've run into the High Sea Fleet!' Collins blurted out. He was clearly no longer impressed. How could he be with over a hundred enemy vessels moving into gun range?

Beatty had obviously been aware of this over ten minutes ago and Evan-Thomas, only just catching up with the game, had decided that now might be the best time to obey the order to follow him back northwards. Whichever of the two of them were at fault – Beatty with his flags or Evan-Thomas with his hesitation – the battlecruisers and the 5th were clearly failing to act as a coherent force.

Soon after that the *Warspite* began taking hits. The sea exploded all about them and the sound of heavy detonations and metal fragments whistling through the air to clatter upon the ship's armour, mixed into a cacophonous fury with the sound of her own guns still firing. The deck trembled and Dollimore was almost blown off his feet by the shockwaves. Great foamy columns of water gushed skyward until gravity dispersed them and brought them crashing down again.

'Be ready, men!' shouted Dollimore. He and his team were awfully exposed right here but there was nothing to be done about that. They needed to be able to react to any damage inflicted upon them just like the other teams that were already at work elsewhere. With the entire High Sea Fleet on their tail he was sure to be needed soon.

Looking out through the smoke and confusion to starboard he managed to ascertain that, in the immediate moment, they were fighting no less than four German battleships that had worked their way up quite close to within a very few miles of them. Heavy shells were falling all about them and they were drenched from the tons of water that had crashed down across the decks.

Dollimore, as yet unneeded in any official capacity, continued to be astounded at the punishment that each ship was taking. Further aft he was aware that some casualties had been taken and astern of them, *Malaya* was a flaming mess. There was fire, smoke and torn steel aplenty. So shocking and real was the carnage that for the moment the objective was of secondary importance. By all the saints, the Germans were hotly contesting the British attempt to deny them access to the rest of the world and the 5th Battle Squadron, drastically outnumbered, simply needed to survive until it could rendezvous with some much needed help.

Explosions continued to erupt all around Dollimore and his team. As one they were thrown from their feet and introduced to an abrupt heat and the horrible smell of burning wood, steel and paint.

Dollimore had been knocked almost senseless. Feeling nauseas, he opened his eyes to see glimmers of daylight poking through the drifting smoke, and when his feelings began to return, he started to wonder that every bone in his body must be broken.

'Get up, sir! Are you okay?' Thank God for the imperturbable Hacklett, who was presently standing over him trying to raise him to his feet. But it could not be Hacklett that had spoken. This man had pronounced his consonants. But then there were no others who looked like him.

Dollimore murmured, 'I knew you were putting it on, you rascal.'

Hacklett smiled with relief.

Dollimore looked about him and saw his men in various states of alertness. Others were still trying to lift themselves groggily up off the deck while others were already wielding hoses and looking to fight the fires which had broken out near to their position. Just inside an open doorway stood CPO Collins talking on the phone. As he hung up the receiver and stepped outside, Dollimore said to him, 'Right, let's get to work.' He immediately knew that it was a daft thing to say but nothing else came to mind.

'Already on it, sir,' reported Collins, not paying any attention to the massive burn on his left forearm that had ruined the tattoo of his 'girlfriend'. 'I've made a report to Damage Control Base and we're to fight these fires up here until further orders, sir.'

'Thanks, chief.' Looking around, Dollimore saw that his men were gradually pulling themselves together. From what he could see nobody was immobile. Good. Although many of the hoses had been allowed to run water over the decks since before the action a couple of them were still laying on the deck waiting to be used so he called the nearest men to him and gave his orders. He ran over to the fire mains and snatched up the wrench thrown down nearby. To try and turn these brass handles without the aid of a tool would be foolhardy. Left is loose, right is tight, he told himself as he put all his strength into it.

Explosions were still sending splinters clattering about them and an impressive piece sliced its way along a nearby bulkhead taking off the paint as it went. It fell smoking onto the deck at his feet. It was the size of a football. How easy would it have been for that thing, travelling at hundreds of miles an hour, to simply tear someone's head off?

Using every ounce of mental strength to push these evil thoughts from his mind, he continued in his work. In some distorted way it was a blessing that he was kept so busy with the fires and wreckage because Warspite's dramatic dash northwards ended up enduring for close to an hour. Dollimore was quite unaware of the time, though, having passed from shocked surprise at the beginning of the action to a numb resignation. Anything that he was aware of just seemed like a confused hell. Doubtless his nerves had been frayed but all would have been fine if that had been the end of it. The battle was, however, about to get worse.

Having just re-emerged from the smoke-filled officers' cabins flat, Dollimore came across his team resting in a lull from the explosions.

They were exhausted and blackened and waiting for their next orders from the Damage Control Base. 'Chief,' he said, looking at Collins, 'Why don't you get below and have the surgeon dress that burn?'

With undisguised scorn, Collins replied, 'Did that already, sir. Bastard used some acid gauze on it so I had to ditch it.' He grimaced at the memory of the irritation to his skin.

'Fair enough,' said Dollimore, 'but don't ever speak like that about another officer in my hearing again. Understand?' Seriously, he thought, you give these people an inch and they take a mile.

Collins looked down, momentarily ashamed. He would probably take it out on the men later.

'E fle's aplo'i', sir!' shouted Hacklett, when he could get a word in between the fresh salvoes from the guns.

'Tell that boy to shut up!' Dollimore said to Collins wearily.

'He's saying that the fleet's deploying, sir.'

That got his attention. Dollimore quickly strode over to the portside railing and look out ahead. There must have been fifty vessels within view with nearly twice as many again beyond his sight. It was the good old Grand Fleet out of Scapa Flow! Now the Germans would rue the day that they had bothered coming out to fight. He could clearly discern the lines of battleships on the horizon trailing their black funnel smoke and beginning to deploy from columns into lines ahead. In front of them were many cruisers and destroyers. Although they were well spread out it still seemed like some sort of mass collision was inevitable. It was for manoeuvres such as this that strict adherence to orders was required so that this muddle of warships did not bunch up and run over each other.

So this was the Grand Fleet at its moment of supreme glory. Some of the men here had seen this before in the more relaxed atmosphere of fleet exercises but this was the first time for Dollimore. Seafaring was one of the two most important things in his life and he desperately wanted to be impressed but, after the experience of the last hour, excitement did not come easy. Before him was the most powerful fleet of ships ever assembled in the history of the world but the splendour had been robbed of him.

The 5th began to turn in line to starboard. Of course, he thought, our job is not yet done. We have to take our place in the battle line and continue to fight. Then the squadron suddenly began to weave back to port. Trying to make sense of where they were going, he realised that Evan-Thomas up ahead must have thought the fleet would deploy to the west. In the event the fleet was deploying to the east, moving out of its multi-column formation into one continuous line that would bring hundreds of heavy guns to bear on the vanguard of the enemy force.

Dollimore's weary interest in the fleet's tactics drove him to the far rail to look out and see if he could see what the enemy was actually doing, but the smoke hereabouts and the mist which it aggravated made everything too hazy. What he could see, however, were two heavy cruisers far out ahead attempting to make their presence felt. It was as though they were detached from everything else going on around them. Each with their four straight funnels, very high masts and turrets, he knew them to be the *Minotaur*-class or something very similar. They were both firing intensely but in turn they were being pounded mercilessly by explosive shots which showed them to be hopelessly outmatched. Get out of there, thought Dollimore. But they stayed and fought valiantly. Perhaps too valiantly.

The lead ship, swaying to and fro with pieces of her flying off at each hit, very suddenly exploded. The fireball burst out and almost instantaneously receded leaving an expanding ball of smoke and a number of splashes in the surrounding sea. The sound and shockwave reached Dollimore after a pause of disbelief and by that point the darkness that marked the area of death was clearing to reveal a terrible truth. The cruiser was completely gone. In her entirety she had vanished. He found out later that he had witnessed the demise of HMS *Defence* .

The display of destructive power was awesome and he found that this made more of an impression upon him than anything else so far. He was stunned and quite sickened, finally understanding how this 'great' war was dispensing with so many lives so quickly. Over seven hundred men had just been obliterated before his very eyes. He now knew more than ever that this was a battle that the Royal Navy could not afford to lose. The Germans must be made to pay.

Not fancying the chances of the other cruiser, which was now aflame and dead in the water, he looked out further to see if he could see anything of the German battle line. The low cloud, mist and smoke were making everything difficult to contemplate. The only thing that he knew for certain was the success of his own meagre work.

The *Warspite* was turning to starboard again. Dollimore was losing track of the developments but he did understand that the ship was not finding her way into the battle line. Collins, through the din of the gunnery, shouted something about almost ramming HMS *Valiant* up the rear. She was indeed a little close as the *Warspite* turned sharply out of the line and headed in the direction of the stricken cruiser and towards the enemy.

There came a large explosion very close by and the steel trembled. They were hit down by the stern. Soon after that the deck beneath their feet shuddered as the engines struggled to respond to the captain's requirements but, whatever was going on down below, they continued to circle towards the enemy. At a range of only two miles, which was next to nothing for these guns, the Germans spotted their new victim. Shifting their fire from the smashed cruiser, they then began an all-out attempt to destroy the *Warspite* .

Dollimore had his men duck back into a nearby hatch as tons of lethal metal splinters ripped their way across the open decks, sweeping away side rails, smashing scuttle glass and wooden boats, and holing all the thin, lightly armoured structures. Fresh fires took hold in the cabin flat aft of them and Dollimore directed his men into the fray, all of them gasping and choking from the thickening smoke and the depleted oxygen.

Collins was close by, backed up by another couple of men, directing the jet of water up into the overhead pipes so that what did not evaporate could smother the flames.

Then, from somewhere along the dark passageway, came an unearthly screaming. Was it a man in agony back there? The high-pitched howl sounded more like that of a small animal being tortured. Then a new, sickly smell was penetrating through the other undesirable odours. Burning flesh. Collins knew it for what it was in an instant. It had not come to them while they were working on the outer decks, but inside it was pervading everything and there was no escaping from it.

Splashing through the few inches of water that had nowhere to drain to, Dollimore bypassed the conflagration that Collins had managed to bring under control and followed the sound to the injured man. In his exhaustion the man had ceased his howling and was reduced to a childish whimpering. Dollimore found him lying half in a hatch, his jacket and hair still on fire. His fingers were already black with red immovable claws.

Dollimore quickly took off his own jacket and smothered the flames, then, using all his strength, he turned the man over. The face was charred. 'Just hang in there. I'll get you to the surgeon.'

'Sir, a 'ish a jus' kill uh,' gasped the man as he fought for breath.

'Hacklett!' cried Dollimore. He had not even recognised the boy who had been aggravating him these past few weeks. His ginger hair, white skin, and chin rash were thoroughly distorted by the heat of the flames. 'Don't worry, boy, I'll get you out of here.'

With shells pounding the *Warspite* until she was nearing the state of a wreck, Dollimore lifted the light, sobbing form of Ordinary Seaman Hacklett down two sets of hatches and ladders to the wardroom where one of the ship's surgeons had been tending to many of the wounded. The smell of burning flesh was intensified in this shadowy room which was lit only by the occasional burst of sunlight through the scuttles and the dim emergency lamps.

Hacklett joined those being calmed by overworked sick berth attendants and other volunteers who had found themselves put out of work through whatever reason. The cries, the shouts and the pleas for their mothers or mercy were unnerving but Dollimore tried to reassure the boy before he left. From this moment onwards, in his mind, Hacklett was no longer the arrogant boy who still had much to learn about discipline and respect for authority. He was a hero, deserving of honour – and a bit of good luck.

His anguished mind whirling with all that he had seen and heard this day, Dollimore climbed back up to where he had left his men still working to assess the damage and control the fires. So dazed was he that he had not even noticed that the shelling had stopped. He saw marred daylight up ahead and stepped out of the hatch. Squinting hard as his eyes adjusted to the brightness, he breathed heavily on the fresh air. The most astonishing thing was that there was a surreal calmness around him. He suddenly realised that the deafening noise had been stifled. That was not to say that the battle was over, however, because somewhere beyond the bow the sound of the big guns still raged out.

Astern, he caught a glimpse of that beaten cruiser steaming very slowly away like a wounded animal. Thank God they had made it. That had been a close run thing. As for the *Warspite*, she was still steaming ahead happily enough even though her smashed decks, scorched paintwork, scattered steel and wooden wreckage begged to tell a different story. The only other thing of note was that she was moving at a slightly reduced speed.

'Sir, I thought you'd copped it!' exclaimed Collins with genuine surprise.

Having stopped their gathering of tools and equipment, the exhausted members of his team were all staring at him.

'Just left Hacklett with the surgeon,' was as much as Dollimore could reply until, 'What's happening?'

Seeing the lieutenant looking around confused, Collins said, 'The rudder was jammed, sir, and we circled round twice towards the enemy. Got a bit windy, that's for sure.' But noting his lack of comprehension, he finished with, 'We're trying to catch up with the rest of the squadron but we're making water down below and can't do the speed. We're waiting for the commander's orders.'

Dollimore took in the words but his understanding was still jumbled up with the image of Hacklett's ruined body lying forlornly in the wardroom.

'Sir?' continued Collins, in a gentle tone, 'Rest easy. I think we're out of it. We made it.' Then after a pause, 'Sir, we've still got work to do.'

That snapped Dollimore out of it. Each of these men had endured what he had endured and if they were not allowed a respite then neither was he. 'Right you are, chief. Let's do it.'

*

For weeks following the battle, which became known as Jutland, Dollimore had been forced to wrestle with the emotions hoisted upon him by all he had seen on that day. He found that everything he had been sure about before was lost in an eddying confusion. He had gone from knowing that the Germans needed to be taught a lesson and that he was a cog in the war machine that was going to administer it, to a lost sheep clinging to service routine as the only thing left that made sense. How could he, a decent, conscientious man, have ever wanted that battle to take place?

As time went on it had become possible to come to terms with that question. He discovered that there were questions being asked many times over by millions of men caught up in equally hideous battles, though each man would inevitably deal with them in a different way. For Dollimore, he found that the strength to face the future came from his wife, Jennifer. Even distracted by battling with all that went with nurturing a baby in the uncertainties of wartime, it was her that had mustered the wits that helped Dollimore reason with his stresses. She helped him bring clarity to the priorities, first by talking and then by a devoted attention to written correspondence.

Some years later, when his son Philip was old enough to ask, 'Daddy, what did you do in the war?' he divulged nothing more than, 'I did my bit.'

It was impossible to elaborate further and it was Jutland that had haunted the muddle of his life.

Then six years ago there had been another pivotal event that he had come to feel sure marked the end of everything. Fair enough, he had not been court-martialled but he had fallen from favour most decisively at the Admiralty and that was very nearly as bad. He could barely stand to think about what had happened.

He cast all that aside and brought himself back to the present, for it was in the here and now where a new hope had emerged.

*

Summer, 1939.

The ungodly shadow which had been drawing across Europe's affairs had almost blotted out all good sense and humanity, but there was nowhere else on earth that Captain Charles Grenville Dollimore RN would rather have been right now. Bad news put aside, a great sense of relaxation and well-being filled his mind and body as he stepped out into the garden, the first typically English garden that he had seen for over six years. He kept his collar unbuttoned and the sleeves of his shirt rolled up in an uncharacteristically casual way and sipped from a glass of cool orange juice. He breathed in the sweet countryside air and looked about at the various healthy shades of green, red, purple and white that made up his surroundings. They were even more brilliant for the sunlight which caressed them from a clear sky.

His wife Jennifer had only been tending to the small plot here for three weeks but she had already worked miracles, turning it from an overgrown hive of neglect to a neat, well-ordered showpiece. He wished he could have done more to help but they had long since acknowledged that she was the visionary when it came to the creation of beautiful things. His talents laid elsewhere.

'There's no place like home,' was a phrase that sat well with him this year, for there were great things afoot. For a time he had been worried that when events began in earnest he would still be skulking about on the far side of the world. Undoubtedly, serving the Empire at a shore establishment on the China Station was important but it held no appeal for him. He was a highly patriotic man but one also needing an avenue for vindication, so he had been more than satisfied when his request to return to British home waters was granted.

In Westminster the politicians were working round the clock to prevent the coming war but Dollimore was nothing if not a realist and he could not see how decent folk could go on continually appeasing the tyrannical likes of that awful German dictator, Adolf Hitler, much longer. He was very adamant on that point. In another not-so-distant age he had also believed in stopping Germany's Kaiser Wilhelm II in his belligerent bid for European domination. He knew the barbarity of the Great War as well as anyone else but it had been necessary, just as this new war must be. It was a crime in itself that Hitler's evil had ousted all that was reasonable in his own homeland, but the result was that Germany was once again a powerful beast that was lashing out at others and needing to be caged. The Royal Navy was one of the world's prime instruments that could help achieve that. They had done it before and they would do it again.

While still in the Far East he had been informed that there was a command waiting for him in England. That had been satisfying but at that point there had still been a chance he would only be given a depot ship or, even worse, another shore establishment. He could not deny that after all was said and done, it did not matter how patriotic or conscientious he was, his career had turned out to be a rather chequered one because he still had as many enemies at the Admiralty as he had friends. So when he finally received word that his command was going to be captain of one of the navy's newest and most powerful light cruisers, everything just fell into place and he took to his new residency in England with a thankful appreciation. His professional life would not now simply fade out, leaving behind an unaddressed blot on his reputation. He felt certain that at the eleventh hour he had been given the best chance possible to be vindicated.

Jennifer could see that her husband was in an excellent frame of mind and welcomed it, for there had been times during the last six years when his turn of misfortune had seen him sink quite low. She had taken great pains to understand everything that made him tick and that had always been invaluable to him. What she had been able to do was help him rationalise his feelings in a way that was not always possible in the tight-lipped company of men. It had been part of her willing sacrifice to always be the dutiful wife to this officer, and so had always been careful never to overburden him with womanly trivialities. In return she had found his devotion to her in real times of need just as she would want. She considered that their marriage, now in its twenty seventh year, to be as close to perfect as she could want it be. Not everybody achieved that.

She stepped outside and stood beside her husband. With all her customary authority, she said, 'You would never have suspected that there were rose bushes hiding under those weeds. They should bloom now they can breathe. You can see that the petals are going to be pink.'

'You've done a wonderful job, dear,' replied Dollimore, his admiration evident. 'It's almost a shame that I shan't be able to see them in all their glory.' For he had only one day left before he was due to leave for Northern Ireland, where his new ship was just being completed in the builder's yard.

Suddenly, the flighty woman that was their youngest daughter appeared in the doorway clutching a handful of letters. 'There's some post in,' she said. 'It didn't take people too long to find out where we went.' Standing an inch or so taller than her mother, this blonde beauty had just celebrated her eighteenth birthday but they still could not help but regard Betty as a child half that age.

Dollimore had long ago learnt to let her comments pass. She did not have the wit to realise that they had informed everybody of this address weeks ago when his friend, Commander Stanley, had rented him the place. But what the girl lacked in brain power was made up for in looks and charm. Hopefully they would be enough to see her through this life.

'There's one here from Phil,' she said.

Jennifer could not suppress her excitement as she took the envelope and tore it open. Sitting down at the table underneath the parasol where she would not have the sunlight glaring back off the paper at her, she read quickly and eagerly. 'Yes,' she said, a huge smile taking over her features. 'The baby has been born, Charles. It's a boy – little Charlie. He arrived earlier than expected but he's healthy. Weighs 7lb 8oz.'

'Mm, big,' Dollimore commented. He knew something of these matters having been interested in the welfare of his own children from the very beginning. He could still remember the birth weights of all three of them.

'Sarah's doing just fine too,' she then said of the baby's mother. 'She comes from good stock.'

'So, you're grandparents at last,' grinned Betty. 'You're getting old, you two.'

Dollimore frowned at her and asked, 'Who runs rings around you twice a week at tennis, young lady?'

Realising that her father had a point and really was better at sport than her, Betty quickly fired back with, 'Well, you've obviously had fifty three years longer to practice, haven't you?' Then, her mind immediately flitting back to her brother Phil and his wife Sarah, she continued, 'You know, if we got a phone line put in we could actually talk to them.'

Jennifer gave her a reproving glance. 'You know full well that we're getting the line put in next week.' Looking over at Charles, she suddenly noticed that he was no longer smiling, that he was lost in deep thought. 'What is it, love?'

'Nothing, really,' he answered. 'It just brought back memories of when Philip was born. The timing just made me think.'

'You mean because of what's happening in Europe?'

'Precisely.'

Another child had been born just at a time when their very freedom was being threatened. Dollimore found himself needing to come to terms with the fact that Philip himself might have the same experience of war that he had done. The young man had followed in his father's footsteps by choosing the same career and was presently at Scapa Flow with the Home Fleet, himself a promising young lieutenant. There was every chance that he would have to learn the same truths that Dollimore had come by at Jutland and beyond.

'There really *is* going to be another war, isn't there?' Jennifer asked as she laid Philip's letter down on the table.

'I can't see how we're going to avoid it,' Dollimore replied. 'Hitler's picking on every weaker nation around him and making himself stronger. It's upsetting the balance.'

Jennifer made no argument. The last war had made her abandon the notion that was forever in the minds of younger women, that surely there was a way of settling the differences peacefully? That sentiment only goes so far, she thought, and then the fighting starts.

But you could always count on Betty to voice it in her own peculiar way. Holding out her hand to a squirrel that was staring at her suspiciously from the safety of a branch in the apple tree, she asked, 'Why are men so stupid?'

This time Dollimore raised his voice just ever so slightly. 'Young lady, I think you'd best keep quiet until you've thought through what you just said.'

Her only reaction was to give him a frumpy look. She understood that if he was getting like this then it was because of something serious – to him at least – so she contented herself to say nothing more.

'Anyway,' said Dollimore, as much to himself as to them, 'try not to worry about the war unless it actually happens.'

Jennifer exclaimed, 'I worry about you!'

'I know you do,' he replied, giving her a little smile.

Chapter Two

HMS Burscombe

Returning to the point where he could once again take command of a warship was very much the prime reason for Dollimore's satisfaction, but he did wonder if there could be a cynical side to all this. He knew that the present expansion of the navy required an 'all hands to the pumps' attitude. This meant that it was perfectly possible that he could have been given this position out of sufferance but, in the end, he had managed to convince himself that this was not the case. There was still plenty of scope for him to have been put in an out-of-the-way place but instead, he had been given command of one of Britain's most anticipated modern light cruisers, HMS *Burscombe*. He would never have been entrusted with this job if their Lordships did not think he was up to it.

He picked up his orders and documents for all matters concerning his ship in Portsmouth, not too many miles from home, and managed to catch a lift to Northern Ireland in the sloop, HMS *Grey Tor*. As she glided smoothly towards the quaysides of the inner end of the Belfast Lough towards the sprawling works of the Harland & Wolff shipbuilder's yard, he saw in the distance a few ships in various stages of completion and was certain that he had picked out the shape of the *Burscombe* amongst the others. He had sat for many hours in the privacy of his cabin studying the plans of this ship and, impressive as they were, he expected the real thing to be even more so.

He had also looked carefully at the list of officers who were already appointed to her, working hard to the requirements of their specialist branches. One or two of the names were familiar, most were not, but one name leapt off the page in a flash.

If this man listed here, Commander Derek Crawshaw, was the same as he who came to mind then Dollimore had not seen him since college in 1904. The two of them had been in the same year together; Crawshaw also having a brother two years their senior. Even though they had studied in many of the same classes they had no particular history together, yet Dollimore very well remembered the fresh-faced bully who had happily made the college a living hell for some of the others. That Crawshaw of thirty five years ago had never seemed to understand the practicalities of the technical bias of their schooling. That he had enjoyed college life was certainly true, but he had chosen instead to place more emphasis on the social aspects, or his interpretation of them, to the detriment of knuckling down to any proper hard work.

As it turned out, this was indeed the same Crawshaw. There he was waiting on the quayside when Dollimore stepped ashore from the sloop.

Crawshaw smiled, saluted and shook the captain's hand. 'Sorry, old boy,' he said. 'Try as I might I couldn't remember the face but I did remember the name. Dollimore's a bit of a rarity, wouldn't you say?' His features were quite soft compared to those of most men their age. There was still a certain youthfulness about him which was helped by the natural charm that he exuded. The charm was at least something different from the constant boisterousness of his youth.

'I suppose,' answered Dollimore, taking a second to look at the jaunty angle of the other's cap. Just like Vice-Admiral Beatty's from the old days.

'I understand that you wish to go straight to the *Burscombe* , sir,' said Crawshaw.

'Correct.'

'Shall I make arrangements to have your baggage taken to the hotel?'

'No, I've already taken care of that.'

They climbed into the car that Crawshaw had parked just the other side of the chain fence and he drove them off along the lanes between the huts and workshops of this extensive yard. He handled the car with a skilful patience, dodging the occasional truck or greasy labourer carrying material or equipment. Once or twice they also observed the presence of bowler-hatted men of authority, the venerated businessmen of the industry.

There was no great distance to go to the place where Dollimore had seen his ship docked but there was still plenty of time for Crawshaw to start saying, 'If I may, sir, I really must make a point before we get stuck in.'

What a way to begin. Not impressed, Dollimore looked at him and said, 'If this has got anything to do with college, I was not one of your

24

victims and, in light of the fact that that was over three decades ago, I wouldn't give a damn if I had been.'

'That's not really what I was going to say,' Crawshaw continued, unashamed. 'It's just that I've never really progressed in the navy quite as I'd hoped, you see. One or two people at the Admiralty have had it in for me all along but I want you to know that I understand the opportunity I've been given here, even if it is down to Hitler, and I'm one hundred per cent dedicated to the ship. I won't let you down.'

Already regretting this man's position, Dollimore asked, 'Is there something I should know?'

'Just please don't let old memories colour your judgment, sir.'

'I'm not much interested in any of that so you don't need to say it,' said Dollimore sternly. 'What I'm interested in is how you apply yourself. Don't do anything to discredit us; try to be slightly less presumptuous and we'll get on just fine.'

'Yes, sir.' Crawshaw could not have received a clearer message. It was just that he did have ambition enough to want his legacy to be something more than the mediocre image that people generally had of him. In this brief moment he had gauged that Dollimore, while severe, at least seemed to have an open mind. That was a good start.

What Crawshaw did not appear to know, which was almost incredible, was that Dollimore himself also had much to prove. Such was his own dubious reputation in some quarters that he too could not afford to mess this up. So it was, he noted, that as long as they stuck to this common aim they should not go too far wrong.

Crawshaw eventually gave a token, 'There she is, sir.'

But Dollimore did not need to be told. He was already familiar with the *Burscombe* after studying those plans and there was no mistaking the long, sleek, dark grey shape topped by two separate sections of superstructure. She had two precisely vertical-standing funnels with flared vents around the bases and a large open space between these and the forward superstructure. Only four ships in the navy had been built with this space. They were the two of the *Edinburgh* class and the two of the *Farecombe* class and the purpose of it was as an open flight deck for the Walrus reconnaissance aircraft. The Walrus was already a sticky subject with Dollimore because production was not keeping up with the demand and there were no aircraft presently available. Hopefully this situation would be rectified before they were due to commission.

Towering above the flight deck and superstructures were the fore and main tripod masts upon which men were at this moment rigging up wireless aerials and halyards, but what really caught his attention were the squat, enclosed armoured gun turrets. The two fore turrets were sitting at the fo'c'sle and higher 01 Deck levels and the aft turrets were situated at corresponding heights. Herein lay her bargaining power. Each turret carried four 6-inch guns and the sixteen of them, handled efficiently, were capable of delivering 128 rounds of high explosive shells onto a target per minute. This was thirty two rounds more than the next best ship in the class.

'If it's alright with you, sir,' said Crawshaw, 'I've taken the liberty of arranging a tour of the ship first and then a chance to meet the chaps afterwards.'

'That'll do just fine,' agreed Dollimore.

After stepping out of the car, Dollimore waited while the commander acquired some overalls. There was much activity on the decks of his ship. Tools and materials were being carried back and forth, sparks from the welding works flashed here and there and the sounds of grinding and hammering were coming from every part of her. Very noticeable was the flow of surplus materials, wiring and steel amongst other things, being disembarked by gangway or crane onto the quayside. This was a positive move for a practically completed ship that he intended to keep to a timetable.

Once they were ready, they walked up the gangway and stepped onto the dirty wooden quarterdeck which was littered with equipment. This mess will have to be sorted out, thought Dollimore, as he surveyed the chaotic picture crowned by the large Red Ensign hanging limp from the flagstaff.

Having removed his jacket before putting on the overalls, he then still deemed it necessary to keep his tie on and his collar fastened.

As a result, Crawshaw, ready to gasp because of the heat, felt compelled to do the same.

Three men immediately approached them. One, a very smart, freshly-shaved young man staring at them almost suspiciously through circular-rimmed spectacles, introduced himself as Lieutenant Powell, Senior

Engineer and Admiralty Liaison. To an outsider he would have looked a bit too young to hold such a position but throughout the course of his service, Dollimore had met many men who seemed out of place yet were exceptional in their respective branches. Such men were indispensable.

The other two were clearly civilians. Smart as they tried to be, they were both silver-haired and somewhat grizzled. The taller of them, Pat McAllister, had a knowledgeable if strangely insane look in his eyes and the other, Rob O'Neill, had his nose and cheeks blotched hideously by broken blood vessels. This gave a good indication of his relationship to the bottle. While McAllister appeared more lithe and healthy, O'Neill moved gingerly. His life experiences had obviously taken a toll on him.

'She's just about ready for your attention,' McAllister said to Dollimore, quickly checking the cleanliness of his hand before offering it to shake.

'Good,' Dollimore replied. 'Let's get started.'

As they began to head off into the starboard waist, O'Neill said, 'We both been workin' on 'er since layin' the first keel plates. I'm sure she'll be 'appy to see the backa me. That said, I can guarantee she's a fine ship, sirs.'

Always astounded by the degree to which a regional accent could mutilate the English language, Dollimore was immediately put off by the man. 'I should hope that she is. I'm more than aware of this yard's recent financial troubles and everything you've been through to secure more Admiralty contracts. There would be no profit in handing over a substandard ship.'

O'Neill's gaze became menacing. 'We never 'and over substandard ships.'

'I never implied that you do, my dear man.'

Then came the confusion. 'Right.'

It took the best part of five hours to make this initial inspection of the ship. With his nose gradually getting used to the familiar mixed smell of oil, grease, paint, ground metal and sweat, Dollimore fired questions at the three men conducting the tour, demonstrating his own knowledge and interest in their expertise.

Everywhere was well lit by the ships own lamps. O'Neill explained that the DC ring-main was now fully operational though electricity would still be drawn from the shore until such time that the boilers would be fired up, a much cheaper option than running the diesel generators.

Moving slowly along the confusing network of passageways and climbing up and down many ladders, they took in keen views of the engines, boilers, generators, crew's accommodations, and the various sections that made up the highly sophisticated systems of Fire Control. Dollimore would never pretend to have known the precise functions of all that he was looking at but he had spent enough time around ships to carry a basic knowledge in his mind. In that way his guides were happy that he was as serious as they.

Civilian workers were hammering, sawing, grinding and welding everywhere in the ratings accommodations. Chunks of lagging were still hanging from the pipes like saggy oversized bandages and a team of men, their hands and overalls covered in powdery asbestos, were pushing it into position in preparation to sew it up. Painters were daubing brilliant white matt onto that already completed.

Their inspection eventually took them up to the bridge. From here Dollimore could see out quite far across the yard of workshops and cranes to the church spires of the City of Belfast in the distance. He then looked down fore and aft taking in the long, pointed bow and the beam which was of no more than seventy feet. These aspects of her build were essential for her hoped-for speed. He remembered Warspite's sprawling ninety foot beam and the fact that she had never steamed faster than 24 knots, but then again she had been an entirely different class of ship. Just by looking at the *Burscombe* he could just sense that she was going to be fast – fast and powerful.

Finally, their tour took them beneath the quarterdeck where many of the officers' cabins were situated. For the foreseeable future Dollimore would be using the admiral's quarters, as was his right when there was no admiral on board. They stepped inside and viewed the dining room, sitting room and cabin. He did not find them immediately inviting. Even with the scuttles open the air was still stuffy because of the sun beating down on the deck above and, from just outside, every word shouted by one of the foremen could be heard as though he was in the cabin itself. However, the fine wood panelling, pleasing cream lamp-shades, soft bunk and the general spaciousness were plus points.

He turned to face the other four. 'I sincerely thank you for your time and patience, gentlemen, but once I've met the other fellows I shall have plenty of paperwork to do. Where's the furniture?'

Crawshaw glanced at Powell who glanced back. It was Crawshaw's problem. 'You're booked into a hotel, sir. I guessed you would catch up on your work there as the ship's not yet fit to be inhabited.'

'I will sleep there but work here, understand? Okay, we have much to discuss and a lot to do if we're to go to sea in two weeks' time. Let's get to it.'

Crawshaw wondered if the captain understood just how much effort he had put into this ship in the last few months. Would he be forced to motivate himself still further?

*

After the many months that some of the chaps had given to this job they had begun to consider themselves part of an exclusive family.

This was certainly how Lieutenant-Commander Stephen Digby felt for he, Peterson, Gailey, Crawshaw and all the others had thoroughly bonded through their professionalism and shared experiences, both of this yard and of the City of Belfast itself. Having been quite recently promoted, he had the task of being the ship's gunnery officer in charge of all the main, secondary and anti-aircraft armaments. Only the operational aspects of the torpedoes fell outside his jurisdiction. That was Brad Gailey's job.

He was pleased when he had heard that Captain Dollimore was on his way to take command. He had been a young midshipman in the destroyer HMS *Stoat* when Dollimore had commanded her back in 1929. He remembered it well. Many officers at the time had not much good to say about the Old Man but Digby had felt otherwise.

Although the Dollimore of ten years ago had been admittedly over-exacting and impatient, Digby's own father had been just the same so he more easily recognised that if you stripped away the temper and the intrusive stare and just concentrated on the words that had been sparingly uttered you would find complete common sense. His old friends from the Stoat's gunroom had thought him bonkers. He had heard that Dollimore had had tough times since but everything had been set right now and he could sense that the captain was back on top.

As the *Burscombe* headed out of the Belfast Lough on calm water and under clear blue skies, Digby stood on the bridge near the captain and his civilian counterpart, Pat McAllister, he with the insane look whose right eye was slightly larger than the left, or so it might have seemed because that eyebrow was permanently raised. Feeling the gentle throb of the machinery through the deck as this great ship pushed forward under her own steam brought to Digby as euphoric a feeling as it did to the others. It was the perfect result of months of high expectations.

'Well, Mr Digby,' said Dollimore as he observed how the instruments were behaving, 'it's come to my attention that you organised a cricket match in the spring. You and the officers of HMS *Belfast* against the best the builders could throw at you?'

Digby grinned. 'Yes, sir.'

'Is it true that you managed 550 for five declared?'

'Absolute travesty!' shouted McAllister.

Digby simply said, 'Our coordination and tenacity won through that day, sir.'

'As I hope it always will,' replied Dollimore. He turned to McAllister. 'Let's increase the speed.'

Shamed at the memory of that match, the grizzled Irishman stepped up to the voicepipe to call down to the helmsman, one of his own people, as there was still only a limited navy presence on board. 'Increase to 120 revolutions and steer fifteen degrees to starboard.'

As the ship completed its manoeuvre the RN navigating officer, Lt-Cdr Gerald Peterson, lowered his binoculars and reported, 'There are two fishing boats two thousand yards off the starboard bow.'

'Thank you, Pilot,' said Dollimore, easily slipping back into his old ways of command.

But McAllister said, 'Don't worry. The buggers'll get out of the way.'

Even though they were but an hour or so into their first journey, Dollimore began to yearn for the day when these civilians were off his bridge so that he could get down to some real exercises in discipline. Turning back to Digby, he said, 'You've come a long way since the *Stoat*. Forever in trouble as a midshipman, I seem to remember.' This was the first time that he had even alluded to the fact that he might have recognised him.

'I must say I don't seem to remember it like that, sir. It was all rather a good adventure.'

'Excelled in guns but completely hopeless at everything else. Wasn't that the trouble?'

Digby allowed a grin to slip. 'Something like that, sir.'

'I hope the cane did no permanent damage?'

'We've all been through it, sir.'

'Indeed we have,' finished Dollimore. There were no particularly happy memories where the thrashing of the cane over the buttocks was concerned. He had been taught, and certainly once believed, that caning was an integral part of a young man's instruction in naval discipline but, in more recent years, he had begun to think that it should not be necessary. He could not put this change in thinking down to his getting older because he could think of a dozen men who had become stricter with age. Perhaps it was part and parcel of the efforts he had put into managing his own patience and temper.

*

The gruelling but satisfying days quickly turned into weeks as the ship's trials became tougher and tougher. Every piece of machinery was rigorously tested from guns to engines and from capstans to diesels.

One sunny afternoon, McAllister took her up to the River Clyde in Scotland and worked her up to full power in careful stages.

His orders, which were relayed to the boiler and engine rooms on the telegraphs via the primary steering position far below, seemed to get sterner the faster she went. Provision was immediately made each time for extra oil to flow into the fuel injectors where it could be atomised in the furnaces which now burned at a temperature approaching 600°F. The throttle wheels were turned in order to redirect the dry superheated steam down onto the correct turbines and the huge engines began shaking on their mounts.

Standing in a central position of the forward engine room from where he could see the men working the throttles for the outer propeller shafts was Commander William Bretonworth. After so long working in close conjunction with the builders and that likeable oddball Powell, he was truly happy to see these machines achieving their full potential. They had been constructed and fitted well with only minor adjustments needed in the weeks leading up to this full power trial.

The turbine blades rotated at high speed within their casings, emitting a surprisingly small amount of noise. As this low noise topped out,

Bretonworth kept his eyes roving about the compartment searching for anything unexpected. There was nothing. He clenched his jaw and gave one solitary nod of approval. Like any reasonable and well educated engineer, he considered these turbines to be cutting edge technology, the wondrous culmination of experimentation with steam engines at sea which had been going on now for well over a century.

Up above, the sun that Bretonworth rarely saw shone down brilliantly upon the proceedings. The surface of the Clyde was flat calm. The time chosen for this test was slack water between the tides so that there was no current creating resistance, helping to push or propel the hull, and good fortune had given them a day when there was only a gentle breeze blowing. With these conditions prevailing Dollimore, McAllister and their guests from the Admiralty's design department would get the fairest assessment of the Burscombe's speed possible.

As she raced ahead, the long point of her bow was clearly defined against the thrashing white foam being pushed out either side and the sunlight began dancing in the spray in the form of a mini rainbow showing off all the colours of the spectrum. Her astounding progress also whipped up a wind of its own, eventually becoming strong enough to steal the breath from the mouths of the men on the upper decks.

On the riverbank was a pair of markers. They took the form of two long poles standing vertically in line down to the river's edge and, when they converged along the line of sight of those occupying the bridge, McAllister set his stopwatch running. He and Dollimore privately willed the great beast to go faster but knew she was happily making the most of her narrow beam and smooth keel.

The whole ship reverberated as the power from the engines thundered from her innards and a distorted, colourless haze of hot gasses pumped from her funnels. All too soon a lad nearby announced the converging of the second set of markers one mile further on and more than one person started furiously jotting down their observations on notepads.

McAllister, a veteran of a hundred speed trials over the years, ordered the helmsman to steer them 180° which, at this speed, made her heel over considerably in the tight turn. The few present who were unused to this sort of manoeuvring wondered how far she was going to roll and found themselves clutching at handrails or fittings in an effort to stay upright. Soon she was racing the opposite way back up the Clyde with the needle of the stopwatch turning. The thrill of the run continued for two more lengths by which time all were convinced she had a hardy soul.

'Reduce to 140 revs!' McAllister eventually ordered.

The relevant orders were relayed to the engineers below who adjusted the throttles, the gears and the flow of oil and steam. As Bretonworth busily logged the facts and figures for his own paperwork, McAllister was reporting the main result of the trial to Dollimore on the bridge. 'Average speed is 33.02 knots. Mean revolutions 299.25. That'll give you 9.06 revolutions per knot.'

'Very good,' nodded Dollimore.

*

The sun was sinking low towards a horizon displaying the hilly, green shore of Northern Ireland straddling a glittering sea. All too soon the trials were drawing to a close and many of the men working on board, civilian or navy alike, were fighting to stave off the need to drag their heels with fatigue. There were just a couple of days left, a final effort to be made and then the ship could be signed over to her new owners. The outcome was not in doubt. In everyone's minds she had already demonstrated that she was the ship they had always intended her to be.

As she steamed south-south-east, Dollimore watched Digby, accompanied by the torpedo officer, Lt-Cdr Gailey, conducting final trials with the forward turrets. Minor issues with the electric motors had been rectified and the turrets were now being turned their 240° arcs from port to starboard and back again.

The sky soon became a deep red and the wind gradually sprung up along with a moderate Irish Sea swell. Before long, the ship's pitching and rolling became more pronounced and one young apprentice, who had been standing with Digby, dashed to the railing to empty the contents of his stomach over the side. The officers chuckled and gave the miserable boy a light-hearted ribbing, encouraging him to consider the army if and when he received his call-up papers.

Then all of a sudden the turrets stopped moving in mid-turn, their barrels trained at odd angles off to port and the officers stared at them wonderingly. Within seconds they were dashing inside to find out what had happened. Those damned motors had failed again – except that the lamps were growing dimmer also.

Dollimore, standing up on the bridge, was already coming round to the idea that the electrical problem was more serious than faulty motors when all the throbbing from the machinery beneath his feet ceased and their navigation lights went out. 'What on earth?' he started, looking at McAllister, but he was just as confused. In the space of just a very few seconds this great ship had gone from being a thriving cruiser to a dead hulk with her decks beginning to fall into deep shadow.

Far down below in the engine room, surprise and confusion had gripped the men working at the throttles as steam had unexpectedly stopped being fed to the turbines and all their lighting too disappeared.

Bretonworth did not panic. Since first going to sea nearly two decades ago, he had participated in Damage Control and Action Stations drills hundreds of times over in eleven different ships so suddenly finding himself in a dark, claustrophobic machinery space evoked no more of a reaction than curiosity.

A few seconds of stunned silence followed during which there was nothing but the sound of other men's worried breathing, then suddenly the emergency lamps flickered on. Dimmer than the main lamps, they vaguely allowed these men to imagine that *Burscombe* was trying to come back to life. But, of course, that was not the case. The engineers looked back and forth at each other.

Their supervisor, an elderly fellow with a thin white face, quickly composed himself and asked, 'Er, talk to me lads. Is anybody aware of what happened?'

Another man said, 'We were losing steam pressure a few seconds beforehand, Joe.'

'You should speak up if you see somethin' like that, man,' said Joe.

The other turned his palms upwards. 'It were just a few seconds.'

Bretonworth, already losing patience, discarded his status as an observer and stepped forward. He firmly moved Joe out of the way and pushed a red button by the throttle six times. For what it was worth, it was standard navy procedure to use this reply gong like that in order to let the bridge know that he could not obey their orders. With his thick Scottish accent quite apparent, he quickly said to the nearest men, 'Open the main engine drains and close the throttles.'

As Joe and his men reacted to this unexpected authority, Bretonworth continued, 'Please tell me that somebody is standing by with the diesel generators?'

'They should be,' was all he got.

'Christ!' he cursed, immediately winding the crank handle on the nearest telephone. As he did this, he said to them, 'Be prepared to get lubricating oil to the engines and gearboxes the moment the diesels give us electricity.' Within the next minute he managed to ascertain that somebody was indeed ready to get the generator going, if rather slowly, and he then made his report to McAllister. The man listened intently and readily deferred any corrective actions to him.

He hung up the receiver and looked at the little crowd standing near him. 'Can anybody tell me anything more about what happened?'

They just shook their heads and shrugged their shoulders. Nobody knew a thing. Not wanting to waste any more time than was necessary, he decided to move his investigation on.

Along the shadowed, deserted passageway that Bretonworth used to get to the boiler room the emergency lamps had worked perfectly. He and Powell, short-handed as they were, had made a conscious effort since the beginning of the trials to keep the batteries in good order for such an eventuality as this and he felt happily justified for their diligence.

When he got to the forward boiler room, the airlock doors were already open. From inside he heard raised voices echoing up from the hot, eerie darkness below. He went in and clambered down the ladder. By the light of the lamps he could see a small crowd of civilian engineers arguing on the bottom plates. Rob O'Neill, the old drinker, was in the centre. A young lad was protesting, 'I dunno what 'appened! Everythin' jus' died! No steam, no 'lectrics, no air pressure! I dunno!'

O'Neill gave him a hefty clip round the ear. 'That tells me nothin'! I left you for five fuckin' minutes and you broke the ship!'

'It weren't me, I tell you!'

Bretonworth walked straight into the middle of them. To O'Neill, he said, 'You left the boy in charge?'

'I did, an' God knows I'm regretin' it now.'

'Tell me exactly what you know. What were you doing?' Bretonworth said to the boy.

'Well, I'd just took a message that we were switchin' over to another fuel tank and then it all went funny. I swear I never touched anythin',' the boy protested, forcing the words out amidst a terrible fear that he had truly broken the navy's newest and most powerful cruiser. He was at this moment fighting an hysterical urge to start sobbing.

'There'll be hell to pay,' said O'Neill.

'Please!' Bretonworth said, raising a hand to silence him.

As he said this, the main lamps suddenly came on, indicating that the diesel generators and switchboard had been brought into action. He looked about at the still confused faces and let some sarcasm run amok. 'Not before time!'

Then, sensing that the ghostly teenager standing before him was almost uncomprehending because he was thoroughly intimidated, he decided to revert to his calmer voice, that without any hint of an accusatory tone. 'I want you to think carefully. Tell me what you noticed before we lost power.'

The lad took a deep breath and sheepishly said, 'The oil pumps did sort o' surge a few seconds before. They didn't sound right.'

'Okay. I don't think we have ourselves a major problem here. We're simply trying to draw fuel from empty tanks.' He turned to O'Neill and asked, 'Who is supplying the oil to the furnaces?'

'Olly Knowles,' O'Neill replied with distaste, thinking of the man who was hidden away in a different part of the ship with ultimate control over the oil feed. 'The fool was brought in at the last minute 'cause my man went sick. I'll have his hide!'

Bretonworth sighed. 'Let's just concentrate on getting the ship underway again.'

As per his next instructions, the men threw themselves into the work of restoring the power and upholding the builders' otherwise good reputation. He then started his way back up the ladder. As he climbed, he heard O'Neill saying, 'You'll all pay for this.' He was struck by the way that O'Neill seemed incapable of seeing his own negative contribution to this little drama, but continued on his way, reasoning that what happened between these civilians now was their own business.

He went straight to the bridge and reported on what had happened to Captain Dollimore and Pat McAllister, both of whom had been waiting for news with as much patience as they could muster. Now furnished with the knowledge that all four boilers had been running on one oil tank up forrard instead of being split into completely separate units, Dollimore found himself needing to suppress the desire to accuse McAllister's team of gross incompetence. Wondering about the possible consequences of any sudden changes that the breakdown might have brought to the turbines, he asked Bretonworth, 'What's your opinion on damage?'

'The risk is not great, sir. We took measures to protect the machinery and we still had some way on. That would have kept the turbines rotating for a while. We're doing everything in our power to get steam back through the engines as fast as we can.'

Still also concerned for keeping to his timetable, Dollimore asked, 'Will you need to open the engines to check them when we reach port?'

The Scotsman shook his head instantly, saying, 'Ooh, the very idea is horrific. That could take a couple of weeks. But I really don't think it's come to that, sir.'

'Who was changing the tanks over?' asked McAllister.

'Some chap called Knowles,' said Bretonworth, but quickly added, 'I think we're going to have to put this one down to experience.'

Turning away, Dollimore said to Bretonworth, 'Go back below,' and could not resist adding, 'and make sure these people don't mess anything else up.' Yes, he was disappointed but to be fair, ninety five per cent of the trials had proceeded without a hitch even if little points of unprofessionalism had irritated him along the way. They really were only little things like downing tools and stopping for a cup of tea in the middle of an important job or slouching around the decks with hands in pockets.

Deliberating over this unfortunate episode, he knew that he had wanted to lose his temper but had fully understood that it would not help matters at all. Six years ago he would have just succumbed. He privately took a couple of deep breaths. Only a few days to go and then the ship would be his. He could finally get these builders out of here and have an elite Royal Navy crew controlling the decks. However much they tried, these civilians would never quite cut it for him.

*

Commander Crawshaw delivered all the final reports on the incident to his ever-busy captain and was immediately dismissed. No comment, no nothing. He had been working for Dollimore for weeks now and still could not understand him. With him it was all business or nothing at all. There did not seem to be room for any social pleasantries and Crawshaw was not convinced that that was how it was all the way across the board. He sensed that the captain had a much easier relationship with the other officers, especially Digby and Peterson. Could this separate standoffishness really be harking back to his memories of how things were at college?

He asked Bretonworth for any insights but the man would not discuss it. So he went to Digby. 'Apparently he was put ashore for a few years. Do you know what that was about?'

Digby also looked duly embarrassed. 'I'd rather not discuss that, sir. Besides, it's common knowledge and I'm surprised you're even asking.'

Crawshaw frowned. 'If it's common knowledge then I shall find out anyway. Why don't you just save me the bother and enlighten me?'

Rarely having seen the commander perturbed by anything, Digby ventured a cautious, 'Very well. Surely you know what happened to the *Spikefish* ?'

'That submarine that was sliced in half a few years ago? Some of the crew died, didn't they?'

'Exactly, sir,' Digby replied, unimpressed that they were even talking about it.

'And Dollimore was the fellow who ran her over,' stated Crawshaw, as though he had just had a 'eureka' moment. It was at times like this when he recognised and hated a certain component of his own character, that of instantly dismissing most, or perhaps even all, information that did not directly concern him or somebody close to him. The tragedy of HMS *Spikefish*, rammed and sunk by the cruiser HMS *Constant* up the River Clyde back in '33, had had no impact upon him and so he had always regarded that story as something of an irrelevant, distant sensation. Until now.

Chapter Three

A Family of Repute

David Clark knew that he would be coming home to a storm. He had consciously made being a disappointment to the family into something of an art but unfortunately he had to concede that his actions had even begun to bother himself. It was just that he was becoming aware that his behaviour brought concern to those he respected as well as to those that he did not. He had yet to discover a way of separating the two so that he could find the closeness that he wished for with the one while thoroughly upsetting the other.

The problem began with the fact that, as father frequently put it, 'the Clark's have been providing Great Britain with successful captains and flag officers for over two hundred years'. Nearly every male in this line had been in the Royal Navy since an obscure captain, Thomas Clark, had supported the Protestant Accession of William III and Mary II to the throne of England in 1688. The family had found favour and never looked back. Only those who had been physically or mentally too frail had not gone to sea for the reigning monarch and the empire.

David, now a nineteen year old midshipman, had been pushed through the otherwise venerated naval system against his will and now faced a life of seafaring if he could not break free of his family's history. Everybody had such expectations of him and all those who came up against his rebellious nature could not understand it. He was a Clark, they thought, born into a life of great privilege. How could he possibly want to spurn his calling?

He had just come home from his last training cruise having left his commanding officer, Captain Howard, thinking just that. Howard was an old friend of his father's so there would be questions, comments and arguments to face. But that could wait until this evening. There was another part of his life which he wanted to reacquaint himself with first before he went through all that.

It was mid-morning when he had reached his family's stately home of North Cedars Hall in Kent. He was pleased to find that most of the family were out at Edenbridge meeting with the reverend at the church where his sister was soon to be married, for it gave him plenty of room to follow his own path for a few hours.

Only his brother, Henry, had been at home. Henry was ten years older and had a serious air of his own. But he was also tolerant and this was due to the fact that he did not have father's desperate need to control everybody, to force a person into a destiny that he would not otherwise have chosen for himself. That he had also been pushed into the navy was something that he had been able to accept much easier.

David spoke to him briefly without alluding to anything in particular, changed from his uniform into something more comfortable and took his horse, Neptune, from the stable to ride off and disappear for the remainder of the day.

So it was that when their father, the rear-admiral, returned home, having heard that David too was in the vicinity, he rounded upon Henry for the details of his whereabouts.

'As you know he's only forthcoming when he wants to be,' said Henry, 'and I don't really like to pry.'

Father took a step closer to him. 'Listen to me. You are not just his elder brother. You are an officer in the Royal Navy and where that boy is concerned, you will pry. You understand me? You will pry!'

Henry, reflecting upon the fact that there was always some sort of problem between father and David, sensed that there was more to it this time, and asked, 'Is there something I should know?'

'He has left the service!' These words were forced out of the old man's throat in a strangely constricted falsetto. His fists were clenched and his face shone a beetroot red.

'No, he hasn't,' sighed Henry.

'Don't you tell me!' Father withdrew a crumpled envelope from his pocket and waved it in Henry's face. 'I received a letter just this morning from Captain Howard, complaining about the boy's bad attitude and his intentions of giving it all up!'

'Father,' said Henry, too much of his own man to be cowed, 'perhaps you should not fret until you've actually spoken to him about it.'

The old man turned away to stalk up the grand staircase towards some seclusion and sanity, cursing, 'Howard's letter is damning, boy! Damning!'

Henry walked desultorily into the sitting room and poured a small whiskey from the bottle at the bar. He had never been a strong believer in taking drink too early in the day so he was sure that he would mend his ways the moment he left North Cedars Hall. Just four more days to go.

He thought sadly about his mother suffering father's bad humour since last Christmas though, thankfully, she had her own ways and means of dealing with it. Father's temper had reportedly deteriorated drastically in the face of every domestic challenge that had confronted him in the last seven months of waiting in between appointments. Although it was clear that things had not been quite right years ago, this prolonged separation from his beloved service had driven him quite round the bend. Fortunately, in the face of Britain's rearmament, there were certainly going to be fresh orders for him soon. After all, he had a reputation as a valued flag officer so it was just a question of when they would come.

Henry then wondered why David aggravated father so much. The youngster was displaced from his three older siblings by a large gap of years so perhaps the difficulties had started there, right at the beginning. He had always been more alone. But then he had always been strong-willed and somehow upsetting father had become something that he considered to be sport.

He forced himself to stop thinking about it. He did not know David as well as he ought so he decided to take a little bit of his own advice, not to fret until he had actually spoken to him.

*

Rear-Admiral Harper J. Clark entered the brightly sunlit study and closed the door behind him. The balcony doors were open and the best of the summer breeze was stirring through the room making the corners of his weighted papers lift and drop again in a gentle fashion. The servants understood well enough that he liked his personal space to be aired frequently throughout the summer months, and a better space he could not have asked for. When his ancestors were laying the foundations of this Kent retreat in the hearty days of the last Stuart monarchs they had fully understood the qualities of south facing rooms with spectacular country garden views. This was the England that he strove to protect, not the people who complicated it, just this wealth and beauty.

He sat down behind his desk and silently stared at the files and books that were tidily placed before him. He sat there for some considerable time while running his mind over the facts of how it was that David was able to be so disrespectful in light of the family's background and standing. What was it he did not understand about his responsibilities? Belatedly, he came to the conclusion that there was nothing he could do until the young rascal showed his face at the hall so he turned his thoughts to matters that might steer him away from the problem and perhaps calm him down. Naval business had a way of doing that.

Therefore he reached into his pocket and drew out a key which he turned in the lock of the desk drawer. He pulled out a file which he intently began studying. It was a very basic appreciation of the strategy that the Royal Navy would set into motion if Britain went to war.

His superiors at the Admiralty had had to think through a few possible scenarios. These were not just concerned with war against Germany but also with war against a combination of Germany *and* Italy, seeing as those two nations seemed determined to have a common destiny. In addition to this was the possibility that Japan might throw in their lot with the European dictatorships, though that seemed less likely.

Where Clark became ultimately concerned was with the freedom of movement of the world's merchant navies of which the British Empire controlled an entire third. There could be no doubt that Britain's prospective enemies would move to block the trade routes in the Atlantic, the Mediterranean and the Pacific. This was an accepted part of the doctrine of economic warfare so the Admiralty intended to protect those routes, their significance prioritised in the order noted, whilst at the same time blockading the enemy's trade. Put simply, one side or the other was destined to be economically ruined and Clark had no doubts about which side that was going to be. The Royal Navy had dominated the oceans and denied all enemies their freedom of movement for generations. They would continue to do so.

*

David Clark, centre of so much family controversy, told his lover everything. Whether or not his problems gave him cause for anxiety, he always let her think that he was completely in control of the situation. It was a bravado that he had learnt from years in the training of the service and an excellent defence mechanism against the attentions of his father. Father, according to the things he had heard, was getting worse. It was going to be an interesting interview that they were to have when the Old Man finally caught up with him that evening.

In the meantime he needed the company of his lover – secret lover would have been the more apt description – to steady his nerves and help him focus on the challenges ahead. She was good at that sort of thing for she had a maturity and intelligence that many of his class believed the uneducated could not possess. These features were much of what made up her beauty because she was not beautiful in the conventional sense that most young men were attracted to. She was a tall girl, her eyes a little oriental in shape, had a small mole on her chin and was not given to wearing any make-up, but she took care of herself and kept herself neat. She always smelled sweet when he met with her.

The reason why they stayed secretive about the affair was that neither of their families would understand the match, his because he was the product of landed gentry and hers because she was an only daughter to dramatically over-protective working class parents. Her father was a strict old soldier of much war experience and now the landlord of nearby Welbury's village inn, *The King's Head*. Her mother was a devoted spouse but a little crazy, seeing sin and depravity everywhere. There was no way there could be open dealing with any of them.

As for the young woman herself, her name was Margaret Gufford.

It was difficult to believe that they had been meeting clandestinely every time he returned home for over three years now. Travelling with the navy, he had notched up a considerable number of experiences though, to date, he looked upon the day that he had reined in his horse on a quiet country lane to offer this gorgeous girl a ride home as one of the best. She was one of the few people who had instantly met him on an equal plane to be neither servile nor demanding. In truth he loved her but unfortunately their circumstances dictated that he could never do anything about it.

When they met earlier in the day, they had sneaked out to old Turnham's barn as they usually did. It was the best place they could think of because it was in a completely secluded place about half a mile from the village, and Turnham himself was getting so old that he could not get about the farm as he once did. It was a wonder that he did not sell off the land or hire help to stop these far corners from falling into ruin.

David thought, if we go to war the government may very well have something to say about the wasted acres.

He told her first of his disinterested approach to the navy on this last Mediterranean cruise and then admitted that he had felt guilty because Captain Howard had treated him with such friendly patience. 'If I were him,' he said, 'I'd have booted my backside into compulsory submarine service or something.' Poor old Howard, he was a chap nearing sixty, dedicated to teaching boys like him with never a chance of making flag rank. 'But it's not about whether or not I should respect him because he's an affable fellow. I simply do not want to be a sailor.'

Then, after telling her of the outcome to the situation, which made her shake her head with a mischievous disbelief, they made love. It was perfect if rushed, but that was okay because she knew what she wanted and she got it.

Then she lay back in the hay and asked him about the foreign women.

'There were a couple of seedy places in Alexandria,' he replied, 'with stage acts that can really turn a fellow off.'

'Well, you seem to know a lot about it,' said Maggie.

'Do you expect me to be in some exotic land with twenty inquisitive young men all harping on one topic and not go ashore to find out about these things? Look, what I mean is, we all went to look at the girls on offer. Some of the boys go for that sort of thing but I think most of us discovered that it was... well, a bit dirty.'

'Don't you think that what we're doing's a bit dirty?' she asked.

'Good lord, no!' he exclaimed without a moment's hesitation. 'I find the idea of sleeping with a woman I know much better than one I know absolutely nothing about. That'd be a bit of a flop, literally. I know you well enough and like what I know. Paying for some quick sexual satisfaction doesn't add up in my brain.'

She frowned. 'In that case I'm glad I come for free.'

'Don't make what we have sound cheap.'

'You know I don't think it's cheap,' she replied and smiled at him knowingly.

That was one of the things he liked about her. She knew when to stop baiting a fellow for a pointless fight. If she had a reason to fight then it would be over something serious and not frivolous. He knew enough of the other type of woman through the headaches one or two of his friends had had with their girlfriends and from growing up with a sister as inexplicable as Patricia.

David rolled over and looked in her eyes with purpose. 'Maggie, you are one of the only things which make coming home worthwhile. Of course I couldn't bear not seeing my mother as well but when I'm sitting in the train heading toward North Cedars, it's you I am thinking about.' Raising his eyebrows, he said matter-of-factly, 'I'd marry you in a second if I could.'

'So why don't you?'

Inwardly, the thought of having this woman as his wife intensified his desire, but he was careful to keep that to himself. 'Come on, think of the harm we'd do. I'd be cut off from the family, perhaps from the navy too, and your parents are well known to hate those of us of the upper crust.'

'A few minutes ago you didn't want anything to do with the navy,' she argued.

'Quite right,' he conceded, 'but I have some good friends there and I don't want to alienate them.'

'You might alienate them but you'd have me,' she said, propping herself up on an elbow and kissing him.

'Yes, I would,' he said, beginning to let his hands wander across her body once more. 'You're a terrible temptress.'

Suddenly looking serious, she said, 'You may as well know that my parents want me married and I'm supposed to be helping them choose my husband.'

'How does that work?' he asked, perplexed. 'They're so protective of you that they've not even allowed you to have a boyfriend.'

'I'm nearly twenty,' she explained, 'and dad – you know he sometimes suffers with his wounds – he wants to be able to hand the business over to someone in the family, and obviously not me because I'm only a girl. So I'm expected to marry so the business stays in the family.'

'He won't let you run the business?' David asked with incredulity. 'Surely your mother must have an opinion on the subject. I mean, we must be doing away with that antiquated sort of attitude.'

Her thoughts briefly wandered onto David's own blinkered view on the idea of their marrying, knowing him to be as much of a slave to society as the rest of them, but on her mother, she commented, 'She's as bad as him, says that the suffragettes back in the last war did nothing but cause trouble and bring disrepute to English womanhood.'

'She sounds barmy!'

Maggie gave him a lazy slap on the chest. 'Don't talk about my mother like that.'

Smiling, he said, 'Let's not talk about mothers at all, or fathers, or businesses.'

'Deal,' she said.

'I'll have to be heading back shortly,' David said, with a touch of remorse. 'Dinner is promptly at eight and, let's face it, it's going to be a sticky reunion.'

She did not envy him the evening ahead but at least he was entering the situation with a little forethought. Perhaps everything would turn out all right for him. 'Well, come on,' she said. 'You can take me back to the edge of the village as usual.'

'With pleasure, my love,' he said, standing up.

'But where did you throw my clothes? I can't exactly go back like this,' she said as they laughed together over their nakedness.

*

After returning home he found himself very short of time in which to make himself presentable for dinner. These affairs were always formal when father was at home, no matter how many people were dining, and the standard never fell below semi-formal at any time. After saying goodbye to Maggie, he had picked up the pace a bit, stabled Neptune, and crept into the hall through the back way via the kitchen. Passing through like a whirlwind, he gave the cooks a wink and a smile and received a look of admonishment from the butler, Felsham. The poor old fellow was probably imagining how the tense atmosphere around the admiral was about to get tenser still.

David sped up to his room, quickly changed into his dress uniform and ran a comb through his hair. He did not consider there to be anything else to worry about, for Maggie had picked the last pieces of hay from him before they had parted. He then flew down the grand staircase and puffed out his chest in order to enter the dining room with as confident and upright a posture as possible. Without pausing, he went in.

The room was very large, designed to cater for a great number of people. His ancestors had known that the Clarks were always to be a sociable family and he had sometimes tried to imagine the original candle-lit soirées that had been held here. These days the room was better lit by a new electric crystal chandelier. This evening, however, they were assisted by the sunlight still available as England plodded through her summer.

He had known that most of his family would be at home but he had not expected to see Patty's fiancé, John, sitting there waiting also. Oh well, he thought, this is just going to have to be slightly more embarrassing than it would have been. David knew himself to be the prime architect of this situation so he would just have to bite the bullet and get on with it. There was no going back now.

It was two minutes past eight by the grand clock at the far end of the room. David had been too late to hear the chimes of the hour.

'So, you had to creep round the back of the house like a peasant thief,' said the Old Man from his position at the head of the table. He was barely holding his anger in check. 'How is it that you dare to come to my dinner table late?'

David sat himself down next to Henry and glanced up and down the table in order to gauge the general mood. His poor mother, Dorothy, looked angry but she could not meet his gaze, just kept her eyes downcast. She had been the one putting up with Harper these long months and she looked worn down. Not that she had been crushed under the weight of his presence, for she had consistently and spiritedly disagreed with him on many subjects from the politics of the nation right down to the colour of the drapes. But she had definitely since exhausted any good humour.

His sister, Patricia, stared hard at him. She might have been a pretty young woman if she did not wear this scowl on her face so much. David fancied that the unnaturally deep lines either side of her mouth were moulded from the constant need to curl her lips in disgust. You never know, though, the lines might just disappear when I'm not around, he thought. She did not like him rocking the boat at all.

Next to her, John Bushey, who unsurprisingly was also a Royal Navy officer, sat impassively, keeping his eyes averted. David knew him a little and liked what he knew. If Patty ever whispered any bad things into his ear about him then he kept it to himself. Bushey was a serious, career-minded man currently at the rank of lieutenant. There was every

47

hope that he would be a welcome addition to the family and oddly, for this troubled brood, the feeling seemed to be universal.

Then there was Henry. When David looked at him, he was looking back with disappointment written all over his face. He was probably thinking that they did not have too much time together and how nice it would have been if the immature antics could have been avoided. But then he was a full ten years his senior and had always been more accepting of the status quo. His desire to keep the peace and do well made him a very different person. This was not to say that there was any discord between the two brothers, but their life experiences were far too separated by the years. Any antics that Henry may or may not have shared in had been left behind long ago.

David looked at his father. 'It's like this....,'

Whatever that excuse was, it was never going to be good enough and would have to wait. The Old Man had greater concerns on his mind. 'Explain the meaning behind the letter I received from Captain Howard.'

'Presumably you read it.'

'David!' came his mother's sharp voice from the further end of the table. 'We are all waiting to dine. Get this business over and done with so we can get on with our lives.' This was as stern a note as he had ever heard come from her.

David did look slightly perplexed as he said to her, 'Then perhaps we should eat and I'll discuss this with father alone. We're embarrassing our guest.' With that he motioned to John, whose face did not change.

'You're embarrassing the whole family,' said the Old Man. 'And what you are doing is a family affair, therefore we will have this out right here, right now.'

David tried to clear his throat a little and waved for a steward, one of the four silent servants of no opinion, to pour him some water.

'Forget the water for five minutes!' shouted the Old Man, making the servant retract his one step and invisibly suck a tooth in annoyance. The Old Man continued at his son, 'How dare you leave the service! You will scratch whatever commitments you have made and return immediately! You will do your duty to your family and to your country in the service of the navy and no other!'

Then David's indignation kicked in. 'Yes, God forbid that I should be allowed any personal wishes, any ambitions of my own. Since I was brought into the world all I have known is preparation for the navy. Do you know that I purposely tried to sabotage my interview for Dartmouth so that they wouldn't accept me? I was so suffocated by your world that I was that desperate to be anywhere else or do anything else. Yes, father, at the age of twelve I was feeling this way and even though I made myself particularly useless in front of the board I was *still* accepted into the college ahead of other, much better boys.'

'That is because you are a Clark,' said the Old Man, 'and we have been providing Great Britain with successful captains and flag officers for over two hundred years and don't you forget it.'

'I'm no particular fan of nepotism,' replied David, then pointed across the table. 'John is the type of man the navy needs, not me. He is the first of his family in the uniform but entirely more suited to it than me because he wants it. Some things in this life should not be a hereditary right. They must be earned.'

That made Henry turn to him and say, 'Come off it, David, that's starting to sound like Communism. Britain's power would be nothing without the great families carrying on their work for generation after generation. Those nations which have done away with their ruling elite are nothing but a shambles.'

Noticing John's face flushing a little red opposite him, David turned to his brother and said, 'Nazi Germany is far from a shambles. I've seen it first-hand.'

Suddenly, Patricia stopped them with, 'The politics and the history are quite pointless. Britain may be at war soon and David just seems to be intent on proving to the world that he is a half-witted coward. End of story.' She always had a way of making a petty observation sound authoritative.

The Old Man proudly said, 'Ah, Patricia, if only you were the boy.' Looking back at David, he continued, 'It's not quite the end of the story, however, because if it is that you are a half-witted coward then you will bring shame upon this family and I will never allow that to happen. I should be dead before you disgrace us in that fashion so you have a choice. Whatever you have done I shall undo and have you placed on another ship at the earliest opportunity...,'

'Or?' asked David with perhaps a hint of tentativeness.

'Or you can pack a bag and leave right now. Go wherever you wish but never think to draw upon the family's name or fortune again.'

'Harper!' gasped Dorothy. There was as much a look of consternation as anger upon her face at the thought of one of her children becoming an outcast. But she would not have given it a second thought if she did not know that her husband was deadly serious and perfectly capable of carrying out that threat.

Funnily enough, being an outcast as the solution somehow appealed to David, but when he looked at the trouble it was causing his mother, he drove the idea away. He had come to the point where making his father angry just for the sake of it was no longer worthwhile. Calmly, he said, 'There's no need to go that far and there's nothing that you need undo. It's true, the last time I spoke to Captain Howard I was in a very negative frame of mind and may have left having given him the impression that I was, in effect, deserting. But I knew it was a rash approach as soon as I'd finished talking with him. I'm here on leave as normal, everything's above board, and I'm awaiting new orders. I'm not leaving the navy, I never was.'

Thinking on the many hours he had wasted fretting over this, the Old Man sat back, stunned. 'Why must we go through this with you, boy?'

David sat silent and unapologetic.

'Answer me this,' continued the Old Man, 'How do you think the men serving under you will ever trust you if you show no respect?'

Actually rounding on his father, David said, 'I do show respect! I show respect where it's due!'

The Old Man stood up, knocking the table with his legs and thumping it with a clenched fist, but before the next challenge could emanate from his mouth, Dorothy interjected, 'Please, Harper! Let us eat! This can be solved after dinner!'

'Funny that, I've lost my appetite.' With that the Old Man stalked from the room.

Once his echoed footsteps had faded to nothing beyond the grand staircase, Dorothy said quietly, 'He's right, David. Why must we go through this with you?'

'Sorry, mother,' he said, this time showing real humility.

Sighing, Henry turned to the head steward and said, 'You may serve the dinner now.'

'Aye aye, sir.'

*

A little over an hour later, after they had eaten their fill, David strolled with Henry and John through the six acre gardens behind the hall, each smoking a cigarette. The day was almost at an end and there was just the faintest light showing over the horizon of darkening trees to the west. Any other illumination for the three men to see by came from the large windows above them. In one of those windows, that of the study, they could see the Old Man intently reading his documents again. Henry had told them that that was where he had taken to retreating to when things began to get on top of him.

As they went forth with lazy steps, Henry said, 'David, you really mustn't give him so much reason to be angry with you. It doesn't do any of us any good, you know, least of all mother.'

'I do know, but I'm sorry to have to say this, Henry. I do not have an ounce of fondness for the Old Man and if he wants to be an admiral rather than a father then I shall respond by treating him as a third rate manager in a dead end job.'

'That's just childish in the extreme.'

'Is it?' asked David, his emotion rising again. 'I wouldn't know what childish is because, as far as I'm concerned, I had my childhood taken away from me. All for an ancient family name.'

Henry glared at him, the light from the hall glinting in his eyes. 'You know full well what childish is because it's how you're behaving right now.' Then, after a pause he raised his hands in a conciliatory gesture and said, 'Listen, I do have some sympathy with you. I can't say that I was overwhelmed with Dartmouth either but the navy grows on you, it really does. As each day goes by I am more and more convinced that the whole thing was worth it. Give it time. You'll feel the same.'

'Maybe,' David conceded, and to John he said, 'I'll tell you one thing. It's you I envy right now.'

John was clearly astonished as he said, 'Envy me? I've struggled all the way for the position I hold.' Then, in a light tone, he added, 'I don't have the birth, you know.'

All three of them laughed together. The brothers liked John tremendously. He was a very confident sort of chap who never felt too out of place amongst the Clarks. That confidence, tied in with quick wits and an invariable devotion to his chosen career, endeared him to the whole family. To some this endearment was seen as strange given that his upbringing could not have been more different from theirs.

John's father had once been a struggling fishmonger at the Billingsgate market in London, only ever having pennies left after he had paid his rent and bills, then clothed and fed his family. One day, a little over a decade ago, he was left a modest sum of money in a will and from then on certain privileges were available to the Bushey family. For John this meant a decent education at the reputable school of Charterhouse and a chance to get into the Royal Navy as an officer through the Special Entry Scheme after he had finished studying. Their backgrounds aside, the main difference between these men walking in the garden here tonight was that, while the Clarks had been bred for the navy with specific training throughout their childhoods, John had not officially come into contact with the service until he was sixteen and then only by choice.

'The important thing,' said David, 'is that you had options.'

John asked him, 'Has the navy done nothing for you? I mean, it's anything but dull.'

'You're right, it's not dull, but there are too many other things that bother me.'

Henry had heard most of this before and did not show the same patience as John, saying, 'Everything bothers you, it seems.'

But David was in a mood to pursue his point and continued. 'Well, consider the Admiralty's leaning towards the importance of the battleship like it supersedes everything else.'

John said, 'But the battleship is the most powerful type of ship afloat. The fleet revolves around it.' He did feel that he had a vested interest in defending the battleship as supreme, seeing as he was presently serving in one of the grandest old ladies of the fleet, HMS *Royal Oak* .

'In some ways perhaps,' continued David, 'but I don't understand the need to centre everything we know upon that type of ship or why the masters at Dartmouth continually flap on about Jutland like it was the only battle that ever took place in the Great War.'

'It was a great victory,' argued Henry.

'It was a victory but was it so great? Ship for ship the Germans did better but we have to realise that the outcome was a foregone conclusion.

We had superior numbers, longer experience and deeper traditions when all the Germans really had was the guts to challenge them. Only a fool could have lost us the Battle of Jutland.'

Henry shook his head. 'You're just being disrespectful now...,' he began to say, but was interrupted before he could remind his brother of the Royal Navy's inferior ammunition and ship design at the time.

'And you're not listening. I know the battleship at Jutland is important but what about the support of infantry landings? What about convoys and anti-submarine work? What about naval aviation? Don't you think the battleship might just be vulnerable to torpedo bombers and that that might be important, too?'

John said, 'Our ships do have anti-aircraft guns, you know.'

'But why aren't we taught about those things with the same emphasis? If we become deficient in those areas then it's because everybody has been spending all their time harping on about the battleship.'

'What are we to do about it?' asked Henry, his tone bitter and his patience well and truly diminished.

But it was John who took up the point. 'David, some of your questions have occurred to me also but there is nothing we can do. We're young and we have a rough ride ahead, so what I suggest we do is serve to the best of our abilities, make and maintain decent reputations and lobby for changes in the future. You can't sweep away a Victorian attitude overnight and you certainly won't change a thing if you strut about like an impetuous schoolboy. The people that matter will remember that you were once like this.'

David threw the butt of his cigarette into a nearby flowerpot and looked at John. He nodded and said, 'A reprimand. But one I am willing to accept. Let's just hope that the Nazis allow us to have a future.'

'And always look on the bright side of life, please,' continued John. 'The next time we all meet will be my wedding. Something grand to look forward to, eh, and balls to the Nazis.'

'Hear hear,' said David as they headed back inside.

David was genuinely looking forward to the wedding but mostly on account of welcoming John to the family. At this present time his feelings for his sister's happiness were not positive and he had not been able to fathom what this level-headed man here saw in that spiteful creature. Perhaps he would never know.

*

A couple of days later, the orders that had eagerly been awaited by Rear-Admiral Harper Clark found their way to North Cedars Hall. They instantly turned his life about. His old energy began returning with rediscovered purpose and the contents of those Admiralty papers that he had been reading now took on a greater value than ever. These orders' arrival certainly did much to break the tension that had abounded in the house for far too long and demonstrated that they had also been eagerly awaited by his family and servants alike.

With the possible exception of Patricia everyone breathed a sigh of relief, especially as they learned that he would probably be away for some considerable time. He himself started to find less fault with those around him, David excepted, as his mind turned upon more important matters and significantly, spent less time at the hall as he travelled about settling affairs before heading off.

Even though he had been testy and difficult these past months, rarely giving anyone a moment's peace, he was still somehow surprised at Dorothy's reaction when he told her that he was soon to be heading north to Scotland.

'I really don't care where they send you,' she said after he had interrupted her morning tea in the garden. She usually liked that time to be for a solitary, sober reflection on life.

'I beg your pardon?' he asked, his temper already fraying.

'Harper, don't speak to me as though we were a couple needing to keep each other informed. That ended a long time ago.'

'It certainly did,' he said, staring at her in disgust. 'One wonders why I didn't cast you out twenty years ago.'

'Well, one needn't wonder,' she snapped and turned her head to look the other way. This was her dismissal of him.

She had him cornered. Blinkered as he was, he understood well enough what she was getting at so he changed tack, briefly saying as a parting shot, 'I shall be securing a berth for that wretched son of ours in my new squadron. If we go to war I want him nearby so that I can stop him disgracing the family name.'

'You do what you feel you must,' she said, still looking away. David was no longer a child needing her protection. She knew perfectly well that he would be able to take care of himself now and very probably give this fool more of a headache into the bargain.

Harper took himself away to concentrate on preparation for his new task. He hated Dorothy more than ever now. This was a time for family unity, not further division.

So why had he never cast her out? It was a little known fact that it was mostly her money that was keeping the house and grounds in this state of good repair. When they were married over thirty years ago he had not been entirely forthcoming about the fragile situation concerning the Clark family finances, but at that point he did not think it to be her business. They had had what they thought was an unconditional love for each other and he had truly not considered using her money to cover his problems, but as time went on and he began talking about closing off parts of the hall and making cuts to staff, she had entered into the game with her own personal fortune.

As Clark had served his country with great skill at sea, he had unfortunately proved himself to be far less skilled when it came to money and domestics, so Dorothy gradually took over more than sixty per cent of the costs of the upkeep of the hall. This was why he had never cast her out. The breaking of this bond would mean too great a loss.

During his last two weeks at home they broached no further subject of a personal nature.

Chapter Four

To Portsmouth

Stepping out into the aisle, Dollimore took his place in the queue of people filing out of the church. He was happy and content. The trials of the *Burscombe* had been wound down in a satisfactory manner and he was expecting to be signing for the ship first thing on Tuesday morning. This was just as soon as the shipwrights had finished their last series of tests on her structure. Fortunately, the extensive checks made by the engineers on the ship's machinery after their little mishap at sea proved that the engines had suffered no significant damage and they were able to go on as normal.

Now his spiritual well-being was also being catered for as he had just listened to a stirring sermon given by the rector of the local parish, who had eagerly expounded the evils of the dictatorships in Europe and called upon God to guide them in the coming confrontation against tyranny, subjugation and persecution. He had seemed pretty certain that this confrontation was unavoidable and Dollimore appreciated the realistic stance.

Walking down the steps between the columns of the portico, nodding pleasantly at one or two of the familiar faces that passed him by, he suddenly heard his name being called. He turned and the lady who was following him down the steps, clutching her wide-brimmed hat to her waist, gave him an unsure smile. 'Captain Dollimore, may I have a word?'

'Certainly,' he replied, keeping his expression stern.

He noticed that she was middle-aged with the beginnings of silver showing in her otherwise fine, dark brown hair. Though he did not let his eyes wander he also noted that her figure and skin were very healthy, which was rare in this city. Belfast was still struggling to recover from a long period of poverty and despair with all the associated ill-health that came with them, and it had been Dollimore's impression that everybody and everything had been run down. This lady, whom he had seen from time to time at the church, seemed to be the exception.

'I've noticed you before and I don't want to be forward,' she said, in well-educated tones, 'but, well, something has happened to me which you may be able to help explain and possibly solve.'

Noticing the troubled look that quite suddenly appeared in her eyes, he said, 'First I should say that you have the advantage of me. I don't even know your name.'

'Of course. I'm a little out of sorts. When I get like that my mouth moves faster than my brain.' Having blurted that out, she then took a breath. 'My name is Mrs Moxham. Er, what I have to ask is a bit awkward... and concerns an officer in your ship.'

'Oh?' he asked, his eyebrows going up. He suddenly found himself hoping that there was not some awful indiscretion at hand but he somehow knew instinctively that there was and the inner peace that he had gained from the sermon was fast disappearing.

'It's just that I thought he was going to marry me,' she continued. 'Everything was perfect and has been for many weeks then last night he was... it was terrible. I never knew he could be so despicable.'

For a moment he thought she was going to cry, though he could have been mistaken, but then she recovered herself with a good deal of grace.

He eyed her uncomfortably and said, 'Mrs Moxham. *Mrs...,*'

'Oh, my husband is dead. Colonel Moxham died from a fever in Alexandria three years ago.'

'I see. And you have recently been involved with one of my officers? You do understand that I consider delving into people's private lives really shouldn't be my domain unless it brings disrepute to the ship. Is this what we are talking about? Which officer is it?'

'Derek Crawshaw,' she said.

'Ah,' he muttered. Why was he not surprised that Crawshaw's name had come up in connection with some possible scandal to do with the fairer sex? Up to this moment Dollimore had considered there to have been some considerable improvement in him since those days of youthful distraction at college and, on reflection, his contribution to the overseeing of the ship's trials had been very good. Also, he had kept this little affair very secret and it had not interfered with operations. Until now? He asked, 'What do you think I can do for you?'

'Well, Derek dropped me quite unexpectedly last night. He was very rude to me, more than I deserved, and now he won't answer my calls.

Captain, I know you're a busy man and I'm not some young fool who is going to whine and beg him to come back. I'm simply owed an explanation.'

He nodded, 'I understand, but I have to tell you that I'm not at all happy about this.'

'I wouldn't have troubled you if it wasn't important. To me at any rate. If he thinks to walk away in such a fashion and not even look back then I shall cause him trouble.'

'Over an affair?' asked Dollimore, with a hint of distaste.

'It was not an affair,' she said indignantly, and reiterated, 'It was an engagement.'

Sighing, Dollimore finished with, 'I'll think it over, Mrs Moxham, but I shall give you no guarantees. Whatever I do will be in the ship's best interests, you understand?' With that he abruptly turned, put on his cap and strode off down the street in the direction of the ship yard. It never occurred to him that his expression and his sudden dismissal of her only served to make her think that HMS *Burscombe* must be in the control of a bunch of immature egotists.

*

Amidst a round of official receptions, the yard's managers wanted to demonstrate their appreciation of the connection that they felt with the *Burscombe* and to wish the officers well for the future. To do this they had organised what they hoped would be a lively affair in the spacious back room of the *Blue Anchor* pub in Ann Street. They were not disappointed with the ensuing intensity, especially as many of them seemed to think that the swift consumption of vast amounts of alcohol was a measure of how Irish they were, so the room was soon full of very happy people.

Dollimore drank cautiously and moved about the room using the occasion for learning more about what drove his officers on as much as for the celebration of a huge and difficult task completed. They were a very mixed bag but they were comfortable with each other. A shared experience like the one that they had had could only bring men closer together. He did not doubt that the trend would continue into active service.

Bretonworth had been attached to the building of this ship for so long now that he was feeling the pangs of deep sentimentality towards many of those present but, never having been blessed with the gift of comfort in socialising, he found that he could only stand to one side slowly sipping his beer. Though he liked the taste, he did not trust himself with too much of the stuff.

Eventually, Lieutenant Powell, whom Bretonworth had always considered more of an oddity than himself, gravitated towards him with a small group of civilian engineers. It appeared that they also preferred more formal behaviour and he very soon found himself enjoying competitive tales of who had encountered the worst engineering problems and the limitless ingenuity that had gone into solving them.

Digby, whilst continuing to observe gentlemanly manners, was swiftly working his way through the beer and laughing with the best of them. Here was a man who believed he had found the perfect balance for a fruitful existence. He had the confidence to know as to when to be serious and when to be comedic, when to be hard working and when to be playful, and even when to be respectful and when to be rude. He was well regarded in both family and professional circles alike.

Brad Gailey stood at his side lapping up the atmosphere that his brother officer radiated, laughing happily yet still jealous at his companion's comfort and skill with the harmless wit. Offering the odd comment here and there, he did not attempt to compete for conveyer of best banter.

Dollimore stood listening to Crawshaw talking for a while. Planted firmly in the midst of a small audience of drooling shipbuilders the commander demonstrated that he was capable of quite staggering crudity. It was just as well that everybody involved were men because the stories of how he seemed to have whored his way across the Mediterranean were wholly disrespectful. However it seemed that those listening were impressed and more than one of them lamented the fact that they had missed a trick by failing to join the navy in their younger days.

Disgusted, but presently not wanting to alter the tone, Dollimore moved away and latched himself onto a high-spirited conversation that was being led by Pat McAllister.

It would appear that just yesterday he had fallen foul of his bitter-sounding wife and had been knocked unconscious when, having taken umbrage with him stating his opinions, she had swung at him with a frying pan. With an even more maniacal look than normal, he then invited all those around him to feel the bruise beneath his thatch of grey hair.

Dollimore resisted the temptation to put his fingers on the bump out of revulsion at the amount of perspiration soiling the man's head but agreed that the bruise seemed to be everything he claimed it to be. The fact that he knew McAllister enjoyed a healthy, respectful marriage and that he seemed far too happy about the incident led Dollimore to believe that something considerably less dramatic had happened to him.

He smiled but wondered what McAllister's wife would make of this performance if she knew about it. The idea of telling exaggerated stories with one's own wife as the butt of the joke was one completely alien to him. He knew that Peterson, standing close by, would be wondering the same thing. He too was married and infinitely less prone to these sort of theatrics.

Then, as Dollimore sipped at his beer, he saw a familiar figure entering the door by the bar. The young man, clad in a royal navy uniform, casually stepped into the crowd, removed his cap and looked expectantly to his left and right.

'Philip!' Dollimore called above the noise of the great revelry.

The young man immediately saw his father and pushed his way through to join him. The meeting was as pleasant as it was unexpected. Dollimore gave a broad smile, shook Philip's hand and clapped him fondly upon the shoulder. 'What the devil are you doing here?'

'I got an assignment to deliver some equipment here,' said Philip. Immediately eager to move away from talking shop, he continued, 'Anyway, I was surprised when they said I would find you in a pub, but you really are slumming it, aren't you?'

Dollimore looked around briefly at the sweaty, wide-eyed clientele and said, 'They're a good bunch, all of them. We're celebrating the completion of the *Burscombe*.'

'I hear she's going to be one of the finest ships in the fleet.'

'You can count on it.'

With small talk fast running flat, Dollimore said, 'It's been four years since I've seen you, boy. You're looking well. How's Sarah? How's the baby?'

'We're all doing well. I spent a few days with them a couple of weeks ago and took them to see mother as well.'

'She mentioned it,' said Dollimore, recalling the elation in Jennifer's voice on the phone at seeing the baby for the first time.

Philip then said, 'It's just perfect that I was able to run into you here. Please take this.' He took from his pocket a picture of the new family. Philip and Sarah were sitting against a plain backdrop, Sarah holding the sleeping baby on her lap and Philip's hand resting affectionately on the infant's gown. Everything was right about it – apart from the world they were bringing the baby into.

'Thank you,' Dollimore said, tucking the photograph away into his jacket. Then he looked at his watch.

'The China Station seems to have agreed with you,' said Philip, 'You still have a tan.'

'It was a decent enough appointment, but here is the best place to be right now.'

'I know what you mean.'

'Come get a drink and some food,' said Dollimore, 'and I'll introduce you round to the chaps.'

As they moved over to the bar where the landlord had laid out some sandwiches for the revellers to pick at, Gailey stepped out from the crowd and, flushed from the drink and the rising heat, announced that Digby was about to play the piano and everybody should give him a hand. With the cheering and the clapping eventually subsiding, Digby feigned a little embarrassment but willingly enough strode over to the piano and sat down. He then led the gathering through a raucous but faultless version of *Madamoiselle From Armentieres* slotting in some comical lyrics of his own that nobody had heard before.

Dollimore was astonished and proud. He said to Philip, 'I had no idea he was musical. It never ceases to amaze me what you learn about people.'

As the song was winding down and calls were going up for another, there suddenly came a shout from the opposite corner closest to the back door. 'I'll kill him! I'll fuckin' kill him!' It was the unmistakable voice of a highly inebriated Rob O'Neill. The crowd parted and soon every pair of eyes in the room was focussed upon him. But he was so staggeringly drunk that he could not focus in return so his gaze wandered back and forth. 'I'll kill him!'

'No you won't!' Pat McAllister angrily countered. 'Go home! You're making a fool o' yerself!'

'Not 'til I've killed him!' O'Neill looked dizzily around the room.

Dollimore stepped forward to where, it seemed, few were prepared to tread. 'What's bothering you, man?'

'You gentleman types make me sick.' His eyes finally found Bretonworth. 'You! Do you take pleasure in destroyin' a person?'

McAllister stepped in front of O'Neill and took hold of his arm forcibly. 'You were only demoted. If you carry on you'll be sacked.'

Bretonworth understood now. 'This must be over that business concerning our machinery.'

Dollimore raised a hand to silence him. 'Mr O'Neill, you're going to solve nothing while you're in this state. What's done is done and the best thing you can do now is go home and sober up.'

'You wanna' give me advice?' O'Neill shouted, his temper well and truly broken. Shaking free of McAllister's grasp, he swayed the few steps forward and took an unbalanced swing at Dollimore.

The captain simply arched his back and let the fist pass harmlessly in front of his nose then stepped to one side so that the lousy drunkard fell flat on the floor. He then reached down, grabbed a hold of his collar and dragged him towards the door. The ease with which he did this – for O'Neill was not the lightest of men – astounded almost all who witnessed it.

O'Neill found himself being thrust into the urine soaked alleyway behind the pub minus some of the buttons from his stained shirt, too stunned to do anything but collapse. Nobody made a move to see if he was alright. Only McAllister mumbled, 'That's him finished. What was he thinkin'?'

Once back inside, Dollimore noted that the drinkers were slowly getting back to their revelling though some of them were still staring at him in wonder. One of them was Philip. Perhaps he had forgotten his father's decisiveness.

Crawshaw stepped over to Dollimore and said, 'I must say that was a brilliant move on your part.'

'Was it?' Dollimore asked coldly. Distractedly looking at his watch, he said, 'It was very one-sided.'

'In my experience a drunk can do a lot of damage.'

Dollimore frowned. 'Well, think on this. I'm fit, he's fat. I'm calculating, he's emotional. I'm sober, he's drunk. What more is there to it than that?'

'And all of that went through your brain in the few seconds before the off?'

Dollimore looked Crawshaw in the eyes. 'Be clear about this. I can't abide any man who reaches adulthood and can't take responsibility for his own actions, let alone one of his age. That being said, no, I have to admit I didn't see that one coming. I shall have to take more care.'

Crawshaw pondered that for a couple of seconds. They were fair enough comments for a man in this business. They all knew that Bretonworth had had nothing to do with this little episode. He had not said a thing to anyone about O'Neill's part in the machinery fiasco. There had been many witnesses and it was all in the running reports, plain for everyone to see. Bretonworth was just the scapegoat in O'Neill's selfish imagination, just as that apprentice and Olly Knowles were on the day of the incident. Crawshaw never considered for a moment that something of Dollimore's remark about responsibility was also aimed at him.

Philip came up beside them, a pint of beer in hand. 'I must say it's a laugh a minute around here.'

Dollimore immediately said, 'Derek, this is my son Philip. Philip, this is Derek Crawshaw, my Executive Officer.' Then he looked at his watch again.

After the cordial, 'Pleased to meet you,' had been said and reciprocated, Crawshaw asked Dollimore, 'Is there something bothering you? You keep looking at your watch.'

'Derek, do you mind if we step outside for a moment?'

'Not a bit, sir,' he replied, suddenly perplexed. He followed him towards the front door after Philip had been left in the care of Mr Digby.

Outside, the late evening sunlight was just beginning to fade. The long shadows made by the buildings stretched out across the road which was all quiet but for the occasional motor car chugging along it.

Crawshaw, taking the cigarette that was offered him, spoke first. 'I say, what's this all about, sir?'

'Something of a delicate matter, I'm afraid,' Dollimore said.

'Oh?'

'Something has come to my attention which I would really rather was none of my business, but... Ah, right on time.'

Crawshaw noticed that Dollimore was looking past his right shoulder to something behind him so turned to see what it was. He was more than a little surprised to see Josephine Moxham striding towards them, her head held high and moving with a confident step. She was just as alluring as she had been the first time he set eyes on her all those months ago, and he even found himself wishing that he could erase the past so that he could begin the chase again. But all that tumbled out of his mouth was, 'You two know each other?'

Dollimore said, 'If you were at all religious you would have discovered that we both had attended the same church. Now, I thank the pair of you for sparing me the details of your love affair but Derek, you are about to do the right thing and talk to Mrs Moxham. It seems that some sort of explanation is in order. I fully understand that there is no relationship to save but you will part amicably. Don't even think about returning to the ship until you've done so. You have until midnight. There's work to be done.'

With that the captain stepped back inside the pub leaving an embarrassed Crawshaw nonplussed and speechless on the pavement.

*

With some little ceremony, Dollimore and his specialist officers put their signatures to the handover documents, the legal proof that Harland & Wolff had done their job to the required standard and that the ship was now part of the Royal Navy. This done, they hauled down the Red Ensign from the staff at the quarterdeck and from the wide expanse of the Belfast Lough, they finally weighed anchor and proceeded southwards, those civilians and their questionable discipline cleared from the decks.

A steaming party had come up to take the ship to Portsmouth, which was two days away at an economical speed. This nucleus of the future ship's company was mostly made up of stokers and engine room artificers but enough electricians, signallers, telegraphists, cooks and seamen were also embarked to ensure the smooth running of operations, even if the routine was only in its embryonic stage.

With this influx of men, Crawshaw had his work cut out organising them all but he was happy enough with the lieutenants, Selkirk and Giles, that had arrived to help him. As he launched himself into the task, he found that working hard was the only way to take his mind off that sorry little episode with Josephine. In part he hated Dollimore for what he had done but at the same time he could not help but admire his neat handling of delicate situations.

They were both the same age, born just a couple of weeks apart in the spring of 1886, but Dollimore was now a captain whereas he, short of there being a change in naval policy or a miracle, never would be. Funny, he thought, back at college he had been convinced that it was the studious Dollimores of this world who had got it all wrong. They were boring and would never make an impact upon anything.

He was just mulling this over when the man himself summoned him to his sea cabin up in the forward superstructure.

'Ah, Mr Crawshaw,' said Dollimore, his expression one of good cheer. 'We're not in any particular hurry to get to Portsmouth.'

'No, sir?'

'A few drills are in order, I think. Collision Stations followed by Boat Drill would be a good place to start.'

Crawshaw furrowed his brow. He had a thousand other tasks. Still, he answered, 'Very good, sir.'

*

More than happy with the amount of shouting he had done at the men during their tentative drills, Chief Petty Officer Doyle headed back to the mess and hung up his hat and jacket, thankful to be able to cool down. He took a clothes brush from his locker and begun removing what he perceived to be dust from them. 'Captain seems a decent sort, as captains go,' he commented.

Ross, the Chief Yeoman of the Signals, glanced up lazily from his almost concealed position, lying on a couch behind the table reading a *Daily Sketch*. He did not seem too interested.

But Vincent, a CPO stoker in his mid-thirties, looked up from the thick, brown stew he was hungrily scoffing down. He had a heavy sweat on his brow even though there was a good breeze coming in through the open scuttles. 'You remember the sub that copped it up the Clyde back in '33?'

'What, the *Spikefish*?' asked Doyle, straight away recalling the blurred photograph of the stern-most quarter of the submarine hanging on by only a few strips of bent steel.

'This is the fella that hit it,' explained Vincent.

'Oh,' Doyle mumbled, not wanting to commit himself to an opinion.

Vincent carried on, 'Got clean away with it, he did, even though he killed three blokes, but then they were only ratings. If he'd killed an officer they might have taken a dimmer view.'

Finishing up with the tidying of his jacket and reaching into his locker for some shoe polish, Doyle said, 'I don't go in for conspiracy stories much. If he was really at fault they'd have given him the push, I'm sure. Anyway, one of the POs reckons he gave distinguished service in the war.'

'Never got no medals, though,' said Vincent, determined to believe the worst.

Without looking away from his paper, Ross said, 'I got the clap once.'

Vincent laughed, 'Yeah, but you have to be a distinguished signalman to get that.'

All three men gave a chuckle. Perhaps it was just as well not to take the issue too seriously.

While Vincent ate and Ross read, Doyle busied himself polishing the shoes which were already polished to a high sheen and thought on another matter that the captain had raised earlier when they were on the flight deck. He had innocently enough singled out a particular able seaman as a man of quality. This he had gauged from his observations of them raising and lowering the cutter. It was a Scotsman with a very smooth and decisive way of working who had seemed to be the man that the younger ratings were taking their cues from. This man, however, was clearly aging. Was he content with his lot?

Doyle had tried to explain without going into too much detail that the man in question, one Able Seaman Bonner, was as content as a man could be when he harboured absolutely no interest in advancement or indeed getting on with authority. The captain had left it there. He did not need to hear any more for he knew the type and accepted the chief's evaluation.

Doyle had known Bonner on and off for the best part of fifteen years. Their paths had crossed a few times, this being the fourth ship that they had in common. Back in the early days Doyle had thought Bonner was clever and funny for his apparent disrespect and strange invulnerability but, as the years went on and Doyle had become ever more serious about the service, Bonner had simply become a headache. They had not seen each other now for a couple of years but, because of what they knew of each other, there remained a simmering gulf between them.

*

Bonner had acknowledged Doyle, obeyed the man's orders, then got on with his life. He obeyed all orders but it did not mean he had to like the men giving them. That was especially so with the senior rates. What was it in this world that made people want to rise above themselves? As best as he could figure it, pure selfishness was involved. He had watched many men grow from raw, idiotic recruits into these masquerading upstarts who really believed that they had developed a conscience. But at the end of the day, the only person who had benefitted was the man himself. Pure selfishness.

Men like Doyle would also have you think that they actually cared about the welfare of the men and the service to which they belonged, but Bonner knew them for what they really were. It was all very simple. If you cared – and Bonner did not think any of them really did – that was your problem, but if you *said* you cared then that was just outright self-righteousness.

However, he still loved being a sailor. He had a thorough understanding of ships and the sea and had a particular penchant for any ship with guns, thus could not imagine himself going into any other profession. In fact he could not imagine any other life at all. He hated women as much as he hated men, so there was no chance of settling with a family, and he had felt compelled to turn his back on his parents before he had even reached his teenage years. No, there had only ever been one thing to do and that was to go through this life serving his ships, attempting to keep in line any man who was thinking of growing a fat head.

Of course the latter business was very difficult and he regularly failed but he did have some notable successes. Over the years he reckoned he had made somewhere in the region of fifteen men reject advancement and keep in their place. A few years ago one man had even committed suicide and some had tried to pin that on him by saying he had bullied the man to his grave, but the case could not be proven so he carried on with his life. If the man chose suicide as a solution then that just showed him up for the coward that he really was and that had nothing to do with him.

It was just about two bells of the First Watch when he came down to the mess. It was a fairly large space which straddled the circular, armoured barbette upon which one of the forward gun turrets sat. It was a large space at the moment because there were not many men occupying it. Once they reached Portsmouth he would see this compartment truly invaded and cramped.

Looking around the mess, which was brightly illuminated by the lamps, the Scotsman asked, 'What does a man have to do to get 'is scran round 'ere?'

Heads were bowed so that they would not have to look at him, all except Pincher's. Pincher Martin threw Bonner's bowl onto the table and said, 'Give it up, Bonehead. If you want it then you're gonna have to say please.'

'Just gi' us it,' said Bonner, sitting down and wiping the sweat from his brow.

Pincher grinned and started dishing up the stew that had been in the pot for the last couple of hours. The two men had something of an accord as Pincher was also an old hand who spurned advancement for the sake of his own peace of mind. But there the similarity stopped. This Londoner came from a good, if poor family who believed in discipline and hard work. It was a large and well liked family and, so far as people could tell, there were no black sheep. Pincher proudly wore his long service stripes on his sleeve and liked to see other men get on and make something of themselves.

'Skipper's gonna make us work for a living,' he stated, undaunted.

'Same shit, different ship,' said Bonner, then piled the stew into his mouth.

*

HMS *Burscombe* steamed slowly into Portsmouth Harbour late the next day and moored alongside the jetty amidst an abundance of other vessels in various states of commission, some old, some new, others midway through their rough lives. Everywhere men and stores trailed back and forth, the activity of a build-up to war. The crew of the *Burscombe* added to this forthwith.

By the end of the Last Dog Watch a sizeable proportion of the ship's company had come aboard. Crawshaw had settled the list of crew requirements with the drafting authorities months ago and they had arrived at a final figure of 802 men. Therefore all decks were quickly thriving as the new men wandered to and fro with personal or pusser's gear, generally just trying to familiarise themselves with their new surroundings. It seemed that roughly half the crew were new, not just to the ship, but to the navy itself, having been sent here after only a few months of basic training, so there was no shortage of blank-faced lads wandering the passageways.

All the senior rates like Doyle had already decided that they would either feign or truly hold a complete lack of sympathy to their plight. They remembered back to when they were the bemused newcomers to the service and had been made to feel that they only had themselves to blame because they had volunteered for it. So now they would treat these lads the same. It was the most proper and fastest way for them to learn.

One of the most serious of adherents to this outlook, and one of the least sympathetic of the lot, was an old, imposing warrant officer given to glaring terribly at anyone who came near him. Everybody knew that anyone who had reached the rank of warrant officer had done so through years of sheer hard work and a thorough devotion to the rules of the service. Anything less would have been completely unacceptable. In that way they were tough, and sometimes uncouth, taskmasters.

This particular man, not very tall but fairly muscular, was even more frightening than most because of the terrible scarring that covered all of his exposed skin. Whatever hair he had was white and wispy and his facial features were completely distorted from having once been melted in some calamity. To the men he terrorised he was nothing but an imposing, sinister mystery. Only he knew that he had become the hard man he was today from believing that he could never be accepted in any other walk of life thanks to his disfigurement.

Captain Dollimore was shocked when he saw him, not because of what he looked like, but because of who he was. 'I had no idea you stayed in the service,' he said to WO Hacklett, when their paths crossed on the quarterdeck.

'Nothing else was the right life for me after the *Warspite*, sir,' Hacklett said, his voice more gruff than once it was. 'Sent Jerry packing that day, we did, sir.'

Dollimore sensed straight away that Hacklett had convinced himself of many things in order to come to terms with what had happened all those years ago and decided he was not going to dredge up any unwanted emotion. He simply said, 'I also see that you've learned how to talk properly.'

'You were right about that one, sir. Seems like I always had it in me.' After a difficult pause, Hacklett seemed to want to say something but he stifled the words and allowed the look in his eye to convey the gratitude of what Dollimore once did for him.

'It's good to have you on board, Mr Hacklett.'

'Thank you, sir.' They parted with a smart salute.

*

At the command of 'Attention!' every man on parade drew himself up smartly then Lieutenant Selkirk turned and saluted their commanding officer. Once Dollimore had returned the salute, all arms came down again and he looked out over the array of uniforms that denoted every rank between boy seaman and commander immaculately presented before him. On the quayside was a Royal Marines band with brass instruments at the ready and a fifty-strong group of civilians. These were families and friends.

Dollimore cast his eyes over the crowd and saw Jennifer staring back at him from beneath the rim of a large blue hat. Her pride in this day, in her husband and in his achievements was written all over her face, and he took extra heart from that look. She had been the one who had been by his side through every trial to date. It was a shame, he thought, that Betty, standing next to her, looked so bored. He suspected that she would remain so until she had free rein to wander among the young officers and engage them in conversation.

Without any further ado Crawshaw ordered the commissioning pendant to be broken and within seconds the breeze took hold of it as it was hoisted upon the mainmast. Everybody saw the red cross on the white background unfurl and then fly. With that Dollimore read out the

Commissioning Order then observed the hoisting of the White Ensign to the pleasing strains of the band's rendition of *God Save The King*.

*

After the necessary religious observances and the obligatory singing of the hymn *Eternal Father Strong To Save*, Dollimore looked at the men. All were stern and serious. This is where it all begins. Projecting his voice, he said, 'Well, men, we have been given the great honour and responsibility of taking to sea the navy's newest, largest and finest cruiser. People everywhere are already talking about her just for what she is, but it now rests upon us to build and enhance her reputation. No one man can shoulder this alone. The work must be done by all of us. I may be the captain but am I more important than the gunner? Or the signaller? Or the stoker? Or the cook? Every man has his job to do and every other man is dependent upon his fellow. This is how we shall go to sea. This is how we shall perhaps go to war.

'It is my resolve that this will be a happy ship. Most of you know the ropes so you know that there is lots of hard work ahead of us. A clean ship is what makes an efficient ship which in turn makes a happy ship. Over the coming weeks we will get to know her and each other through this hard work. Those of you who have worked up a ship before will know the benefits of working and sweating and then working and sweating some more. For it will not do for *Burscombe* to be just the newest and largest cruiser. She must be the very best before all ships.

'You and I, we have a lot to prove. To go forward, we must do so without fear and without regret. This is what I am going to do and I am counting on you all to do the same. I'm sure you will make me proud.'

He had spoken clearly and concisely and now, as he looked about at the faces of his men for the umpteenth time, he noticed their expressions were already beginning to fill out with a sense of the determined pride that he had asked for. The *Burscombe* had finally passed from being pencilled ideas on a drawing board to a fully active warship, and Dollimore had given the men their motto: *Forward without fear or regret*.

Chapter Five

Joining the Home Fleet

For Rear-Admiral Clark the journey north consisted of a long, uncomfortable train ride in a rather suffocating heat. The breeze coming in from the open window, which was sometimes mixed with greasy smelling steam, offered some relief in the enclosed first class compartment but he had still felt compelled to remove his jacket and sit with an unbuttoned collar like some slumming peasant. While studying his documents he actually fell asleep and when he awoke he did not feel particularly well. This had never happened before. But then he knew that he was no spring chicken so it did not overly concern him. As it turned out the feeling was temporary and not bad enough to flag his spirit. Indeed the orders summoning him were the best thing to have happened to him in a long while.

He wiped his handkerchief across his brow and continued turning the pages of the file that he held. A new squadron was about to be formed, the 25th Cruiser Squadron, which was to be based on Rosyth. That was why he had been asked to come north by Admiral Forbes, Commander-in-Chief of the Home Fleet, to take command. He had been given a heavy cruiser, HMS *Godham*. She was an older type of ship, maybe a little worn out, but was known to be a sturdy workhorse. What more than made up for it, though, was that he was also being given those two new light cruisers that people could not stop talking about, *Burscombe* and *Farecombe*. The prospective power of eight 8-inch, thirty two 6-inch and thirty two 4-inch guns between just three ships was not to be scoffed at. Looking over the facts and figures he knew immediately in which ship he was going to raise his flag. Unfortunately, it could only be the *Godham*. Much as he liked the idea of going to war in one of the new ships, she was the only one which was a fully worked up vessel having been engaged on her present commission for over a year.

While he perused these documents his mind turned onto what it was he should do with David. Should he keep him under his watchful gaze in the *Godham* or should he send him to earn his keep under one of the other skippers of the squadron? His eyes wandered onto the particulars of those who had charge of HMS *Burscombe* and caught sight of the names Dollimore and Crawshaw. Well I never, he thought. Both names were familiar to him and more of an unlikely pairing he would never have imagined. There was not much positive he could think about either so, with a chuckle of mischievousness, he decided that that was where he would put his insolent son. That should set the cat among the pigeons.

The day was beginning to draw to a close and he found himself looking out over the glistening waters of the Forth estuary as the train rumbled slowly across the great Victorian bridge, a structure which he was more used to seeing from the deck of a ship. Looking out eastwards he saw a beautiful sight, a small fleet of ships steaming out to sea grouped in their various squadrons. Just a couple of hundred miles beyond the horizon lay the approaches to the Baltic Sea. That was the one region dominated by the German Navy and it was perfectly possible that they possessed large warships built in contravention of all those painstakingly negotiated post-war treaties. Whatever power they had, Clark still held them in scorn. Let Hitler have his toys. They will do him no good.

The train pulled into Inverkeithing a short while later and he happily climbed down onto the platform. It would be good to get some blood moving through his stiff body again. As the porter dealt with his baggage, he observed the throng of healthy sailors of all ranks with kit-bags slung over their shoulders, coming and going amidst the hissing steam. He noted the business-like air of the men arriving and the grins of the men leaving. That was always the way.

'Admiral Clark, sir?' asked a very young man dressed in the neatly pressed uniform of an ordinary seaman. As he spoke he came smartly to attention and saluted.

'Yes,' Clark replied, returning the salute but noticeably without the precision and verve of the rating's.

'Ordinary Seaman Symmonds, sir,' the man introduced himself. 'Your driver, sir.'

'Very good. Lead the way. I have business at the base before we head to my lodgings.'

'Aye aye, sir. I have all the instructions.'

Too much information, thought Clark. 'Get on with it then,' he snapped.

*

On the outskirts of Rosyth was a large, white-washed cottage with a thatched roof, dark oaken beams and lattice-framed windows. It was one of a staggered row that stretched along a road which carried the traveller northwest out of the urban sprawl and into the expansive green of the rolling countryside. It was quiet. It was discreet.

OS Symmonds drove his car up the near pitch black lane which was flanked by hedgerows and trees and eventually pulled up into a gravel driveway, though he had done so hesitantly because he was in unfamiliar territory, not entirely certain that he was in the right place. It did not help that Rear-Admiral Clark was not sure either, though it could only ever be Symmonds' fault.

It was the right place.

'Put my bags on the doorstep and then you're dismissed,' said Clark.

'Aye aye, sir,' Symmonds replied, hiding any bemusement and moving as swiftly as possible. He was already more than aware that he was not liking this assignment. The admiral was largely uncommunicative but when he was, he was just rude and now he was being shifty about this cottage as well. One of his mates had said that the Clarks were well respected as being amongst the foremost families of the nation. Well, now he would go back and have words because he certainly did not respect him.

Once he had placed the bags on the step by the light of the overhead lamp, the young sailor jumped back into the car and started up the engine.

'Come back at 0800 tomorrow morning,' ordered Clark.

'Aye aye, sir,' answered Symmonds. With a few gravel stones flicked up by the tyres, he drove the car out of the driveway and was gone.

Clark rang the bell and the door swung open straight away. The lady inside had been waiting behind the door until the bell had signalled the all clear. 'Diane,' he said.

She smiled her wholesome, almost innocent smile. She was a highly voluptuous woman, almost a vision of saintly perfection. She wore her blonde hair neatly pinned away from her brow and the back flowing about the nape of her neck. Her mascara-lined eyes were large and oozed seduction without effort. They seemed to have a mystical light shining from them. Her lips she kept reddened with a light lipstick but this only needed to be subtle because of her natural beauty.

She wore a cream and white summer dress with sleeves stretching respectably down to her wrists and the hem reaching down to her ankles. The ankle was as much as Clark was willing to allow her to display when she was not in the bedroom for he still clung to those same things which had attracted him when he was a young man. Of course his mind had modernised to a certain extent but he was essentially a Victorian gentleman and held the old standards dear to his heart. The younger generation seemed determined to break down everything that the Victorian citizen had taken for granted but this girl, twenty years his junior, would follow his instructions to the letter.

'I have tea ready in the lounge,' she said.

'Good,' he said. 'I have paperwork to do but that can wait until later.'

As they walked through to the pleasant room with its armchairs placed before an unlit fireplace, walls lined with bookcases and decorated by tasteful paintings of naturalist themes, he was pleased to note that the cottage was airy, clean and well furnished. 'You made an excellent choice,' he said of the place.

'Thank you,' she replied and bade him sit down in the most inviting chair.

He watched her pour the tea into the small china cups and loved the image before him. Diane played the role well. She had built herself up into being everything that Dorothy had long since ceased to be: happy, useful and compliant.

She was just what he needed when he was away from home. The small fortune that she was costing him was worth it, even with the dire situation of his finances concerning the hall. This was the only time that Clark would admit that he had a frailty – and then only to himself. But it was a frailty shared by men and women alike the world over. It was one of the basic instincts of the human no matter what culture they belonged to. Whatever the economic or political circumstances a person found themselves in, from the richest to the poorest, from the most responsible to the most aloof, there was always enough money and reason to feed a vice.

*

Now that the liaison with Diane Greyforth had satisfied particular needs, Clark was well fortified to be able to launch himself into his work. He raised his flag in HMS *Godham* and immediately ordered the ship up to Scapa Flow in the Orkney Islands.

The *Godham* was a bulky ten thousand ton heavy cruiser with three vintage funnels and a high freeboard running the full length of the ship. There was nothing sleek and romantic about her like there was with some of the other classes, but Clark knew her for the tough ship that she was and refused to be disappointed.

Captain Nunn kept everything pristine, as did most commanding officers, and it did not surprise Clark to smell fresh paint as he stepped aboard. Seamen and marines were parading on the quarterdeck to welcome him with all due ceremony and he was appreciative of it. They were well turned out and he decided that today would not be the day that he need find fault.

Nunn himself had added a couple of pounds to his waistline in the two years since Clark had last seen him but the unassuming, bespectacled gentleman was as alert as ever and eager to make something of this commission. He listened patiently to the explanation of what the composition of the 25th Cruiser Squadron was going to be and what Clark expected of him as his flag captain. He accepted this graciously but inwardly felt uneasy when the admiral hinted that Captain Dollimore and Commander Crawshaw should bear watching for they had chequered pasts and dubious reputations. He did not know those men personally and had a revulsion to reacting precipitately to hearsay. He wanted to make his own mind up so he made no comment or expression as Clark said this.

After a short cruise northwards the *Godham* was steaming casually in through the opened boom defence of the Scapa Flow anchorage. It was a familiar place to Clark. The flat surface of the water stretching miles to the north with Royal Navy ships scattered across its expanse was a welcome sight. The whole area was completely surrounded by the low hills of the Scottish Orkney's with all the channels and gaps plugged by booms, sunken blockships or natural tides of intense ebb and flo, making it an impregnable defensive position. It was the perfect place for the battlefleet to use as a haven from the attentions of an enemy. Clark felt safe here.

They had not long anchored near some other cruisers when a flag signal was hoisted upon the foremast of the imposing battleship HMS *Nelson*. The Commander-in-Chief, Admiral Sir Charles Forbes, was summoning all admirals present to join him at 1800.

*

The Chamberlain government's present requirement was to have the ships of the Royal Navy gradually and cautiously brought to their war stations. To avoid provoking Hitler's aggression the Admiralty decided that a fleet exercise would be reason enough to cover their movements. All available ships of the Home Fleet would be placed on a war footing and, under the terms of this exercise, it would be the perfect opportunity to test further their readiness, quality and flexibility. Everything was done openly and above board. After all every government in the world had a right to pose problems to their various fighting arms and play them out.

HMS *Nelson*, the great but aging thirty four thousand ton battleship sat motionless at anchor in the huge bay. From various directions small motor boats skimmed their way towards her as the admirals congregated for the meeting.

Clark looked up at the huge ship as his boat sped towards her. He had had the pleasure of commanding a battleship a few years before and never tired of seeing these majestic old ladies. Some people had commented on the unconventional design of this particular one, of having three great gun turrets on an over-extended fo'c'sle and its superstructure in a comparatively cramped position aft, but this had never bothered him. All he saw was the power.

He soon climbed up the lowered stairway on her portside and was piped aboard amidst a slow-moving procession of other admirals and one or two senior captains. He recognised almost all of them as they bade each other the compliments of the day. Shortly afterwards they were ushered below.

Seated at the large table in his plush quarters in the stern of the ship, Admiral Sir Charles Forbes, now facing these dozen or so subordinates, reiterated the prospective aims of the fleet. All were acquainted with the general defensive strategy for protecting the British Isles but he felt that it would be good to go over it again because then they would be in no doubt as to his intentions. This was an essential part of the old Nelsonian tradition that Forbes fully invested in and something that had been sadly lacking at the time of Jutland.

'Now, our exercise,' said Forbes, swiftly moving onto that subject. 'The ships of the fleet will be strung out on their extended patrol line in a blockade of Germany all the way from the Faeroes down to the Orkney's or waiting to sortie from here in Scapa. One ship – and which one I've not yet decided – will be given the task of taking on the role of the German heavy cruiser *Hipper* and starting from a specific point in the North Sea, will be attempting to break out into the Atlantic as a prospective raider. You all know the threat posed to the merchant routes by these large ships so your job will be to find and prevent our designated ship from achieving its aim. It's simple but it should be interesting.'

'And should war break out right now the fleet will be assembled and ready for action,' commented Rear-Admiral Hallifax, putting his cigarette out in an ashtray.

'Yes,' agreed Forbes. 'I'm sure all of you are feeling, as I am and along with most of the country, that the crisis point is near.'

Clark gave a harrumph which made all look at him. 'I'm not easy with all this pussyfooting about. If I had my way I'd jump in and show the Hun a thing or two right now.'

Forbes furrowed his brow. His personal attitude towards Clark had never been particularly pleasant but that was only because the man made such an issue of everything. He had sent for him because he knew exactly how to wield a squadron of ships as a potent force. That was what was going to be of paramount importance in the coming months.

Hallifax said, 'I'm usually all in favour of leaving the politics to the politicians but the only problem is, it's always us who have to clean up the mess.'

'Remember,' said Rear-Admiral Blagrove, speaking in precise tones, 'We only hesitate because we do not want war. Chamberlain is superb in that he reflects the mood of the country on that point.' He was a man known for understanding matters beyond his remit.

'And that helps absolutely nobody,' said Clark. 'Since when has the country been expert in foreign problems? Anyway, as Hallifax suggested, it's in all likelihood that we shall be at war before the

78

completion of this exercise anyway. Mark my words, bank on Hitler. He'll force the decision.'

Always careful to avoid any personal commitment on political matters in front of subordinates, Forbes jumped in at this juncture with, 'That eventuality would, of course, be ideal for us as it would save us from dispersing the fleet only to have to reconfigure it again at some later date. But we shouldn't bank on it, I'm afraid.'

Clark's eyes narrowed slightly as he soaked up the rebuke.

Hallifax, clearly enjoying the conversation, leaned forward in his seat. 'If only Chamberlain, God bless him, had the guts to shove his boot up Hitler's backside then we would all know where we stand.'

'What are the chances,' asked Blagrove in a calmer tone, 'that Hitler will see us gathering our fleet as a threat?'

'It's our thinking that he's too preoccupied in the east to pay us too much attention,' answered Forbes. 'But, gentlemen, Hitler, Chamberlain and the east are subjects you or I can do little about. Let us just make sure that we have done everything in our power to be as ready as possible. Now, the exercise... As the ship attempting to break out into the Atlantic is supposed to be the *Hipper* we need to select one of a similar size to take on the role. Who should have the honour?'

A few mouths moved to open but none were as fast as Clark's. Without a second's pause, he said, 'I believe it should be the *Burscombe*.'

'Oh?' Forbes rolled his eyes for a moment as he sought to remember her whereabouts. 'Er, isn't she just commissioning in Portsmouth?'

'As we speak, taking on her crew and stores.'

'But she is completely untried and has done absolutely no working up.'

'And as such would be the least effective in contributing to the blockade. The point is she's brand new, new design, most of the men have never been to sea before and the captain himself has been shore-based for six years or more. I believe the experience will be invaluable for them.'

'Captain Charles Dollimore,' stated Forbes.

'The very one.'

'I've heard that name,' said Blagrove. 'Wasn't it something to do with being relieved of command? That's right, I remember now, the incident with the *Spikefish* in the Clyde.'

'To be fair, he was exonerated though it was deemed he needed a break,' explained Clark. 'This exercise should demonstrate once and for all whether or not he's fighting fit.'

So the decision was made. Forbes accepted the idea and instructed Clark to issue the orders forthwith. What he did not divulge to anybody was that a month previously he had received a copy of a letter which had long since been lodged at the Admiralty concerning that particular captain. It had read thus:

To Whom It May Concern,

Regarding the possible transfer of Captain C.G. Dollimore to the HOME FLEET. He is one of the most loyal officers to have served in my command. His knowledge of the navy and its organisation is excellent and his handling of the establishment has been without fault. The base is always neat and clean and the men serving here are always well turned-out and of good morale. I give full credit of these accomplishments to Dollimore. He has kept himself fit and has been in good health the whole time and encourages those in his command to do likewise. I believe it is time he was given a sea-going command again.

Rear-Admiral S.F.T. Plowton

Forbes had returned this letter to the Admiralty having noted upon it that he did not agree with the last sentence, but it been a gesture only since Dollimore was already in command of his ship. Thinking on the situation, Forbes was pleased that Clark had made the suggestion that he had. As he had said, it would settle the matter one way or the other.

*

Young David Clark was admitted to the Burscombe's gunroom on the evening before the ship was due to sail. It was an easy transition thanks to the fact that he knew some of the other midshipmen already assigned. Most notable amongst these was his good friend Robert Barclay-Thompson, or Beatty for short.

Beatty had an excellent spirit and a great, energetic decisiveness. At college, Clark remembered, his grades had been brilliant and his actions always well thought through. His character had an enviable mixture of cool intellect, courage and highly disciplined independence which allowed him to be liked, respected, or both, by practically everybody. If he did have a shortcoming, it could only be that he did not easily sympathise with anybody beyond the confines of his class.

The coincidence of the initials of his surname had led him to being called Beatty within fifteen minutes of his arrival at college. Of course he welcomed it. After all, was Beatty not a great naval name? He and Clark, with two or three other boys in tow, had sustained each other through all the tough years at Dartmouth.

The gunroom was a bit of a cosy affair. Once the dining table, armchairs and coffee tables had been taken into account there was not much room left, but its decor was bright and aided by the usual strong electric lamps happily burning away. Close to the connecting pantry door one's eye was drawn to a particularly good painting of King George VI in his uniform of Admiral of the Fleet. He stared down at the midshipmen with solemn dignity as though forever reminding them of their obligations.

But not everything about the gunroom was inviting. Unfortunately, one of the other fellows he found here was one who had not been such a good friend during those long school years. Farlow was his name, the middle son of a mediocre aristocratic family who dealt mainly in land and other people's business. Much as he did not like Clark, he had been and was still wary enough of him not to consider being too bullish. Just a bit rude was how he wished to play it.

'Well, Clark,' Farlow said, unimpressed when the 'new boy' stepped into the gunroom. Looking up patronisingly from his comfortable position sunk deep in an armchair, he lowered the copy of the *Daily Mail* that he had been pretending to read and continued in exaggerated upper class tones, 'You've missed all the hard work but don't worry, we've victualled the ship in your absence.'

Clark frowned and glanced at the other's waistline. 'It hasn't helped you shed the extra pounds though, I see.'

Ignoring the muffled sniggering from other parts of the room, Farlow said, 'The point is, little boy, we're all serious about this business and the *Burscombe* doesn't carry passengers.'

'Even those who can't fit through the hatches?'

Beatty laughed. 'Come on. You two can catch up on old times later.' He led his friend back out of the room and headed off down the passageway. Being a few inches taller, his black hair was almost scraping the overhead trunking. To counter this he walked with a slight stoop.

Having made no secret of the fact that he'd been very happy to see Clark posted on board, he took it upon himself to show his friend around the cramped living spaces. Once past the wardroom, where they were most certainly not welcome, he led the way up a ladder to the next deck. There was much bustle as men of all ranks and departments walked this way and that, chasing after a thousand and one unfinished tasks before the ship could leave harbour. They found themselves in a thin lamp-lit passageway which looped itself around a clump of bathrooms, heads and storerooms. Lining the outer edges were rows of cabins and offices.

Stepping out of the way of two ratings carrying boxes of files – for it was one of the unwritten rules of the service that a man must make way for another who was working – Beatty explained, 'This is mostly lieutenants and subs up here but the Paymaster and Engineering Commanders have got offices and cabins just over there on the starboard side. Oh, and keep the language clean; the reverend is berthed just over there on the left. As you might expect, we midshipmen don't get cabins...'

'Don't tell me,' said Clark. 'We have to sling our hammocks in the passageway.'

'Spot on, though I'm afraid you've got the draughty spot by the door at the fore end. You're the last in so we others have seniority.'

Clark gave a chuckle. 'You make it sound like you've been on board forever.'

'Eight days actually.' Before he continued, he looked at his old friend and said, 'Here listen, Clark. I heard you got into a spot of bother with Captain Howard. Are you still trying to fight the system? There are ways and means of doing these things, you know.'

'I know I must be embarrassing to you...,' began Clark, holding up his hands in a helpless gesture.

'That's not what I'm getting at, old boy,' Beatty said. 'I'm on your side no matter what happens. Got that? It's just that you're one of the smartest chaps I know and I really want to see you do well. Of all of us you have the gift.' He had concluded many years ago that they both possessed a similar wit even if they did not always agree on everything and he clearly hoped that Clark would try and settle.

'I have the gift?' asked Clark. 'Don't undersell yourself, Beatty.'

'Would I ever?' said Beatty with a mock frown. 'I intend to be Admiral of the Fleet before I'm done.'

*

Crawshaw and Selkirk came up to the Paymaster Commander's office and carefully stepped around Felix, the obstinate black and white cat that would not move from the doorway. 'What's all this I'm hearing about the surgeon-commander?' Crawshaw asked of Pay directly.

'Ah, yes, he died of a heart attack this morning at a hotel,' replied Pay matter-of-factly, even blandly. At his time of life there was not much that could happen to excite him. It was said that he had been present at Dogger Bank, Jutland, and had been torpedoed twice on convoys in the Great War.

'Bloody hell,' replied Crawshaw, screwing up his face in consternation. 'We'll have to put in for another straight away.'

'Already done,' said Pay. 'Of course we still have two lieutenants to run the sick bay.'

This was true but if there were any emergency operations needing to be done at sea, these men were theoretically not yet qualified to perform them. Still, there was nothing more to be done. Every branch of the navy were needing more and more men as the fleets expanded so they would just have to be patient.

That being said, it was a shame that they had still not embarked a Walrus aircraft because, as Pay then pointed out, he could not see why they were keeping Lieutenant Hanwell, the air officer, on strength with hardly anything to do. Hanwell had arrived on the day of the commission and had simply been helping to load stores. He had done hardly anything related to his specialist qualities as a pilot of the Fleet Air Arm.

'Shall we see him off?' asked Selkirk.

'No, no, no,' replied Crawshaw. 'You know what'll happen if we do that. The second we get rid of our pilot we'll get a plane. Then we'll have no one to fly it.'

'Yes, you're probably right.'

'Keep at it, Pay,' said Crawshaw, stepping out of the office with Selkirk in tow. He had not gone far when he saw two midshipmen engaged in conversation a few feet away. One was Barclay-Thompson but the other he had never seen before. It stood to reason that this must be David Clark.

Crawshaw had received notification a few days ago that, not only was this boy's father to be their squadron commander, but that Midshipman Clark was also to join the Burscombe's crew. He was not best pleased about either of the appointments because he was not enamoured of the Clark family in general. They played about with people's lives including his own – but that was a deeply personal matter.

To demonstrate further that the Clarks were a law unto themselves, the young man's being drafted here was next to pointless. The *Burscombe* already had a full complement of 'snotties' so Midshipman Clark was just superfluous.

Both young men straightened themselves up as they saw the commander coming towards them. Clark looked him in the eye. There was no apprehension, no fear. The boy was as sure of himself as all his family were and that annoyed Crawshaw even more. 'Clark, is it?' he asked.

'Yes, sir.'

Then, in a tone which surprised all about him for its venom, Crawshaw said, 'Well, you can forget all about your silver spoon comforts here, boy. And we'll have none of the bother you gave Captain Howard either. He may be a soft touch but I'm not. Clear?'

'Yes, sir,' said Clark, his expression unchanging. He had half expected to have that business thrust in his face by his superiors at some point, but not so quickly and not so malevolently.

Crawshaw decided that he had already seen enough of the new boy and started on along the passageway again. He had barely taken two steps when Lieutenant Giles appeared in front of him.

The busy man's short fringe clung to his forehead with perspiration and his cheeks were reddened from exposure to the sun. He quickly stated, 'Ammunition's coming over, sir.'

'Thanks, Bosun,' replied Crawshaw. He did not need to worry any more about it than that for Giles was more than capable in clearing the lower decks and organising the work parties. Even though there were motorised hoists in use to load the shells down into the four stowages there was still much manual handling needed to be done and the men, who had not worked this hard for a while, were discovering muscles they never knew they had, or were rediscovering those that they had forgotten about.

'Oh, Bosun,' Crawshaw said as though it was an afterthought. 'Those two men there can help you.'

'Very good, sir,' said Giles, sizing up Beatty and the other one whom he did not recognise.

As they walked out on deck to begin unloading the tons of ordnance sent over on a barge from the Priddy's Hard depot, Beatty looked strangely at his friend. 'Listen, old boy, I know you can be a bit of a troublemaker but surely you must have insulted the commander in a former life or something.'

'Never met the bastard.'

*

Dollimore read the signal concerning their next move and immediately sent for Crawshaw. 'What do you think?' he asked the commander, who had just stepped into the small, basically furnished sea cabin which was situated high up in the forward superstructure.

Crawshaw, inwardly cursing for the fact that he still had so many other things to contend with besides this, scanned the slip of paper. It read:

To Officer Commanding 'BURSCOMBE'
Proceed to position – Horn's Reef as soon as crew and stores embarked for participation in HOME FLEET EXERCISE. Further instructions to follow,
Rear-Admiral Commanding 25th CRUISER SQUADRON

Barely disguising his ill-humour, Crawshaw said, 'Sounds like a bit of a hoot.'

'Yes, that could be one way to describe it,' said Dollimore. 'Something the matter, Exo?'

'Just the usual, sir.' Quickly wanting to change the subject, Crawshaw asked, 'Don't you think that sending us over to Denmark might be a bit risky?'

'In what way?'

'Well, just supposing that war is declared while we're over there? With half the German Navy parked up nearby we'll be a sitting duck.

Don't you think we should at least have the chance to practice firing our guns first?'

Dollimore smiled one of his rare smiles and repeated the other's words. 'Sounds like a bit of a hoot.' He was to be no more forthcoming than that apart from saying, 'Well, tie up all the loose ends. We're departing tomorrow morning at 0730.'

'Very good, sir,' said Crawshaw and left the cabin, his mind full of plans as to how he was going to cram forty eight hours of work into twelve.

Dollimore watched him go then turned back to his paperwork. Crawshaw did have a point, he thought. It would have been a matter of greater wisdom not to send a completely untrained crew in a brand new ship right in close to Germany at such a time as this. Anyway, there was nothing to be done but obey and do the best that they could in the circumstances. Their concerns, he decided, would be noted in his final report.

*

The next couple of days saw them cruising steadily up into the North Sea, first with the coast of England clear to port then with an almost unblemished panorama of flat blue-grey sea about them. Early in the voyage they sighted plentiful shipping in the usual lanes between England and France, but later this dwindled to the occasional lone merchantman.

With the ship rolling gently and a generous sun beating down on busy men still conducting drills, Dollimore had the bosun's mate pipe some of his officers to meet him at the chart house. In this small office just below the bridge he happened upon Midshipman Clark and Able Seaman Barrett poring over a chart of the surrounding sea.

Barrett was about as common as a man could be, not well educated and always working hard not to swear as he spoke. The reason that he was a welcome presence in the chart house was because of his inexplicably natural grasp of mathematics and navigation. When posed a problem in this area he was swift to solve it and never wrong. The navigating officer, Lt-Cdr Peterson, who was also a dab hand in this sphere, had quickly decided that he could rely on Barrett one hundred per cent.

Clark and Barrett both straightened up when Dollimore suddenly entered.

'Is he getting it?' the captain asked the AB.

'Once 'e understands the f... earth's not flat, sir, 'e'll be fine, sir,' replied Barret.

'Well, Clark,' said Dollimore, 'it seems as though we might make a navigator out of you.' After a pause, he continued, 'The chaps won't be here just yet so we've got a minute or two to talk. What was the nature of your problem with Captain Howard?'

That was direct, thought Clark, and he doesn't seem to like me either. I suppose there's nothing for it but to be direct in return. 'Captain Howard was a fine man, sir, but I think he and many other officers are blinkered in their scope of what to teach cadets and midshipmen.'

Immediately provoked to disgust, Dollimore asked, 'Do you think I'm blinkered?'

'I don't know you, sir.'

'Well, do you think the training on board thus far is up to your standards?'

'The training is perfect, sir,' said Clark, realising he was not going to fight his way out of this corner.

'I'm glad you think so,' Dollimore said bitterly. 'You know, all the other young men don't question what they're taught. They listen and learn. I haven't much time for boys who steamroll over others just because of who they are. Admiral's son or not, if you question me I'll put you ashore. And you can count yourself fortunate that we don't cane senior midshipmen.'

Clark was not even going to attempt to start on the fact that he was not the way he was because he felt confident that he could get away with anything. Far from it, but that would take too much explaining.

'Yes, sir,' he said, with enough capitulation to end the attack.

Dollimore stared at him for a few seconds. 'You're obviously a boy of considerable opinions even when they're not welcome. Well, okay, let's put your intelligence to the test. When the others get up here, you stay.'

'Yes, sir,' answered Clark.

'Barrett, you may leave us.'

'Aye aye, sir.' He happily squeezed past Clark and fled the room.

Crawshaw, when he arrived with Peterson, Digby and Irwin, the new 2nd Officer of the Watch, was surprised and somewhat dismayed to find that Clark had also been invited. He wondered what the object of that could be. In the meantime he prepared himself to listen to the captain with his arms folded and a serious expression on his face.

Even with just the six of them in attendance it was uncomfortably tight here in this room, and everybody shuffled a bit in order to be able to see the chart on the table. The only one that held back was Peterson. Obviously he was already in the know.

'I'm sure most of you know why I've gathered you together,' said Dollimore. Glancing over at Clark, he then said, 'For those of you who don't, this morning I was furnished with the final details of this Home Fleet exercise in which we are to play a central part.' As he started running his finger along the significant points of the chart, he continued, 'Now, we have been heading towards the Horn's Reef off the coast of Denmark and I can tell you that it is because we have been chosen to assume the role of the German cruiser *Hipper*. Pretending that we have just come out through the Kiel Canal we are then to try and break out past the British blockade of the North Sea in order to menace the merchant shipping in the Atlantic. I have already discussed with Peterson my thoughts on how to achieve this but I would invite comments and suggestions from any of you before I explain them.'

'Why did they choose us, sir?' Irwin asked.

Crawshaw commented, 'Probably because we're not yet much good for anything else.' This squarely indicated his disgust for their lack of preparedness.

Dollimore shook his head. 'Gentlemen, all of that is irrelevant. Although I'm always interested in what the powers-that-be are thinking, that knowledge can't help us now. One thing I know for certain is that, when we succeed in this mission and turn up in the Atlantic with a smart, tidy ship, completely ready for action, their Lordships will know our worth. Now, how do you think we should do it?'

There was silence for a few seconds as each of the officers digested the challenge, then it was Crawshaw who piped up with, 'I would favour heading up the Norwegian coast and cutting across to break out between the Faeroes and Iceland. I know a bit about what the dispositions of the fleet should be and whatever forces there are at that point will be very spread out. That's our best chance.'

'Very time consuming,' said Dollimore, thinking of the many days it would take to cover the distance.

'And fuel consuming too,' said Clark.

Each pair of eyes turned on him in either surprise or disgust. It had been assumed that the midshipman had been invited to listen, not contribute.

Dollimore was the only person whose expression did not change. 'Go on.'

Clark had already correctly figured that he could not be any more despised so he fearlessly continued, 'Well, I know the endurance of our ship is getting on for nine thousand miles but, as a commerce raider, we would necessarily need to do a bit of dashing about, so that would be considerably reduced through fuel consumption. The führer wouldn't be best pleased if we were worrying about refuelling even before we'd sunk any merchant ships. Granted, if we were German then we would make provision for having our own tanker at sea but we couldn't count on that. What if *it* got caught in the blockade? We'd be stuffed, so we'd need to conserve our own fuel.'

Crawshaw stared at him. 'Smooth argument, young man, but you fail to take into account the fact that the fleet's concentration will be thicker the further south you go so it'll not be fuel consumption that you're worrying about, rather your very survival.'

'Do you have an answer for that, boy?' asked Dollimore.

Clark decided that he literally had nothing to lose by speaking his mind. 'There is a very direct route to the Atlantic that it would be worth taking a chance on.'

'Oh?'

'Sir, I'm sure you're more familiar with the Pentland Firth than me.'

Dollimore said nothing, just stared at him.

'Well, it's not as well patrolled as the other routes, is it?' Clark said.

Crawshaw immediately exclaimed, 'That's because it's in full sight of the Orkney's and the Scottish mainland, you fool!'

Dollimore looked at Clark and said, 'That's a very bold manoeuvre that you're suggesting.' Then after a pause, he announced, 'It's also the very manoeuvre that I have decided upon.'

'What?' Crawshaw said in disbelief.

Peterson gave Clark a confirming nod and there were stunned looks all around the chart house.

'It just remains to inform you of the details,' said Dollimore. 'We will arrive at the Horn's Reef tomorrow afternoon at which point we shall inform the Commander-in-Chief that we are starting the exercise. We shall obviously want to break through the Pentland Firth under cover of darkness so we'll time that for the middle of the second night after that. Any questions?'

There were none.

Dollimore left the room after first giving Clark a glance which could have been interpreted to be something sinister. But was it? Why was he so enigmatic?

There was a mixture of feelings about the audacity or the foolhardiness of the plan, but all of them were equally curious to see if it would work. As the other officers went back to their duties Crawshaw lingered alone for a few moments longer staring at the chart. For somebody who wanted to re-establish his career as a seagoing captain, Dollimore was taking a considerable gamble. Nobody would have thought the less of him if he had played a safer game. Surely what they were about to do was not worth the risk. He went back to his work full of indignation at the fact that he had been made to look a fool by both the captain and that upstart boy.

Chapter Six

A Bold Manoeuvre

At the age of thirty four Douglas Bonner was beginning to find that this constant exercising was tiring him out quicker than it used to. They had gone from Actions Stations to Boat Drill, from Towing Fore and Aft to Prize Crew Drill, from Damage Control Drill to Air Defence Stations and much more besides. It was exhausting, but what gave him confidence was that he noticed how hard pressed a lot of the younger men looked. He swore that he would never give any hints as to how his body was slowing down and even let them know that they were making him feel like an Olympic athlete.

He had decided to be particularly unpleasant to Ordinary Seaman Gordy because he was the skinniest, whitest, sickliest looking specimen who had ever been placed below decks on any of the ships he had served on. What made matters worse was that this hapless young Irish lad had been assigned to his mess and division so they had to live in very close quarters with each other.

Gordy was more commonly known as Les. He had started out as Paddy to his messmates but they came to notice that each night he tried to read a little of a huge volume of *Les Misérables* before he went to sleep. The funny thing was, it was clear that he was getting absolutely nowhere with it. The heavy book lay open, faced down on his chest every night with hardly a page turned. Why did he bother? 'My dad says it's a classic,' was all anyone could get out of him.

So he was a skinny, white, sickly Irish boy with no mind of his own and Bonner hated all of that. The navy was supposed to have standards. On this evening, when Bonner stepped through the hatch into the mess, he immediately said, 'Who ever 'eard of tightenin' up a bottle screw usin' 'is finger as a marlin spike?'

One or two men laughed as they looked from him to Les.

'God, boy, you're a disgrace,' Bonner said to him.

Les looked up at his antagonist with an expression of extreme concentration on his face.

Pincher, who was just closing up his locker, grabbed his own crotch and said, 'I did up a bottle screw with this once.'

Les was jealous. He would never have thought of that as a retort.

'It doesn't paint a pretty picture, does it,' continued Bonner to Les. 'An' yer still never told us how you upset the commander either. Is this how it's gonna be? You making this mess look like shit?'

Les, still concentrating, looked over at another figure sitting on a bench a couple of messes away. There sat Able Seaman Smith looking back at him with a huge grin on his face. There was no way that he could tell anyone what Smith had done to him. It was far too embarrassing, how it was he had been conned onto the commander's report.

Smith, or Smudge as they called him, was well known in the service. He only had four years on ships behind him but, everywhere he went, he carried with him an infectious sense of good humour backed up by a major dose of mischievousness. With the reputation of being the only man in the ship's company who had yet managed to make the captain laugh at a joke, he was practically untouchable. Even Bonner could not get to him. But what had he done to Les?

It was back on commissioning day when everybody was standing around in their best uniforms that Les had encountered Smudge for the first time.

Many officers and ratings alike had family and friends present that day and Smudge had noticed Captain Dollimore step ashore once the ceremony was over and usher his wife and daughter towards the gangway. Smudge immediately knew them for who they were because he too had recently served on the China Station and had seen them entering an official reception in Shanghai. So, when he had quite indiscriminately turned to Les and said, 'That's the captain's wife and daughter,' he was telling the truth.

It was the next bit that had slid seamlessly from his imagination. 'She's a right saucy one, the girl. I saw her once before on another ship, she always wears these knee length skirts. I swear to God, just to wind us up, she put her foot up on the capstan as though to check a scrape on the side of her shoe or something and all you could see was this massive great, hairy muff.'

With that Smudge had walked away. His work was done.

Les had then been caught by the humourless Lieutenant Irwin staring stupidly at Betty Dollimore's legs and bottom and, when ordered to get lost, had still spared the girl's figure another gawping look. That was enough for Irwin. He had dragged Les in front of the commander for his indiscretion and so the lad had found himself on report.

This was what he was embarrassed about, what he could not tell anyone, especially as he had since found out that Smudge's repertoire was nearly entirely made up of neat fabrications. He did not know what to do about this situation and felt that it was beginning to get out of hand. He had both Smudge, the most loved, and Bonner, the most hated, members of the crew on his back.

*

About half an hour after Dollimore had commented on the execution of the latest drill, he retired to his cabin to continue with the many reports that he had to work on. The activity went on without him. He knew that his standing order to clean the ship regularly was being enforced right now. Where there were eight hundred men living together in a confined space special attention had to be paid to hygiene. He was pleased that Crawshaw understood this and was pursuing the matter with due diligence.

Not having got far into his first report, he suddenly heard Peterson's voice coming through the voicepipe in the corner of the cabin. 'Bridge to captain.'

'What is it?' he asked.

'There's a cruise liner about six thousand yards off the port bow, sir,' came the tinny reply.

'Anything we should be concerned about?'

'She's flying a swastika.'

'I'll come take a look.'

He casually climbed out onto the bridge and observed the vintage ship steaming in the opposite direction at speed. She cut her way gracefully through the flat sea leaving a foamy torrent in her wake and a black cloud of smoke behind her tall, red and black funnels – clearly a coal burner. She was of the medium variety of liners, her freeboard a full two decks higher than Burscombe's but her weight not exceeding thirteen thousand tons. Old as her frame was, she boasted a recent paint job the length of her hull, a simple black below with white above.

As the two vessels neared each other it became apparent that the liner's side rails were crammed with hundreds of people waving and cheering at them.

Once opposite, Crawshaw and a few others waved back although feeling a little odd at doing so. They were on the brink of war with these people! 'Holiday makers, sir?'

'I expect so,' said Dollimore.

Peterson, taking a closer look through his binoculars, pointed out, 'Some of them are taking photographs of us, sir.'

'There's not a lot we can do about that, I'm afraid.' He hid the frustration that was crowding in on him.

Crawshaw looked at him then back at the liner. This was just one such indiscretion that had preyed upon his mind since they had been ordered to bring this brand new ship to within spitting distance of Germany. The worst case scenario right now would be war being declared but fortunately the politicians on both sides still wavered on the subject. He gave a cynical laugh, for the moment did require some sort of comment at least. 'Just think of it. Britain's newest cruiser in all her glory is going to appear before the Hun's intelligence services courtesy of a bunch of women and children holidaying in the sun.'

As one or two of the younger officers smiled at the remark, Dollimore gently thumped the bridge casing, saying, 'Well, that's life. At the end of the day they're not doing anything wrong, but then neither are we so there's nothing more to be said. Get her name and note it in the log.'

'Her name's *Trier Stern*,' said Clark, whom nobody had noticed appear beside them. 'She's used to give working class families cheap cruise holidays up and down the Norwegian coast and around the Baltic. Hitler's quite hot on the whole deal.'

Dollimore looked at him. 'If you don't mind, Mr Clark, but would you explain how it is you seem to know so much?'

'I find the Germans fascinating, sir.'

'I generally find them to be a bore,' commented Crawshaw.

'I was given the opportunity to travel there a couple of years ago. Naturally I couldn't pass it up. I actually saw the *Trier Stern* herself moored up in Lubeck. She's part of Hitler's *Strength Through Joy* programme in which a family can go on a state subsidised holiday which they would otherwise never be able to afford. The idea is that every

German from the highest to the lowest must be made to feel that he's included. Through shared experiences the German nation can only profit. Do you see the logic? It's also a good way for Hitler to thank them for all the rubbish he expects them to put up with. Oh, and of course they love him for it.'

'*Every* German, you say?' asked the young Lt Irwin with disgust. 'What about the Jews? Or the Gypsies? Or what about the...?'

'We've got the picture, Mr Irwin, thank you,' Dollimore cut in.

'There is that,' said Clark to Irwin, duly humbled. He supposed he must have sounded so enthusiastic about the positive part of Hitler's policy that it must have seemed like he had forgotten about that awful, darker side to the dictatorship.

'Well, now they've got lots of lovely pictures of us,' said Crawshaw. 'And of Norway too.'

Peterson asked, 'What are you getting at?'

'I'll eat my hat if these holidays are not simply a cover for intelligence gathering.'

'You think they've got their sights on Norway too?'

'Never underestimate the Hun.'

'Or the matelot,' smiled Clark. 'There were many places in Germany that we were forbidden to take photographs but I made quite an art of sneaking a few in.'

'Like what?' asked Peterson.

'Like a view of the countryside overlooking the point where the Moselle meets the Rhine. You see, the Siegfied Line is not too far away from there. It was quite a sticky situation, I don't mind saying. Do you know, our tour guide was an SS man.'

'Presumably they didn't search your luggage when you left?'

'They did actually,' replied Clark, thoroughly pleased with himself. 'But I hid the roll of film in my shoe.'

Dollimore looked at this young man carefully. The distaste that he had felt after reading the boy's reports was beginning to dissipate. Perhaps he was even beginning to like this individual who was showing himself to be so independent and bright. But 'individual' was still the correct word for it. It would be nice to see more indication of a team spirit. The most important thing now was that he should appreciate receiving the right training and be directed in his career in the best way possible. Dollimore left the bridge thinking on it.

The *Trier Stern* continued on her way leaving her trail of smoke rising high into the blue sky.

*

'Pilot, send a signal to the Commander-in-Chief Home Fleet and repeat to Admiralty: *Burscombe* in position Horn's Reef. Shall commence Operation Hipper,' said Dollimore. 'Once it's sent we shall observe radio silence.'

'Very good, sir,' replied Peterson, writing down the message and handing it to the waiting runner.

Then, for everybody within earshot, Dollimore announced, 'Make sure all the lookouts understand we are searching for submarines and air patrols as well as ships of the fleet. We should expect them to throw everything they have at us. Not that it will do them any good because I intend to be in the Atlantic the day after tomorrow.'

There were smiles and short laughs all around. He then broadcast a message of the same sentiment throughout the ship and the men began to wonder appreciatively about the captain's audacity.

So, they had finally come to that point off the coast of Denmark where the submerged shoals of the millennia-old glacial deposits lay hidden beneath the shifting surface of the sea. With the ship leaning over the opposite way to her tight swing to port, they adopted a north westerly course and picked up speed as they prepared to steam across that stretch of water that Dollimore knew and remembered so well. It was this very stretch where he and HMS *Warspite* had received their baptism of fire so many years ago, and the weather that day had been very much like this. With some effort he put that memory out of his mind and applied himself to the task in hand.

Soon the western skyline off the port bow, with its light scattering of cloud and setting sun, was deeply reddened as the tired and well-exercised crew were resigned to respond to the clang of eight bells. Men moved quietly as the Last Dog Watch changed to the First Watch.

Peterson looked out across the sea with satisfaction. He could be forgiven for sparing the evening a moment's thought because the sunset was a truly wonderful sight. He had always felt that being on an open bridge when the scenery was like this, alone with no other ships around, brought him closer to God and creation. It was relaxing and he was at peace.

His retreat, however, was short-lived as one of the lookouts suddenly announced, 'Aircraft approaching red-one-nine-five.'

Peterson sighed and turned in the direction indicated, raising his binoculars to his eyes. Scanning the sky off the port quarter he almost immediately picked up the slowly growing silhouette of what appeared to be a boat plane with a single engine mounted centrally above the wings. He was instantly at the voicepipe, once again alerting the captain to the new situation.

'It better not be the Fleet Air Arm,' answered Dollimore, although he already knew that it could not be. It would surely be ridiculous if the *Burscombe* were to be observed by the searching forces just half an hour into the exercise.

'I don't think so, sir,' said Peterson. 'I've never seen this type before. It could be Danish... or German.'

'Right, I'm coming up. And pipe for that Hanwell fellow to come to the bridge as well.'

Dollimore appeared on deck with Crawshaw trailing just behind. Looking about he saw some more of his men gathering on the flight deck and aft superstructure, throwing long shadows across the decks, all trying to get a glimpse of the aircraft. It began to circle them to the south and west at a distance of about two thousand yards.

By the time Hanwell, the air officer, appeared on the bridge it was edging round to the north. He had black rings around his eyes and his skin was a pasty white colour. On top of this, his eyelids appeared droopy and his face betrayed a certain contortion from discomfort. It did not take much to imagine that he was suffering from seasickness.

'What's the matter with you?' Dollimore still felt bound to ask.

'It must have been something I ate,' he almost sputtered.

'Perhaps you would have been better off on dry land.'

'Just get me in the air and I'll be right as rain.'

'Sorry, I can't do that for you,' said Dollimore, drawing his attention to the circling machine, 'but you can tell me what aircraft that is.'

Hanwell followed the point of the captain's finger to observe the machine gently buzzing along in the distance. 'Ah, that's a Dornier-18, no doubt about it.'

'A what?'

'A German reconnaissance aeroplane.'

'Cheeky bastards,' muttered Crawshaw.

As they watched, the plane turned and angled in closer towards them before resuming the circling pattern. As it passed ahead of them to starboard it ceased to be a blackened silhouette and the sunlight showed off its paintwork. Dollimore looked through his binoculars and could now definitely see that distinctive German cross painted upon the grey-green fuselage, the cross that they had become so conditioned to hate in the last war. These days, though, there was the added swastika adorning the tail-plane. That was a symbol of true menace.

Peterson remarked, 'Look how interested they are in us. I'd wager the captain of the *Trier Stern* signalled Kiel in order to send them out to get a closer look.'

'I'd love very much to shoot him down,' said Crawshaw. 'That'll teach him a lesson.'

'Belay that!' snapped Dollimore. It should not be too much to expect gentlemanly behaviour from the officers on the bridge, especially from the executive officer.

The aircraft turned in again and settled in a tight circle. They had closed to a range of less than five hundred yards. Very close. Part of the canopy then slid open and a man was quite clearly leaning out holding a camera. Before long he would have a nice collection of definitive shots of his future adversary from every angle.

'Our friendly Hun certainly has some gall,' said Peterson, shaking his head with admiration.

Hanwell tutted then said, 'We've rather handed ourselves to him on a plate, haven't we?'

Feeling that very thing himself, Dollimore could only reply, 'He's welcome to take as many pictures as he likes. He'll learn no more about us than the publishers of half a dozen magazines, or the ship enthusiasts we saw in Portsmouth.' Still, he thought, we should never have been in this position in the first place.

Eventually, the plane had circled them more times than any of them could remember and on its final pass it straightened up and flew very close down the starboard side from stem to stern. The co-pilot leaned out and waved quite amiably.

'What should we do?' asked Irwin, who had been standing quietly trying to comprehend the details of this unexpected situation.

'Wave back,' shrugged Dollimore.

But Crawshaw had already taken matters into his own hands and had unceremoniously stuck up two fingers.

Dollimore, starting to move towards the hatch to descend the ladder, gave him a disappointed look. 'Must you?'

'At least I didn't do it to the women and children, sir.' He grinned to himself as the jolly would-be foe flew back towards Germany, taking its valuable intelligence with it.

*

Over the last few days the ships of the Home Fleet had been steaming from their scattered anchorages around the British Isles to concentrate in the wide stretches of sea north of Scotland. Rear-Admiral Clark wished that he could have seen all their ships drawn up together but they had only managed to gather five battleships and a couple of battlecruisers with their attending destroyers in Scapa. There was no armada, no parade or review. Today's requirements called for the fleet to be extended along a line covering five hundred or so nautical miles.

Once at sea, Clark ordered Captain Nunn to take the *Godham* to a patrol position just off the cold, windswept Faeroe Islands. After sighting the dark peaks of the islands' rocky hills they began steering a search pattern across the sea, now and again glimpsing the cruiser HMS *Farecombe* as their courses drew them closer together, then eased them further apart again.

The *Farecombe*, under Captain Craine, had come up from the Clyde on its very first commission and Clark eagerly tried to make out the detail of her structure through his binoculars. She might be under his command but he had not yet had a chance to even see the ship properly. Even now the heavy mist was generally preventing that from happening.

Up here, almost on top of the world, the summer was considerably cooler and Clark made sure that he was wearing his duffle coat before stepping out onto the captain's bridge. He found Nunn comparing notes with his gunnery officer on emergency repairs that had just been carried out underneath X-turret. Such was the lot of a captain who only had an aging ship like the *Godham* to play with.

Clark, considering his own position, knew that nobody was forcing him to fly his flag in this old ship so the only solution was to transfer it over to the *Burscombe* or *Farecombe*, both of them having less mechanical difficulties. One other issue that arose from this was the fact that, if he did make this transfer, then he wanted to take Nunn with him as his flag captain. Of the other two captains Dollimore had the worst reputation, so that was who could be most easily removed. His tenure as captain was still in its infancy so the disruption should hopefully be minimal. Once he had been caught trying to break through into the Atlantic and had been shown up to be as unimaginative and dull as Clark suspected the killer of the *Spikefish* to be, nobody would bat an eyelid at such a transfer.

'Good evening, sir,' said Nunn once he had finished conversing with his gunnery officer, and finally noting the admiral's presence.

Clark nodded and immediately pressed the thin faced man with, 'So, what do you think our friend Dollimore will do?'

Taking out and opening a gold-plated cigarette case, Nunn offered it towards Clark and, remembering earlier comments made about the Burscombe's captain, replied, 'I've only met the man once so couldn't predict much from experience, but I've heard tell that he's a very efficient and precise man.'

'What would you do if you were him?' asked Clark, accepting the cigarette and a light.

Nunn wondered if Clark was the type of man who fished for an officer's thoughts in order to blame him later on for bad decisions made. But he did not like thinking this way so he immediately cast it from his mind and answered, 'Go north and break out as close to Iceland as possible. That's exactly what any self-respecting German would do.'

'Somewhere not too far from here then?'

'That's what I would do if I were German,' Nunn reiterated.

'But what would you do if you were Dollimore?'

'The same thing would be a fair bet, but then...,'

He had been about to say that he considered there to be a more direct route but Clark suddenly smiled one of his rare smiles. Was there something mischievous about it? 'I think one of our ships will be seeing Mr Dollimore sometime this coming week, if the air patrols don't pick him up first. Give him a bit of a surprise, eh?'

'I understand one of your sons is in the *Burscombe*,' said Nunn, wanting to change the subject because he was not sure that he cared for the direction that the conversation was beginning to take.

'That's right,' replied Clark. Why did he have to mention him? He had been enjoying the day and now it was all but ruined. But he supposed it was just the cross he had to bear, for it had been him who had decided to keep David close by. Hiding his disdain, he said, 'Since this may well become our principle theatre of war I thought it would do the boy no harm to serve here instead of some far flung corner of the globe. I have high hopes for him, a very spirited lad. We Clarks have been producing some of the country's greatest captains and admirals for over two hundred years.'

Nunn gave a short smile. He could not argue with that statement at all but he had it on good authority that things were fairly feudal within the Clark family. Apparently this man here tried to rule the roost with an iron fist but the youngest son had become a bit of a discipline case, having been caned more than once as a junior midshipman. Would the Clarks continue to produce great men or were they washed out? Looking at the admiral's thinning frame, pasty white skin and black bags under his eyes, this was indeed a possibility.

*

'So far so good,' said Dollimore.

As the last cloudy smudge of sunlight had given way to the black of night he ordered the number of lookouts to be doubled on the bridge. It soon became a crowded space but it buzzed with the excitement of the moment.

The biggest surprise guest up top was Commander Bretonworth. Rarely seen above decks, he had come up to personally deliver his latest status report but, in all honesty, he was always eager to catch a glimpse of his native Scotland; that and his curiosity had got the better of him.

Dollimore graciously tolerated it.

The ship had been heaved to for a couple of hours and Bretonworth's stokers had been keeping the steam up in the boilers for the moment that the captain ordered them to be on their way. But for the noise of the intake fans, pumps and generators working far below them the whole ship was dead quiet as the men waited in anticipation for what was going to come next.

Finally giving voice to everybody's surprise that they were now staring at the black line of the Scottish nighttime coast dotted here and there by house lights, Bretonworth said, 'It's nothing short of a miracle that we've got as far as we have.'

Digby agreed. 'It beggars belief, it truly does.'

In the twenty six hours since they had been observed and photographed by the crew of the Dornier they had seen neither hide nor hair of any Royal Navy vessel or any evidence of the existence of the Fleet Air Arm. Their various encounters were comprised of two merchant ships and one fishing boat, all of whom were unaware of what they were looking at. In this way the *Burscombe* had casually cruised along finding time and seclusion enough to stop in order to put into effect another Boarding Party Drill, and even to allow some of the ratings to have a refreshing swim in the sea!

On the black bridge of the completely 'darkened' ship, Digby asked, 'Sir, do you really think our luck will hold out through the Pentland Firth itself?'

'Part of me sincerely hopes not for the sake of the fleet,' replied Dollimore. 'But then a little bit of success and credit for the audacity of an untrained ship could hardly go amiss, could it?'

'Certainly not.'

'Remember,' Dollimore said to all those around him, 'our whole plan relies on the fact that their Lordships think that the Germans would never dare try to break through here.'

'Well,' laughed Crawshaw, 'tonight I hope they're going to get something of an education.'

Dollimore, pleased with the upbeat spirit, said, 'Pilot, we'll wait here for two more hours until the locals are quite sure to have bedded down for the night, then set course and speed for entering the Atlantic by dawn.'

'Very good, sir,' replied Peterson.

*

When those two tense hours had finally dragged themselves past, Peterson ordered the ship on its way. Rejoined by a surplus of officers on the bridge, he guided the *Burscombe* into the narrow channel which had the Scottish mainland in view to port and the Orkney Islands, with their major naval base of Scapa Flow, equally as clear to starboard. As they proceeded it seemed that the intermittent beam flashing out from the Stroma lighthouse must illuminate them at every turn. Digby murmured how even more disgraceful their success should be because of this. At least if the war had actually started then the lighthouse would be blacked out along with every other light along the coast, giving them even more cover of darkness. But as it was, anyone to the north or south of them must surely see this suspicious, gigantic shadow gliding through the channel.

Clark and Beatty wandered forrard along the port side of 2 Deck, past the torpedo tubes and the unused catapult apparatus for the overhead flight deck. Finally they came to a stop near the cutter hanging from its davits alongside the galley. Here and there stood small groups of men in the blackness. They were all caught up in the excitement of the moment.

It was here that Clark spotted the bulky figure of Bonner standing alone at the side rail. He was busily rolling a cigarette with all the speed and nimble fingerwork usually applied to his rope handling.

'This fellow Bonner, he's the most interesting chap,' Clark whispered to Beatty.

'Really? Can't see the fascination myself.'

'A first class sailor but refuses to accept any responsibility.'

Beatty, knowing that his expression could not be seen, frowned anyway. 'Sounds almost like someone else I know.'

'I'm not afraid of responsibility,' said Clark. 'I just need it all to make sense.'

'Good luck with that.'

Just then CPO Doyle stepped out from a nearby hatch and walked past Bonner. Noticing the cigarette between his fingers, he warned, 'Don't even think about lighting that up.'

'Good God,' replied Bonner, as shocked as he was insolent. 'What d'yer take me for?'

'You'll get yours, Bonehead.'

After Doyle had moved on, Bonner muttered to himself, 'That's nice, that is. If it were not for the Swilkie I'd jump ship right now.'

'Thinking of deserting, sailor?' asked Clark.

Bonner shuddered suddenly and very nearly swore in his surprise. 'Sir? I didn't see yer standin' there. Would never desert, sir. Not me.'

'I didn't think so,' said Clark. 'So, what's the Swilkie then?'

'Only one o' the most dangerous whirlpools o' the channel, sir.'

'That's right,' Beatty cut in. Usually very conscious of the class difference, he did not find it so valuable to communicate with ratings on a personal level, but tonight he seemed quite relaxed. 'It's because of the way the currents flow around Stroma Island. It's a fact that the seabed is littered with wrecks around here – fifty at the very least.'

'Aye, sir,' said Bonner, adding a hint of sarcasm, for the young officer had imparted nothing more intelligent than a decent seaman should. 'You seem to know your Swilkie, sir.'

'Yes, Bonner, I do,' answered Beatty with rebuke.

Trying not to let the conversation be ruined by animosity, Clark carried on amiably with Bonner, 'Close to home, are you?'

'Aye, sir, I am. My ol' ma will be fast asleep right now, just a few miles away over there past the Dunnet Head. A dainty house near Thurso, she's got. She's a grand ol' dear, would invite us all round fer breakfast if we were not up to this noshyenannigins.'

'Has it been a while since you've seen her?'

'Aye,' replied Bonner with an exact finality. The midshipman had overstepped his boundaries.

'Forgive me, I didn't mean to pry,' said Clark with compassion. Not wishing to make him any more uncomfortable Clark decided to move further down the deck with Beatty trailing him. But before he was too far away, he turned back and asked, 'By the way, is Bonehead simply a play on your name, or is there something more to it?'

Bonner tapped his head. 'Many 'ave tried to crack this skull but it's not happenin', sir. I never go down in a fight.'

'I'll remember that,' said Clark, and finally left the man alone.

A few seconds later, Beatty said, 'I say, we really shouldn't be fraternising with the men like that.'

'It's not fraternising, Beatty, they're people just the same as us. Look, while I understand the need for discipline and the social hierarchy and all that, I can't see it as the be all and end all of life in the navy.'

The frustration in Beatty's tone was quite evident as he said, 'David, I could never stress enough the difference between them and us. It's a matter of breeding. I mean, we have been brought up to take on the responsibility of leading these men. Just imagine what life would be like if they were left to their own devices, or if they were responsible for us. It would be sheer anarchy.'

Clark understood all too well the differences between the classes but he could not help feeling that the lack of common ground was based not just in experience but also in prejudice. Surely, he thought, they were writing off large swathes of the population who could amount to something more if given a better chance. This was where the Royal Navy could make a real difference. 'I believe,' he said, 'that the navy has a responsibility to these men. Everyone who serves must be given the chance to leave a better person than when he joined. Everyone, not just the officers.'

'I'm telling you the navy already does enough for these men and there's an end to it.'

Enlightened humanist as Beatty sometimes was, he had been known to launch into diatribes on the French and Russian Revolutions, two episodes in history which he maintained marked just how low people could stoop to. He held both the French Republic and the Union of Soviet Socialist Republics in complete contempt. Clark, on the other hand, had once ventured to suggest that if the English Revolution of 1649 had succeeded then a much better balanced society might be in existence today. Both had been dismayed with each other for weeks.

The bottom line was that Clark believed there was nothing wrong with men like Bonner that a little understanding would not cure for the sake of trust and cooperation. Certainly there was respect in discipline, but was it the truest respect that men could have between one another?

*

From the bridge the lookouts kept the most vigilant of watches on the various shadows which silently cruised nearby. With all these vessels lit up in comparative splendour and showing off their navigation lights, this operation was child's play.

Under the silent, watchful eye of the captain, Peterson gave the occasional steering orders which calmly guided them through the night. As there was hardly any wind, the water's surface was flat-calm and the watch keepers looking out in every direction from the bridge were acutely aware of the lighter hue of the wash being pushed out either side of the bow and from the stern. Of course, their swishing wake was one of those unsolvable problems but it did make them wonder at their continuing success. Every time the beam from the lighthouse shone out or the moon appeared from behind the clouds it was illuminated clear as day.

Then they were practically through the firth and the land was dropping away behind them. Dollimore sensed the tension easing but still said, 'Stay sharp. We're not out of the woods yet.'

How right he was for it was only a matter of minutes later that one of the lookouts reported a group of destroyers passing them on the starboard side at a distance of about fifteen hundred yards. They seemed so close and so clear that it was almost as if they could hail them.

The men gathered hereabouts on the decks of the *Burscombe* stared at those silent ships, some imagining that those machines must be unmanned and propelling themselves through the water. But for the course they were steering there was no other sign of life. What were their lookouts doing? They were in the middle of a major fleet exercise.

'They have to spot us!' gasped Crawshaw through his excitement. 'They just have to!' It stood to reason that the game should be up in a very few moments. So then why did those destroyers continue blindly, not deviating from their easterly course?

After what seemed like an age they were gone, enveloped by the night and a light mist which had started to spring up.

'God's teeth!' said Crawshaw, as though he had just let out a long held breath. 'If I were over there I'd have my watchkeepers' guts for garters. We could see their wakes as clear as day. Why couldn't they see ours?'

Dollimore shared his commander's indignation but, less prone to outbursts, he simply answered with an, 'Mm,' of agreement. There certainly was some incompetence being displayed over there and it perfectly demonstrated that a lack of vigilance was going to make somebody the loser in the coming war.

'I do believe this is going to work,' said Crawshaw, his tone betraying the fact that he had not been entirely confident.

'Here is the lesson, gentlemen,' said Dollimore, again so that all men about him could hear. 'Nobody is searching for us in the Pentland Firth because it stands to reason that it should be suicide to try and break through here. What we have all got to realise is that in wartime any captain with an ounce of daring is going to attempt to do things which in peacetime would seem stupid and reckless.'

With that their faith in their captain was complete. He had shown cool judgment and skill and had more than passed the tests hoisted upon him from above and below. There was not a man present who was not happy to be here at this moment, even Crawshaw.

The night ebbed away slowly after their encounter with the destroyers and the temperature began to drop, sending much of the crew back below decks to await the official news of their success. Some even went to sleep as the night became easier and the hope turned into certainty. Finally, at 0400 almost the entire ship's company roused itself with the change of the watch. They would not have to wait too much longer for that which they wanted to hear.

On the bridge, Crawshaw grimaced with the stiffness of his muscles brought on by the inactivity and the chilly air. His hips and spine were crying out to tell him that he was no longer young and the odd jarring pain came upon him so suddenly that he could not conceal them from the captain.

'You really don't look after yourself, do you?' said Dollimore, his breath passing his lips as white vapour. 'Keeping fit is more essential the older you get.'

'I'm afraid I'm a bit too old and long in the tooth to start worrying about all that now, sir.'

'Rubbish. There's plenty you can do about it,' said Dollimore. 'We're the same age, you and I, and hell will have to freeze over before I give up running and tennis.'

'You know I'm still a dab hand at cricket.'

'Not quite the same thing, old boy.' Slightly changing his tone, Dollimore said, 'Derek, we have a markedly different approach to life, but I do appreciate your winning spirit. Which brings me to my next point.'

'Oh?'

'I do believe the exercise is just about over. Isn't that right, Pilot?'

Peterson glanced over from where he had been checking the compass and what he could see of the stars. He had regularly been calling down to Lt Irwin and AB Barrett in the charthouse and making a few calculations on a piece of paper. 'We'll be at the western extremity of the exercise area in under five minutes, sir,' he reported. 'We've done it.'

Dollimore turned back to Crawshaw. 'I'll give you the pleasure of informing the crew at the appropriate moment and, when you're done, send a signal to Admiral Forbes informing him of our success and giving our position. At the same time you can turn the navigation lights back on and order the deadlights opened. I bid you all a good morning, gentlemen.' With that he unceremoniously climbed inside the hatch and disappeared below.

'And just like that he washes his hands of the whole affair,' muttered Crawshaw. He stepped over to Peterson and said, 'If I were him I'd want to share something of the victory with the men.'

'I don't think he's interested in the egotism. His mind has already moved onto the report he's going to write. And you can bet your life it won't be very complimentary to the C-in-C.'

When the time came, Crawshaw addressed the crew over the broadcast system and a great collective cheer came up from the darkest recesses of the ship. Morale was high and everyone felt that the *Burscombe* was going to be charmed. Those who had served for years understood that some ships had a feeling about them, a feeling of stealth and invincibility while others were simply destined to be unhappy hulks. This ship was well on the way to being a champion of the former.

Perhaps the only man on board whose brain did not register that fact in its fullness was the captain. Dollimore, who understood morale but was not aware how much his men were beginning to revere him, buried himself in the construction of his report and did not sleep until he had finished it.

*

HMS *Burscombe* entered Scapa Flow for the first time through the Hoxa Sound, a channel on the south side of the bay. But for the Royal Navy's presence and the many ships that came and went each day this sprawled, low-lying and windy muddle of islands would have been even more bleak and desolate than they already were. Unfortunately, this lack of charm was a necessary evil, for Scapa Flow was of paramount importance to the security of the British Isles.

This natural defensive anchorage here in the Orkney's was considered to be impregnable. On only two occasions during the last war had the Germans tried to breach the defences, the result being one U-boat sunk and another lost without a trace. The one that disappeared must have succumbed to the treacherous tidal currents, all part of the Pentland Firth's mean reputation. Even a ship with the power of the *Burscombe* lost a little way when pushing against these currents.

The day was bright and there was almost perfect visibility as she passed slowly through the sound. The way ahead was clear, the long single line of linked buoys marking the length of the anti-submarine boom having been dragged to one side by a sentry tug to allow them to pass inside.

Noticing that the boom had been opened before they ever came within sight of it, Dollimore looked back afterwards and saw that it was not being put back into position now they were through. A quick scan of the surroundings showed him that a pair of destroyers was steaming towards the vacant exit. They should be through it within the next ten minutes. He then raised his binoculars to his eyes and observed a distant vessel heading up towards the Flow, following the course the *Burscombe* had taken. That one, he estimated, would be passing the open boom perhaps another ten minutes after the destroyers. So the entrance was open for long periods?

Crawshaw, who was becoming adept at knowing when something was on the captain's mind, appeared next to him and asked, 'A problem, sir?'

'No,' replied Dollimore.

'Really? When you stand there muttering to yourself there must be something up.'

Dollimore frowned and said, 'Alright. In my opinion I don't think this anchorage is as secure as everybody thinks it is.'

Immediately Crawshaw was appalled.

Dollimore went on. 'Take a look at how long they're keeping the boom open for. They wait for ships that are miles apart from each other to pass through before they close it.'

'It's broad daylight,' said Crawshaw, his tone argumentative, for he fully believed in this particular wisdom.

'Do they keep the same procedure at night?'

'Well, I don't know. But come off it, we're not even at war yet. Cut them some slack.'

Dollimore persisted, 'We've been gearing up for war for weeks. Security should be taken more seriously in my opinion.'

'Sir, I'm sorry, but this time I cannot agree with you,' said Crawshaw, shaking his head. 'This is Scapa Flow. It's impregnable – and that's been proven. No German in his right mind would dare to attack us in here.'

To be fair, thought Dollimore, the odds were stacked against a German incursion. But had he not taught Crawshaw a lesson just this morning concerning what men would dare to do? He walked away to the front of the bridge and begun to discuss where their designated anchorage was with Lt Irwin.

Crawshaw cast a look at the string of buoys pushed away from the Flow's entrance and pondered the captain's fears. Could he be right? Could Dollimore always be right?

Chapter Seven

Scapa Flow

Over the course of the next four to six days the ships of the Home Fleet began to appear in Scapa Flow and drop anchor. In effect, while the ships stayed close to their war stations, most of the blockade was disbanded. The Burscombe's victory had been so swift that many officers felt that Hitler had not been given the chance to start his war while the fleet had been in its advantageous position. Still, you cannot win them all.

Midshipman Clark was in charge of the motor boat that delivered Captain Dollimore to HMS *Nelson*. Once the captain had taken the stairway to the quarterdeck of the battleship, they tied the boat to a line that was thrown down to them and there they waited. A minute or two later, just as Clark was settling into a conversation with his stoker, another boat passed them bearing his father to the same place. He saluted but the bitter admiral just stared ahead, pretending that he had not seen him.

'Miserable as sin, that one,' muttered the stoker to the coxswain.

'Silence there!' said Young Clark sharply. 'Keep your opinions to yourself!' Still, he was aghast at his father's rebuff of him. No matter what problems they had on a personal level, a professional indiscretion like that was surely out of order.

Rear-Admiral Clark had been nothing short of mortified when he had received a copy of the signal stating that the *Burscombe* was in the Atlantic, ready to begin operations against merchant shipping. He had not even considered the possibility of a ship of that size breaking through the Pentland Firth right under the nose of the fleet's main base. It was bad enough that this had been done by a questionable officer who had not held a seagoing command for six years but, as a result, he could not even think about removing Captain Dollimore from his command now. Everybody was so impressed that he would never be able to build a case for it. He would just have to be content to keep his flag flying in the old *Godham* for the time being.

As he had approached the *Nelson* in his motor barge, he found that he could not bring himself to acknowledge his son in the other boat. That boy just reminded him of everything that was wrong in this life, of a family that would not listen to him and of subordinate officers who would best him. However, it was worth finding out how much of a headache David was causing his commanding officer.

'How is my son doing, Mr Dollimore?' he asked once he had introduced himself.

The answer was, 'He's shaping up to be something of an asset, sir. Just give it a little time.'

How was that possible? thought Clark. How could a boy like that go from being a discipline case to an asset in less than two weeks?

*

The dozen or so men present in Nelson's admiral's quarters were drinking their tea and chatting softly about the fleet's shortcomings when Forbes entered, looking none too pleased. He carried with him a handful of thin paper files which he threw down onto the table, saying, 'Please hand these around, gentlemen.'

Rear-Admiral Hallifax leaned forward, took one and passed the rest on until everyone was perusing the contents. The only person who flicked through the pages and immediately closed it without reading was Dollimore. All it contained was a copy of the report that he had written at sea and forwarded to Forbes. The only difference was that the C-in-C had signed it as read and understood.

'Well,' said Forbes, staying on his feet and pacing while the others stared at him. 'We've learnt a thing or two these last few days, I think you will agree.' Waving his hand in vague indication, he continued, 'Gentlemen, you have before you copies of the report written by Captain Dollimore here – and I thank the captain for its thoroughness. It should be quite apparent to you all that he has demonstrated we are not as organised as we thought ourselves to be in the event of war breaking out with Germany. Let's take point one, his passage all the way across the North Sea without being spotted by a single air patrol, ship or submarine. Unacceptable.' He stared back at them but nobody said anything. 'Point two, the forcing of the Pentland Firth, the shortest route through to the Atlantic barring the English Channel. Unacceptable. Point three, the *Burscombe* passing within a mile and a half of a group of destroyers in the firth who abjectly failed to spot her. Hallifax, they were some of yours. What do you have to say about that?'

'Sir,' said the officer, betraying some shame yet not breaking eye contact. 'That was Commander Fulton-Stavely's group in that position. I've already had words with him. His report for that morning obviously states that he believed the firth was clear, but I shall bring this new evidence to his attention directly. I can guarantee you we'll shake up his men.'

'Good,' continued Forbes, with a scowl, 'because we're not playing a game here. I don't need to tell you what could happen if the Germans got ships like the *Hipper* out into the Atlantic Ocean. If the balloon goes up then we'll be starting the war very short-handed and if the real *Hipper* did manage to get into the merchant shipping lanes she could do a very serious amount of damage before we could subdue her.' Forbes' point was well and truly made so he decided enough was enough and sat himself down at the head of the table, resting his hands on the paperwork before him and lacing his fingers together.

Giving Dollimore a quick glance then going back to the text in front of him, he said, 'Well, at least we have a list of things here that we can get to work on which brings me to point eleven: "...Concerning the lack of Fleet Air Arm presence that allowed us to traverse the North Sea without being spotted. When *Burscombe* takes up station in the blockade I would deem it very necessary to have embarked at least one Walrus. Addressing the shortage of these planes throughout the fleet is of paramount importance. My air officer cannot remain a useless mouth to feed indefinitely." Captain, more intelligent men than you are well aware of the situation.'

'Yes, sir,' replied Dollimore. But had the point been absorbed?

Suddenly, Clark piped up with, 'Yes, Charles, these reports are not for the purposes of airing grievances and being flippant. They are for recording facts and making suggestions.'

As he said that, Dollimore fancied that he saw the man's nostrils flaring a little as though he was smelling the blood in some sort of hunt.

Forbes, completely ignoring the interruption, continued to speak to the captain, saying, 'That aside, I appreciate that you've shown considerable skill and initiative in what you did. Your forcing of the Pentland Firth was well done.' He paused for a second or two while he looked round at the other faces. 'Needless to say, gentlemen, that it would be in our best interests to keep this one under our hats. The last thing we need to do is give Jerry a tutorial in dynamism. He'll be trouble enough without us prompting him. We'll simply act upon the lessons that we've learnt and otherwise forget that this episode ever occurred. Understand?'

There came nods and replies of acknowledgement from all.

'All of you take a look through Dollimore's report and come back to me with any comments and suggestions that you may think proper.'

Leafing through the couple of pages before him, Rear-Admiral Blagrove said, 'The most obvious thing I can tell you now - that would be to commit more ships to the Home Fleet.'

'That's not an option. I'm sure I don't need to tell you how we've failed to build enough ships over the past ten years so much of our hardware has been in service for two decades or more. Then there are the deployments across the whole globe. Our presence in the Far East has suffered greatly in order to keep us and the Mediterranean bolstered up. No. No more ships for us. Now, is there any other business before we get back to work?'

Without a pause, Dollimore looked the admiral in the eye and asked, 'Would it be pointless for me to ask for more time to work up my ship? We had not even fired a gun until a couple of days ago.'

Forbes had not expected the sudden change of subject or the candour but it was something for which he was not entirely without understanding. Still he answered with the same frankness, 'That is a matter between you and your squadron commander.'

'As it so happens,' said Clark, his face now growing red with irritation, 'you have the coming two weeks to exercise here in the Flow. Beyond that, who knows? And do not think that your position is unique.' This is what happened when you admitted lower officers into these conferences.'

Dollimore nodded in dubious acceptance and, spurred on by what he deemed to be arrogance from Clark, then asked, 'And just to clarify, would it be pointless to expect delivery of a Walrus anytime soon?'

'Yes,' Forbes cut in, himself becoming exhausted. 'Mr Dollimore, is there anything else you wish to add on *fleet* matters? Your personal trivialities are to be handled separately.'

'There is one more thing. It concerns the defences here at Scapa. I think they're inadequate.'

'What?' said Clark, with a short, derisive laugh. 'This place is impregnable.'

'So everybody keeps saying,' returned Dollimore.

'What's your point?' asked Forbes with more patience than he was truly feeling.

'I've been observing the operation of the anti-submarine booms in the sounds. They seem to be left open for considerable amounts of time while traffic goes in and out. I know there are lookouts and trawlers patrolling, but they're no guarantee that a submarine couldn't slip inside while the boom is open and the nets lowered. Also, to the east and west you have blockships sunk in the smaller channels. To my mind, not enough. The strong currents in those channels would have driven an older type of submarine onto the blockships but the Germans are beginning to produce quite powerful ocean-going boats now. Plus, there seems to be a distinct lack of anti-aircraft arrangements here.'

Clark said, 'You presume to know an awful lot about it. More than the men who actually work here. Not enough anti-aircraft guns? Our ships are bristling with them.'

'And if the fleet is at sea? What about the protection of the less well-armed vessels then?'

'Okay, thank you, gentlemen,' said Forbes, raising his hands to stop the conversation. 'Captain, your observations have been noted but I can tell you with good authority that all of these things have already been considered and are being reviewed. Now there's an end to it.'

'Thank you, sir,' said Dollimore. Better than nothing, he thought. The admiral could have been much less receptive than that. It just remained to be seen now if the name Dollimore became synonymous with dynamism or trouble.

Anyway, whatever unpredictable challenges the coming weeks held he would not let it be said that he had not done his utmost to make his ship ready. That was at least one thing he could control and he set about working his men hard in the short time he had been given.

*

The fighting condition of HMS *Burscombe* then improved only marginally in Dollimore's estimation. He acknowledged privately that there was only so much they could do in the short space of time allotted but being on a high from their victory during the exercise, all the men needed now was the skill to go with their luck. Understandably, the biggest deficiencies lay with target practice.

As a result of the Orkney's being of the region where the warm gulf stream from the Americas met with the cold of the Arctic, mist and fog frequently hampered their gunnery exercises. In the end *Burscombe* only got in an average of two and a half hours of practice per day, and this included 4-inch, anti-aircraft and torpedo firing as well as the main armament. Lt-Cdr Digby got what he could out of the men in these restricted times then took Dollimore's reproaches in his stride.

Firing the sixteen 6-inch guns started out as an exhilarating business. The officers on the bridge felt the shock waves and displacement of air acutely as the guns spewed out their shells, flames and smoke. Below, the messes and stores shook violently, steel cable trays and fittings came loose, bottles smashed in the sick bay and violent reverberations were felt all the way down to the engine room deck plates.

Warrant Officer Hacklett was in command of the big guns of B-Turret. All the men that were crowded round the polished breaches worked themselves hard as much from pride as a wish to escape the retribution of their scarred officer. He cursed them and cajoled them as they built up a sweat ramming in the shells, then ramming in the cylindrical bags of cordite, slamming the breaches shut and inserting the primers.

The first few practices were sub-calibre firings. The turret only had two sleeves – thin, portable barrels which slotted inside the main ones in order to preserve the effectiveness of the rifling – so only half the men could work at a time.

The target, which presently consisted of a float being towed by a tug, was being monitored up in Fire Control and the information sent to the mechanical computer of the Transmitting Station. The final calculations were delivered to the gun crews by means of small pointers indicating which direction to train the turret and what angle to elevate the guns to. This was as much as the gunners ever knew. They were otherwise blind.

Hacklett easily convinced them that all they had to do was load and be ready as fast as possible, a task which became even more difficult when they came to the final shoot and Lt-Cdr Digby ordered a full-calibre fire without the barrel sleeves, all guns engaged at once. Now they were ramming home the full 112lb shells. This meant a certain amount of manual handling which could be a terrible torment to those men unused to lifting the weight. As it stood the 6-inch shell was the largest that the Admiralty said a man was allowed to lift by hand.

'This is going to be the fastest and best turret on this ship!' shouted Hacklett, his voice never drowned out because, contrary to popular belief, the noise of the guns did not actually penetrate to the inside of the turret other than as a dull plop. 'Come on, you lot! Those bastard marines don't look like they're pissing themselves when they lift a shell! What's the matter with you? Are you Royal Navy gunners or shall I put in a request for you to be transferred to the bleeding RAF where all you get to do is pull on a joystick?'

Then he finished with, 'As fa's a's'n te' 'us ora bun'a us's 'as'ars a'y'ay,' a comment which confused and worried them more than anything previously spoken.

Later, when the gunners were exhausted and could think of nothing more than getting below away from *him* and having a rest, a message came down from Captain Dollimore that they would have to do better, that they had been granted an extension of one hour with the target to do some improving.

One lad, a teenager who was usually the perfect image of fitness, was covered in sweat and his shoulders were drooped. He gasped, 'Why don't 'e come down 'ere an' show us 'ow it's done, then?'

Hacklett rounded on him with clenched fists. 'The captain knows more about guns than you ever will, boy! He was killing Germans before your mother ever knew what having children was! Don't ever talk about your officers like that again or you'll know what it feels like to have that shell rammed up your arse! 'U'n 'asar!'

'Aye aye, sir!'

*

One evening, a tired Clark was given charge of the boat that skimmed across the water carrying Burscombe's libertymen to and from the jetty. It was quite noticeable that he was ferrying to the canteen eager young men who were anxious to relax after their gruelling day of work and, upon their return, they were in all states of merriment, ranging from the simply satisfied to the near-paralytic. Those of the latter, of whom there were thankfully only one or two, would be in trouble the moment they stepped on board the ship but that was not his concern. He just needed to deliver them there.

It was past 2300 when an officer appeared on the jetty as Clark's stoker was mooring up the boat. 'I'm told you're from the *Burscombe*!' his voice thundered in an angry Cornish accent. Though his face was fairly shadowed, the lines of his rage were more than apparent.

'Yes, sir,' replied Clark, noticing the stripes and red rings on the sleeve denoting his commander's rank of the medical branch.

'Then there's my belongings,' continued the newcomer, pointing at two suitcases lying nearby. 'Get 'em loaded and take me over there straight away.'

Clark nodded at the stoker and pointed. The man jumped out of the boat and passed the cases across.

It was just as this officer was climbing into the boat that Bonner, Pincher, Smudge and Les appeared. What bad timing, except that it could not have been otherwise for they were the last four libertymen dutifully arriving to catch this last boat back to the ship. It did not help that the first three were staggering along, laughing privately over some immature joke while Les trailed behind like some lost puppy. Bonner made to climb in the boat when the commander said to Clark, 'I'm not travelling with the likes of them. I've had a gizzard full of their sort since Rosyth. They'll have to wait until you come back.'

'But they're due back on board, sir,' Clark protested. 'If I don't take them they'll be reported as adrift.'

'After the week I've had, I really don't care.'

Bonner leaned forward and pointed drunkenly, Smudge keeping hold of his other arm so that he did not topple into the boat. 'Listen, pal, I got no idea 'oo you are, but this is not 'ow it works, see.'

'Hold your tongue!' shouted Clark. 'I'll be back as soon as I'm able. If you're late I'll speak to the Quartermaster myself.'

The commander added, 'And that man is to be charged for insubordination as well.'

'Yes, sir,' replied Clark, sighing, and ordering his two-man crew to get the boat underway before anything else went wrong.

Surgeon-Commander Albert Lawson was a clean cut but wrinkled man who, until a year ago, had been a depressed General Practitioner who had decided to broaden his horizons before he got too old. Of the

118

three services he had chosen the navy because he had always been impressed by the discipline and the stories of those of his patients who had served. The realities of what he had then found fell far short of his expectations and he was discovering that he was as unable to deal with these new complexities as the old.

When the Quartermaster tried to welcome him on board ship Lawson refused to look at him. It turned out that he would speak to no one until he had vented his anger upon the captain.

The worried QM passed the word for the Officer-of-the-Day and so it was that he did not get Captain Dollimore, but a young lieutenant by the name of Eddington.

Although Eddington approached him respectfully enough the old officer instantaneously decided that he appeared as disagreeable as that awful midshipman in the liberty boat.

'Well, I'm afraid that the captain is indisposed at the moment, sir,' said Eddington with all the authority his position required, for he was no weak-hearted fool, 'so you'll have to make do with me.'

'Do you know what sort of a week I've had?' asked Lawson, his teeth gritted. 'All up and down the country I've been sent! I was at the hospital in Invergordon when I received my orders! Portsmouth, they said, so I went there and you'd gone! Scapa, they said, so I had to come all the way back north again! Then my bags went missing at a connection in London! It's because of the European crisis, they said! Tosh! Utter tosh! Then one of your men was rude to me in the boat! There's no excuse for it! It's not on! It's simply not on!'

Eddington's face remained unchanged as he let Lawson wear himself out then looked at Clark with an expression of enquiry.

'Able Seaman Bonner, sir,' Clark said solemnly. 'I'm dealing with it.'

With no further ado, Eddington turned back to Lawson. 'Well, sir, we're pleased you've arrived at any rate. The present sick list sits at four and your opinion is desperately required. Come, I'll show you your berth and then let's see about getting you a drink.'

As if by magic Lawson's anger disappeared and he followed Eddington meekly through the hatch on the starboard side. He suddenly felt that somebody was taking an interest in his plight, though he had made too much of a fuss to say anything other than, 'You've got a lot of work to do to convince me that you're not an idiot too.' But all his conviction had gone. It seemed as though his little tirade had helped release all the pent-up anger like a valve letting out steam.

Clark exchanged a quick glance with the QM then turned back to his business and, as he did so, was suddenly confronted with the three merry seamen and Les Gordy standing right there before him. But he had left them stranded on the jetty. As they advanced happily across the deck, Clark exclaimed, 'How did you get here?'

Smudge, unable to contain his grin, said, 'We hitched a ride, sir, with the admiral, sir.'

'Admiral Forbes,' said Bonner.

'True, sir, every word of it,' added Smudge.

The fact that Smudge had said that instantly made Clark disbelieve the story, for if you took Smudge's tales at face value you would believe that you were facing a multi-lingual athlete, a survivor of the world's four most inhospitable terrains, pacifier of the worst undiscovered tribes that a man could conjure up and father to fifty eight children – all whilst serving with his majesty's ships.

'If you don't believe me, sir, take a look for yourself,' said Smudge.

Clark took the few paces over to the side rail and looked down. In the dim light thrown out from the scuttles he could see a pinnace heading off into the night with Admiral Forbes sitting casually on the stern. He turned back to the four men in surprise.

'You see, sir? Admiral Forbes. Lovely fella,' smiled Smudge.

'Mm,' muttered Clark. Bewildered as he was, he did muse that he would have loved to have been a passenger in that boat to be able to hear what sort of conversation these men must have had. 'Here listen, Bonner, you're still going to have to be brought up on a charge over your insubordination, you know.'

So started the unpleasant proceedings against that man in order to satisfy, Clark considered, the temper of an arrogant man. So he spoke up for Bonner and was thankful it did not have to go any further than his chief petty officer.

The Scotsman was given extra duties but the true negative effect of the episode was that the lower rates, who were none too keen on Bonner anyway, began to see Clark as a soft touch. The young man did not always act like the other officers. Was he looking for friendship beyond comradeship? Was he going to be a 'popularity Jack'? The jury was out on that one.

*

Next day, the department heads were quite suddenly asked to gather in the captain's sea cabin, which was just big enough to accommodate them all at a squeeze. Dollimore wanted to talk to them out of earshot and they stood or sat staring at him intently if somewhat bleary eyed. The only person who seemed to be in the know besides the Old Man was Commander Crawshaw, who kept looking back and forth at them, knowingly raising their expectations. His look of barely concealed excitement spread a positive feeling about the cabin.

'Well, gentlemen,' said Dollimore, looking in disbelief at the effect Crawshaw was having on them, 'Hitler's game plan is gradually being unveiled. But before you jump to thinking that he's moved on Poland, he hasn't. Not yet. What he has done is concluded a pact of non-aggression with Stalin of all people.'

Digby and Peterson whistled their amazement and glanced at each other, both immediately appreciating the brilliance of the move, but also wondering that it was the very last thing any of them had expected. Were the Nazis not rigidly opposed to the Communists in almost every way possible?

Bretonworth, his face smeared with oil, and Gailey and Irwin, all being less politically aware took a couple more seconds to catch up with their realisations of the seriousness of the news. This was not surprising as their respective worlds mostly revolved around the ship's machinery or simply trying to survive the navy.

Digby said, 'But I'd had it on good authority that Chamberlain sent an embassage to Moscow so that *we* could do a deal with Stalin. Whatever became of that? An understanding between Britain and Russia would have been the best thing for everybody. Then Hitler would have been caught powerless between all the other major countries. He might have been stopped.'

'Hindsight is always twenty-twenty,' said Dollimore.

'Well, it was obvious to me,' the young man went on.

Crawshaw, with a look of distaste, said, 'It's likely that Chamberlain was appalled at the idea of treating with Stalin. As far as I'm concerned it's a travesty that we ever recognised the Communist revolutionary scum as a legitimate government in the first place. I once knew a lady who lost everything because of them. They murdered her husband and chased her from the country.'

Dollimore frowned. Everybody present was well aware of how Crawshaw might have known the lady and why he knew her no longer.

Then Bretonworth said, 'But if I'm understanding Digby's thoughts, Hitler's free to go after Poland with impunity now, isn't he?'

'That's how I see it,' agreed Digby.

Dollimore said, 'I've been informed that Chamberlain is making guarantees to the Poles about assisting them if they are attacked.'

'I'd be interested to see that happen,' said Crawshaw, with a little chuckle of pessimism. Then he brightened up with, 'Anyway, we've been talking for months about whether we will or won't go to war with Germany. Now we're on the brink of the war we've all been waiting for. Just pray to God that Chamberlain doesn't dither anymore.'

'He doesn't dither,' said Irwin, whose personal feelings about war and peace were on a par with the prime minister's. 'He's just cautious, wants to do the right thing.'

'He dithers,' Crawshaw said, effectively silencing the opposition. 'When Hitler goes for Poland we have to declare war.'

Dollimore put up his hands to calm them all down. 'However we feel about all this the essential truth is that the Home Fleet is going onto a war footing for real this time, and we'll probably find ourselves on patrol very shortly so expect our training to be cut short at any moment. It's also important that we keep the lower decks properly informed of developments about what we are doing and why we are doing it. It's not enough that they should decipher our policies from the newspapers.'

With purpose, Irwin nodded and said, 'Now that things are moving faster we should hold briefings with the ship's company, say, in one of the hangars every few days or so.'

'Well volunteered, Mr Irwin,' said Dollimore. 'In the meantime, gentlemen, tell your men the news. We will be at it for real very soon. Let's get back to work.'

With a chorus of 'Aye aye, sir,' they happily picked themselves up and headed off back to their parts of the ship, each planning how best to disseminate the news to the men.

*

During a short break in the proceedings, Young Clark, pleased that the training schedule was enough to take his mind from his father's arrogance, obtained permission to take a boat across to the *Royal Oak* to see his future brother-in-law, Lieutenant John Bushey. The small craft had to chug its way across at least two miles of the anchorage to reach her and, as they drew nearer, he became more and more impressed by her size. Perhaps she was no more length than the *Burscombe* but she was much wider and boasted almost as many 6-inch guns in her secondary armament as the other ship had in her main. Of course *Royal Oak* was a battleship, also carrying eight huge 15-inch guns and as many decks in just the superstructure as *Burscombe* had in her entire height. Whilst still harbouring doubts as to why the Royal Navy should centre its thinking upon the supposed supremacy of these ships, he understood why they left people in awe.

The '*Mighty Oak*' was acknowledged to be past her prime but she still gave off a strong sense of worth. She was well known to have been one of the heroines of Jutland these twenty three years past, firing into the German forces from her place in the battle line right behind the flagship, HMS *Iron Duke*. The only problem was that she had more modern and faster ships to contend with now and there was a rumour that she struggled in her efforts once she exceeded twenty knots. Just imagine if the grand old girl had a speed to match her firepower.

But whatever her condition, she was still well looked after. The crew had been taking care to conserve the steel from rust and keep the paint-work up, the superstructure and the decks were washed down and the brass and copper brilliantly polished. Everything was as it should be for the ship that carried the commander of the 2nd Battle Squadron, Rear-Admiral Blagrove.

'She's very pretty,' Bushey was saying of his beloved *Oak*, after gaining eventual permission from his fellow officers to allow Clark, the 'snotty', into the quiet and spacious wardroom anteroom, 'but I'm not quite sure how the old lady will fair in action.'

'No longer one of the best, eh?' said Clark.

'Don't you worry,' said Bushey, nodding. 'When we get into a scrap we'll give a good enough account of ourselves. It's just that a hearty scrap might well finish her off. Every time we fire the guns we spring a leak somewhere. But keep that to yourself. As far as the rest of the world is concerned we are still a force to be reckoned with.'

'Of course.'

They sat in their comfortable leather armchairs and sipped at the drinks that the steward had just brought them. Clark supplied the cigarettes and they enveloped themselves in a soothing haze of tobacco smoke.

Bushey pointed at Clark with a look of pride on his face and said, 'The *Burscombe* is all the talk at the moment. We busted a gut setting out our blockade and there we were, not expecting to hear anything for days, only to discover that you were already in the Atlantic. Game over. Well played, David.'

'Don't think it had anything to do with me!' exclaimed Clark with a grin, knowing he could not take any credit for his own meagre contribution. 'The captain hatched the plot in its entirety.'

'I know what you're saying,' said Bushey, 'but when we think of you we don't think of just one man. We think of HMS *Burscombe*. You all act as one, which puts me in mind of our last meeting. I seem to remember you were very conflicted. How are things now? You look more content.'

David thought for a moment, then said, 'Well, I know I'm a hard-headed bugger, but I think I've realised that I'm not so vain that I can't admit that I need someone to look up to. Believe me, Captain Dollimore has been far from sweetness and light with me, though what should I expect with a record like mine? However, I can't help trusting him. He may come across as a stuffy gent from a past age but I can tell you, his brain is not stuck in a rut of tradition and convention. He understands that if we go to war, it's going to be much more than plain sailing. Jerry's going to give us the fight of our lives and if I have to follow anyone into battle then I should be glad if it was him. It's just unfortunate that he in turn has to take orders from my father.'

'Well, I can't agree with you on that last point but let's not pursue the matter now.' As Bushey said this he noticed, beyond Clark's shoulder, another officer stepping into the room. 'Ah,' he said, holding up his hand and catching the other's attention. 'David, there's someone here you should meet.'

Clark looked round and saw a lieutenant in his mid-twenties walking over to them. There was something strangely familiar in the walk and the look in his eyes that he could not quite place. He stood up and held out his hand which the officer shook.

As they did this, Bushey made the introductions, 'Philip Dollimore, meet David Clark.'

To the newcomer, he said, 'Clark and I are shortly to be brothers once I've marched his sister up the aisle.'

Of course, thought Clark, the walk and the mannerisms were just like his captain's though this younger version of him was noticeably more laid back.

'Pleased to meet you,' smiled Lieutenant Dollimore, his face also holding a look of surprise. 'My, but it's a small world. You're the fellow who predicted the Pentland Firth breakthrough.'

To counter Clark's stunned look, Dollimore said, 'I popped over to see my father last night and he mentioned this midshipman, son of Rear-Admiral Clark, who sized up the tactical situation with great clarity and sense. Said something about you showing great promise as long as you can keep your nose clean. And here you are, the man himself, standing right before me on the *Oak*.' Sitting down he finished with, 'I trust my father will be letting you get away for the wedding?'

There was a slight pause as they sat back down then Bushey broke the silence, saying to Clark, 'I've asked Phil here to be my best man. I've known him since training ship days.'

'Well, what about it, Clark?' said Dollimore. 'We've only got four weeks to go until the big day.'

'Of course,' Clark replied, 'I've put in the request so I'll just have to wait and see what the Old Man says. We have to bear in mind, though, that the commander absolutely hates me so he might be something more of a stumbling block and may yet get his way.'

'What, Derek Crawshaw?' asked Dollimore. 'I met him in Northern Ireland. I found him to be a thoroughly agreeable chap.'

'Yes, that's what everybody else keeps saying, but I'm beginning to think that I must have run over his dog in a past life or something.'

'Anything I can do to help?'

Clark considered that for a second. This connection to his captain seemed very handy at first glance, but he decided to say, 'Better leave that as a last resort.'

*

He returned to the *Burscombe* in high spirits. Talking with Bushey had helped him to clarify in his mind some of those points about his future which had for so long frustrated him. The little adventure of the Pentland Firth and Captain Dollimore's incessant reality checks were things that made sense to him and, as a result, he felt less indignant about matters. But it was just as he was beginning to feel this when he received a letter that carried with it the potential to change everything.

He did not immediately know the handwriting upon the envelope to be that of Maggie Gufford because she never wrote to him. He never wrote to her. There was complete secrecy surrounding their relationship so, once it dawned upon him who it was from, he became alarmed. It was not her style to break with their accepted confidences. What was going on? It was a little over six weeks since he had seen her. Could she have fallen pregnant? Good God, no!

He looked at her unpractised scrawl and simplistic language. This was the product of her education and no reflection of her true intelligence.

He read:

My dearest David,

Please do not get angry with me for writing. You know I wouldn't if it wasn't important. When we were last together we talked about my father's expectations about me marrying and, to cut a long story short, a man has approached him to ask for my hand in marriage.

In the past I'd always felt that I would say no to any sort of offer because I still had these childish fantasies that me and you would find a way to be married. When I thought it through I realised what was fantasy and what was reality and so I accepted. He's a lovely man. His name is Tom. He is not you but I will learn to love him,

Yours forever,
Maggie

Clark looked away from the page with his mind whirling. It was an unpalatable truth that he had to face now because it very suddenly hit him that she was one of the few things in this life which had made it all seem worth it. Where life at North Cedars Hall was concerned she was the pinpoint of light in an endless void. But now forced to consider the matter, how could this have ended any other way?

Finding himself at a loss as to how to proceed, he decided to take the plunge and explain the whole situation to Beatty. That turned out to be a big mistake. Really, he should have predicted what his good friend's standpoint would be seeing that he had always been such a staunch advocate of the sensibilities of his class. It was simple, said Beatty, more amused than shocked, 'If she loves you as much as you say, she'll be easy to corrupt. Whatever you do, though, don't go declaring your love for her or anything stupid like that. A barmaid? Oh, my dear Nobby.' He always used Clark's naval nick-name when he was tickled by something.

Clark's reaction to that was obviously not good. Here now was his best friend completely misunderstanding him, unable to see that his blinkered outlook on life had caused offence.

But true to form, Beatty was then in turn dumbfounded by Clark's ensuing bad humour and could not shake him from its grip, even when he pleaded with him, 'Come on, David, old boy. Please don't let this girl turn you into a sour drip.'

Chapter Eight

The Northern Patrol

Ships began to leave Scapa Flow. The men of the *Burscombe*, bursting with the suspense of the situation, watched them go and wondered where their orders were. The latest news coming out of the east had created a proper stir and things looked hopeful when the captain was summoned to the *Godham*. The plan for the 25th Cruiser Squadron must surely be about to become known.

Dollimore stepped onto the flagship's quarterdeck and acknowledged Captain Craine of the *Farecombe*. That tall, middle-aged man with his hair greying a little at the temples stood with a loose but respectful posture, one hand in his jacket pocket. 'Good morning to you,' he said, smiling.

'And to you,' replied Dollimore.

These two men had not met until a week ago and in that time the squadron had already practiced manoeuvres twice. The three ships keeping station together abreast or ahead, and especially where the battle line was concerned, was most important. They had subsequently struck up an easy acquaintance in the debriefings. Dollimore wished the same could be said of relations with the rear-admiral.

Not too many seconds had passed before Captain Nunn appeared on deck. Next to his more robust counterparts he could have been regarded as looking a little daft with his short height and rounded shoulders upon which his four gold stripes hung at a sad angle. However, Nunn had a reputation for his keen intellect and seafaring abilities. On top of this he was the only one of the three who had been at sea consistently for the last decade and the *Godham* was the third cruiser that he had commanded in that time.

After the basic pleasantries had been dealt with they climbed down into a hatch just abaft the imposing double 8-inch turret. Down below their eyes adjusted quickly enough from the sunlight to the electric bulbs and they filed through the thin passageway and straight into the admiral's quarters. The wallpaper and wood-panelling in the dining room were all fresh and new. It was a good enough impression for a ship of her age even if it still felt somewhat antique next to the more modern quarters being used by both Craine and Dollimore in their respective ships.

The door leading to the sitting room opened and Rear-Admiral Clark stepped out. His hair was white, his face wrinkled and the skin blemished by odd dark patches about the cheeks. While a good sense of intelligence could be detected in his eyes there was still something distinctly tired about them. Dollimore had noticed this during their previous encounters and the man did not seem to be improving at all.

Clark tried to muster a smile but failed. Instead, he ended up barking, 'Good day to you, gentlemen. Thank you for coming.' This was always an interesting greeting. Was there ever any choice but to respond to the summons? 'Please take a seat. I will pour the drinks and if anybody wishes to smoke, please do so.'

Dollimore pulled his pipe from his pocket as he sat down and took a small quantity of tobacco from his pouch. Drawing on the smoke was going to be an important factor in keeping him calm because he had already developed the type of relationship with Clark where he was considering pre-empting a clash.

As the other two captains lit up their cigarettes Clark circled the table with the decanter and poured three small glasses of port. Dollimore noted that he did not pour a drink for himself.

The admiral sat at the head of the table and said, 'Well, gentlemen, the Hun has crossed the border into Poland so it's only a matter of time before we are called in to help them.'

Craine, excited but unsurprised, immediately commented, 'One wonders that we haven't declared war then. I mean, we have made guarantees to the Poles, haven't we? We must honour them.'

'Chamberlain,' said Nunn without elaborating, since that one word said it all. The prime minister had done what he could to avoid war and failed so why was he still needing to prevaricate further?

'Well,' Clark continued, 'we must assume that we will be at war at any moment. In the meantime we have received our orders to head out on patrol with the other squadrons, enforcing the blockade across the North Sea.'

'But without a declaration of war,' said Craine, 'we'll be severely limited as to what we can do. We need to have the freedom to challenge German ships.'

'Just restrain yourself for the time being,' said Clark, though not in a reproving tone, more one of sympathy. 'What we must do is note what vessels pass us by. If they happen to be German warships then we shall shadow them with a view to opening up an engagement the moment war is declared.'

'That should be interesting,' said Nunn. 'Most of the opposition carry larger guns than ours. The *Hipper*, *Moltke*, *Prinz Eugen*, not to mention the *Deuschland* or the *Graf Spee*. They're all much heavier ships than ours.'

'And that is why we must work carefully as a squadron if we run into them. Hopefully they will be operating singly in which case we should outgun them. Hitler doesn't have that many ships and it is our well-considered opinion that he'll keep most of them in the Baltic protecting that shoreline and his trade routes there.' He then looked straight at Dollimore who had been sitting tight-lipped and only taking the occasional puff on his pipe. 'What do you think?'

Without a pause, Dollimore looked the admiral in the eye and said, 'Our crews need more time to work up.'

Clark's eyebrows rose in surprise. 'I'm sorry that the cogs in your machine are not as well-oiled as they might be but the blockade comes first. Eventually it will be enforced by the Armed Merchant Cruisers but they are not yet ready, so we have to do it. Understand?'

'Of course, sir,' said Dollimore, keeping his calm beautifully and thinking about those AMCs, commandeered ocean liners with guns hastily fitted to them. 'I support the notion whole heartedly but, much as I'd like to express a blind bravado, our men are simply not yet ready to face the enemy.'

Both Craine and Nunn squirmed in their seats. For the *Farecombe* as well as the *Burscombe* what he said was the truth but there was nothing anyone could do about that now. What was clear was that there was something of a standoff between Clark and Dollimore, which Nunn uneasily put down to the Burscombe's forcing of the Pentland Firth. Instead of the admiral being proud of his captain, his nose seemed to be out of joint.

Clark said, 'All I can say is, work your men harder. But I was in fact asking if you had an opinion on strategy, seeing as you've displayed such a flare for it in the past.'

'I haven't given it much thought, but let's see...,' Dollimore paused for a few seconds, then said, 'I agree that we shouldn't see too many forays of the German battlefleet from the Baltic. Though if they did decide that they wanted to come out I think you could do worse than to mine the Kiel Canal. That would be a start in limiting the Germans in their options of getting out of the Baltic in the first place.'

Nunn's eyes lit up at the idea while Craine kept his face expressionless.

Clark frowned yet again. 'Mine the Kiel Canal? So that they could sweep it and have it open again in twenty four hours?'

'Have the air force drop hundreds of bombs with timed fuses. Some could go off today, some tomorrow, some next week and so on and so on. The Germans would try and clear them but the uncertainty would hamper their operations for some considerable time.'

'Do you realise the scope of what you're suggesting? The resources required would be incredible not to mention the fact that repeat raids would have to go up against heavier and heavier opposition.'

Dollimore raised his hands to back down. 'You asked me what I think. That's what I think, but then again I understand that we're still being asked to err on the side of caution – which in turn prohibits a British incursion *into* the Baltic, which itself might be an idea if we were actually serious about our guarantees to the Poles.'

Clark stared hard at him and said, 'If you wish to continue to be part of this squadron, then you should seriously consider modifying your tone.'

'Of course. Sorry, sir.'

'When war is finally declared,' said Clark, turning back to the others, 'we have been instructed to take any opportunities for scoring small tactical victories but our main mission will be to enforce this blockade. Understood?'

'Yes, sir,' came the replies from around the table.

*

A couple of days later the struggling sun rose above a grim sea which was much colder still than that around the Flow. Its intermittent rays found HMS *Burscombe* steaming at a leisurely cruising speed of thirteen knots in and out of heavy banks of patchy fog and rolling on a swell that was making the less hardy amongst the crew a trifle uncomfortable. The officers and lookouts on the bridge had already seen more than a dozen men dashing to the rail below and heaving the contents of their stomachs out over the side. There was even one man who seemed to be having difficulty parting from the rail at all.

Looking down at him, Peterson gave one of his rare smiles and said, 'There's always one on every ship.'

'No hope for that particular man, I'm afraid,' said Crawshaw. 'He's a stoker.'

The other officers and the lookouts chuckled. There was nothing like a little humour to bring some warmth to these northerly climes.

Aside from the odd chatter, the rhythmic crash of the bow wave, the subdued vibration of the ship's machinery and the occasional retching from below, all was silent at sea. *Burscombe* was alone. Rear-Admiral Clark had already reluctantly been compelled to disperse his ships to operate over quite a large area, so each was independent unless they happened upon a situation that they could not handle, and then a short radio message would bring the other two racing towards them at high speed. To this end nobody should be more than an hour away from assistance.

Very soon after the six bells of the Forenoon Watch had sounded Captain Dollimore's voice echoed throughout the *Burscombe*, announcing that the ship's company was about to hear some important news. Then the BBC was patched into the broadcast system via the Sound Reproduction Equipment Room, that tiny little radio station stuffed into an unpleasant position underneath the forward boilers' air intakes. The whole irregularity in the timing of the broadcast immediately told the men what to expect.

Very soon the prime minister was introduced and the man himself came on the air, speaking in his particularly precise upper class tones which played down his Birmingham ancestry. He spoke strongly but not without a hint of solemn resignation. It was the voice of a man whose endeavours for peace had been shattered by the politics of an increasingly dangerous world, and the words confirmed the rumour that

132

the Nazis had no intention of quitting their lightning attack on Poland. Britain was at war with Germany.

No cheers rippled through the ship. Chamberlain had set the tone.

Within the hour a CPO Telegraphist handed Dollimore an envelope. The man tried to be as dispassionate as possible but he had the real shine of excitement in his eyes.

'Thank you,' said Dollimore. He let the chief go then ripped it open. The message upon the slip of paper simply read: 'Commence hostilities at once with Germany.'

They could now be dealt with accordingly, when and where they were found, with no prevarication. The time for observation and note-taking was past. It would be the guns and the proficiency of their crews that made the decisions. From the highest to the lowest it were the words 'At last!' which were spoken or thought throughout the ship.

*

Looking over one of the latest signals to come in, Dollimore decided that 'Winston is back' was a bit vague. Far away from the North Sea, their Lordships of the Admiralty were welcoming to their London offices a new First Lord and boss in the person of Winston Churchill. His staunch anti-appeasement and warnings about the Nazis had kept him out of office for many years but now, everything being different, he was the man of the hour.

Crawshaw did not see what Dollimore meant at first but was soon put straight. They could see the words but they could not judge the tone. Was the Admiralty's message sent out of joy that they had received a leader who was not afraid of aggressive action, or apprehension because they had received a leader who was sometimes known to be reckless and difficult to control?

Such were the emotions over this one that the discussion was taken into the wardroom by some of the officers later that evening and continued over dinner.

Irwin stressed vehemently that the last time Winston Churchill was trusted with the office of First Lord of the Admiralty he had thoroughly messed up the 1915 Gallipoli campaign, which had resulted in the deaths of tens of thousands of fine men.

'And you think Lord Kitchener had nothing to do with that one going south?' asked Crawshaw, getting agitated, but then he found it easy to be

133

agitated by Irwin. 'Churchill was the scapegoat for the whole war cabinet's mismanagement. But then he's a man of action and doesn't allow himself to be put down. When he was fired from the cabinet, did he not go and fight in the trenches? He worked his way back up to where he is now the hard way.'

Irwin tried to counter that with, 'Some say he's as much of a warmonger as Hitler.'

'I'll tell you one thing for free,' said Crawshaw, guessing that Irwin had been overhearing the gripes of one or two of the lookouts. 'He was the only politician who spoke the truth about Hitler the whole of the last six years. All the others ignored him and look where we are now.'

Irwin wanted to continue by stating that this 'man of action' was also a man of excess who enjoyed a fight and liked being shot at. He himself thought that was completely stupid but, gauging that his sympathies were not the same as any of the men about him, he did not want to be called a coward into the bargain so backed down quietly.

It was no surprise that Crawshaw should idolise Churchill if the story that had been put about the ship was true. As a 'man of action' himself, Crawshaw had supposedly once saved the lives of some men from a burning oil tanker by placing his destroyer underneath the vessel's bow and persuading them to jump. The trouble, apart from the fact that the tanker might have exploded at any moment, was that it was still underway and out of control, the Portuguese masters having already abandoned ship. The men left on the bow were all Indian and Crawshaw's own officers had counseled that it would be as well to leave them to their fate than risk his whole crew.

Crawshaw, with gravity, was reputed to have said, 'They may be only Indians but they are still human beings. My conscience would not be clear if I let them perish just for their low birth.' So, he performed the reckless manoeuvre at speed much to the chagrin of those around him and was completely successful. That had happened not too far from Calcutta at the end of the last war, if the story was true.

Bretonworth tried to put the latest situation in a nutshell. The Scotsman said, 'We obviously need a man of action at the helm and that's why Churchill was appointed.' Less confidently, he added, 'Aside from that, I'm a bit of a political dunce so I'll just keep her upright and keep her moving.'

'I trust you're talking about the ship?' grinned Digby.

His face flushing red, Bretonworth said, 'There's no need to be crude.'

'I beg your pardon,' Digby said quite earnestly, though glad to have got more from the engineer than his usual clinical sayings such as 'Warfare is maths, fighting is physics.'

*

The ship was now running with the lookouts doubled and all navigation lights extinguished. As the crew labored with their usual round of exercises and routines, in the back of everyone's minds was the knowledge that a German warship, submarine or aircraft could appear at any moment with the express purpose of killing them. They were going to take no chances. They were going to call the ship to Action Stations every day at dawn, for that was traditionally the most dangerous time of day for any vessel, and keep the ASDIC – the anti-submarine device – echoing away as a matter of course in the depths below them.

The news that a German U-boat had already sunk a passenger liner, SS *Athenia*, in the Atlantic with heavy loss of innocent life was enough to make the message clear to all that their new enemy meant business. It was a terrible piece of news which disgusted all who heard it. Was the Royal Navy not supposed to be in command of the oceans? The Germans were going to pay dearly for this.

*

The *Burscombe* was coming up fast on a small, rusty black-hulled merchant ship of no more than six thousand tons which was crawling painfully eastwards through the heightened sea at about nine knots. Its low superstructure should have been white but was dull and spotted with exposed steel and the red funnel, which belched far too much smoke, was in a similar state of disrepair. It was not all a dead loss, though, for at least she was still afloat.

Those looking across at her through their binoculars did wonder that pieces were not falling off her, especially as she was pitching more violently than the sea suggested that she should. Her crew was most probably suffering terribly from her being in service long after she had passed her prime.

Chief Yeoman Ross was busy with his flags and halyards, hoisting signals in an effort to get the ship to stop. Another of his men repeatedly asked for information using the morse lamp but both were unsuccessful.

What was more, the telegraphists down below in the wireless office had not been able to raise her over the radio either. Was her captain somehow hoping that ignoring them would make this great warship go away?

Irwin climbed out of the hatch onto the bridge that was intermittently being swept by a rain which came in sideways on the wind. He immediately said to Dollimore, 'She's definitely the *Signhild II*, sir. She's registered as Danish according to the *Lloyd's* and we haven't received any signals warning us of any potential contraband in her hold. She should be okay.'

Dollimore nodded and studied the ship again with his binoculars. 'She may very well be okay but her master should know better than to ignore our instructions. I don't care who he is, everybody knows what's going on out here.' Turning to the officers the other side of him, he said, 'Pilot, ensure that we don't get any closer than five thousand yards until I say. She may yet be hiding torpedo tubes. Mr Digby, you have my permission to put a warning shot across her bows.'

'Sir,' acknowledged Digby in a flat tone, superbly hiding the excitement he was feeling. This was to be Burscombe's first shot fired in the war! Who would get the pleasure of dealing it out? He picked up the telephone, turned the handle to alert the operator, got connected to one of the secondary Fire Control stations and ordered, 'Port One 4-inch is to fire one shot across the bow.'

Four decks below, the first port 4-inch mounting, which was situated outboard of the forward funnel and flight deck crane, was immediately turned onto a forward bearing, her twin barrels simultaneously being elevated. The shell that was to be fired had already been loaded so in a very few seconds the crew was declaring that they were ready.

The officer in charge quickly looked at the *Signhild II* through his binoculars. Happy that his spotters, trainers and layers had done a fine job, he ordered, 'Shoot!'

An AB pulled on the white lanyard that was attached to the trigger and the right hand gun thundered, belching its shell and smoke out across the water. Instantly the crew opened the breach making the large brass casing eject itself out onto the deck. Smoke swirled around the crew smelling of putrid sulphur and another shell was quickly slammed into place.

Shortly, in front of the *Signhild II*, a tremendous geyser of water rose up in the air and the belated sound of the explosion rolled past on the wind.

On the bridge of that distant, dilapidated little steamer a man was observed to appear on the wing and shake his fist but the desired effect had been achieved. He finally surrendered to the inevitability of what was happening and stopped his engines. As the ship's speed dropped to almost nothing, Dollimore had the *Burscombe* circle her, gradually moving in closer until he was happy that they were in a good position to lower the cutter for boarding. At no time were the 6-inch guns turned away from their potential target.

'A first taste of action,' said Beatty, grinning from ear to ear as the boarding party waited in the port waist.

Young Clark smiled back. The excitement was infectious. They shook hands.

'No hard feelings?' asked Beatty.

'No hard feelings,' Clark replied, for this moment seemed to pale their misunderstandings into insignificance. A solution to his problem had far from presented itself to him as yet but he had accepted that he would need to search for it alone.

He was pleased to discover that he was not frightened of what might happen on this boarding party. He was about to be lowered into a rough, unforgiving sea in nothing more substantial than a thirty two foot wooden boat and be transported over to the deck of a foreign ship whose captain was, if not hostile, at least unsympathetic to the British cause. The only thing that bothered him was the cold.

'Away boarding party!' came the order from the bridge.

Lt Eddington, the officer commanding this little foray, leapt to his task with all the fervour that his dedication demanded and soon they were on their way. Taken from their stations at the anti-aircraft guns, Bonner, Les Gordy, and Pincher Martin were joined by AB Barrett, a wireless operator, a stoker, and a handful of smart marines under the firm control of the stocky Sergeant Burroughs. These were the men that the boat's crew was going to deliver to the Danish merchantman.

The boat, commanded by Beatty, was dropped the last couple of feet off the ropes onto the crest of a wave on the leeside of the *Burscombe*. Here they were relatively sheltered from the wind and the worst of the sea that was all but battering her other side. As soon as the lines connecting them to the davits were cleared, Dollimore ordered the ship to continue circling, her guns still diligently trained.

As the double-banked oarsmen pulled with all their might, everybody was soaked within seconds. Up ahead on the unstable looking *Signhild II*, more men had appeared on the deck and the captain had finally ordered one of them to lower a rope ladder over the side so that the British sailors would not be impeded in their efforts to get on board.

It took quite a bit of concentration and strength for each man to get hold of the ladder and begin the ascent. Lieutenant Eddington was the first to make it onto the ship's deck followed closely by Sergeant Burroughs, who was less than impressed when he split open the back of his hand on a worn rivet as the ladder swayed back and forth. As he cursed and pulled a field dressing from his pack three more marines arrived on the deck followed by the seamen. Clark brought up the rear leaving Beatty and his oarsmen in the cutter, its fenders just about preventing it from being dashed to pieces on the ship's side.

Eddington was a bright-eyed, fit twenty three year old who took pride in the fact that he thought he moved with all the grace of a Hollywood star. It was certainly true that he had more spirit and gusto than most men. He unhesitatingly pulled a revolver from the holster at his belt and walked straight towards the dusty old man in the black cap who was standing with his hands on his hips, staring at the invaders, furiously defiant.

'Now listen here, old chap,' Eddington snapped, 'what's the meaning of the commotion?'

The captain started shouting in Danish and such was his rant that it seemed as though his bulging eyes would pop out of his head. The language barrier was already creating problems so, after all the blustering, the only thing that was certain was that the man felt he was hard done by. Here and there stood other dirty members of his crew attempting to look just as aggressive but it was quite clear that any confidence they were showing was drawn from their leader in its entirety. But he had as good as lost the argument already.

'No point in babbling,' said Eddington, leaning over the man. 'Now you will bring me your cargo manifest and open your hold so that my man Clark here can take a look at what's inside. Understand?'

'Don't think they have the education to understand, sir,' grumbled Burroughs as he tied off the last end of his dressing.

Clark was momentarily struck by the hypocrisy of the statement. Why should a Dane be ridiculed for not understanding English when it was perfectly natural for the Englishman not to understand Danish?

'Cargo manifest!' Eddington shouted at the captain. 'I want to know what you've got, who's shipping it, and where it's going!'

The man launched into another tirade at which Eddington rolled his eyes. Then came through a word which everybody understood. 'Pirate.'

Looks of surprise and anger went around the British men at the insult. Eddington poked his finger into the captain's chest but deigned to lower his voice a little. 'Get this clear. We are not stealing your cargo. If you're carrying goods bound for the Germans we shall confiscate it, but if you're above board you can go on your way. What's so bloody difficult about that?'

In the ensuing pause the captain looked from one to the other of his unwelcome guests and finally said, 'I open the hold.'

'Oh, so you do speak English!' exclaimed Eddington. 'Get a move on! We haven't got all day!'

Burroughs muttered, 'I knew it wasn't for no reason that it's us what's got an Empire, sir.'

Who could argue with that? wondered Clark.

In short order the paperwork was produced which Eddington and Clark quickly reviewed. According to this the ship was carrying a mixed cargo of wheat and dairy produce for a company based in Copenhagen.

'There's no evidence that the goods are destined for further shipment to Germany,' said Clark.

'No,' agreed Eddington. 'Apart from this fool's unwillingness to co-operate we don't have much on him. However, take a rudimentary look down below but don't spend too long on it. The sea's getting worse so it's going to be very difficult to get back to the *Burscombe*.'

Inside the ship everything seemed to have been permeated by coal dust and Clark felt that if he stayed on board for too long then it should permeate him also. He went below into the dimly lit bowels followed by Bonner, Les and one of the marines.

The captain of this vessel was really running his operation to the limits of retrenchment. It was clear that the decks, bulkheads and deckheads were being kept as clean as was possible in the circumstances, but they were mostly unpainted and drab. This gave the impression that she was dirtier than she actually was, something which was exacerbated in Clark's mind by the fact that the *Burscombe* was so spotless. It was also his impression that the lower decks smelled of their unwashed crew and, to top it off, the most scrawny-looking cat that Clark had ever seen was sitting on a pipe by the forward hold staring at him with brazen dislike.

Bonner heaved open the hatch whilst commenting, 'Eh, Les, maybe we could leave you 'ere. It's more your style than one of 'is Majesty's ships, wouldn't yer say?'

Les just shrugged.

They climbed into the dark space, the low-watt bulbs not making much of an impact for the sake of their visibility. There were countless crates and sacks holding all manner of foodstuffs and, as he supervised the inspection, Clark was pleased to note that the hold at least was not so bad by way of hygiene. 'Still, it's just as well that the consumer won't see how this stuff is being transported.'

'What's this?' asked Les as he shifted sacks of grain against a bulkhead. Everybody looked at him, it being one of the rare occasions that he actually made any sound.

'What have you found?' asked Clark, climbing over the sacks to get to him.

Bonner was already there. 'Well, as I live and breathe,' he said as he shined his torch into the space made by the items they had disturbed. 'There's copper pipin' under here, sir. Tons of it.'

Clark smiled and looked at them. 'That, my friends, is what you call contraband. Well done, Gordy.'

Closing the hold back up again, they hurried to the bridge to report to Eddington the pathetic attempt at the concealment of the items that did not appear on the manifest, and wondered that there were probably more things hidden around the ship. It did not take long to round up the twenty one men that made up the crew. They looked rather appalled at what had happened. It seemed likely that the bad hat was the captain and that he was just trying his luck at making a bit of extra money regardless of the fears of his crew.

The Dane appeared furious but was necessarily deflated in front of the marines who each carried .303 rifles as well as sidearms. There was nothing he could do now and he knew it.

Eddington told him, 'I have perfectly good reason to suspect that the cargo of this ship is ultimately bound for Germany. There would be no other purpose in hiding the metals. I'm taking the *Signhild II* into Kirkwall for further examination.'

To the wireless operator that had come along he said, 'There's a morse lamp on the bridge wing. Signal the *Burscombe*, "Contraband found. Taking the ship into Kirkwall."'

'Aye aye, sir,' said the man, and immediately stepped out into the biting wind that came at him mixed with the odd splattering of sea spray.

Without delay, an acknowledging signal was flashed back from the bridge of the circling warship. A silent conversation sprung up which minced no words: "Are more men required?"

"No."

"Proceed with despatch. What speed can you make?"

"10½ knots."

After this their position was flashed to them. This was to ensure that AB Barrett had an exact point of reference to start from. It would not do if the Danish navigator had purposely pencilled the wrong position on the chart in order to mislead him.

Beatty and his men in the cutter had been sent back to the *Burscombe* as soon as the decision had been made. As much as anything else, if they had waited too much longer then the sea would have become too treacherous for the boat to be recovered.

Finally, under the supervision of the prize crew, a certain number of the Danes were put back to work so that the *Signhild II* could be taken south to the Orkney's.

*

The storm spent the rest of the day gathering strength. Even the *Burscombe*, superior to most ships, was beginning to labour under the difficult conditions. Peterson was trying to keep her on a definite course which corresponded to a pre-arranged plan but this just meant that she was destined to roll heavily, her hull groaning and her masts swaying violently.

Any daylight which penetrated the layer of grey cloud did not help much with the visibility, so the lookouts became keenly aware that an enemy vessel could easily steam straight past them within a couple of miles and never be seen.

Then the dreaded seasickness returned. Below decks the atmosphere was fast stripping away the lustre of Burscombe's renown as a clean ship. In such circumstances Lt Irwin was glad to be able to get up top and take over the bridge. He was one of the lucky ones. Although he had felt sick with the worsening of the storm, the feeling eventually disappeared, leaving him able to function without any difficulty.

Clad in dark waterproofs, Digby suddenly clambered out onto the bridge holding a camera. Making sure that he had Irwin and a couple of the other lookouts in the shots, he took a few photographs before returning the camera to its case and protection from the elements. 'For posterity!' he shouted to Irwin, raising his voice above the howling wind. 'It's my full intention to end up with a gaggle of grandchildren looking over these and wondering just what the hell we went through!'

To Irwin, Digby's optimistic sense of adventure and future well-being was truly enviable. It was as though he knew that they were destined to get through every scrape to a glorious conclusion. Irwin said, 'I hope the world ends up to be the sort of place you're dreaming of!'

'Chin up!' grinned Digby. 'Adolf needs to subdue Britain before he can really spoil everybody's fun and let's face it, he's not going to get past the navy, is he? He certainly isn't going to get past the *Burscombe*!' Laughing heartily, he made his way back inside the hatch.

Irwin looked out at the white-topped, stirring mounds of water and tried to do away with his doubts but it was not an easy task.

Just below him, in the relative comfort of the chart house, Peterson was jotting down a few calculations on a piece of paper. He had long ago learned how to continue doing this most difficult of tasks single-mindedly, even with the din of the sea and wind buffeting the ship.

In the corner of the room sat a wretched figure hunched over a bucket making some awful noises. Peterson had not quite given up bothering with the young lad who was currently throwing up his breakfast and more, though he had decided it wise to just give him a moment until he had emptied himself out.

Dollimore suddenly appeared, holding onto the doorframe for support. 'How about it, Pilot? Where are we?'

'About ninety five miles north west of Bergen,' Peterson said, without a pause. It was the very question that he had been working on knowing that the captain was lurking nearby. 'Although we've spent enough fuel oil in the last twelve hours to have covered 165 miles, if you take into account the wind and the current, I can quite guarantee we've done no more than a hundred.'

Dollimore nodded his acceptance of the situation. As bad as things were now he knew that they were in for a worse night. 'The sea is starting to come up over 2 Deck now as well. I'm going to have Irwin reduce our speed to eight knots to prevent damage to the boats and fittings.'

'Yes, sir.'

'It's at times like this when you find out what your ship is capable of.'

Peterson gave the captain an amiable sort of frown and joked, 'I'd be tempted to put in for a few extra feet on the beam next time we're in dry dock. It might do something about this rolling.'

Dollimore said, 'The thought had crossed my mind as well.' He looked at the lad sitting in the corner. 'What do you think, boy?'

The white-faced youth only managed to stare helplessly at the captain. His hands, holding fast to the stinking bucket, were visibly shaking and his saliva-coated lips quivered with every troubled breath.

'When you've seen waves twice the size of these,' Dollimore said, 'then you can say that you know something of the power of Mother Nature.' After a pause he added without reproach, 'Come on, boy, get back to it. You're not being paid to sit there.'

As the captain disappeared up top, the lad picked himself up from the corner and leaned once again over the chart.

Peterson screwed up his nose at the smell which drifted along with him. 'Do me a favour and go get rid of that first,' he said, pointing towards the bucket.

Even though they reduced the speed, Dollimore very soon judged that the situation might require drastic action. Crawshaw came to him in his cabin with a concerned CPO Doyle in tow to report that the waves sweeping along the exposed sections of 2 Deck had now holed the forward cutter, sheered some of the bolts from the practice breach in the starboard waist, bent some of the catapult frames, and almost taken the galley door off.

It had been Doyle himself who, trying to time a dash along the waist, had opened the door to notice a solid wall of water heading straight towards him. He had pulled the door closed in a hurry but the waves had slammed it repeatedly until the steel was bent and the galley had shipped plenty of water.

Dollimore was just digesting this report when Selkirk, the first lieutenant, appeared at the door. Even that hardy young man was looking a bit green around the gills.

Seeing Crawshaw already in attendance, Selkirk said, 'Ah, sir. I thought you might be here.'

'Well, come in,' said Dollimore, his patience beginning to be tested, 'the more the merrier. What do you have to add?'

'There's something very wrong with the plumbing in the forrard heads, sir,' Selkirk reported somewhat morbidly. 'Not only is sewage coming back up out of the bowls themselves, but it's finding its way through the vents into the seaman and stoker's messes a couple of decks below. What with everybody being sick as well it's becoming highly unsanitary down there. We're trying to locate the problem but it could take some time, sir.'

Dollimore nodded and stood, grabbing his waterproof coat from the hook beside the door. 'There's nothing else for it then.' Expertly negotiating the swaying ladder, he climbed out into the open and was immediately hit by a barrage of heavy rain. He moved forward to where Irwin kept station by the compass. 'Heave to!' he shouted.

'Very good, sir!' answered Irwin, happy for the decision made. He swiftly gave the orders which abandoned the patrol pattern. Turning the ship head on to the sea it was apparent that the wind was still striking her just on the port bow so he ordered the rudder to be held at an angle to port until further notice. Then he ordered the speed reduced again until they literally only had enough way on to keep the rudder barely under control.

*

The *Signhild II* was being tossed around as though she was a toy in a bathtub.

Clark, who had just been relieved from an eight hour stint on the bridge, clambered down to the mess that had been designated for their use. He was tired and feeling dreadfully sick. He could not remember ever being in a vessel that pitched and rolled as this one did. Slumping down on the shifting sofa and loosening his muffler, he listened with concern to the creaking of the bulkheads. He was thoroughly unimpressed.

'Here, sir,' said Pincher, carefully passing a cup of tea and a ham sandwich into his hands. 'It's as much as I can muster with this sea, sir, so no hot food, I'm afraid.'

'Thank you,' said Clark, not alluding to the fact that any form of meal would probably not stay inside his stomach for very long anyway.

After regarding the look on the midshipman's face, Pincher said, 'She's perfectly seaworthy, sir. I've served on much worse than this.'

Clark looked back at him. Pincher's face was well weathered and the coal dust from these boilers was already finding its way into the creases about his mouth and eyes. But the expression on his face was calm and compassionate, a bit of a contrast to the macho look he always put on around the other men.

Clark asked, 'You've been in the navy since you left school?'

'I was actually three years in the merchants before joining your lot, sir, working ships wherever my dad could get me in. He's still out there somewhere, near Singapore at the moment, I think. I catch up with him once in a while,' he grinned. 'I sort of feel sorry for my mum, you know. Me, my dad and my brothers treat her more like a landlady than a mum. You know what, sir? Thinking on it, I've been at sea for seventeen years now.'

Clark could not imagine being at sea for seventeen years.

'That's nothing in the scheme of things, sir,' added Pincher.

The door slid open and two tired marines stumbled into the room. One of them was soaking wet from having done a patrol on the outer decks in the pouring rain. Both men in their turn fell exhausted onto a sofa or bunk and the wet man grumbled, 'This has got to be the worst ship I've ever served on.'

Clark gave a chuckle and, when he turned back to Pincher, the AB had already gone off back to the pantry.

*

That night in the *Signhild II* amounted to the most uncomfortable time Clark had experienced in his life to date. For an ocean-going merchant ship her stability was really rather poor though, for some reason, the Danish captain thoroughly defended her seaworthiness.

Later, on the bridge and holding onto a pipe for support, he looked out of the window into the solid blackness of wind and rain. The ship was darkened and there was only a faint glow coming from the instruments and the chart table. Clark was not prone to panic but because of his fatigue, his imagination did not serve him well. He feared the ship would founder and could not help but envision himself shortly to be discovering the secrets of Davy Jones' Locker.

Barrett had been having much the same navigational difficulties as Peterson whilst not being able to see any stars for a fix. However, he gave Eddington his best estimate which was accepted without question. Clark understood and appreciated that.

While a sickly marine stood guard over the Danish helmsman, Eddington began making notes for his report. 'How would you describe the sea?' he asked Clark.

'Bloody rough,' commented the midshipman as he wiped some moisture from his nose with a handkerchief.

'Now would be a good time to start being serious,' said Eddington, unimpressed.

'Of course, I'm sorry, sir,' Clark replied. 'Twenty foot plus waves, er... Sea State Seven. Severe gale blowing. Force Nine.'

'Very good,' agreed Eddington. 'We might make an officer out of you yet.'

Yet another comment on his reputation? Clark tried to disregard the slight, which was something of a development for him. Still, why the comment? Had he not been working hard to fit in? He thought he had.

Sergeant Burroughs entered the bridge from the interior hatch and immediately began speaking matter-of-factly, which was quite incredible seeing that the news he was imparting was of a very serious nature. He said, 'We're shipping rather a lot of water under the fo'c'sle, sir. The Danish fella says we're okay but I reckon we might sink.'

'Thank you, Sergeant,' said Eddington, who turned straight to Clark. 'Get on it, will you? Bonner and Gordy are off duty at the moment. Take them and sort our little problem out.'

'Sir,' Clark acknowledged, quickly moving off towards the mess.

Having passed down to the deck below, Clark approached the ragged door to the mess and reached out to slide it open. It being already ajar, he could hear the voice of Bonner coming from inside raised above the rumbling of the old tub's frames. The words were enough to make Clark pause.

'Don't worry,' Bonner was saying, 'the bastard don't 'ave the gusto. I'm tellin' yer, 'e's not long for this service. 'E'll get so far, act like a martinet then be buggered off to some low key job outta the way. An' buggered's probably the right word. It's because 'e's a brown hatter. You can tell a mile off. Come to think of it, most officers probably are. All they do is get in the way and when they mess everything up they blame people who know what they're doin', like me.'

Clark grabbed hold of the door handle and pulled it open forcefully. The sharp crack of wood against wood made both Bonner and Gordy jump.

'Don't stop talking on my account!' said Clark, more enraged than he had been in a long time. 'Just which officer are you referring to? Should I be concerned that it's me? Am I the brown hatter who doesn't know what he's doing?'

'Tha's not what I meant, sir,' said Bonner pathetically.

'No, it's exactly what you meant. Why don't you explain to me your suspicions? You never know, perhaps I will concede that you have a point.'

Bonner just scowled, knowing that anything he said now would just make the hole he was in that much deeper.

Clark continued, 'Sowing discord amongst the men is a very serious offence. It completely undermines the happiness and efficiency of the ship in which you are serving. Does your divisional officer know the extent of your arrogance or are you the type who just whispers in corners? A bloody coward.'

Eyes flashing with anger, Bonner cried, 'I'm no coward!'

'Perhaps, perhaps not,' said Clark. He never took his eyes away from those of the wretched Scotsman. 'But I rather think you exaggerate your own importance. I can quite guarantee you, man, that you are no more use to this company than the martinet you spoke of.' Suspecting he had shamed the man enough, he said, 'Now, there's an end to the matter and it had better not come up again. Follow me, both of you. We have work to do.'

Heading off into the bows to confront the flooding problem, Clark tried to make sense of what had just happened. This infernal Scotsman, who was a brilliant seaman and proficient craftsman, who enjoyed the benefits and protection of the Royal Navy, seemed intent to cause trouble and make a mockery of everything. Why would a man so want to destroy something that could only be for his own good? He stopped with a horrid realisation. This was exactly how people looked at him.

*

The crews, British and Danish both, ended up working throughout the night to keep the flooding to a minimum. Just like so many other ships caught by this terrible September storm, she was hove to until the morning brought lesser winds and a calmer sea, allowing Eddington to let her proceed again.

She was eventually anchored in choppy waters amongst the northern islands of the Orkney's and there waited for the crew and cargo to be dealt with by officials from the Ministry of Economic Warfare. The dilapidated merchantman's captain assured Eddington that a complaint would be made against the British government for the detaining of his ship which was going about its lawful business and, of course, Eddington invited him to do his worst.

Chapter Nine

Relationships at North Cedars

Although autumn was coming to the southern counties it was still much warmer here than anywhere in the latitudes beyond Scotland. Young Clark could hardly believe the contrast. A few days ago he had been cold, soaked, hungry and sick all at once, unable to switch off his tired brain due to the pressures of keeping a near condemned ship afloat and guarding against retaliation from its waylaid crew. Now here he was on horseback in his old surroundings of absolute quiet and serenity. It was almost as if the war did not exist in this part of Kent. Nobody but the locals used these roads, not even the army on its way to the channel ports. The land around North Cedars Hall and Welbury were insignificant to all but the few who lived here.

He rode his horse, Neptune, in a seemingly casual manner down the winding lane, giving the impression of being someone who was out for nothing more than a breath of this pleasant morning air. The truth was that he had been cursing himself from the moment he had stepped aboard the ferry in Kirkwall, working against Beatty's and his own better judgment that he should let these affairs take their natural course. He had not stopped fighting with his conscience for the remaining eight hundred miles.

Not wanting to draw unsolicited attention to himself, he had changed out of his uniform at the hall and had slipped on a comfortable tweed jacket with riding breeches. He somehow felt that he did not want anything of the service to encroach upon this matter.

All too soon he saw the village ahead of him and shortly he would be in view of *The King's Head*, that small public house that he suddenly realised he had never set foot inside. It was one of only nineteen grey brick or wooden buildings that made up this small, quiet community. The little Norman church with its square bell tower and point-arched windows was very much the only other thing that stood out from the rest of the surrounding structures.

There were two familiar old men strolling along, both whom doffed their caps to the youngest son of the squire, and a motley collection of small children of varying ages seeing what sweets they might be able to buy with the few pennies that they had managed to lay their hands on. Their presence was odd. This was something new. Then he remembered reading that thousands of children had been evacuated from the cities in the last couple of weeks for fear of them being caught up in the expected bombing. These particular children looked like they were having themselves a thoroughly good time out of the whole affair. One could almost envy them the simplicity of it all.

The King's Head was at the opposite end of the village to the church and Clark took a deep breath as he tied Neptune's reins to a post in the barrel yard behind the building then pushed open the wooden door. Once inside, his eyes took a few seconds to adjust to the dim light. As his mind whirled with the dreamlike nature of it all, he prevaricated with the thought that the windows at the front could have been made much larger to let more light in. But that had obviously been overlooked centuries ago so the landlord was now required to keep a lamp or two burning throughout the day.

Clark was not particularly tall but he had to stoop a little in order to get past some of the overhead beams as he approached the small bar which held two pumps for the local ales. On the shelf behind were the usual bottles of spirits and wines which he had seen in other establishments in busy ports. This place was tiny. It was as though the builders never expected there to be more than fifteen customers at a time. They were probably right.

'Hello, sir? Can I help you?' The voice came from a man sitting smoking a pipe in a cubby hole to the left of the bar. As he looked up from the ledger that was laid upon the table before him, the smoke drifted about him in the weak light. He was a good looking fellow with neatly combed blond hair which looked as though it had a touch of cream applied. He was not a lot older than Clark himself and immediately seemed very approachable, smiling in the most agreeable way. Was this Tom? It had to be. Maggie had no brothers.

Now Clark felt very awkward. He had not expected this, either to meet him or to discover he might be a decent sort. But there was no going back now. 'Where is Mr Gufford?' asked Clark.

'He's in the cellar 'tending to the pipes,' replied the young man.

'Would you be so good as to get him, please? I would very much like to talk with him.'

The man looked him up and down for a brief moment to gauge his authority. He noted Clark's expensive clothes, the riding boots and breeches. It must have been him sitting on the horse he had heard outside a few moments ago. He also noted the posh voice and confident manner. The unexpected visitor was evidently high born so therefore most likely carried some weight. He nodded respectfully at Clark's request and slipped out through the small door behind the bar.

After only a few short seconds the landlord stepped into the room, wiping his hands on a dirty rag. His face, one Clark remembered only because it was so noticeable, drooped terribly on the left side. This was not through any natural cause but through the fact that a shell splinter had mutilated his features while he fought at Ypres in 1917. Another splinter had opened up his left forearm at the same moment. You could see the ten inch scar of the wound and stitches but, if he had ever suffered any debilitation, then he had obviously since regained full use of the arm as his movements now showed. Even if he did not know him personally, Clark knew of Gufford in the usual way that people living in a small community always knew of each other. Any deeper facts had been told to him by Maggie during one of their clandestine meetings.

'Yes, sir?' said Bob Gufford. His throaty voice held a forced affability. Otherwise he could not hide a certain need to be hostile. 'You're young David Clark from North Cedars. What can I do you for?'

'Well, it's rather a delicate business,' said Clark, feeling the man's cool approach to be somewhat inexplicable but making sure he kept eye contact. He worked hard to keep his voice level and confident as he spoke. 'I don't want to beat about the bush so I'll just say it. I want to ask for your daughter's hand in marriage.'

'You what?' Gufford said, an intense fury suddenly and visibly mounting up within him.

Clark stood his ground. 'I wish to wed Maggie... er, Margaret.'

'How the hell do you know my daughter?' growled Gufford, but before Clark had a chance to reply, he went on, 'I don't know who the hell you people think you are. Good God, I really thought those days were over. Everybody in these parts knows your family for rubbish.

151

Gutter rubbish! We don't want nothing to do with you! Get the hell out of my place!'

Clark was thoroughly taken aback by this verbal assault but he was nothing if not stubborn. 'That's completely out of order! How can you justify this? I've come to make an honest woman out of her and you insult my family.'

'With good reason!' Gufford was now standing right before Clark, his fists clenched and ready to fight. 'Now go. I know exactly how to pull a man's brain out of his skull. I've done it before and I'll do it again.'

Clark absolutely believed him. The man looked, and probably was, physically powerful and was known to have spent three whole years on the Western Front in the last war. You do not live through that and become a man to make idle threats. To top it all off, Clark had entered the situation nervous so now he was completely rattled. He retreated through the door into the yard and quickly untied Neptune's reins. Without any further ado he was riding up the road in the direction of home aware that Gufford had followed him outside with fists still made, his eyes boring holes in his back. What was that all about? How was a man supposed to do the right thing in the face of that?

*

At one o'clock on the following day Patricia Clark wholeheartedly submitted herself to the act of becoming Mrs John Bushey. As well as being visibly the happiest she had ever been, her dressmaker had done such wonders on the gown and her personal maid had styled her hair so magnificently that anything of the arrogance that resided in the girl was completely suppressed. It was as though a temporary shell had encased and trapped the old Patricia within.

David felt that he could easily be fooled into thinking her as all sweetness but, as it turned out, a situation quickly arose which dispelled the false image. Due to operational requirements, father had not been able to get away from the squadron, a circumstance which was fully understandable to all who heard so. Also their brothers, Henry and Thomas, were absent for much the same reason, though their situations were exacerbated by the realities of geography, for Henry was in the Mediterranean and Thomas was on the China Station.

This opened up an obvious question for Patricia. Who was going to give her away? Should the honour fall to David? Not a chance. She staunchly stood by the fact that she would never allow her perfect day to be marred by such an eventuality. He was not surprised and accepted the decision with no fuss.

When John found out, however, he tried to make a case for David – via a servant of course, because he was not to lay eyes upon her until she was walking up the aisle – but she was not to be persuaded.

'Sorry, old boy,' he said to David as a manservant brushed down his uniform. 'Your Uncle Geoffrey will be giving her away.'

David, who had popped in to see how the preparations were going with the groom, appreciated that John had tried to put in a good word for him, had known from the start that it had not been worth it, and was now seated by the window puffing away miserably on a cigarette. They could not know that his melancholia had very little to do with the bride's wishes. 'It's really not a bother,' he said. 'I'm not at all surprised she doesn't want me for the job.'

Philip Dollimore, standing nearby, fighting with his cuffs, said, 'It's still a shame.'

David managed a grin but there was no depth to it. 'There are things that happen between siblings that cannot be understood, sometimes by the siblings themselves. That's just the way it is. John, enjoy the day and don't spare it another thought, I beg you. Patty's not the problem.'

John turned away from the manservant and stared at the young man. 'Then why are you so down? If she isn't the problem, then what is?'

David paused and tried to put on a brave face. 'I think I've gone and made a fool of myself. It's over a woman.'

Both John and Philip laughed. 'We've all done that,' said the latter.

'It's a little worse than that,' David said, looking awkwardly down at the floor. 'Anyway,' he suddenly continued, 'I'll not let my stupidity ruin your day.'

Philip looked at his watch. 'Good, everything's done on time.' To John he said, 'How are you feeling?'

'I have butterflies in my stomach and I'm going weak at the knees.'

'Ah,' said Philip, thinking back on those two short years ago to when he had married his Sarah. His apprehension had manifested itself in much the same way. It had nothing to do with regrets or second thoughts but more to do with the excitement of changing his life forever in front of a hundred people, and the fact that that change was as yet uncertain until the very moment the bride actually appeared in the church to walk down the aisle. 'I think a stiff drink is the order of the day. It'll calm the nerves.'

'Better make it a brandy,' said John to the manservant.

The old man nodded and left the room.

John looked back over at David. 'So, this girl of yours,' he said. 'Who is she?'

Thinking about how Beatty had reacted to this information, he replied, 'I couldn't possibly say.'

'Fair enough, but is it serious?'

'Yes,' said David, miserably.

'Then ask her to marry you,' said John quite definitively. 'That'll solve all your problems. Girls like that sort of thing.'

The face David pulled then was somewhere between amusement and outright perplexity but John was too preoccupied with his own arrangements and nerves to really register the fact.

*

The ceremony went without a hitch and, at its conclusion, John was pleased to hold his new wife in a keen embrace at the altar and kiss her enticing lips.

Her expression was one of real happiness. For once there was no hint of any ulterior motive, no hidden agenda. She had wanted to marry this man with all her heart and, now that she had, her day had turned out just as she had planned, father or no father. There was nothing that could possibly tarnish it.

Before long the wedding party and guests made their way casually in a procession of vehicles from the church in Edenbridge back to North Cedars Hall. The most exquisite buffet had been set out in the dining room. There was chicken, beef, pork and lamb – only the finest cuts – a grand choice of fresh fish, salads with oily dressings, freshly baked bread still warm from the oven and much, much more besides. Nobody batted an eyelid at the extravagance even though all were fully aware that rationing had already begun as a war measure. Much of the food had appeared on silver service platters and was surrounded by garlands of bright flowers, a sight which would not be quickly forgotten.

All of this was surrounded by the hum of many voices engaged in topical discussions fuelled by the extraordinary times, and the gentle strains of the string quartet, playing with due grace in the corner of the room.

At the other side of the grand hallway the library had been given over to the more low-key entertainment of gambling, so for those who preferred a quiet card game coupled with a bit of risk this was the place to be. As the weather was still fairly pleasant the patio doors leading off the sitting room at the back of the hall had also been opened and the guests were free to walk in the gardens as they chose.

Betty Dollimore wandered around the whole place spellbound. It was not that she was completely alien to such finery, after all she had attended one or two important soirées in China thanks to her father's position, but more that these experiences were too few and far between. When they did happen she was entirely captivated by the moment, the people and the wealth, and wished that her own family was not so modest.

Her sister-in-law, Sarah, was also around here somewhere. They had arrived together but both had at one point or another become engaged in conversation with some old gentleman who was only too pleased to spend a few moments in the company of a beautiful young woman, and so they had lost sight of each other.

Again between conversations and pleasantries, she stepped into the dining room and looked through the crowds of well-dressed people, noting with frustration how so many of them were middle-aged or older, and then most of them women. She could not understand where all the handsome young men must be. There being a war on, most eligible bachelors would be in uniform, but where on earth were they? In a couple of hours there was going to be the opportunity to dance and she was afraid that her choices were going to be very poor.

Where was the young man whom she had seen with Philip and the groom a short while ago? Ah, there he was. He was dressed in his dashing naval uniform, just the way she liked it, and was talking with a small crowd of 'oldies'. From what she could tell he did not have a woman in tow. As he was pretty much the only prospect for a youthful liaison, perhaps she should talk to him and discover who he was. Looking about to make sure neither Philip nor Sarah could see her, she took a glass of champagne from one of the silver trays and inserted herself carefully into the group.

An old white-haired man in an army dress uniform of days gone by was in the middle of speaking. His cheeks were rosy with age and drink but otherwise he was properly turned out, smart and precise. The right sleeve of his red coat was empty and pinned to the front near his waist and in his left hand was a glass of whiskey. Upon his chest were the medals of almost a dozen campaigns and acts of bravery. He was saying, 'I don't quite see where we're going with this war. I keep hearing that we're busy concentrating our forces and that's all well and good, but somehow we're still doing nothing about Herr Hitler.'

'It's a bit much to say we're doing nothing,' said the handsome young man in the naval uniform testily. 'We're very successfully conducting economic warfare against Germany.'

'Economic warfare?' laughed the old man. 'What baloney is all that? When we went to France in 1914 we immediately sought out the Hun and brought him to battle. I remember it as clear as though it was yesterday. We marched forward until we found him then we let him know in no uncertain terms that we were not putting up with his mischief. So what's all this peering at him curiously across the border business? That's what I'm asking. And what have we done for Poland? Nothing, nothing at all. None of our forces seem to be taking the initiative.'

'I can't agree. Obviously I can't speak for the other services, but our ships are out there twenty four hours a day, seven days a week blocking all of the enemy's seaborne trade, and doing it damned well, I might add.'

'I say,' said the old man, giving his young antagonist a reproving look, 'there's no need to use bad language in front of the ladies.' With that he gave Betty a wink and a smile, thinking that it was wonderful that today's outing had produced such fine young creatures as this. Gentlemanly as he was, his look brought a reaction of disgust to the face of the elderly lady standing at his side. His wife, undoubtedly.

Suppressing a giggle, Betty saw that as her cue to speak. To the old man, she said, 'I could never mean to do you disfavour, sir, but I must side with this young officer here.'

'Oh?' he asked, feigning disappointment.

Feeling the young man's eyes now staring at her to her left, she continued in her most sophisticated voice, the one that most gentry seemed to like, 'I will always put the navy first. You see, my father's captain of a battleship and has been hard at work capturing Germans since the war began.'

'In that case, I am truly humbled,' said the old army officer, nodding subtly at the pleasure of being rebuffed.

At that point his wife cleared her throat. She appeared to have passed a threshold so said, 'Algernon, you told me you were going to introduce me to Lord Worth.' With that and a guilty grimace from the old soldier, they moved away across the room. The three or four other people who had been listening also moved away, leaving Betty with her officer. The meeting had gone much better than anticipated.

'Thank you,' he said to her. 'I'm a little out of sorts at the moment so you rather saved poor old Algernon from a bit of a lecture. It would have been disrespectful of me, I think, to have subjected him to a rant. He was one of our very first men ashore in France in 1914 and spent the whole war on the Western Front. The poor duffer lost his arm just as it was ending. I really should let him enjoy his opinion.'

Not wanting inexplicable matters to put her off her stride, she gave him her best smile and said, 'How could you be out of sorts on such a wonderful day as this?'

Smiling back, for he felt immediately at ease with this young lady, he replied, 'It's an awfully long story so surely a boring one, but I find that I'd like to know more about you. You've quite literally appeared out of nowhere and if you were anything other than what you are I'd be quizzing you on how it was you came to be here. Walk with me and tell me who you are.' He held up his arm so that she could hook hers into it and they started strolling arm in arm through the crowd towards the gardens.

'Well,' she said happily, 'my brother is the groom's best man and he was good enough to bring me along today.'

'Ah,' he said with a full and sudden realisation. 'I would never have thought it. You're Betty Dollimore. I'm David Clark, brother of the bride and until now wishing I'd not bothered coming home. So, there's another thing I've got to thank you for, brightening up my day.'

She felt a flood of warm satisfaction course through her body. 'I'll let you into a little secret,' she said. 'I was not really enjoying myself all that much either because, apart from you and I, the bridesmaids and a few

157

others, everybody's ancient and boring so I sort of hoisted myself on you. I hope you can forgive me.'

'Forgiven,' he said without a pause.

They stepped outside into the bright sunlight. The day had a slight chill in the air but neither found it uncomfortable so they walked and talked, putting the bustle of the reception behind them.

David asked, 'So, your father's the captain of a battleship, you say?'

'That's right. He's got a big ship up in the sea somewhere.'

'HMS *Burscombe* just happens to be a light cruiser, not a battleship, and it's one of the best ships in the fleet.'

'Oh, you know it, then?'

'Yes,' he said, smiling happily. 'I serve in her. Your father is my commanding officer. Good lord, I wonder what he would think if he knew I was chatting so with his daughter.'

'He would have to cope with it,' she said, with more than a hint of her rebellious nature surfacing for the first time. Another misunderstood youth.

He laughed and she then laughed with him.

*

The mother of the bride looked around at the splendid work the servants and florists had done on the grand old house and was pleased that so many people had attended for the big day. The place had been transformed so wonderfully that it was difficult to equate it to being that of where so many years of hatred and tension had developed. This now was how Dorothy had always wanted the hall to be, full of jovial and lively people. How many times had she seen anything like this since she had taken up residence? A dozen times? A dozen in thirty one years? Yet half of those times had been the work of Harper's late mother before the last war.

When all was said and done she still wished Harper could have been here. Patricia was his only daughter and this day would never come again. He had missed the only opportunity there would ever be to give her away and set her on her new life. But did he care? She had not quite decided that Harper despised all his children equally but it was certainly a possibility.

Anyway, Harper's brother Geoffrey had stood in to give her away and fulfilled the role well enough. He was one of those pleasant types who moved easily in any setting without causing any controversy whatsoever. Beyond that, he was unremarkable to the extent that he had been overlooked for promotion in the service years ago and was destined to die an elderly, obscure lieutenant-commander. His strange lack of the Clark family ambition saw to that. Everybody liked him.

She looked out across the garden from the patio, where she was being paid a kind compliment by a Canadian naval captain, when she saw the butler having words with David. Felsham was talking, David was looking down at the grass in deep thought and a frumpy girl – that would be one of the two that came with John's best man – was standing a short distance away waiting impatiently with her arms folded, staring daggers at him.

David then spoke to Felsham as though issuing some sort of instruction and motioned for him to lead the way back to the house. So the two men walked away leaving the blonde girl forgotten, alone and embarrassed amongst the flowers. For David to have been so rude, surely there had to be something amiss. Though to be honest, wherever there was David, there usually was something amiss.

Dorothy wondered for a moment that she should leave this alone. Perhaps some unforeseen circumstance had arisen that Felsham thought David would be best placed to handle, being the man of the house presently. No, the butler was under no illusions that she and she alone was completely in charge of everything that was happening today. Since David had come home yesterday, he had done nothing but disappear for long hours, follow the wedding party dutifully but absently, or skulk about the house miserably. Felsham would certainly come to her if there was a problem to be sorted out with the reception. Something else was going on. When they started heading off round the west side of the house where the kitchens and servants' entrance was situated, her suspicions deepened.

She smiled and thanked the Canadian officer for his wonderful compliment and, picking up the hem of her glamorous floor length gown, turned to move discreetly into the hall. She moved quickly along the corridor behind the grand staircase, being careful not to bring any undue attention to herself, and soon she was at the inner kitchen entrance. There was Felsham, looking slightly perturbed but giving instructions to one of the cooks.

'Is there anything wrong, Felsham?' asked Dorothy.

'Of course not, ma'am,' he replied, momentarily surprised by her unexpected appearance in this part of the house.

She frowned, 'I saw you talking to David in the garden. It looked rather serious.'

Felsham nodded his capitulation. Nothing ever escaped the notice of the mistress of the house. There were few people in this world that he could think of who were so attentive and observant. 'Master David took the young lady up the back stairs.'

'What young lady?' Dorothy asked sternly, already sensing the presence of a scandal. 'For it certainly wasn't the one that he left so discourteously outside.'

'No ma'am,' replied Felsham, clearly ill at ease. 'She is a girl from the village.'

Dorothy swiftly made her way up the stairs. Her blood was boiling. What did David think he was up to? There was a time and a place for such behaviour and it was not at home under her roof within a stone's throw from a hundred guests on the day of his sister's wedding. She did not care what sort of macho egotism he had developed that he could not be discreet. This was not the way she had brought him up.

Once upstairs, she walked along the corridor, hearing the faint murmuring of many voices and the music of the strings coming from below. Then she heard voices coming from Harper's study. It was David and whoever this girl was. She heard anger and distress in their tones. Clearly the trouble was deeper than she thought. Without hesitation, she reached out, pushed open the door and walked inside, instantly silencing the two youngsters.

'What is going on?' she enquired outright, looking at David's companion and wondering where she had seen her before. 'Why are you in your father's study and who is this girl?'

David and the girl were locked in an embrace, but not one of passion, it appeared. His face held a deep look of concern and she had been crying. Her face was reddened, her eyes puffed with smudged, wet outlines. When she looked over, Dorothy could then see by the light entering from the great window that her right cheek was hidden beneath a terrible, dark bruise. So there really was deep trouble and it could only have been David to bring it home. No one else, only David.

'Mother...' David began to say through his surprise.

'Well?'

'It's not at all how it looks.'

'I wasn't born yesterday. Don't you think I have some idea at the games you men must play?' Dorothy's temper was really getting the better of her now and it was just as well that there were so many people making noise downstairs, otherwise their business here would be common knowledge to the whole household. 'It is your indiscretion that I cannot abide. You stalk away from the reception in full view of everyone, sneak this... village girl in the back way, drag Felsham and the kitchen staff into the collusion and now it looks like she's imparting some sort of bad news. What do you want me to think?'

'Mother,' said David, having finally regained his posture. 'I'm going to need your patience on this one.'

'I don't know how much patience I have left. Between you and your father you're going to drive me into an early grave. Of all my boys, you have turned out the most like him.'

David let his arms fall from the girl, who stepped back from him, understanding that that statement had just shocked him to the core. 'You didn't have to say that,' he said. 'We have not been doing anything untoward. This is the girl I love, the girl that I want to marry.'

This having come out of nowhere, Dorothy barely understood what she had just heard. Proudly keeping her chin up, she asked, 'Then why the secrecy? Why did you not invite her to the wedding and introduce her properly? No, let me answer that. It's because she's a nobody from the village and you knew that she would not be accepted here.'

Indignation swept over the girl's blemished face as David said to his mother, 'I could count on snobbery from some of the others but not you, mother.'

'It's not snobbery,' she countered. 'It's fact. There's more to life than your petty desires. The family and its business comes first.'

'There had to be a reason why you and father are still together,' said David, disgusted. 'I just never thought it was that simple.'

Dorothy stepped forward and lashed out, intending to slap him firmly on the side of the face but he easily caught hold of her wrist and held her arm still.

After she relaxed her muscles, he let her go and said, 'We're not going to do this anymore. I'm deeply ashamed that I laid a hand on you, mother, but this is the girl that I *am* going to marry with or without the family's blessing.' There it was, an ultimatum. What would mother's counter-blow be?

Dorothy broke off eye contact and walked over to the window, contemplating the situation as she went. Looking outside she saw John and Patricia together, speaking to their guests as a happy couple. That was how these things were supposed to be, not like this. It was going to take much more consideration. She turned and looked straight at this dark haired girl in her cheap, plain dress and reasoned that she would be very beautiful had she not been crying or punched in the face. 'I take it you have a name?'

'Margaret Gufford, ma'am,' Maggie replied, her voice calm now that things seemed to have changed a little.

Dorothy suddenly looked concerned. 'Gufford?' she said. 'Oh good God. If it doesn't rain it pours. That is a name that I had hoped never to hear again.' She raised a hand to her face and rubbed her eyes, wondering what sort of curse had come down on this family. She walked slowly behind the desk and slumped down into the chair.

David looked at Maggie then looked back. 'What is it, mother?' As he said this, the words Bob Gufford had spoken the day before were coming back to him: 'I really thought those days were over. Everybody in these parts knows your family for rubbish. Gutter rubbish!'

'Let's just say that our two families don't see eye to eye,' said Dorothy.

It was the turn of David's temper to fray this time. 'No, let's just say a little more than that. What is going on?'

'My dear,' Dorothy said to Maggie, with something of pity in her voice, 'do your parents know about your little relationship with my son?'

'Yes,' she replied. Pointing to her bruised cheek, she said, 'That was why my father did this. David came to propose marriage yesterday...,'

'I'm sorry, Maggie,' he butted in. 'That has to have been one of the most ill-judged plans I've ever come up with, but it's just that I couldn't let you marry Tom. I want you to marry me.'

The two of them locked themselves into another embrace, this time not of solace but of love, to the disparaging sound of Dorothy's, 'Please!'

Then she continued, 'So David, in all his wisdom, asked your father for your hand in marriage?'

'Yes,' replied Maggie.

Knowing that the two of them would keep pressing for an explanation to her stance, Dorothy said, 'I have to tell you, young lady, that our two family's history is not a good one. Before either of you were born, your parents had such a disagreement with my husband that they have the perfect right to expect us to stay away from them forever.'

They were appalled. David asked, 'What happened?'

'Something so awful that it cost us a lot of money to buy their silence and I beg you, with every fibre of my being, not to look for the answer to that question. It is done and dusted and will do nobody any good at all to dredge up the past.'

'Except that it stands in the way of our happiness,' said Maggie with a strength that frankly surprised Dorothy.

She could see that these two youngsters really were in love in the way that they professed to be but this was definitely a problem that was not going to be solved here and now. As she had decided before, more time was going to be needed for consideration. 'Here's what we are going to do,' she said, firmly taking control. 'Madam Gufford, you shall stay here tonight, but in one of the servants' rooms and out of sight of my guests. Tomorrow, after David has gone back to his ship, I will take you home and speak to your father to see what we might arrange.'

David's eyes lit up with surprise. 'Do you really mean it?'

'Well, you are both serious, are you not?'

'Yes. Yes we are.'

'Right then,' Dorothy continued, 'David, you will go back to the reception now and carry on entertaining in the way that a man of North Cedars Hall is expected to. Do not do anything to ruin your sister's day or that will be the last thing you ever do under this roof.'

David raised his hands in submission. He had not been handed a perfect solution but it was a manageable one and at least there was now some hope. Somehow, someway, he and Maggie would be together and, with mother's help, they would make it respectable so that even the likes of Beatty would understand.

Also, he found that knowing his father had another hidden aspect to his sordid history did not surprise him one bit. It filled him with curiosity but he decided he would not press the matter for fear of ruining what progress they had made so far. If what happened was so awful then the truth would emerge one day. It always did.

*

The bride and groom continued their evening by dancing merrily away to the music provided by an extended band of woodwind and strings that had joined and complimented the original four who had been playing earlier. David chatted amiably enough to all he encountered, even giving Algernon an easier time when he next raised the issue of the conduct of the war. He drunk wine moderately so that he should not lose his wits in any way and all the time he wished he could be away from here and with Maggie.

Philip Dollimore, happily mingling with his wife by his side, saw him and asked, 'I say, aren't you going to ask my sister for a dance? She's quite taken with you, you know.'

Sarah smiled and added for good measure, 'She's spoken of nothing but you these past two hours.'

'Is that so?' asked David, wondering how that could be. He had been rather rude to her. 'In that case, how could I leave her on her own?' With that he looked across the room and caught her eye. A beautiful girl, he thought, but nothing compared to Maggie.

*

Hundreds of miles away, HMS *Burscombe* was anchored amongst other ships of the fleet at Rosyth. She had been ordered there to make right the damage that she had suffered during the great storm. Although there was as much hard work as ever to contend with, being in port was still considered a welcome breather.

Here their post caught up with them and it was from this that Midshipman Farlow was able to continue in his family's great love affair with other people's business. He had just read a letter that had been sent by his father and was overjoyed to find that it contained some excellent gossip about the Clarks amongst other people, written in answer to his own snooty observations of life with certain people in the gunroom.

On board ship, knowledge of David Clark's excellent conduct in the *Signhild II* affair had been applauded and that had bothered Farlow so how wonderful it was now to finally have some tangible dirt on the little pipsqueak, dirt that could very well make life around here interesting. He wasted no time in whispering this gossip into the ears of his friends.

Chapter Ten

Disappointments

'Well, Jock,' said Doyle, who had by chance found Bonner crouched over the urinal in the CPO's heads up forrard. 'Aren't you a bit old to be doing this sort of punishment? When are you going to start growing up?'

Bonner did not even grace him with the pleasure of a glance as he scrubbed. He just said, 'Ah, get lost.'

'I'm pretty well at the point when I'm not going to take that from you anymore,' said Doyle. 'For old times' sake, I've been trying to understand you. Why can't you get it together? You know that everything's changed now. We're at war.'

Bonner then looked up. There was a look in his eyes that was somewhere between hate and sadness but there were things that he was not going to give this man the satisfaction of knowing. Moving over to the sink in order to give that a scrub, he said, 'You're gettin' right above yer station, you are, so like I said, get lost.'

'After I've taken a piss.' Doyle immediately moved into the space just vacated by Bonner and started to pee onto the spotless enamel. 'I could quite easily give you the chop if I wanted, but then I know you're a first class seaman. That's the only thing that's saving you. You know that, don't you?'

It was hard to imagine that fifteen years ago he had thought Bonner to be one of the cleverest men he knew. But now there was the distinct possibility that the Scotsman was going to be a liability when the time came for action. One of the key elements of any ship at war was that every man should be as useful and important as the others. By all reports, he and the other men from his anti-aircraft team had acquitted themselves well aboard the *Signhild II*. That had been a job of supreme importance requiring certain diplomatic responsibility from all concerned so a last benefit of the doubt for this man surely should be extended. Doyle walked away thinking it through.

*

The impounding of that Danish merchant ship was another high profile achievement for the *Burscombe*, made even better for the fact that, upon closer examination, it was found that she was carrying iron ore as well as the copper and foodstuffs. What with the secrecy and the behaviour of the crew, it was pretty clear that the cargo's final destination was Germany. It had thus been decided that if that greasy little ill-tempered captain wanted to continue to work then he was going to have do something a little more honest with his time.

Achievement though it was, the British officers involved still felt that they could be doing more with *their* time. Not only had the news come through that the fighting in Poland was over, that half of that country had been occupied by the Nazis – the other half by that treacherous Stalin and his Communists – but a couple of weeks ago an old aircraft carrier, HMS *Courageous*, had become the first British warship to be sunk.

Churchill's idea had been to bring the war to the U-boats by demonstrating air power at sea, a perfectly reasonable concept until a U-boat put two torpedoes into the carrier's side destroying the ship, two whole squadrons of aircraft, and killing over five hundred men.

Commander Crawshaw had recently been heard more than once to say, 'We've got to get at them!'

*

While at Rosyth Captain Dollimore was pleased to finally be able to embark a Walrus reconnaissance aircraft. The plane was landed on the flat water in the Forth estuary not too far away from the Victorian railway bridge and its pilot carefully brought it alongside the *Burscombe*. Dollimore was so happy with this eventuality that he stood on the flag deck with Crawshaw and Digby looking down upon the operation as the starboard crane was swung out over the side and ropes were hooked up to the aircraft so that it could be raised up onto the flight deck. The Walrus bi-plane was rather flimsy in appearance, its wings set very wide apart, and its strangely overlarge tailplane attached to a thin body. However, it did boast a steel frame and aluminium body and was designed by the same man who had created the Spitfire, so all concerned had no doubts that they were onto a winner.

'Better late than never, sir,' said Digby.

'Absolutely,' Dollimore replied. 'It will finally give that air officer of ours something to do. Come to think of it, did you know that the Edinburgh's been putting to sea with an aircraft and no pilot?'

Crawshaw gave one of his frowns and said, 'And all the while... These are crazy times.'

'Aren't they just?'

After some considerable time the Walrus was seated on its catapult trolley. It had taken some effort on the men's part to secure it, there having been only one person who seemed to be familiar enough with the machinery. But that was fine. Drills involving the plane were obviously the next order of business.

While they were working, the cutter serving between the ship and the shore appeared from behind a nearby destroyer and approached to pull up alongside the Burscombe's quarterdeck.

Crawshaw looked through his binoculars and saw Midshipman Clark seated in the stern. The boy was back on time. Good. The captain had become aware that the boy was taking something of an interest in the lower rates in such a way that was not usual. The diaries that all midshipmen were expected to write and submit to their commanding officers regarding their service had revealed, in this particular case, heavy hints that the navy should benefit the ratings more than it did. This, coupled with the fact that some of the other officers considered Clark to be a bit of a soft touch, had prompted Dollimore to raise the matter with Crawshaw.

The commander immediately saw the opportunity of making a point by using a case of defaulters that should be of interest to Clark personally. Afterwards, Dollimore would tell him that his diary was not meant for making complaints, but if he wanted to highlight things that he thought could be changed, then he should do so with a list of recommendations. Commenting on the navy's procedures with no reference as to how to bring about a positive change was next to useless.

*

Hardly having had time to stow his gear away, Clark found himself standing in the passageway near the Regulating Office silently waiting while Lieutenant Eddington, rostered as Officer-of-the-Day, finished jotting some notes in his pocket book. Eventually Eddington looked up from the lectern at which he was standing and called through the open hatch, 'Bring the first one in!'

First to enter was CPO Doyle, looking very official in his best uniform and wearing a grave expression on his face. Behind him came Able Seaman Bonner. Also attired in his best and having scrubbed up all clean and smart, he took a few steps forward and stopped expressionless in front of the desk. Though he performed a faultless salute, he otherwise acknowledged nobody's presence, just stared blankly at the bulkhead. Then there followed the Master-at-Arms, the man responsible for lower deck discipline.

Clark wondered what must have happened. Bonner had obviously been detained, but as to the seriousness of the situation? The case had been referred to the OOD so it was bad enough that it could not be dealt with by the senior rates.

Clark cast his mind back to that night aboard the *Signhild II* when he, by rights, should have charged Bonner for his disgusting comments. Had his leniency been a mistake? For then there was that other occasion when Bonner had been rude to the new surgeon-commander...,

Lastly, another lieutenant stepped through the hatch, a bearded gentleman called McPhee whom Clark knew only by sight. This man he understood to be Bonner's divisional officer and, from the look on his face, had been completely exasperated by him.

'Off caps,' McPhee ordered, with a resigned air.

Bonner reached up and removed his hat in precisely drilled movements.

Eddington looked up at him and paused while he judged the mood. Then he looked over to Doyle who was standing out of arm's reach of the defendant, a precautionary measure aimed at not allowing the man to make matters worse by having the chance to lash out at him. Finally shifting his gaze to the Master-at-Arms, he said, 'Would you please tell me what happened?'

'Yes, sir.' Then, in a tone which suggested he was trying to make something posh out of a northern accent, the man said, 'Able Seaman Bonner is charged with conduct prejudicial to good order and naval discipline in that on the evening of twenty second September 1939, he did come aboard at the end of liberty a little the worse for wear and, when Chief Petty Officer Doyle told him to sort himself out, he took umbrage at the fact and started by calling him a 'fucking idiot', sir.'

Eddington tutted reprovingly and jotted it down. 'And there are witnesses that he called him an idiot?'

'Yes, sir, one of them being Surgeon-Lieutenant Fraser, who was smoking on deck at the time, and that would be a *fucking* idiot, sir.'

'Yes, yes!' snapped Eddington.

But the Master-at Arms, unchanging in his stance or expression, said, 'The 'effing' part is, I think, integral to the case, sir.'

'Yes, yes, yes! I've written it down! There's no need to keep referring to it! And you can wipe that smile off your face!' This last order was directed at Bonner who, knowing he could only push these people so far, quickly shifted his grin back to a look of blank seriousness.

After a few more seconds of consideration, Eddington continued, 'Right, you said he called him an idiot. Well, you said that's how he started. But something more must have happened for the matter to come before me. How did it finish, I wonder?'

Now the man relating the story had a deadly serious look on his face. 'Doyle said to him, "You don't go about talking to a chief petty officer like that," to which he replied, "Chief petty officer? Don't make me laugh. You're nothing to me. By definition the word 'petty' means 'small and insignificant'." And all the while he was pointing at him like this.' He thrust his finger forward to demonstrate the aggressive pointing.

Both Clark and McPhee looked down with slight shakes of their heads. How childish was all this?

But Eddington did not flinch. He was giving away no more emotion beyond that which showed his desire for professionalism. Calmly, he said, 'I'd like to know something more of the man's state. You said that he came aboard the ship 'a little the worse for wear'. Was the fact that he was drunk established at all by any authority?'

'No, it wasn't,' the Master-at-Arms answered, realising that he should have seen this question coming. 'Surgeon-Lieutenant Fraser did rule that, although the man had been drinking, if called upon to work, he would fully be able to do so without being a danger to himself or those around him.'

'Thank you,' said Eddington. 'Nothing more will be said about the involvement of alcoholic drink.' Then looking up at Bonner, he asked, 'Do you have anything to say for yourself?'

'No, sir,' said Bonner, stooping from his pride to at least show a hint of regret.

Eddington looked at him in disgust. 'All I have to say to you, Able Seaman Bonner, is that a man of your years and experience should have advanced to something a little more useful by now. It's about time you started showing the proper respect for your officers and senior rates. They are your superiors by law and you will consider them as such without exception. You know well enough that this is more than just me telling you. The *Articles of War* have been read to you and the act of insubordination that you have displayed carries with it a maximum penalty of 'Dismissal with disgrace from His Majesty's Service'.

'However, it is not lost upon me that your seamanship is excellent and you have been most efficient in your work, but there is much more to life in a ship than that. Your personal behaviour has to be on a par with your professional behaviour. I find that I have to put this matter forward to a higher authority. Just know that, if you are removed from the *Burscombe*, you will suffer forfeiture of pay, allowances, pensions and decorations. Plus there will be no hope of receiving any prize money from the sale of enemy ships captured. Now, you will present yourself at the next Commander's Defaulters. That is all.'

'On caps,' ordered McPhee.

A moment later the four men left leaving Clark standing nearby, a little stunned, watching Eddington finish with his jottings in the pocket book.

Once this was done Eddington said, 'The best way of describing this whole business, I think, is infantile. That man may be good at his job but he absolutely does not represent the true attitude of the lower deck. Apart from one or two like him, we have ourselves a good bunch here on the *Burscombe*.' He now looked Clark squarely in the eye. 'But that's not to say we should be their friends. One or two of the chaps feel that you do not have a clear grasp on that fact and the commander wanted you to sit in on this session because Bonner is one of the men you've been trying to... understand.'

Clark held up his hands in frustration and said, 'Where's the harm in trying to understand them? And you think I'm looking for their friendship? I'm looking for mutual trust. I can't escape the feeling that we're selling the men short and losing out on some of that trust.'

Eddington frowned and said, 'If it's mutual trust that you're looking for then you must look for it within the confines of naval discipline and the unalterable understanding that we have been bred to lead and they have been bred to follow.'

He sounds like Beatty, Clark thought. Inwardly, however, he was beginning to wonder if Beatty might be right since his friend did not seem to suffer any internal conflicts and appeared to command perfect obedience and respect from the men under his command all the time. What had just happened with Bonner made this even more pertinent.

After receiving a lecture from Captain Dollimore on the same subject, he eventually made it back to the gunroom thinking he could finally relax in the presence of his friends. Then Beatty started on him as well.

He had just settled himself, running his eyes over an article in *The Times* concerning important German dignitaries abroad trying to get home through the blockade, when Beatty said his piece.

'Alright, I get it, I truly do!' Clark exclaimed, raising his hands in submission.

Then, of course, that pompous idiot Farlow, who was sitting close by, allowed one eyebrow to hook upwards in a condescending manner and said, 'There are easier ways of making yourself popular with the lower decks. I suggest you look to the submarine service. They're much more comfortable in their snug environment, plus they're a lot more apt to take the odd types such as yourself.'

Clark rounded on him. 'At least I wouldn't be classed as unneeded ballast!'

'Enough, enough,' Beatty said, carefully watching Clark's body language that he might be ready to restrain him if he was to do anything stupid.

Oddly, Farlow was looking much too happy with himself for someone who was not adept at winning arguments. Beatty wondered if it was just because Clark was more than usually worked up, or did it have something to do with those damaging rumours that had somehow recently found their way onto the ship? Clark knew nothing about them yet and Beatty was wondering exactly how to broach the matter. In the meantime he had ruthlessly warned off anybody he had caught spreading them. Apart from the risk of personal insult to Clark, they were potentially detrimental to the harmonious running of the ship.

'Now,' he said, regretting his part in causing the upset and forcefully changing the subject, 'tell me about the wedding. What were the bridesmaids like? You know I can't resist a bridesmaid.'

Clark answered his questions but remained guarded.

*

The atmosphere in the seamen's mess was considerably improved once Bonner was no longer part of it. There had been two types of men who existed on that deck when it came to dealing with that volatile man, those who hated him and tried to have nothing to do with him and those that tolerated him and shared the odd conversation or joke with him. Friendly as some of them were, none were actually his friends.

Les had not understood that before but he found that, no matter where anybody stood on the subject, all were pleased that he had finally been ousted. That was not to say that Bonner had truly been given the chop, but he had suddenly been sent on a gunnery course and there was a rumour that he might be drafted to another ship.

Even Smudge and Pincher, men who seemed to have got on well with him, did not mourn his disappearance. It had been bound to happen sooner or later, was the general consensus of opinion. Not only had Chief Doyle had it in for him from the word go but, as Les told them, that midshipman, Clark, had decided to put the boot in as well. He told them all how that big-headed 'snotty' had sounded Bonner out after he had caught him talking about Lieutenant Irwin behind his back.

Oh yes? What had he been saying about him?

That he was as bent as a nine bob note.

Smudge was unimpressed. 'There's more than a couple of *them* round here. Are you gonna tell us something we don't know?'

'But it's illegal,' said Les, who had never spoken so much in his whole time aboard the ship.

'Only if you get caught,' said Pincher. 'So you better make sure you don't. We don't want to have to break out the buggerboards.'

Les looked thoroughly shocked, somehow not registering that a lot of the other lads were laughing. 'The what?'

'Well,' said Smudge, taking up the explanation since he considered himself the better bullshitter of the two of them. 'Just supposing they try to cram many more men inside this barge, and believe me it's looking likely 'cause they keep doubling the watch and what not, then the newer members of the crew, being the junior etcetera, have to give over half their hammocks to those incoming. This is where it gets uncomfortable, and I've seen it happen more than once and it still makes me shudder. Just supposing we have to stick another man in your hammock with you because there's nowhere else for him to sleep?'

'But we only get a regulation twenty one inches as it is!' protested Les, his Irish accent getting stronger the more indignant he became.

'Whoa!' said Smudge, raising his hands, 'Slow down! You're getting way ahead of yourself, boy. So, you're in your hammock with this other big, hairy fella and you've got one of two choices.' With that he held up three fingers. 'You can make sure you lie back to back but if your new friend is insisting that he turns to face your back, you can break out your buggerboard to prevent him from getting too familiar. You catch my drift?'

But Les just stared back at him, shocked and upset.

Pincher suddenly said, 'Leave him alone, Smudge, he's had a respectable upbringing and doesn't want to know about all that stuff.'

'What, reading stuff like *Les Misérables*?' asked Smudge, again making no attempt to form the proper French pronunciation of the name. 'What was the names of those two fellas you told me about who started that uprising?'

As Les shrugged, Pincher said, 'What, Marius and the other one?'

'That's the ones. I bet they shared an 'ammock once or twice together, or haven't you got up to that bit yet?'

'Smudge,' said Pincher with a hint of warning in his voice. 'He's only just got Bonehead off his back.'

'You're right, you're right,' said Smudge. He turned back to Les and gave him a friendly little slap on the shoulder. 'No, seriously now, when we turn to at eight bells I need you to go to the store to get the oil for the capstan motors. Now remember, I need the red can for the port motor and the green can for the starboard. Think you can do that?'

'Don't see why not,' replied Les.

He had no idea why the petty officer started shouting at him at the stores but knew that the only oil he received was in a grey can. Things were not going well, but at least Bonner was not around to make matters worse. Or could it be that Bonner had been the one keeping Smudge off his back and things were about to get an awful lot more difficult?

He did not get a wink of sleep before having to start work at midnight and he still did not manage to get any rest before he was due to turn to again at 2000 the following evening. Beginning to get anxious that there was something very wrong, he quickly went along to the sick bay before reporting for duty to complain to the attendant that he could not sleep. Surgeon-Commander Lawson just happened to be seated in the adjoining office and peered round the edge of the open door.

'What time do you next come off watch, lad?' said the twitchy old Cornishman, scowling because he had been disturbed from studying a colleague's medical notes on a recently performed amputation.

'Midnight,' replied Les feebly.

'Perfect,' said the surgeon with ill-disguised discontent. Seriously, these servicemen were turning out to be as irritating as his civilian patients had been. 'Well, if you're still suffering from your little problem at midnight then come back to me. I have plenty of work for a young chap such as yourself. Got it?'

'Thank you, sir,' said Les.

At the end of his watch he slung his hammock amongst all the others in the mess and listened to the men snoring around him as they swayed gently back and forth in the dark. Lying awake, he came to the conclusion that he was not going to go anywhere near Surgeon-Commander Lawson ever again.

*

It was only a few hours that he had been able to spare but that was what Rear-Admiral Clark allowed himself for another meeting with his mistress, Diane Greyforth. He arrived at the cottage on the quiet lane outside town and they were soon taking tea together in front of a welcoming fire in the lounge. He had told her to light it because he was still feeling something of a chill within, one that he had not been able to shake since that horrendous storm had nearly wrecked the *Godham* a couple of weeks ago.

'I didn't manage to get back to North Cedars for the wedding,' he said.

'That's unfortunate,' Diane said. 'I'm sure that Patricia felt your absence keenly.'

Clark smiled, 'Yes, she's a good girl that one. Not particularly bright, though. No matter, we've palmed her off onto that Bushey fellow. They go well together; they'll make each other happy. From all reports he'll make a fine commanding officer one day and with my backing, he might make flag rank.'

As he talked he thought about how he had not made any special effort to get away for the wedding but seeing as how there was so much to do here it was the easiest thing in the world to make everybody suppose that operational requirements were keeping him too busy. North Cedars Hall was no place for him at the moment anyway. He had spent months waiting for orders to get him out of there and away from his disrespectful wife so he was not about to rush back, not even to give his daughter away to her new husband.

As it was he suspected that the whole affair had probably proceeded a lot smoother without his input. Essentially his stance had been an act of kindness.

'Harper, are you well?' asked Diane, for she had noticed his appearance and energy slowly deteriorating of late. She was truly concerned for, although there was no love between them, she had grown to be fond of him. Furthermore, her uncertainty as to what she would do next when he finally sent her packing was changing to what she would do when he died.

'Of course,' he said. 'Do I not seem well?'

'If I might say,' she said, 'you are not as spritely as your usual self.'

He gave a short laugh. 'Diane, when you get to my age things will be bad enough for you. If you get to my age and have to live through the hell of the last two patrols that I have just done, then you, too, will not be your usual spritely self. Don't you worry, I have plenty left to give and more to do before I'm done.'

'I'll start preparing some food in a moment,' she said. 'What are your plans for our time?'

He looked straight at her when he said, 'We shall not be making love tonight. We shall eat and then I shall go.'

She nodded and accepted it without comment. It was her job to be compliant, not inquisitive, so she did not speak of her concern. This was that it was strange he would not be touching her because she knew there was something about her that made him mad with desire. But he was evidently going to be tight-lipped about it. When the moment was right she took her leave from him and started work in the kitchen.

Clark stared after her as she went. How perfect she would be as a wife, he thought. The problem was that he knew full well that any such bond would put her upon a pedestal and give her thoughts of grandeur that would destroy everything of this homely image in a second. No, it was not really her that he considered would make a perfect wife, it was the concept of her. It was the concept only that he was paying for.

Cherishing the warmth reaching him from the flames, he picked up his document case and pulled out the letters which he had picked up at the base. What was this? Here was something out of the ordinary. There was an envelope bearing his name in Dorothy's handwriting. Just imagine thinking of his concept of a good wife then immediately receiving a communication from the one who had ruined everything. She hardly ever wrote to him.

He opened the letter and read the words with interest:

Dear Harper,

I don't know where this letter will find you but I hope it finds you soon. I know that the very idea of me writing to you has either intrigued you or set alarm bells going but, quite frankly, there is a matter of importance that I must bring to your attention.

'Just get on with it, woman,' he muttered and read on, digesting the sordid little story about David and his girl with incredulity. He went through the thing twice to make sure he was happy with the facts and finally gave a chuckle. What a state of affairs. For once he managed to look upon his wife with something approaching admiration. There was hope for the woman yet.

*

Finally everything was in order to get back to sea. Commander Crawshaw had been working very hard making sure that all was just so. During this last short time of maintenance and exercises in and around the Forth he had got away into town as much as possible. This meant evening runs ashore as much as routine would allow. His reputation being what it was, the word that had gone around the ship was that he had performed another conquest with the fairer sex and all who said so were inevitably correct. The only person who seemed to be none the wiser was the captain.

For Crawshaw, things were not quite the same as they had been when he was younger. He was in his fifties now and it was not as important as it once was to take a woman straight to bed. Not only was he slowing down physically but his tastes were maturing as he matured, which he considered to be a good thing, because then he could not be vilified for attempting to chase girls who were thirty years his junior. By latching onto women in their forties he concluded that there was an air of respectability about his games. Plus, if they were or had been married, they understood things that the younger ones did not.

Anne was a beautiful Scottish lass who had become estranged from her violent husband a decade ago and had dedicated herself to looking after her two single brothers ever since. She may very well have stayed that way for the rest of her life had Crawshaw not noticed her and made her succumb to his considerable charms. This had been aided by him feigning a penchant for Dickens novels having discovered her interest in the subject. What he actually knew or cared of Dickens had only come about by way of Digby's odd appreciation.

The relationship with Anne started in the usual cynical fashion and it would eventually end in the same way, but for now he had impressed her and was going back to sea with the affair open-ended. Her phone number was carefully tucked away in his wallet.

After reporting that the men were all present and accounted for and that the ship was ready to weigh and proceed, Dollimore caught him off guard by saying, 'Very good. By the way, the lady has feelings so you had better conduct yourself better this time.' Did that man know everything?

*

With *Burscombe* at the head of the line, the 25th Cruiser Squadron steamed past the open boom of the Firth of Forth and out towards the North Sea. Some of the Fo'c'sle Part of Ship men were gathered to stream the paravanes. OS Gordy, still unnaturally tired, was at least satisfied that he was becoming handy with the sledge hammer as he put the pins into the blake slips that would hold the great anchors in place while the chains and capstan were used for the paravanes.

The odd little torpedo-shaped floats, with fins designed to keep them streamed out on their cables at either side of the bows, were lowered into the water and the men waited to see if any contact mines would be snagged by them.

Today they were lucky. None were found.

But with the tension only just subsiding over that procedure completed, Chief Yeoman Ross informed the captain that the flagship had signalled that she would be taking over the lead position of the column and that speed would then be increased to thirty knots on the course that she dictated. This just went to show how quickly the immediate future could be turned about in wartime. Moments later a typewritten message came to the bridge indicating what the emergency was. The German battlecruiser *Gneisenau* was at sea.

As the ships sped out to an ever worsening gale, Dollimore felt memories stirring of that day back in 1916 when the *Warspite* had left this same anchorage heading unknowingly towards death or glory. Here they were, twenty three years later, and the same two nations were at it again.

It was understood that just the *Gneisenau* and a few attendant destroyers were at large so the British were going to hit them with everything they had spare. These three cruisers were coming out of the Forth and, up at Scapa, Admiral Forbes was venturing out with the battleships *Nelson* and *Rodney*, a couple of battlecruisers and a whole host of cruisers and destroyers. Furthermore, ships of the Humber Force were heading out from further south. Excitement was high. With a sudden pang of well concealed guilt, Dollimore realised that it was all too likely that every generation might just need its own war to understand what it was all about.

As the ship pushed through the waves at speed, the spray once again drenching her fo'c'sle and forward turrets, he was forced to consider another point of irritation, that of Burscombe's aerial reconnaissance capabilities. Hanwell may have got his much sought after Walrus and may have managed one test launch off the catapult before putting to sea but now being the time it mattered the most, the hideous weather made it too dangerous to launch. The helpless thing presently had its wings folded back and had been stored in the starboard hangar. Even if they did manage a launch they would never be able to retrieve it because it would simply crash into the confused swell of the sea.

Dollimore glanced around at the windswept lookouts on the bridge and up at AB Smith, his eagle-eyed man up in the foremast, and cursed the weather. That Walrus could have increased their relative visibility by over two hundred miles. All was not lost on that front, however, since a squadron of bombers had been sent up from shore – an infinitely safer option than a shipborne launch – to locate and attack the *Gneisenau* force.

*

The operation dragged into its second day. Nothing was seen or heard of the enemy and Rear-Admiral Blagrove's flagship, *Royal Oak* , was ordered out from Scapa Flow to join in the hunt. With two destroyers escorting her she took up a patrol position to the west, closer to home than the main bulk of the fleet. It was the best place for her since the old girl, with her maximum speed of 21 knots, would not be able to keep up with the newer ships anyway, and if the *Gneisenau* did get past the searching force then perhaps the two of them would meet and do battle.

The men were all eager for that eventuality to come to pass. However, if it was not for this infernal weather then the operation would not so fast be becoming synonymous with disappointment and misery.

Lieutenant Bushey made his way aft to inspect the portside 6-inch guns which were part of the ship's secondary armament. Reports had come up to the bridge that, through water having penetrated the mountings and the general deteriorating condition of the bulkheads, the guns were out of action. The deck was swaying violently under his feet as he made his way uncomfortably along the internal passageway. Above the crashing of the waves outside he could hear the groaning of the Oak's hull. Such was the screeching of metal in places that it sounded almost as if she was tearing herself apart. Near the guns he found some men sloshing around in a few inches of water, battling with some trunking that was threatening to collapse from the deckhead. What a mess.

'What do you think, chief?' he asked the young ordnance artificer, who was busily inspecting the outlets for the shell hoists.

The grim faced man shook his head. With his voice raised above the surrounding din, he answered, 'Aside from the state of the guns, sir, I think we'll be lucky to make it back to Scapa. Even if we manage that, one hit from the *Gneisenau* and we're going straight to the bottom.'

'Nonsense,' said Bushey. 'This is the *Mighty Oak* . She'll surprise all of us yet.'

'John,' came another voice from behind him. He turned to see Philip Dollimore standing in the hatchway, keeping himself supported with one hand and clutching a clipboard in the other.

Wearing a grimace as a result of seasickness, Dollimore asked, 'What's it like in here?'

Moving out of the artificer's earshot, he replied, 'It's a bloody mess. If we meet the enemy the main guns will have to do most of the work.'

'Mm,' agreed Dollimore, shaking his head. 'I've got the marine's barracks back there shipping considerable amounts of water and the store beneath that is flooded as well. Listen to that horrendous noise. It sounds like we're breaking apart.'

'You're right,' said Bushey. 'I'm beginning to think we might founder. Just joking.' But he did look concerned.

The reports they submitted to Captain Benn did not make for inspiring reading but the ship steadfastly ploughed on nevertheless. He, along with Blagrove, was determined that she should not fade away into an obscure end, obsolete and worth nothing but scrap.

Time was slowly dragged away from them and, after putting up with their uncertainties for the whole of the next night and achieving nothing but sustaining more damage and losing her destroyer escort in the storm, *Royal Oak* was ordered back into the safety of the Flow. Bushey and Dollimore felt the disappointment of their poor performance keenly and vowed that the next time out they would do much better.

*

In the meantime, the 25th Cruiser Squadron continued searching a few miles away from the rest of the battle fleet. Rear-Admiral Clark kept his ships at visibility distance in an effort to see as far as possible while keeping help close at hand. If a ship as powerful as the *Gneisenau* caught one of them out alone it would be an unforgivable, suicidal waste. The doubled watches of lookouts scanned every inch of horizon in silent hope, each man wanting to be the first to spot a smudge of funnel smoke against the constantly changing horizon of blue to grey and back again. But it was from the sky that the first threat came. One of Burscombe's lookouts reported a formation of aircraft appearing from bearing green zero two five. Alarm bells rang and flag signals were hoisted to the other two ships but they had already caught on.

It did not take much time to get the men fully closed up. By that point the formation of bombers was almost upon them. But there was still a strange pause. Could they be another patrol of friendly shore-based bombers sent out to look for the enemy?

'Definitely Heinkels and Junkers 88s,' announced Lt-Cdr Peterson calmly. His voice was a little higher than normal but he was satisfied that he had controlled himself well. Not bad for someone who had never seen anything like this for real.

'Mr Digby,' said Dollimore, as though he was running a drill, 'You may open fire when ready.'

'Aye, aye, sir,' Digby replied and the order was relayed forthwith.

Amidships, at the starboardside battery of 2-pounder pom-poms, young Clark and his team of gunners had been stood or sat at Defence Stations wearing life-jackets, white anti-flash gear and tin hats for some hours already. They had until now been damp and chilled to the bone but as soon as it was clear that they were facing enemy aircraft, all thoughts of the cold were quite suddenly banished. Some of them had even started perspiring. 'Fire as soon as you have the range!' ordered Clark.

Pincher, Les and the rest of the team only had to wait a couple more seconds and then they set their anti-aircraft guns firing a steady stream of shells up into the sky. The sudden noise was deafening for it was not just their battery going off but the whole line of 4-inch and Oerlikon guns were also spitting their fire. These were joined by the rattling of many smaller machine guns. The bright white tracers went off into the overcast sky and black bursts of smoke and shrapnel appeared all around the bombers, quickly to dissipate and be carried away by the wind.

Looking at the ten or so aircraft through the binoculars, it seemed to Clark that the thunderous mass of explosions sent up by the guns were going off all around them. But they continued on their course without making any attempt to take evasive action. Surely they must be destroyed soon.

Then small dots started dropping from underneath them. Bombs!

Until now the unreal feel to the situation had only been half eliminated by the knowledge of who they were facing. Finally, here came the full realisation that these men up there in those machines actually wanted to kill them and the whole thing suddenly took on a desperation that had been conspicuously absent during the gunnery exercises back in Scapa.

Unbeknownst to the anti-aircraft gunners the squadron had already increased speed and now the ship heeled over sharply as they obeyed the admiral's signal to follow him to port. As the gunners of the *Burscombe* adjusted their aim it seemed as though the bombs must fall directly on them but somehow the great explosions occurred in the sea a long way off each beam. In their turn the *Farecombe* and the *Godham* received the same treatment and again, none of them were hit.

Then the enemy were casually making good their escape with a distant turn to starboard so that they could head back to base. Just like that the action was over. The guns were silently smoking and the enemy formation had disappeared, completely unbroken by the barrage sent up to deter them.

Nobody spoke. There was a collective disbelief that such ordnance had been disposed of in both directions and neither force had suffered so much as a scratch. Was this war? There had to be more to it than that. Only Dollimore and those few who had fought in the last war realised how minor and insignificant this little engagement had been. But that did not matter right now. The *Burscombe* had had its first taste of action and now nobody could deny the fear that that engendered. To those around him on the bridge, he simply said, 'If we find the *Gneisenau*, her aim won't be nearly so blind.'

The squadron continued to steam very slowly in an easterly direction all night, making periodic changes to the course in order to baffle any enterprising U-boat commanders that might spot them. Finally, on the following day a signal came from Admiral Forbes for all the searching parties to start heading for home. It was incredible. None of the extensive British forces had happened upon a single clue as to the whereabouts of the German ships. More wasted time.

*

In the preceding hour, a bitter and disappointed Admiral Forbes had stepped into his sea cabin aboard HMS *Nelson*, stripping off his oilskin coat and hat. Salty water streamed from the garments as he hung them up, then he wiped his hands dry on the towel which swayed back and forth on its peg.

The steward that he had just called for appeared at the door and the admiral immediately said, 'Get me some tea.'

'Aye aye, sir,' replied the steward and disappeared toward the pantry forthwith.

A steaming hot cup of sweet tea would certainly help him get over the annoyances of the moment. There was a lot to digest and still more to consider. He was not best pleased that they had pushed their way through this severe gale for two whole days and received no hint as to the whereabouts of the *Gneisenau*. That she had been at sea was a given for she had been spotted leaving harbour. He did not believe that she had sneaked past the blockade into the Atlantic; more likely that she had simply sneaked back home after stirring up everybody's expectations. Still there was a doubt. It was not commonly known that more than a few British ships had also just been committed to hunting another large German raider that was happily causing significant problems in the South Atlantic. Whatever that ship was must have slipped through the Home Fleet blockade and Forbes was not best pleased about that either.

The tea was placed before him as he studied the documents and signals related to this *Gneisenau* foray. He sipped it gratefully, savouring the warmth and sweetness. Drawing no further conclusions, his mind turned towards something else that had been bothering him. It was about Scapa Flow. His own personal instincts had been telling him that the defences around the anchorage were still not adequate, that the whole subject had been treated in a rather blasé manner by the authorities concerned. He was uncomfortably aware that the defence procedures around the Flow had not been shaken up enough and that the extra blockships which were to be sunk in the approaches had still not arrived.

Furthermore, he could not help but remember the unsolicited interest taken in the subject by that irritatingly precise fellow, Charles Dollimore, a few weeks ago. Although it had been none of his business, the man had made perfect sense and his voice would not evaporate from his conscience.

He mulled over the dispositions of his ships. The Humber Force and the 25th were obviously nowhere near the Flow so they did not matter, but what of the rest of the fleet? On a hunch stirred by his doubts he ordered the force in company with *Nelson* to head for Loch Ewe, a safer anchorage on the other side of Scotland and a few more hours steaming from Scapa. But he generated no such orders for any other ships operating independently, ships such as HMS *Royal Oak*.

Chapter Eleven

The Sinking of the Royal Oak

It was a strange shudder accompanied by what sounded like a distant clap of thunder drifting away on the wind which made Lieutenant Philip Dollimore wake with a start. There was a faint rattling of vibrating glass and a minor pause in the hum of the generators. Then everything returned to normal, as though nothing had happened. He decided that he must have been dreaming and as soon as he realised that he was tucked up comfortably in his warm bunk aboard the slumbering *Oak*, rocking gently at anchor, he began to drift back off into his much needed sleep. As his mind started to wander back into the land of the subconscious, creating a strong sense that he was taking a relaxing drink of brandy in the wardroom, there suddenly came a knock at the door.

'Yes?' he called softly.

His door slid open to reveal the silhouette of John Bushey standing against the dim electric light. He had a slovenly appearance, the collar of his blue and white striped pyjamas hanging undone, his blond hair askew. 'Did you feel that?'

'What?' asked Dollimore, trying to piece together the information in his fuzzy brain. The only thing he was certain of was that he had heard no alarm. That was the only thing he would have responded to without hesitation.

Bushey said, 'Sounded a bit like an explosion to me; and the lights went out for a second.'

Dollimore sat up and regarded his friend with an odd expression. 'Then why aren't we being called to Action Stations?'

'Beats me,' replied Bushey. 'One of us should go up forrard and see if anything is going on. Flip a coin.'

This was their usual way of distributing non-essential tasks and whoever lost the toss would have to bite the bullet, get dressed and shift themselves. Sighing, Dollimore sat up and reached into a drawer. He retrieved a sixpence, flipped it, and wearily announced, 'Tails.' Dollimore was tails, always was.

'Okay,' grinned Bushey. 'Do let me know when you find out what it was.'

'Righto.' Dollimore quickly put on some semblance of uniform and headed out onto the deck where he could make his way to the bow. Part way along he was joined by a couple more curious officers who had also been disturbed.

Eventually Dollimore and his companions became aware of some commotion up ahead as they passed the great gun turrets lying silently in shadow. There was quite a gathering of officers and men on the fo'c'sle which, but for the moonlight intermittently shining down, was in complete darkness.

'What's happening?' Dollimore enquired of a petty officer who was walking hastily back towards an open hatch.

The man, looking fairly bothered and perhaps a trifle worried, said, 'It seems like there's been an explosion in the paint locker, sir. Some chemical's gone up maybe. It's a bit smoky down below.'

So, something had happened internally. There was no evidence at all that an enemy may have managed to get near the anchorage to target them? That at least would explain why the crew was not being called to Action Stations.

He noticed Captain Benn walking amongst the throng of sailors looking at some damage on the deck. Somebody was telling him, 'The cable has broken, sir. The chain has run out.'

'Damage to the capstan machinery?' Benn asked.

'Checking now, sir.'

How was it possible that a minor explosion in the paint locker could have severed the anchor cable? It seemed to Dollimore that nobody had a clue what had actually happened. He looked up suspiciously at the black sky with its extensive banks of fast moving cloud which let the occasional shaft of moonlight shine through. Was there a lone airman up there somewhere who had risked everything to drop one solitary bomb on the ship and, in so doing, notched up a near miss? You had to admire the gall of the man if there was. The only thing that was certain was that, if it was an attack, it was over.

Looking more closely at the fo'c'sle itself to see what damage the captain was inspecting, he noticed that much of the deck before him was wet. That was suggestive of an explosion in the water that would have sent up a geyser to come crashing back down again. If the paint locker was the true scene of the incident then it must have been one hell of an explosion which had broken the steel cable and sent up a geyser of water at least forty feet in the air. Also there would have to be a hole in the bow, enough to put them out of commission for a while.

The whole thing was very mysterious and he knew that various rumours were going to be flying round the ship by now, so hopefully Benn would get at the truth quickly and speak to the ship's company forthwith.

Apart from this almost casual gathering here, all was still quiet. It did not seem real. Dollimore looked at his watch and guessed that a full ten minutes had passed since the incident occurred and, as there was no immediate cause for alarm, he decided to go back and tell Bushey that there was nothing to worry about.

*

Bushey had already gone back to sleep. He had had a busy few days since the *Oak* had crawled back into Scapa after her gallant attempt at supporting the battlefleet. There had been plenty of inspecting and report writing to do as that storm had caused a fair bit of minor but significant damage to her old hull and the force of the sea had also nearly wrecked some of their secondary armament. Although hopes were still high, the idea of the ship being able to give a good account of herself seemed to be creeping away.

That aside, she was still something of a power. Her 15-inch guns were always important and her anti-aircraft guns were currently providing an essential defence of the Flow, so Bushey had strenuously been helping to organise the revictualling so that she may be ready for anything. That was the reason why sleep had overshadowed a bit of excitement on deck.

He was suddenly jolted awake by a terrific thunder clap, as frightening as it was loud, and the cabin leapt a few feet in the air, bodily throwing him from the bunk. He landed with a sharp crack on his left shoulder in the corner of the compartment and let out a yelp of pain. He stood up very quickly, fighting the urge to empty his bladder here and now, and instinctively reached over for the light switch. The cabin appeared before him, if only dimly, and he saw that the drawers beneath his bunk were open and some of his possessions were scattered on the deck. His framed photograph of Patty, with her thoughtful stare, was lying amongst the mess, the glass smashed.

Rubbing his shoulder and moving his arm back and forth to gauge the damage, he put his head out the door and saw other officers, as confused and dazed as himself, emerging from their cabins. There was a scattering of voices all asking the same sort of question, 'What the hell was that?'

'Attack,' Bushey managed to say. 'Jerry must be bombing us.'

As if to emphasise the meaning of his words there was another great explosion and the lights flickered and almost extinguished themselves for good. 'That one was closer!' somebody shouted, though not necessarily panicked. Thick black smoke began drifting along the corridor from somewhere up forrard and it swirled upwards, feeling its way menacingly along the trunking and pipework.

'Damage control officers to their stations!' came another call from the further end of the corridor, given as though it was a parade ground command. 'The rest of you should think about getting under the armour!'

That was the only sensible thing to do, Bushey thought. Many times they had performed the drill of what to do in an air attack. Get down below under the armoured deck. Why had that thought not come to him in the midst of the emergency? He cursed himself for his lack of clear thinking. He and the rest of these men depended upon each other. He would have to do better so he resolved to calm himself and think all this through properly.

Before he did anything else he reached down and took the photograph out of the broken frame, folded it and slipped it into the pocket of his pyjama jacket. He did not know why but he had had a sudden feeling that if he was going to come to grief tonight, then he did not want to be parted from the memory of his beautiful Patricia.

Suddenly there was another explosion and everything shook so violently that he was knocked again to the deck. A pipe above the bunk cracked with multiple metallic chings and water began pouring out. Thank God it was a water pipe, he thought, and not a steam pipe! In a space of seconds the cabin had gone from being a cosy refuge to a completely uninhabitable wreck.

Mindful of the debris and glass strewn upon the deck, he quickly pulled on his shoes and, without lacing them up, he was suddenly running down the corridor. 'Keep going there,' a frightened midshipman was saying to the men waiting at the ladder, but the truth was that there were too many of them trying to file down below. Somehow the Germans had already scored three definite hits on the ship. They should expect more and the safety of the armour was still two decks away.

As Bushey's turn came to slide down, he fancied that the deck was beginning to slope to starboard. Indeed he ended up with his feet negotiating rungs which most certainly were not level. That set new alarm bells ringing in his head.

*

Just ten or so minutes before, that first minor explosion had disturbed a few of the sleeping sailors below decks, just as it had done the officers, but again most had remained where they were, unwilling to leave the comfort of their hammocks for something which did not constitute an alarm.

Able Seaman Bonner's old instinct of self-preservation had told him that something was afoot with that original distant thud and had been one of those to pull on some clothes and go up on deck. Having almost reached the fo'c'sle, he then decided he should not go near for the simple fact that, in the middle of the group gathered there, he had recognised his new divisional officer standing with those about the captain. This wretched Lieutenant Dollimore had only turned out to be the son of his last captain and had already given him a stern warning that those antics he had performed on the *Burscombe* would not be tolerated here. Bonner was very much on a last chance before he faced a Court Martial and a possible prison sentence.

So he decided to go back to the mess down below and, careful not to draw any attention to himself, he slipped through the hatch and down into the shadows. Whereas the decision to go on deck and investigate could later be said to have saved his life, the decision to go back almost ended it.

He was walking towards the open hatch of the mess and could see the dark, motionless forms of his new messmates slumbering in their hammocks when the almighty sound of a close, cataclysmic detonation rattled his eardrums painfully. The passageway shook and he was brought dizzily to his knees by the shock wave. To the sound of the explosion and the tearing open of thick steel armour, the whole ship seemed to lift with a tremendous force right out of the water then settle again, albeit with a painful groan.

In a frame of time spanning less than a few seconds blue-orange fire coursed violently amongst the bewildered sailors and it was only by some miracle that it did not head in Bonner's direction. As he regained his senses he stared dumbfounded at the scene before him, at the human torches trying to scramble through the inferno, no one knowing which way to go. The screaming was horrifying and barely human. Theirs must have been an unimaginable pain and, whatever it was that they felt, it was more than he was prepared to know. He leapt to his feet and started running away along the passage. More explosions knocked him down as he went, though they seemed a bit further away, and eventually he found himself in pitch darkness with the sound of death only haunting the distant background.

He breathed hard and widened his eyes to see something. Anything. All he was aware of was his rising panic fed by the thickening smoke until there were suddenly other men pushing their way past him. Out of nowhere an authoritative voice cried, 'Hold it, lads! Here!' Then a match was lit and others, realising that they too had matches, added to the thin illumination.

All around Bonner men were appearing, some in scrappy uniforms, some in their underwear. One or two of them were naked. All were struck with an intense confusion. Apart from being stuck here with them, he felt no affinity with them. They were faceless, strange men on a strange ship.

He who had lit the match, probably a CPO by the way he appeared, was trying his best to calm those around him, saying, 'They're bombing us! We've gotta stay here!'

But Bonner's mind was silently screaming at him in objection. That instruction was lunacy. Could no one feel the deck already sloping to starboard? After a pause, he said to those nearest him, 'I'm getting out. Where's the hatch?'

A bare-chested man nearby, holding a burning match up in front of his pale face, pointed along a thin passageway and said, 'Let's go that way.'

They pushed their way along. Bonner's left knee collided with an unseen hydrant and he cursed with the sweat-inducing pain. A tear came to his eye, born as much from anger as anything else, and he limped his way to a ladder up ahead.

All too quickly the deck was becoming a steep slope which he and the couple who had decided to follow him were desperately trying to ascend. He grabbed hold of the ladder and then they were in darkness again. The man who had pointed them this way coolly lit another match and looked at their means of escape. The hatch above was closed so he and Bonner hammered at the clips with the flats of their hands. It was all to no avail.

Bonner shouted, 'The list has distorted the deck already! Shit!'

His calmer companion said, 'We were only at Air Defence Stations. Other hatches were left open for communication. We just need to find one.' With that he began edging his way back down the slope.

Bonner did not want to go after him. Back to where there was obviously hundreds of tons of water pouring into the ship? Coughing on the smoke, he suddenly became very claustrophobic. How is it going to happen? Am I going to drown, burn or suffocate? Please God, put me out of my misery now! Fighting the urge to cry, he followed the other two men.

*

The full meaning of war came to Philip Dollimore in what was quite literally a flash. He had no time to think, no time to act. In a split second a great white light erupted before him, bathing him in a heat as intense as the sun. It felt like his skin was being flayed as the breath was dragged out of his lungs and his body was heaved through the air. He came to land in a heap a fair few feet away, deafened and numbed.

A great torrent of water came cascading down out of nowhere, battering him and drenching him to the skin. He worked quickly to try and gather his thoughts then began to try and pull himself up. His legs were like jelly and he had to support himself before he could take a step. When he reached out to steady himself, the steel he touched was quite hot and the water immediately began to rise from his jacket as vapour. Looking into the inexplicable, fiery maelstrom that had erupted but fifty feet away he saw a slumped body burning. The dead man's black hat complete with gold-embroidered tally was lying nearby, now also being consumed.

He staggered back the way he had come, his thinking not coherent enough to even begin wondering what had happened or what he was to do next.

Then there was another explosion further aft which was very shortly followed by a third. What the hell was going on? A man came to him, a man whose cap was missing but had the three buttons of a chief petty officer on his sleeve. The voice that reached his bursting ears was somehow unnaturally calm. 'Are you alright, sir?'

Dollimore could not answer.

'Don't worry about it, sir. I'll get you up forrard. Not so much amiss up there.'

He was led along the deck away from the fire. The kindly chief opened up a hatch and helped him into the cover of a passageway. 'Take a pew on that generator just there, sir. Catch your breath. There's some other blokes to 'elp.' With that the strong, guiding man was gone.

Dollimore's senses were slowly returning to something approaching their full soundness but he was suddenly shocked into full awareness when he felt himself sliding off the machinery. Quite a few men had run past outside the open hatch. There had been some shouting though not as much as one would expect in the middle of a disaster area. He suddenly realised that he did not want to be in this passageway any longer because sea water was beginning to lap up over the deck at the foot of the guardrail outside.

He heaved himself up and almost fell out of the hatch, such was the sloping angle of the deck. Slipping and sliding on the deck as his legs were gradually immersed in freezing water, he clung onto fittings with a view to pulling himself towards the fo'c'sle. Further aft, fire and smoke was billowing out of holes in the deck or bulkheads but that would be short-lived since the whole area was slowly sliding beneath the waves. There was much gurgling and hissing as air escaped from below and water turned to steam on the red hot steel plates.

Looking up, Dollimore saw the dark grey hulk of the superstructure bearing down upon him. There was a clear distinction between this and the black moonlit sky with its heavy scattering of clouds and shining stars. He absolutely understood that if he did not move right now then the ship was going to roll on top of him and keep him pinned there until his lungs burst in his chest and filled with water.

The only way he could go was into the sea itself. He threw himself into an unwelcoming mess of salty, black oil. *Royal* Oak's furnace fuel oil tanks had ruptured and were spewing their crude filth all around the dying hulk. He had the taste of it in his mouth. He sputtered and vomited a quantity of it back onto the churning surface as he put his strength into escaping. He started rhythmically turning his arms in the forward stroke yet somehow the job seemed harder now than it had been back in the days when his father had insisted he learn how to swim. In his desperation he did not even register that his difficulties were founded in the fact that his uniform was weighing him down.

The crashing of steel and swirling of the water was filling the night all around him so he kept going, not calming down until the oily water did so as well. The superstructure had slipped under the water and somehow it had not taken him with it. It took nearly all the strength he had left to tread water but there was nothing else he could do for he could see no wreckage, no life belt, no raft, nothing to cling onto. He turned to look back at the ship and what he saw made his heart race and his stomach squirm with horror.

The fires seemed to be extinguished now. The points of damage were deep below the water and the *Mighty Oak* was lying on her side, stricken, helpless and dying. There was much movement, of the ship herself as she continued on her inevitable course of capsizing and of men walking or running along the levelled portside hull. Dollimore was in the middle of the worst of nightmares and he felt physically sick with horror at the suddenness of the disaster and the impotence of the crew. How could this have happened?

*

Not too long after the pyjama-clad John Bushey and his fellow officers had clambered down below the main armoured deck to shelter from further 'air attack' he realised that they had all made a terrible mistake. The ship had tipped onto her starboard side in a very short space of time and now men were trying to force their way back through hatches which were turned into unfamiliar obstacles. On top of this, many hatches were now jammed shut with the buckling of the bulkheads and he had seen one instance of where a sliding hatch had slammed closed and sliced a man in half. Awful as the unfolding scene was, he was too terrified of

194

being trapped inside this steel coffin to really register what he had just seen.

There was a distant explosion somewhere inside the hull and the passageway shook again. In the illumination of a nearby fire which crackled menacingly in the torn steel, the officers looked nervously at each other. If nothing else was going to spur them into action then the water which they could hear gurgling somewhere near them certainly would.

I've got to find a way out, Bushey was telling himself, I've got to find a way out. The cross passage where he next found himself had become a long vertical shaft which he and his colleagues cautiously looked over. It was at least a fifty foot drop down which someone had already fallen, and was lying groaning in agony at the bottom.

'We've got to see if he's alright!' shouted Bushey.

The looks he got from the others were of incredulity. The man below them was already being submerged by the inrushing water and he did not seem to have the strength to raise himself up nor even keep his head out of the frothing foam.

'Alright,' Bushey said, resignedly prying his eyes away from the sight of the drowning man. 'Where to from here?'

They looked about in the near-black shadows and saw a figure appearing from the passage opposite. It was a muscular fellow with an older man's face. He was wearing the uniform of a lower rate.

'Hey, you there!' shouted Bushey over the roaring of the water and metallic howls of the ship breaking apart. 'Is there a way out?'

'How should I know?' came the desperately angry reply in strong Scottish tones. 'It's your fuckin' ship!'

Just as Bushey was about to shout back at the man's disgraceful insolence, the Scotsman suddenly looked at something above his head. It was at an open door of the sliding, light, unarmoured type. 'I can see stars!' he shouted. 'An open scuttle!'

Bushey ordered, 'Give us a hand to get across to you!'

But the man was already leaping up with his best spring and clutching at the metal door frame. Then he was gone. Bushey was going to remember that man's face, find him and bring him to justice if it was the last thing he ever did.

He informed the others that he was going to climb across the shaft to the passage opposite and then help them to follow. 'Better make it fast, Johnny boy,' a young lieutenant said, for the water was rising fast and the ship still appeared to be capsizing.

Uncomprehending of the growing pain in his shoulder, Bushey clambered across to the other side, never once thinking that he should have let one of the more able-bodied go first. Holding onto any fitting, pipe, handwheel, firehose or lamp he could find, he finally reached the other side. Then the next man started across and Bushey reached out to grab the collar of his pyjama jacket, hauling him into safety.

'Thanks,' the officer said, 'though you seem to have hurt your arm.'

For the first time Bushey actually felt bound to acknowledge this fact. But there had been and there still was no time for it.

The young man went on. 'Let me give you a step up and I'll help the other chaps here.'

Bushey stepped into the clasped fingers that were provided for him and immediately felt himself propelled up into a dark space where, by the struggling moonlight coming in through the open scuttle, he could see lots of broken boxes of cardboard and wood, and tins of food lying scattered everywhere. What a mess!

The slope of the bulkhead under his feet was pushing further and further towards a complete inversion as he slipped and tripped on the wreckage. That other man, the Scotsman, was not here. He must have already climbed through the open scuttle past the hanging window and deadlight. Climbing up the collapsed shelving unit, he glanced back to make sure that his fellow officers were following and pushed himself up out of the small, round hole into the cold night air. One last effort on his damaged shoulder and then he was sitting on the rim, on the sloping grey side of the ship.

Before he could do anything else there was another rumble from somewhere inside the ship, another catastrophic explosion killing men trapped within, and he was tumbling into the freezing water of the Flow. With a groan, the ship turned upside-down and the scuttle where his friends should have been emerging from was disappearing beneath the waves. First the suction threatened to take him, sea, oil and all into the opening, but then a blast of air pushed him away. The others had no chance, none at all, and the pain of anguish in his heart became the worst pain of all.

*

The dark-reddish bottom of the *Royal Oak*, complete with men staggering across the clinging seaweed and barnacles, did not linger on the surface of Scapa Flow for long. Such was her condition after the explosions that she was committed to foundering without any stay of execution whatsoever.

Dollimore had been treading water for over ten minutes now, this whole time drifting away from the bow of the wreck. However, such was his awe at what was transpiring that he had lost all sense of that time. He felt numb to almost everything except what was happening before him, even the cold and exhaustion. Shortly he would know all about it but, for the moment, the sight of the flat-bottomed ship slipping violently below the surface with her motionless propellers and rudder pointed skyward was tearing pieces of his soul out. He had loved the *Oak* with all her camaraderie and glorious history.

But all too soon she was gone and what replaced her was the stupendous bubbling of the water's surface and men shouting amongst the wreckage. The light was fading in and out as the fast moving clouds crossed the face of the moon and Dollimore tried looking out for the small steam drifter, *Daisy II*, that he knew had been moored along their portside earlier in the evening. But he could not see her. He turned about, surveying the dark scene. Lights from a very distant vessel played out across the water but he soon realised that he had drifted to a point where he was closer to the low cliff of the eastern section of the Orkneys' mainland.

So, bolstering his worn body for a final effort he fought off the aches, the pain of his raw skin and the growing cold to start swimming for the shore.

*

Bushey gasped over and over as he swum like a possessed madman through the thick oil slick that surrounded and clung to everything as the *Oak* began to make the final dive to her eternal grave. He had put all his strength into getting well clear of her stern as she slipped away and barely looked back to see what was happening.

Eventually he slowed down and became aware of another man panting his own heavy breaths, the effects of performing his own superhuman exertions. 'She's going!' that man gasped.

But Bushey was looking the other way, his eyes tired and fuzzy, his head light and wandering. Desperation was beginning to well up inside him. What he would give for possession of a life belt right now. But life belts had never been issued. What an oversight. He looked about to see if there was anything close by that he could cling onto but all was just blackness, except the other swimmer and...

In just the few seconds that the light conditions were correct, with the moon peeking out from the clouds and possibly a searchlight sweeping nearby, he thought... No, he knew he could see the conning tower of a submarine! It was clearly defined for that period long enough to imprint itself on his memory. There was the thin, grey tower raised up from the low silhouette of the long deck and there were the shadowy figures of men moving about at its top. He was seeing it at a fair distance but there was no mistake.

'Do you see it? Do you see that?' he shouted.

'What, sir?' returned the other man, knowing Bushey to be an officer because of his tone and the fact that he was wearing pyjamas.

'There, there!' Bushey said, splashing the oily water's surface with an outstretched arm.

'I see it!' the man gasped, almost disbelieving his own eyes. 'A submarine, sir?'

'A submarine! A bloody U-boat!'

Turning back the other way once they were satisfied that that sinister apparition had finally been swallowed by the night, they saw the drifter, *Daisy II*, moving distantly amongst wreckage and frantic swimmers, smoke pouring from her tall funnel. She was getting closer as her decks filled up with hundreds of exhausted men. They needed to get to her. They needed to live and pass on the information they had, to tell everyone that they were mistaken about the security of the anchorage. They needed to alert the other vessels at the other end of the bay that there was a German U-boat in their midst and try to avert further bloodshed.

The other man started swimming to safety and Bushey lifted his heavy arms to follow, willing almost beyond willpower to forget his burning shoulder, but he seemed to be getting nowhere. 'Keep going!' he told himself. 'Keep going!'

*

Bonner was not as fit as the younger men but surpassed many of them in determination. After he had dived into the water from the slippery keel of the ship he had swum away with every ounce of strength he could muster. The horror story behind him was already evaporating from his memory as he pushed on. He would not look back at that awful sight. He could not. He knew he would not like what he saw if he did so and was not going to do that to himself. The distance between him and the treacherously churning waters around the wreck was the only thing that mattered now.

He hated this war and had known as much the moment he had heard Chamberlain's speech on the radio. The navy had been an adventurous place until then but now everything had become too serious. Those bloody officers had been conducting their business with an exaggerated earnestness and many of the ratings had been just as bad. It was a combination of all those busy-body fools who thought they knew what they were doing that had led to him swimming around in the freezing cold water of the Flow, having barely escaped from a fiery deathtrap by the skin of his teeth.

His mind was a whirl of these recriminations as he continued along in the darkness, his hand eventually touching something solid, something fixed. It was not a piece of wreckage. It was a rock! He immediately relaxed as he slowed his brain in order that his eyes could start doing some of the work.

Gentle waves were lapping about the rocks of the shore and a short distance ahead was the looming blackness of a low cliff face. Breathing a sigh of relief he put his feet down and found that he could raise himself up and stand waist-deep in the water. Proceeding carefully amongst the hidden obstacles he waded ashore and clambered over the uneven ground to the heights before him, hardly registering the jabbing of stones beneath his numb feet. Looking closely at the almost vertical wall and feeling his way carefully, he discovered that it should be quite easy to climb.

Suddenly, a voice from behind startled him. 'Hello, there! Who is that?'

He turned and saw another man pulling himself out of the surf in a laboured fashion. Finally being at a point of safety, Bonner found that he could afford to start to rejoin the human race and so had no problem responding to the cry. 'Able Seaman Bonner!'

'Bonner!' came the voice again. 'It's me! Dollimore! Am I pleased to see you. Give us a hand, mate.'

I'm not your mate, Bonner thought, but held his tongue and retraced his steps. He picked Dollimore up out of the water and assisted him in walking up the rocky beach. 'You coulda drowned wearin' that rig,' he said.

Dollimore looked down at himself and realised he was still clad in his whole uniform but for his shoes and cap. 'It didn't even occur to me,' he gasped as he suddenly understood the weight which had kept threatening to drag him beneath the waves. Looking at the cliff which seemed impossibly high, he asked, 'What now?'

Fighting back the urge to vent his disgust, because these bloody officers were supposed to know what to do in any and every situation, Bonner gritted his teeth and said, 'We climb.'

'I hardly have any strength left.'

'Same goes for me but I'm climbin' anyway.' Already having conversed more than he was comfortable with, he raised his arms, found a toehold part way up, and started hauling himself up the cliff.

Dollimore meekly followed.

For both of them every contact with the cold rock sent more pain through their frozen hands and feet and they had to test every grip they made before moving on, as they could not be sure that their fingers and toes were actually doing what they wanted them to do. Many times they wanted to stop but they knew that that was sure death and as they proceeded, they did so with a slowness that made them feel that they had been scaling this rockface for hours. Perhaps they had. Incredible considering the thing only appeared to be between twenty to thirty feet high.

But just as they were about to reach the top, Dollimore's faint voice drifted up from near Bonner's legs. 'Bonner, I can't go on. I can't. I've nothing left... I... I...,'

Bonner, understanding the pain but not the despair, said, 'Well, the only other way is down, pal.'

'I've got nothing left...,' said Dollimore. 'Help me.' He grabbed hold of the Scotsman's trouser leg and immediately Bonner felt that he was about to be torn away from his tenuous hold on the rocks.

'Leave go!' Bonner growled in as much agony as annoyance.

'Nothing left...,'

'Leave go!'

An inner fight broke out in Bonner's conscience. This fool below him was going to drag them both to their deaths. He needed to shake him off, but when Dollimore fell his body would be smashed and that would be the end of everything – for him at least.

Bonner suddenly wondered whether he had what it took to do this. He had done a lot of doubtful things in his life. He had bullied, cajoled and insulted many people regardless of their age or sex. He had beaten up scores of people – a couple of them women – and had even put some of them in hospital. But he had never murdered anyone. Dark as his life was, he had never had the taste to murder.

But was this murder? They were in a life or death situation already, one not of his making, and the man below him was threatening to end it for both of them if he did not let go of his leg. So was it murder? Or was it simply a necessary sacrifice? He did not start this war. These smart-talking lunatics higher up the chain had done that. He was in this position because of them. He would have to let this man go or they would both be dead.

Chapter Twelve

Fighting the Good Fight

The news of the destruction of that grand old ship hit the navy hard from top to bottom, and by the following evening a statement had been issued to the whole country, thus to the whole world, that she had been sunk within a 'secure' anchorage due to U-boat action. More horrific was the death toll – over eight hundred, including Rear-Admiral Blagrove, who was last seen handing out life-buoys to men on the quarterdeck.

A couple of days later, Captain Dollimore was taking ten minutes away from business to stand and smoke a pipe near the ensignstaff at Burscombe's gently sloping stern. Work continued all around as though the collective consciousness was oblivious to the disaster, but he knew that everybody's minds were in fact full of what had happened. He wished that he could be closer to the scene and not here at Rosyth because the one vital detail that continued to elude him was that of whether his son was still alive. He had never realised it until now but one of the greatest fears he had harboured as a parent was that one of his children should die before himself.

His indignation over the whole dire situation was exacerbated by the knowledge that he had personally spoken to Admiral Forbes weeks ago about the defences of Scapa Flow. How the words of that man effectively telling him to mind his own business were now ringing in his ears. Even so it was not lost on Dollimore that Forbes had suddenly taken the fleet round to Loch Ewe on the day prior to the disaster leaving the *Royal Oak* almost alone in the eastern part of the anchorage. He had doubtless saved many a ship but had also left that helpless, vintage girl and her crew to their fate.

As his pipe began to burn out he started to walk back down the deck for there was no chance that he should skulk about here commiserating with himself forever. It was more than he would allow for any of the other men.

Then he noticed his old acquaintance, the old scarred warrant officer, Hacklett, walking almost at a march along the starboard waist inspecting the ratings' efforts at polishing the handrail and commenting dourly here and there at a slovenly piece of work. It was difficult to equate that stolid, upright, proud man with the boy who had been so grievously wounded aboard the *Warspite*, but it was him still.

Hacklett looked over and saw Dollimore. Their unspoken connection had never been abused by either of them and, until this moment, they had performed their respective tasks in the *Burscombe* with mutual professional respect. Hacklett may have been going out on a limb this time but he crossed the brass bar and approached the captain nevertheless.

'I remember the day he was born, sir,' he said comfortingly, casting away entirely the tough character with which he had been terrorising the men these last couple of months. 'We stood you a drink and you sent cake to our mess.'

'I bet the slices were so small that you only got crumbs,' replied Dollimore, in a way glad to have the distraction.

'It wasn't the cake that mattered, sir. It was the thought. I don't know your son personally, sir, but I'd wager he's a chip off the old block and a survivor to boot. He's alright. I've got a gut feeling he's alright.'

'Thank you, Mr Hacklett. I mean that. Thank you.'

'Aye, aye, sir,' nodded Hacklett and turned back to his duty, almost immediately screaming at a man, 'Who gave you permission to drop polish on the deck? This teak belongs to the king! Scrub that off right now 'fore you feel my wrath!'

Appearing from the opposite waist while this was going on was Commander Crawshaw. He had noticed the brief but familiar way that Dollimore had spoken to Hacklett and wondered what was so important about the man beyond the fact that they had once served together in the same ship. It was not as if they could have been friends in that past life because their backgrounds were too dissimilar. Crawshaw wished for a moment that he could be the one to be in the captain's confidence.

'Has there been any news yet?' he asked.

'Nothing,' replied Dollimore. 'It shouldn't be too long now, though. News is beginning to filter through. Thank you for asking.' He then made to climb down the ladder into the cabin flat below but was stopped by Crawshaw continuing.

'Forbes should have taken more notice of your warning about Scapa's defences. If it's true that a U-boat did get in there then that makes this hash all the worse. The men in charge should be ashamed of themselves.' He paused for a second, making nothing of Dollimore's unchanged expression. 'Oh well, I suppose Nelson doesn't exist in all of us. It's what we aspire to but, let's be honest, his type are few and far between.'

Dollimore smiled for the first time. 'How right you are,' he said, giving the commander a friendly slap on the shoulder.

What was the meaning of that smile? thought Crawshaw. Surely there was something of sarcasm there.

But both of their thoughts were suddenly interrupted by the sound of an explosion. They turned about and saw a great geyser of water crashing down upon the vulnerable form of the cruiser HMS *Southampton* where she sat at anchor a few hundred yards away, dwarfed by the iron arches of the Forth Bridge.

All too quickly the distant droning of aircraft engines that they now acknowledged had been creeping up on them in the seconds before the detonation was directly overhead. The two officers had originally paid the sound no mind because Royal Air Force and Fleet Air Arm squadrons had begun regular exercises and patrols in this area, so they were completely duped by this sudden raid. What was more, there was no precedent set for it. No German bomber had until this day ventured across to the British Isles so their surprise over Rosyth was complete. There had been no warning siren and anti-aircraft guns everywhere remained silent.

'Jerries!' shouted Dollimore, starting to run forward along the deck. 'Call the men to Air Defence Stations! Tell Digby to get some flak up there right now!'

The three unopposed aircraft that they could see, flying in formation thousands of feet overhead, had casually dropped their bombs amongst the ships and were now turning away as one.

Then another formation was spotted far above the estuary to the east. The attack developed quickly, more bombs being dropped. One of the smaller destroyers a bit further out beyond the bridge was under way and tried to turn but seemed to receive a direct hit. She shook violently but kept going whilst churning up a frothing wake.

'Get under cover!' yelled Hacklett at the men who were hurriedly but carefully collecting up their tins of polish and cloths. For fear of his wrath they were making sure that nothing dropped onto the wooden deck.

They quickly dived into the hatch as a bomb screamed down nearby. The sound was so shrill and awful it sounded as though it was going to be a direct hit on the quarterdeck, but there was suddenly a huge explosion in the water some eighty feet off the starboard side. The roar was almost deafening and Hacklett saw the red flash of the high explosive going off in the centre of the torrent. But he stood his ground as though daring the bomb to try and finish him off and was thoroughly drenched by the geyser as it came crashing back down.

Witnesses would come to testify that splinters of shrapnel sped past the unperturbed man but the only evidence of that were three blackened nicks in the paintwork of the hull. Once the resulting wave had subsided he turned to look at the brass handrail and sighed with the understanding that it would have to be dried and polished once more.

Soon the guns were firing and it became clear that more bombers were appearing over the Forth, but the lightning raid was already drawing to a close. These bombers, no more than a dozen in number, had no reason to stick around once they had expended their payloads, especially as the Rosyth anchorage must have been somewhere about the limit of their range out of Germany.

Crawshaw, racing up onto the aft superstructure, shouted at them, 'Hope you run out of fuel getting back, you bastards!' He was filled with disbelief that this had happened. Was nowhere safe?

'At last!' commented CPO Doyle strenuously. He had just climbed the ladder with a furious look on his face and was hastily putting on his tin-hat. With the Oerlikon gunners finally blasting away ineffectively at the escaping bombers, he pointed to a target low in the sky and announced, 'Spitfires!'

'About time,' Crawshaw agreed.

With the fleet's anti-aircraft guns gradually falling silent as the enemy flew out of range the two squadrons of friendly fighters got to work on their adversaries. Those swift machines danced merrily amongst the heavier aircraft causing the previously tight formations to break up and take an 'every man for himself' attitude. The fight was far overhead and drifting off to the east at hundreds of miles per hour as the enemy tried to make his escape.

On Burscombe's bridge, Digby had long since ordered a ceasefire and watched the tiny black dots of the aircraft getting even tinier through his binoculars. Suddenly a black smoke trail was left suspended behind one of the enemy bombers as it slowly fell from the sky, mortally wounded. He did not see what happened next as the distance had become too great, but he was certain that one of them had gone to his death. Without giving it an extra thought he knew that he had never seen a sight so gratifying.

But when they looked back over to the ships that had been hit they saw that one of them was pouring smoke from her deck. It was a destroyer, HMS *Mohawk*. Figures were racing back and forth on her upper decks engaged in damage control work. All the while the little vessel steamed ahead to the dockside.

Digby looked over as he saw Dollimore and Peterson climbing out of the hatch.

'Captain on the bridge,' said one of the sub-lieutenants, and Digby immediately said, 'By God, sir, we'd better find a way of getting back at them soon! The *Courageous*, the *Oak*, and now this!' He pointed at the damaged *Mohawk*.

Digby received a warning look from Peterson and the younger man instantly reined in his temper. Looking over at Dollimore, who clearly needed no further reminders about what had happened to the *Royal Oak*, he said, 'I beg your pardon, sir.'

'I understand your sentiments, gentlemen,' said Dollimore to all around him. 'It may seem like Jerry's closing in on us but he'll soon put a foot wrong. Mark my words.' Such was the men's confidence in him that he saw them take comfort from those words. Inside his own tortured heart they echoed hollow.

Then, with the tension of the air attack quickly subsiding and men called to Action Stations being stood down, a PO telegraphist appeared on the bridge, saluted and handed Dollimore an envelope.

The captain ripped it open and read the signal. Betraying only the slightest relief, he suddenly turned to Peterson and Digby and said, 'My son is alive.'

*

'I'm awfully sorry, old chap,' Beatty had said to his friend when the news came through that John Bushey had lost his life in the *Royal Oak* disaster.

Clark, puzzling over how so definitive and swift had been the end of so promising and enthusiastic an officer, had replied in all sincerity, 'Thanks, Beatty, but it's my sister I'm worried about. There's not much she appreciates in this life but John was everything to her. My God, but they were married barely three and a half weeks ago.' He had heard how his brother-in-law's body had been retrieved from the water some hours after the event, stiff with rigour mortis and the effects of exposure. He had literally frozen to death, a crumpled photograph of his wife clasped firmly in his hand.

This disaster must transcend all the mindless animosity of the past so Clark settled to write a heartfelt letter to Patricia offering his condolences. He found that reaching out for peace and understanding based on a mutual loss helped him to confront his own sense of grief and he hoped that they would find it easier to work through this as a family instead of as individuals engaged in a useless conflict.

A couple of weeks passed and then came a reply. Clark recognised his sister's handwriting on the envelope and opened it with high expectations. Astonishingly, there was no heading addressing him by name, just an angry scrawl which ranted on like this:

Words of comfort are nothing of the sort when they come from the likes of you. John was a man the like of which you never will be. He was an honourable man who knew his duty and this he put before every selfish whim. You are exactly the opposite and to read your words of condolence reaffirms just how fake and superficial you are.

Good God! What bile was this? He always knew that they did not see eye to eye but surely the bond of siblings, no matter how frayed, should suppress this sort of feeling. He read on in horror:

Every time I listen to you talking about what you want, every time I hear that you have acted in a way to bring shame to the Clark family name I care less and less for you. You have a real talent for causing your

*brothers concern, mother heartache and father outright embarrassment,
but then I should not be surprised given I know the truth about you.*

*I was eight years old when I learned what you are. Mother and
father's arguing has often disturbed us but the theme of this one I have
kept to myself until now. Do you want to know why we live in such an
angry house? You do not have the right to bear the name of Clark at all.
You are the product of mother's disgusting meetings with another man.*

*So you can see how you are so different from us. Your impertinence
comes from mother's underhandedness and your father's dishonest
characters.*

*Don't ever offer me words of comfort again. They are as hollow and
as fraudulent as your identity.*

She had not even signed the letter. She had evidently sat and scribbled
out this entire message and sent it in a fit of anger and grief, not even
paying attention to the formalities.

He felt sick and confused. In a space of seconds he and his mother had
been unforgivably attacked and their very lives and characters called into
question. He realised in that moment that there would never be an accord
between Patricia and he. This ended everything.

He needed to speak to father right now. But, damn it all, the *Godham*
was not in port.

*

The *Burscombe* went out on her next patrol alone. The *Godham* and
the *Farecombe* had been required to plug holes in the blockade up near
the Shetland Islands for a week or so. What this meant to Clark was that
he was not in a position to do anything about this awful business that had
been hoisted upon him.

It seemed ironic that he had spent the last few months trying to stay
out of the Old Man's way, but now he needed to confront him and no
opportunity was at hand. As a result he found himself withdrawing from
the social circle of midshipmen and subs while at sea. It was painful
because Beatty was his best friend and he wished that he could tell him
all about what was happening. But, aside from worrying about Beatty's
previous lack of understanding, how could he repeat to anybody such
libel as this until some satisfactory answers had been found?

His insular mood had started to become a noticeable problem on the morning that he found he just could not digest anything that CPO Stoker Vincent was trying to explain to him about the diesel generators down on 4 Deck.

'Suck, squeeze, bang, blow,' the earnest chief had been busy explaining but he had long since begun to wonder why he was bothering. There was no way he could make the understanding of the scientific processes of a working engine easier but his words seemed to be having little impact. His first reaction was to scream at the young gentleman but he bit his lip and managed a simple, 'Something on your mind, sir?'

'I beg your pardon?' asked Clark, suddenly realising that he had been asked a question.

'It's just that I've been talking to you for over ten minutes now and, well, frankly you're not listening, sir.'

'You must forgive me. Please continue.'

Vincent carried on with the principles of induction, compression, explosion, exhaust and much more besides as the two of them clambered first through the generator and switchboard rooms then the machinery of the aft boiler room and that of the corresponding engine room.

Clark was doing everything in his power to grasp the intricacies of the subject, but when he was faced with the need for observing the procedures for ensuring that the oil fuel had the required viscosity, and then minding that the boiler airflow was correct and what he could do to increase or decrease this or that he felt as though he wanted to strangle the chief. Once they had finished, Vincent was as relieved as Clark that it was over.

However, Commander Bretonworth had been less than impressed with Clark's attitude when they had been stripping and cleaning one of the oil heater valves yesterday, so he discreetly observed the pair on their rounds and patiently awaited Vincent's report. He knew it would be in the negative before the chief opened his mouth but he listened anyway and then took Clark away from the log book where he had been set recording pressures and temperatures of certain lubricating oils.

Three decks above in Bretonworth's cabin, which also doubled as his office, he sat on the edge of the desk while he had the midshipman standing before him. Until now he had considered Clark to be a lad of promise so that was why he was taking the stance that he was. 'As I've had no complaints about you from anywhere else,' he said in his respectable Scottish tones, 'I must assume that I am the first to pull you up. What's the problem?'

Allowing his legs a certain amount of elasticity to counter the swaying motion of the deck beneath his feet, Clark uttered the usual dumb answer of, 'No problem, sir.'

'Don't give me that.' Bretonworth had always come across as a humourless, unimaginative man and this interview started with him giving the same impression. He was a man who was known to be decisive in all solutions to all problems so long as he stuck to engineering. Now here was the first time that Clark had seen something different. 'I'm speaking to you first, man to man, in the hope that whatever's bothering you can be solved without me having to make a fuss. Do you understand?'

Clark looked down ashamedly for a second then looked the commander in the eye once more. 'No fuss needs to be made, sir. I'll pull myself together and I guarantee nobody will have to speak to me again.'

Bretonworth sucked on a tooth, nodded and sighed. 'If only it was that simple, boy. In my experience every man carrying baggage would guarantee 'til the cows come home that he'll knuckle down and do better, but at the end of the day he's still carrying that baggage. I don't give a monkey's if you can't talk to me but do talk to someone.'

'I'm sure I shall be alright, sir,' said Clark, working hard to suppress his agitation. It would be a wonderful world if he thought he could talk to someone on board about his particular problem.

Crossing his arms, Bretonworth continued, 'I hope you don't think that you're the only person that's ever had a problem. Believe me, I can actually remember what it was like to be a teenager. I had ideas about where my life should lead and this wasn't exactly it. I sometimes fought the system. I once got a bit silly over a girl...,'

Clark's stare locked onto Bretonworth's for a split second. He wasn't about to tell him his life story, was he?

'I got myself into a rare flap over someone who didn't even want me.' The commander paused while trying to discern any anguish on the other's face.

Clark thought that he was fishing for information and that he suspected there was a woman involved. Had this little talk taken place just before his sister's wedding he would have been bang on the money but, of course, things had moved on since then.

'The point is,' continued Bretonworth, 'there were one or two officers whose heads weren't buried too far up their own backsides that I could talk to and they taught me that they were family of a sorts, too. The navy looks after its own. No problem's too big that it can't be solved. Then you can settle down and serve, if not the country, then us, and yourself.'

'I appreciate what you say, sir,' said Clark. 'Again, I guarantee that I shall pull myself together and do what I need to do.'

'Okay,' Bretonworth conceded, though he was not altogether convinced about the young man's sincerity. 'What did you learn about the machines these last couple of days?'

'Not a great deal, sir.'

'What type of boilers are we carrying?'

Screwing up his face in concentration, Clark said, 'Admiralty 3-Drum Boilers with super heaters.'

'Which water tubes are relevant to the super heaters?'

'Erm, vertical large-bore…,'

'Wrong. Remember, you may find yourself in command of a tub like this one day and the more you understand about what makes her work the better you'll be able to make her fight. Now get yourself back below, find Chief Petty Officer Vincent and let him know that you are taking him seriously. I'll not have you bugger him about.'

'Yes, sir.' Clark came to attention, saluted, then left the cabin.

*

Another laborious six days passed before *Burscombe* finally streamed her paravanes and came cruising slowly into the Rosyth anchorage. Clark was on the bridge scanning the many and varied ships anchored here when Dollimore gave the word: 'Finished with main engines.'

There was the *Godham* about a mile away, close to the actual dock itself. Clark raised his binoculars and double checked what he was seeing because that ship did bear an uncanny resemblance to the County class of heavy cruisers. Yes, it was definitely the *Godham*. This would be the day when he would be able to put the matter to rest, or at the very least start the chain of events that should give him disclosure concerning Patty's absurd and disgusting accusations.

He soon managed to ascertain that his father was not presently aboard his flagship. Disappointed, he got permission to go ashore and track him down at the base, HMS *Cochrane*, starting to wonder at how his father was becoming so difficult to find. Eventually, one of the flag-lieutenants insisted there was no mystery, that the admiral frequently went ashore for a few hours but was always back with the ship by 2200. He then provided a telephone number which was the admiral's means to be contacted in the event of an emergency and even gave him the name of one of the drivers who more than likely knew where he was.

So it was that after questioning Ordinary Seaman Symmonds, who had had something of a troubled look on his face and gave his information in a hesitant fashion, young Clark set out to find the little cottage on that quiet back road which led out northwards from Rosyth.

He tentatively walked up the gravel drive which was still wet from the recent rainfall. With the overcast sky holding the countryside down under a blanket of gloom, he somehow felt colder the closer he got to his destination. He would have done anything not to have needed to be here except that this was a matter that had festered and affected his work for a whole week or more. It had to be confronted now. After a pause he rang the doorbell.

A woman opened the door. He was immediately struck by her elegance. Boasting smooth skin and alluring eyes, her blonde hair was tied up in an impeccable bunch and her rich, burgundy satin dress sat about her in loose folds all the way down to her ankles, that it should only give a hint of her desirable figure. At seeing him she betrayed a very quick look of alarm before she composed herself.

Removing his cap, he said, 'I've been given to understand that I would be able to find my father here.'

'Your father?' she asked defensively.

Suddenly, there came a voice from the living room. It was unmistakably that of the Old Man's. 'Don't worry, Diane. Let him in. It only stood to reason that somebody should catch up with me eventually.' He even chuckled.

Diane stepped aside and David entered the cottage. It was a lovely place, clean and inviting. A warmth grew in the air as he approached the living room door. After the low temperatures he had been experiencing at sea and the autumnal dampness outside right now, the air actually became stifling as he walked into the room. He quickly shed his coat and scarf while regarding the figure of his father sitting in an armchair in front of a roaring fire, wearing a thick sweater but still looking chilled and pale, black rings around his eyes and with a strange blue tinge to his lips. All that aside, his eyes were as sharp as ever, as was his tongue.

'So, you've been doing some snooping about,' said Harper. 'I suppose it was only a matter of time before you started looking into my affairs. You have a natural leaning towards trouble which you can't control. I don't know, perhaps it's a family trait. Well, you've discovered my little secret. What's your intention?'

'She's your mistress!' David suddenly stated, looking angrily over at Diane, who lowered her eyes.

'Ah,' Harper said, in turn showing surprise. 'That's why I thought you were here. You don't want to expose me? Demand terms and conditions? Insist I stop?'

This was worse than David could ever have thought. If this was possible then why not what Patty thought she knew? No, Mother was not capable of anything this low. He found himself saying, 'Quite frankly, I don't give a damn about this. I'm not going to bother mother with petty things that she probably already knows about and cares about even less.'

Harper snorted with disgust. 'Don't ever presume that you know *anything* about your mother and I. But you obviously went to some trouble to discover my whereabouts so what do you want?'

'Firstly to talk to you in private.'

Harper immediately nodded and looked at his lady. Pointing towards the door, he said, 'If you please.'

She left the room without a change in her expression, accepting the curt instruction and obeying without thought or comment. That was strange but, after a moment's reflection, it made sense to David. This was probably father's dream woman, someone who would say, 'Yes sir, no sir,' without hesitation, someone who would never encroach upon his authority or think to take control. This was someone who was not his mother, with his mother's free spirit. But who would subordinate themselves to a man in such a fashion? A prostitute?

'Well?' said Harper.

Still standing so that he retained the dominance of height, David reached into his pocket and pulled out Patty's letter. He handed it over. 'Read this.'

Harper ran his eyes down the hate-filled words and frowned. This would certainly explain why she was so dispassionate to her brother, something that even he had wondered about across the years. 'Oh, my darling daughter,' he sighed. 'She's a good girl but so misguided. She's obviously so distraught over John she's decided to turn your life upside down, too. She has a lot to learn about family politics. I suppose that I ought to teach her one or two short, sharp lessons.' He leaned forward, took up the poker and turned a collapsing log in the fire. Then looking at David's troubled face, he said, 'What do you believe?'

Almost thrown by the fact that the Old Man was speaking to him in a calm, civilised fashion, David said, 'I believe she's mistaken. Mother would never have had an affair.'

'But I would, as you can see...,' Harper motioned to their surroundings, the very place where he had been caught in the act. 'Sit down and I'll tell you a thing or two. I'd be the first to admit that you've earned very little in your life, but you've earned this.'

David now sat down on the sofa opposite. A sweat was breaking out on his brow. He knew it was as much from apprehension as from the heat of the fire. 'The truth,' he demanded.

'The truth,' Harper agreed. 'However the breakdown began to happen between me and your mother is irrelevant. We were happy when your brothers and sister were born, but by the end of the last war we had both changed. I was not yet at the point where just hearing her voice could raise my blood pressure but things were not right and I'm sure she felt the same.

'At the beginning of 1920 I had a time when I was without an appointment so I worked on the estate for a couple of months. Of course it transpired that she'd been having an affair. Had been I suppose since the year before. The man concerned was a friend of mine.' He gritted his teeth and demonstrated an unprecedented level of hurt. 'We had served together in the Indian Ocean during the last year of the war and afterwards I had invited him into my home as a guest on more than one occasion. Believe me, boy, when you've been betrayed like that there can be no thought of trust ever again.'

214

'What happened?' asked David, shocked and desperately willing himself not to be drawn in by the Old Man's apparent emotion. He must remain objective.

'Who knows how these things get started?' Harper continued. 'But they were sneaking around behind my back, that's for sure. Late one night I'd fallen asleep in the library after the three of us had been dining together and an hour or so later I awoke to hear them laughing and...Well, I went next door and they tried to separate themselves from each other but I'd seen enough. I grabbed him by the collar and threw him down the front steps. I sent him off into the night, him protesting his innocence all the way up the drive. Bastard. And she? All I got were floods of tears and more protestations of innocence. Did she think I was born yesterday?'

David listened aghast, wondering at the conviction in the Old Man's tone. This sordid little history also seemed to correspond too uncomfortably with Patty's accusations. Was she right? 'Was that man my father?' he asked.

'No. I am,' Harper said without a pause. 'There's no doubt upon that point. But she would have preferred you to have been his. She said so at the time and, let's face it, whatever your lineage you're nothing but a constant reminder of all that happened.'

Mortified, David barely managed to say, 'So I'm guilty just because I happened to be born at the wrong moment?'

'That much is clear,' said Harper, staring hard at his son as though he really was the cause of all the problems. 'However, I've not forsaken you. I've given you the chance, the same as your brothers, to make a name for yourself, so the rest is up to you. If you can't live up to the family name then you will always just be that last unwanted offspring from a dying marriage.'

David clenched his fists. Being born and bred for a future in which he had little or no interest was what his father termed not being forsaken? He was now literally shaking with the rage at the idea that his life had been worth nothing to his family even before it had begun. Perhaps it may have been better if Patty's deductions had been more correct. He fought back his desire to hurt this unflinching man who was barely a human being, stood up and made to leave but before he got to the door, he turned back to his father and said, 'How do I know that everything you've said is the truth? You would do anything to put mother in her place.'

Harper stood up and walked over to the desk that sat by the window at the back of the room. 'Still believe in your mother more than me, do you?' He opened a drawer and pulled out an envelope. Handing it to David, he said, 'Perhaps this will help you to understand what she is capable of.'

David tentatively opened it and looked at the words, hardly wanting to know what their content was.

Dear Harper,

I don't know where this letter will find you but I hope it finds you soon. I know that the very idea of me writing to you has either filled you with intrigue or set alarm bells going but there is a matter of importance that I must bring to your attention.

When David was home on leave for Patricia's wedding I happened upon the startling revelation that he is in love with and wishes to marry the daughter of old Bob Gufford from the inn in the village. I have managed to ascertain that he had met her three years ago and they have held a secret relationship since that time.

To make matters that much worse, by the time I knew what was happening, he had already taken it upon himself to see Mr Gufford and ask him for his daughter's hand in marriage. I know that you are imagining what sort of reaction the man would have had to that and what you are thinking would be right. Gufford's objections were evident upon the face of the silly girl involved.

I do wish that this was a situation that I could have seen coming but how could anyone have predicted this? Anyway, I have sent David back off to the Burscombe with the promise that I will sort everything out in as positive a way as possible. I had to appear as though I was on his side. The repercussions of the opposite stance might have had considerable consequences. You know we could not have David doing something rash like neglecting his duty in time of war, and I'm sure he is airheaded enough to do that.

I have been to see Mr Gufford and we have agreed upon a course of action. Gufford by now will have sent his daughter off to live with a relative at a location which will be mercifully undisclosed to us and we

*will all maintain to David that she ran away of her own accord. You can
also be sure that it has cost me another small fortune to smooth this
matter over.*

*I hope this letter reaches you before you next see David so that you
can play your part. I know that, for once, you and I will see eye to eye on
the matter, that I have acted for the best,*

Dorothy

'Acted for the best?' gasped David, feeling faint from an anger which
was laced with the effects of betrayal. 'Is nothing sacred to any of you?'

'This is the Clark family. This is who and what we are. You are not so
different,' said Harper. 'Examine your own life for a second. You bring
trouble and consternation to all around you because you have impulses
which you can hardly control. You've been a thorn in the side of your
college masters and your commanding officers since the beginning and
all because you think you know best. To that point we are all one and the
same. You just need one or two lessons in discretion.'

'*I* need lessons in discretion?' asked David incredulously.

'You think to bring a ragged working class wench into the family?'
continued Harper, not to be put off, and his old temper beginning to get
the better of him. 'This oversteps the mark, boy. How did you think you
were actually going to achieve that over the will of the rest of the family?
I'm not sorry that your dreams of harmony and bliss have been shattered.
Welcome to our world. It's about time you woke up and started playing
the game. Just you remember that we Clarks have provided the country
with...,'

But David cut in, '...Successful captains and flag officers for over two
hundred years. How could I forget?'

Harper looked solidly fanatical when he said, 'Because that one thing
overrides all other considerations. Forget the girl and do your duty. You
realise we have been given the gift of war? And not some side show? A
real war? This is the time for us to shine. Do well and make the family
proud of you.'

'You are no longer my family,' said David in haste and with
undoubted conviction. But then he was suddenly very calm and fully
aware that he was finished doing battle with his father. He had always

thought that he was fighting this one man but now it was clear that he should have been spending his life fighting the lot of them. But could he ever have won against these odds?

'One last thing,' said David, his tone flat with hatred. 'What happened between you and the Guffords? What was so terrible that things should be positively feudal?'

Harper, giving his son a final look of malicious amusement, replied, 'If you've not found that out by now, you probably never will.'

Knowing that he would not get his answer here, David gave a token, 'You're a disgrace.'

'Do you want to test the credibility of that statement in public?' asked Harper, chuckling.

He was right, David knew. Reputations counted for a lot in this business.

He made his way slowly back to the *Burscombe*, back to the people for whom he was discovering he truly held respect for. Bretonworth had been right about that. From that moment he was undeniably committed to that ship's company and the leadership of Captain Dollimore. That would be the only way of staving off his mounting loneliness.

Maggie Gufford was the one person in the world that he really wanted to talk to right now, but he had absolutely no idea how he was going to find her. Was she gone forever?

*

Douglas Bonner was given fourteen days leave. He should have been overjoyed but he found himself to be agonising over what to do with the time. Given long leaves in the past, he had gone into Glasgow, Edinburgh, Portsmouth or Plymouth, always depending on where his ship was docked at the time. Once, just to change things up a bit, he had gone into London. That had been an experience into debauchery he would never forget.

This time, however, he wanted to go home. He had just survived a terrible disaster and it had made him think all about the sins of his life. Bad character as he was, he had always been religious to a fashion. He had never stopped believing in the existence of God even though he had scorned the idea of going to church for many years and had found the navy's Church Parades something of an inconvenience. Now he just could not shake the realisation that He had intervened on the night the

Royal Oak was sunk, not in guiding him out of the wreck, but in making him incapable of killing that officer when it had seemed the only logical thing to do in order to save himself.

Clinging onto the rocks that night he had very nearly let Lieutenant Dollimore plunge back down onto the stony shoreline. But in the last second an inspirational warmth had suddenly coursed up through his body putting the strength in his muscles to haul the officer up the last few feet of the forbidding cliff face and into the arms of a squad of men patrolling the summit, looking for survivors. That otherwise inexplicable strength and inspiration had been so profound that it could only have come from God. That was why he and the other man were alive and why he was a free man with a clear conscience.

He knew hardly anything about his parents and they hardly knew anything about him. His childhood had been tough and strange to say the least. He had never been loved. So it was that he had run away from home at the age of twelve and had made his own way ever since, at first living rough then providing muscle for a gang, finally joining the navy as a means of escape after he had fallen foul of his dubious companions. He had been there ever since, quite literally having had nowhere else to go.

It was a dark night made darker by the blackout and the cloud-filled sky. A soft but persistent rain blew against his face. His hat and coat were soaked. In the distance he could hear the violent tides of the Pentland Firth throwing their angry waves against the shore and recalled that night when the *Burscombe* had 'darkened ship' and sneaked through this very channel. He had lied to that midshipman about the sweetness of his mother. She had been anything but sweet. That all seemed like an act in another lifetime now.

It had been over twenty years since he had walked up this lane but he knew it well enough. The mud beneath his shoes was wet but solid even with the autumn leaves lying where they had fallen. No traffic had turned it all to slush. This place, a few miles outside Thurso, was still almost as untouched by human activity as it had been all that time before. Up ahead he saw his parents' cottage. Everything looked the same except for that, years before light from the gas lamps would have been seen illuminating the latticed windows. Tonight, all was black.

He walked apprehensively up to the front door, took a deep breath and knocked.

'Come in!' called a woman's frail voice from within.

Mother! He resisted calling out as he thumbed down the latch, pushed open the door and stepped inside. He drew aside the heavy curtain which blocked his path and squinted at the sudden light. It was electric. That was different. The little old lady who was lifting herself up from the armchair by the fire, clutching at her aching back, said, 'Well, come inside and be mindful of the blackout, my dear.'

'Aye,' said Bonner, quickly closing the door and drawing the curtain back across the space just before it. Turning back to face his mother he found himself speechless. It was not his mother. Her face was far too thin, her cheekbones were higher and her faded hair still showed signs that it had once shone ginger. His mother had had a fuller face and blonde hair. Also the furniture was different and there was carpet as well, not the bare boards that he had once known. 'I... I'm sorry,' he stammered. 'I was looking for Mr and Mrs Bonner. They live here, no?'

'Bonner?' repeated the old woman with a frown. 'Ol' Neil an' Glad? They've been gone these last eight years, my dear.'

'Gone? Where did they go?'

'Well, they've passed away. Both came down with influenza an' died within twenty four hours of each other.' Even as she finished her sentence it dawned on her that the effect her words were having could only mean one thing. 'Are you Dougy? Little Dougy Bonner?'

Through gritted teeth, he said, 'Aye. I didn't know..., I just assumed..., I came to reconcile...,'

Understanding everything, the lady took another step forward. 'I'm so sorry, young man. But come on in an' stop that drippin o' water on the carpet and remove yer boots. It'll take me all of fifteen minutes to put a hot supper on the table.'

'No, you musn't,' said Bonner. 'I'll take my leave an' bother yer no more.'

'Rubbish, it's nearly nine o'clock an' you're miles from the next meal an' warm bed.'

After a little more protesting but with an ever weakening resolve, Bonner sat down and talked to this kind and generous person, wondering at her immediate acceptance of him. Nobody had ever shown him such favour. His new-found faith in God and the strength that it gave him must have been evident.

As for this lady? Yes, he now remembered her. She was Diedre Morton, the late mayor's wife, who had once chased him halfway down Thurso's main road when she had caught him stealing carrots from her garden. Again, that was all in another life.

'Your ma and pa always wondered what had become o' you,' said Diedre as he ate. 'They shed more than a tear over you, boy.'

A feeling of resentment began filling his body. 'I canna' believe that. They never cared for me when I were here.'

'Aye, I'll not lie. They were distant, private people an' it must 'ave seemed as though they didn't care but they did, boy. They really did. What had become o' you were in their thoughts in their last hours. They'll rest easy now knowin' that you came back.'

Bonner eventually agreed that he should stay the night and was calmed by Mrs Morton's generosity and spirit. Before too much time had passed her ownership of the place seemed perfectly natural and acceptable, a welcome turn in the sequence of events.

Later, when he tried to explain to her that he had been aboard the *Royal Oak* he was startled to find that she was completely ignorant of the way the war was being conducted. She explained that as long as she kept her blackout curtains closed at night and accepted the terms of the rationing she was left very much alone. At her age, she had decided, what was the worth in getting into a pickle over who was fighting who? She knew from the last time round that Britain had exceptional young men like Bonner who would fight for her freedom and anyway, it seemed that fighting off the Hun was just another facet of the natural way of the world.

Bonner ended up staying at his old home for over half of his leave. It was as though this lady was the mother he had always wanted and when he finally took his leave of her, he pledged to her that he would do all in his power to ensure her liberty for the rest of her days. It was something worth fighting for and he never went down in a fight.

*

Jennifer Dollimore travelled into Fulham, near London, where her son had gone to convalesce. In so doing she had left Betty in dubious charge of two youngsters that they had taken in at the cottage, evacuees from the Portsmouth Dockyard area. She had not been entirely happy about it but Betty was nearly eighteen and a half years old now, therefore an adult, so it was about time that she was expected to take on some adult responsibilities. Fortunately the two children, brother and sister Jake and Janet, were pleasantly mature for their pre-teen ages so they should be able to keep Betty from getting into too much difficulty.

The large white Victorian house planted firmly in the middle of a rich terrace was Sarah's family home, the result of her father and uncle's combined efforts as doctors to the gentry. The place was large enough and empty enough that Philip and Sarah had not yet been obliged to find separate lodgings of their own. Back in September she had moved down to the country house near Heathrow Hall but, when the air attacks did not materialise over London, she had stubbornly moved back to the place she loved. Philip would allow her this reprieve until the end of the winter, and if the war was still on then he would move her away again.

Even though he had assured his mother that his injuries were not too bad, Jennifer had prepared herself for the worst because there was something of a general current of stoical understatement that ran in the line of the Dollimore males. So she was very well relieved when she discovered that he had been telling the truth. By the time she came to see him the hair that had been burned from his face and scalp had started to grow back. In fact he now had a beard, but this was because his skin was still much too sensitive to attempt shaving.

Jennifer, Philip and Sarah took tea together in the lounge. The room was brightly lit and the maid had stoked up a good fire in the grate. It would have been homely and inviting but for the atmosphere which seemed to suggest that there was something false about the young couple's pleasantries. The baby started crying in the next room and Sarah was far too obvious in her haste to get away and see what the problem was.

'Philip, I know that you've had the most dreadful experience,' said Jennifer, putting down her cup and saucer and deciding that she had better come straight to the point, 'but to cut Sarah out of your suffering can only do further harm.'

'I'm not cutting her out, mother,' protested Philip. 'Well, what I mean is, I don't want to cut her out...' He stood and reached up to the high mantelpiece. From there he picked up his new pipe, a black one very similar to his father's, and took tobacco from the pouch which resided just beside it.

Jennifer felt a strong sense of déjà vu as she observed him standing there lighting it, his back turned to her while he battled with his thoughts. Just the way he stood was so much like Charles. 'Please talk to her,' she said. 'She so much wants to help you.'

'There's no way I can heap my problems onto her shoulders, mother,' said Philip with some apparent anger. 'She has so much to contend with already, what with the baby and the rationing, and how much do you think she would worry if she knew what was really going on out there at sea?' He gave a short laugh. 'It's wrong of me even to worry *you* with this, mother. I must simply get better and go back to continue the fight. That's all that matters.'

'No, it's not all that matters,' Jennifer said scathingly. 'To my mind it's disrespectful that you should suppose she is unable to bear some of the burden of your fight. She would like to understand your situation, now and in the future, so that you can fight the war together. Don't mistake her for some faint-hearted little girl who would bleat and cry at the very thought of you going back out there. She is made of sterner stuff.'

After a long pause, during which Philip could not even look at his mother, he said with an air of finality, 'I don't want to worry her.'

'You don't want to worry her? Or you can't face what happened yourself?'

He turned and stared hard at her, his expression a stark look of horror. 'What is there to face but the sheer stupidity of it all? That anchorage was supposed to have been impregnable. How the hell did the Germans get a submarine in there? Some awful, terrible mistakes have been made here by people who ought to know better and they have cost us over eight hundred lives! My best friend... My best friend was amongst them!' He was visibly shaking with rage and perhaps even terror.

But pleased that she was so swiftly getting to the heart of the matter, she said, 'I understand the pain that you are going through. You must share this with Sarah and look to how you're going to turn this emotion into the strength you need to fight this war.'

'Really? And how can *you*, a woman, possibly understand the pain?' asked Philip. He had never spoken to her like that before.

She remained undeterred and kept eye contact. Hurt as she was she would not bite back, for it was he who had been through the traumatic experience. It was he who had had no avenue to letting go of his pent up feelings until this moment. As well as stern guidance, he also deserved patience.

He had doubted that she could possibly understand so now she must make him know of the experience that she had to offer. She explained, 'You know that your father was in the *Warspite* at the Battle of Jutland?'

'Yes, yes, I know all that,' Philip said irritably.

'His experiences brought him back to me in very much the same state you are in now, but I convinced him that I was able to share the load that he was carrying on his shoulders. It took some while but he opened up to me and we worked at it together. Admittedly, it's not all been plain sailing. He has lapsed into periods of anxiety or impatience since then, one episode of which I hardly need to remind you resulted in tragedy.'

'The *Spikefish*?' Philip asked, calming himself. He had always been given to understand that the blame for that accident lay perfectly with the officer in charge of the submarine. He had never dreamed that his highly methodical father actually hid fears and doubts which might have clouded his judgment.

'Yes, the *Spikefish*. Things were not going so well with him at that time. He was losing his patience and that morning he acted precipitately. The tugs which were supposed to tow the *Constant* down the Clyde were late and he decided not to wait for them. Apparently the mist was becoming heavier as he proceeded so he kept the speed down accordingly. It was just unfortunate that an inexperienced submarine captain put his boat right across his path.'

Philip nodded, 'So that's why one of his favourite pieces of advice is to keep your vessel the right side of the buoys.'

'Exactly,' Jennifer continued, 'but the point is, through everything I have supported him, and he has kept no secrets from me for over twenty years.'

'Father is recognised as one of the most able captains in the fleet,' Philip said proudly, glad to be learning something new about him, and also glad to be deflecting the conversation away from himself. 'He has an instinct which a lot of the chaps are envious of. It was brilliant when he took his ship through the Pentland Firth. That put everybody's noses out of joint, I can tell you. They say he gave the admirals a hard time over that. I saw myself what he's capable of when there was a bit of a to do in the pub in Belfast. This drunken Irishman tried to punch him...,' He suddenly realised that he was almost laughing at the memory, and that his mother was looking at him in surprise.

'Your father brawling in a pub?' she asked. 'How distasteful. That one I've not heard about.'

Then, taking on her more authoritative look, she continued, 'Look, what I'm getting at is that it's debatable that your father would be in the position he is if I had not helped take the burdens of Jutland and the submarine accident from his shoulders. He might seem larger than life to you, he might seem like a tower of strength to all around him, but he is very much human and he is not infallible. You and he are so alike, and in that way you must not try to go on alone. Speak to Sarah. Let her into your thoughts. You can rely on her. You must let her help give you the peace of mind you need to continue fighting the war. I can guarantee you that, thanks to Herr Hitler, there is much worse to come than what you've already seen. Don't believe anybody who says that it'll all be over by Christmas. That's nothing more than reckless naivety.'

Philip looked at his mother in wonderment. He felt like he had learned more about his family in these last few minutes than through the rest of his entire life, and he knew that she was absolutely right in what she was saying. He would not scoff again at the idea that she might know what she was talking about when it came to war. How could he have ever thought that she could live through the last war and not understand something of its trials and tribulations?

He was completely sincere when he thanked her for just pushing open the door to this elusive house of healing, wondering about the many men who never had anyone who could help them with such sense and clarity. He had previously been given to understand everything was simply black and white, that a man was either courageous or a coward, but he was discovering that the mind was a little more complex than that. He knew his duty and he did not fear the Germans but the sense of injustice and the guilt of living when so many had died was actually debilitating. Thank God his mother had helped begin the process of unleashing these emotions.

Chapter Thirteen

The Blockade Runner

The patrols were ceaseless. Men and ships alike were becoming tired and the feeling was exacerbated by the failures which appeared to outweigh the successes. With all the bad news it was easy to lose sight of the fact that thousands of tons of German goods were being brought into Scottish harbours and that, to all intents and purposes, the Royal Navy still dominated the seas. Otherwise, it seemed that any daring being displayed in this war was all on the part of the enemy.

HMS *Belfast*, that great cruiser which was only the same age as the *Burscombe*, was laid up in a dry dock at Rosyth with her keel smashed and large amounts of her machinery damaged because a magnetic mine had exploded beneath her hull. But worse still was where it had happened – in the Firth of Forth. That estuary was now being contested from above and from below. *Belfast* herself had been a major player in the blockade and her loss would be keenly felt.

Hundreds of miles further north, the Armed Merchant Cruisers had begun to take over much of the work of intercepting contraband and taking prizes. These ships were little more than passenger liners with large guns fitted to them and manned almost exclusively by enthusiastic reservists who had not seen proper service for many years, if at all. They hunted for the enemy's merchant ships while the real warships guarded against U-boats and surface raiders. That was why insult was added to injury when two such raiders, the battlecruisers *Scharnhorst* and *Gneisenau*, found and destroyed the AMC HMS *Rawalpindi* then proceeded to escape clean back into the Baltic.

Lieutenant Irwin had small but attentive audiences in the starboard aircraft hangar on board the *Burscombe* where he gave his little lectures on the progress of the war. He had managed to keep these talks going every week no matter whether the ship was in port or out at sea, and the chiefs reported that the ship's company was pleased for his attention. Everybody knew that this odd introvert did not have much stomach for a fight but appreciated the efforts he went to in explaining the navy's circumstances for the good of the whole ship. Because the news that the men were subjected to through the radio, the papers or the latest buzz had not been inspiring, Irwin saw it as his job to help put it into perspective.

He maintained that the patrols they were currently embarked upon were the only way forward at present. The Royal Navy was not yet powerful enough to be chasing the enemy back into his own waters. The tactics could only echo the strategy, which had never changed, to economically ruin Germany through blockade while keeping open British trade routes and safeguarding the home islands. 'We have been hurt,' he told the weary sailors, who sat in that cold, grey venue listening to the words made bleaker by the sound of the wind and waves hammering at the sides of the ship, 'but we will never be beaten. We still have mastery of the oceans and don't doubt that for a second.'

*

The weather was on everybody's minds. There was no escaping its relentless ferocity, and the men had to muster all their mental and physical strength together when they received orders that the *Godham* and the *Burscombe* were once again required to plug holes in the blockade near the Shetlands. Steaming about 120 miles apart from each other, the two ships rode the waves in and out of freezing fog banks with snow intermittently falling to settle on the film of ice that covered almost everything.

A lookout, shivering on the open bridge of the *Godham*, caught sight of something approaching them through the thinning fog and immediately alerted the Officer-of-the-Watch. Action Stations was sounded and before long Captain Nunn was climbing out of the hatch. Quickly having cleaned the condensation from his glasses, he observed through his binoculars the shadow, which now proved to be a passenger liner. 'It's not one of ours,' he declared. 'The nearest AMC should be fifty miles off. Come two points to starboard and signal her to stop.'

The bridge came alive as his orders were relayed and carried out.

Rear-Admiral Clark appeared behind him and watched the proceedings with interest. This was probably a routine interception but he was feeling less and less well and had to keep himself moving. He feared that any form of inertia like slumbering unduly in his cabin would be lethal to him. As far as he was aware Nunn suspected nothing and if anybody did have any thoughts on the subject it must have just seemed like seasickness was getting the better of him.

He drew a deep breath of the salty wind that was swirling about him and joined the captain in the fore section of the bridge. Raising his binoculars to his eyes, he asked, 'What do you think?'

'Probably Norwegian, sir,' said Nunn. 'At least she's obeying my order. Norwegians in fast ships have a tendency to think they can do what the hell they want.'

Soon the *Godham* cut across the liner's bow at a distance of about a thousand yards and started to circle her. Keeping her target on the port beam with her 8-inch guns trained and ready for action, her old, rusting deck plates shuddered as she pitched and barely stopped creaking when Nunn ordered the speed to be decreased. He looked closely at the name which was painted upon the white strip at the ship's bow. The red lettering spelled SS *Hoddøyafjord* .

Some men wearing dark oilskin coats appeared on the liner's bridge wing and Nunn looked at his signalman who was standing by with a portable hand-held lamp. 'Chief, signal "State your business".' The message flashed across was short and curt. Apologies and pleasantries had faded from this campaign a long time ago.

There was no pause before the answer started coming back. Obviously the signalman opposite was as professional as an RN man.

On the bridge of the *Godham*, the message was read: '"We are SS *Hoddøyafjord* out of Kristiansand bound for New York via Esbjerg."'

'Esbjerg is in Denmark,' said Nunn. 'That would account for their north-westerly course.' He then had the question "Cargo?" put across.

'"Passengers only though business could be better",' read the signalman.

Apart from the men on the bridge they could only see a dozen or so other people wandering along the decks staring out at them.

Clark said, 'I guess everybody else is more interested in staying warm and dry instead of coming out to see us.' He was already finding this encounter tiresome and was inwardly fighting the urge to lose patience and stop the chill coursing through his bones by going back below to where he too would be warm and dry.

Nunn was silent for a few seconds and Clark saw him staring hard through his binoculars, his face screwed up as he struggled to see more. 'What is it?' asked the admiral.

'Well, I...,' Nunn began but turned to the Officer-of-the-Watch. 'Pilot, what does the *Lloyds Register* say?'

'Norwegian, 12,700 tons, seems to check out okay, sir.'

Nunn still looked puzzled, 'I happen to know that an old friend of mine took command of the *Hoddøyafjord* this summer. I can't see him there. Could mean nothing but...,' He turned straight back to the signalman. 'Ask him, "Where is Captain Brevik?"'

The answer came back with no delay: "Brevik is in hospital. Appendicitis. I am Halvorson."

'There, you see,' said Clark. 'Nothing to make a fuss about. Your friend is ill.'

Nunn looked over the whole ship from stem to stern but could not put his finger on his aggravation. This ship was one of a dozen Norwegian liners that were probably at sea right now ferrying passengers back and forth across the Atlantic to and from the Americas. There had been no specific intelligence about this one and there was evidently much less to suspect about one heading in a westerly direction than about one that was heading east.

'Well?' asked Clark. 'Are you going to send a boarding party across?'

'No, sir,' replied Nunn.

'That's that, then,' said Clark. 'Don't worry, it's good to be suspicious. That's how we'll catch the Hun. Signalman, send "Give our regards to Brevik. Carry on."'

As the last of the morse signals were flashed across the water Clark staggered back to the hatch and climbed inside, stopping to pause for breath before climbing down the ladder. He was now struggling to hide the shivers which were threatening to overtake his body. He cursed the weakness of his aging form. Why could his body not be as strong as his mind?

*

Captain Dollimore took the *Burscombe* into Sullom Voe, in the Shetlands, for oiling and a couple of days of rest for the crew. Snow laid thick upon the islands surrounding the anchorage, which was presently also occupied by Commander Fulton-Staveley's three destroyers, awaiting news of some friendly merchantmen that they were expecting to escort. Fulton-Stavely was the non-jealous type who greeted Dollimore like an old acquaintance rather than the man whose report from the Pentland Firth breakthrough had caused him to be ticked off like a naughty schoolboy. For it was his group that had passed this great ship in the night and had not noticed her moonlit wake.

It was firmly acknowledged by all sailors of the *Burscombe* that this 'rest' was only going to be a relative affair as there was not much recreation or comfort on offer. The men were cold almost all the time, even tucked up in their hammocks, and in one or two parts of the ship they even discovered ice forming on the inner bulkheads. Young and fit as they were, a few of them discovered that the cold weather played hell with old muscular or joint injuries that they may have picked up at any time in their lives, and more and more of them soon discovered that Surgeon-Commander Lawson was not a man worth complaining to when you had a problem.

To get some of the men's blood circulating a bit more Crawshaw organised a short series of boating competitions between the different departments and was amused at the way the onlookers abused each other as the cutters sped through the water. The rivalry was evidently friendly to a fashion, the stokers easily being the most coarse bunch, but the seamen, gunners, signalmen, writers, the whole damn lot of them were far less than angelic.

Everybody was happier when the captain authorised a tombola to be set up whereby the prizes were selections of decent meats, cheeses and biscuits that he had managed to acquire ashore. Of course, only the men of four messes materially benefitted but the moral effect of running the tombola in the first place was profoundly positive.

Smudge, who had pulled his oar in the races with gusto and later managed to get his hands on a tin of biscuits even though he never had a winning ticket in the tombola, still managed to lament that they could not play a football match and happily remembered the time when they had played a friendly against some of the townsfolk at Grimsby. Again, had he left the story there, people would have been able to accept his sincerity, but he was very soon telling a wild tale of how he had recognised a professional player in the home team and had exposed him. This had led to some sort of physical disagreement, which he won, but created a situation that was made all the worse when he later snogged the saucy girl who was there selling pies. Apparently she was the respected caretaker's daughter but, reasoned Smudge, 'What could I do if she was quiverin' for me?'

*

All too soon the *Burscombe* headed back out into the vastness of the unforgiving sea and the desolate area up near the Faeroes. After cruising sullenly through a bitter wind for a day or so, it was only once she was turning back onto a more southerly course that one of the lookouts on the starboard side of the bridge called out that he could see a shadow against the grim backdrop. 'Bearing green one two five, sir.'

As they all trained their binoculars round, Peterson asked, 'Range?'

The answer was a couple of seconds in coming: 'Four thousand yards, sir.'

They scanned the horizon through the shifting squalls and were on the edge of telling the man that he had been mistaken when, in a sudden burst of weak light, there appeared the dark silhouette of a twin-funnelled ocean liner belching smoke into the sky. It was no mean feat to see it even now with the visibility the way it was.

'Well spotted, son,' said Peterson. 'Pipe the crew to Action Stations! Starboard full rudder!'

The *Burscombe* leaned heavily out of her turn and gave a shudder until he ordered the rudder back to midships.

'First catch of the day,' said Dollimore as he took up his position near Peterson. He raised his binoculars to his eyes and gritted his teeth as the icy wind pushed through his scarf onto his neck. After looking at the slowly approaching vessel for a few seconds, he mumbled, 'Mm, I wonder.'

'What is it, sir?' asked Digby, who had already ordered his guns to be trained.

'Inform Midshipman Clark that his presence is required on the bridge,' Dollimore ordered quite inexplicably. Then, 'Chief Yeoman, signal to that ship to heave to and not to use their radio.'

'Aye aye, sir.' The chief immediately set about flashing across the signal with the morse lamp as the sound of the Director Control Tower's motors whirred above his head.

No reply was forthcoming and the liner, her bow rising and plunging to the running of the sea, continued on her way.

Having hastily dragged on his duffle coat and tin hat, Clark had ascended the ladders to the bridge as quickly as he was able. His muscles were now so fine-tuned to the exertions put upon him by this service that he pushed on up the four decks with ease and hardly broke into a sweat. He closed the bridge hatch behind him and crossed the wet, rolling deck. 'Sir?'

By the time he was letting the captain know that he had arrived, Dollimore was able to read the name painted on the bow of the ship. In any case, he asked, 'Young man, what ship would you say that was?'

Clark looked out across the water at the approaching ship, her blacks, whites and reds all coming up grey in the gloom. 'Good lord, that's the *Trier Stern*!' he gasped.

'You're sure?'

'Either that or another ship of exactly the same class. Either way they're German.'

'Then how do you account for the name on the bow?' Dollimore asked, handing his own binoculars over.

'SS *Hoddøyafjord*,' read Clark. 'She's painted out her real name, sir.'

'That's what I think. Chief, tell them they have one last chance to heave to then I shall open fire.'

The Chief Yeoman flashed across the signal eagerly. He was the same as everybody else, wanting to get back at the Hun for what they had done to too many of 'our' ships already. He secretly hoped that they would not respond so that the captain might yet be compelled to sink her.

Still there was no reply. There was absolutely no chance that the liner's crew had not seen this great warship bearing down upon them. That she was trying to run through the blockade and evade capture was a given, but what was her game now? As was usual, Dollimore kept the *Burscombe* moving at a certain speed and preparing to keep a certain distance because this otherwise innocent-looking peacetime vessel could still have been hiding guns or torpedo tubes.

Even as Clark said, 'Sir, a snow storm moving in from the north!' the penny dropped with Dollimore as to what they were up to. With a swift turn to port, the sleek liner picked up speed and began to be consumed by the wall of whiteness that had descended with startling rapidity.

'Open fire before they're gone!' shouted Dollimore.

Almost as soon as Digby had given the orders the eight guns of the forward turrets blasted out their fiery shots, making everybody jump with surprise.

No sooner had the salvo gone than the captain angrily cried down the voicepipe, 'Steer red zero one five!'

Great geysers of water exploded about the space where the target had just disappeared and settled quickly in their impotence.

While the guns and DCT now turned to compensate for the last manoeuvre, Dollimore gave the order to increase the speed and added, 'Make sure that Bretonworth understands that I needed every knot he can squeeze out of these engines!' The thought that the *Trier Stern* with her vintage machinery could outrun the *Burscombe* was completely ridiculous but whoever was in command over there had smartly sought to make Dollimore look stupid. He vowed that that would come at a price. Everything between now and the final interception was simply a prevarication as far as he was concerned.

He turned to Clark and, now much calmer, said, 'If you'd like to return to the waist, young man, and be ready with the boarding party.'

Clark immediately took himself away.

As the Burscombe's dark grey shape slid roughly into the squall, visibility dropped to practically nil. A heavy dusting of snow quickly coated the lookouts whose eyes were straining to catch sight of anything before them. So involved were they in their search that they did not recognise that the cold air was seeking to chill their hearts.

After fifteen minutes nothing was seen, but a clear and close radio signal was picked up. Deciding that the captain of the *Trier Stern* was playing a very dangerous game, Dollimore ordered the ship turned onto a course of one three five degrees, a mean bearing for enemy territory. But was it a fair bet that the target would immediately run for home?

After another half an hour of pushing her way through the heavy sea, slicing the waves aside with the odd shudder here and there, the *Burscombe* suddenly came out into clear daylight. A fortuitous gap in the clouds had allowed the sun to illuminate everything for miles ahead, leaving only a thick ring of grey bordering the horizon.

'Target bearing red zero one zero, sir!' shouted Peterson triumphantly. 'Range five thousand yards!'

A cheer went up around the bridge as everybody turned to take in the sight.

'Look back to your quadrants!' Dollimore berated them but no one was deflated by his sudden temper. The captain had done it again.

He looked at his gunnery officer. 'Mr Digby, a shot across the bow if you please.' Then he had the Chief Yeoman repeat his signal for her to heave to.

With her far superior steam turbines allowing the *Burscombe* to gain on the plucky liner with ease, one shot cracked out from A Turret sending a shell to explode in the water just ahead of the other's bow. The game was up. In short order the thick black, coal smoke being pumped from her funnels lessened as did the froth of her wake. It took a little while but soon the *Trier Stern* was stopped.

At first no movement could be discerned anywhere on the decks of this passenger liner. The lookouts only saw the seemingly deserted vessel pitching through the sea, her white structure now standing out beautifully against the bleak background.

Then, looking through his binoculars, Dollimore eventually saw the figures of two men becoming quite animated on the liner's bridge. What could that mean? It seemed that perhaps there were two authorities on board having an altercation over what chances they needed to take on this matter. Surely the big guns pointing at them should be making any decision an easy one. Or was there something more worth taking a chance on?

Down in the port waist, the boarding party awaited the order to be on their way. The patient marines and seamen stamped their feet and slapped their arms to keep from getting too cold as they observed the liner hove to a short distance away. It just remained to turn the *Burscombe* so that port would be the leeside and then the task would be all theirs.

On this occasion the cutter that was going to transport them was to be commanded by the podgy little Midshipman Farlow. He looked fatter than he actually was, wrapped up in all his layers of clothing, and his red face looked as miserable as ever. He glanced over at Clark and hated the way that he appeared so heroic and at ease with everybody, even with his rotten reputation. Nothing had changed since they were at Dartmouth.

Also, why did he always get the lion's share of any excitement when there was a ship to be boarded?

Thinking in his usual haphazard way about the gossip that his father had written to him a couple of months ago, he straightened his back, adopted a pompous air and took a couple of steps toward where the other young man was standing. 'Enjoy being in the middle of everything, do you?'

'What are you talking about now?' asked Clark, immediately sighing and wishing this bothersome man would go away.

'Have a special relationship with the Old Man, do you? You always seem to have your fingers in the pie. I mean, there are plenty other midshipmen on board who are as good as you at this work.'

Clark frowned and said, 'I hope you don't class yourself amongst them, my dear Farlow.'

But Farlow pushed on, unstoppable. 'I just thought to say that I know that you wouldn't be so favoured if it had anything to do with the commander. God knows how anyone from your family can look the poor man in the eye.'

Thoroughly confused, Clark turned to look at him. 'What's that suppose to mean?'

Ah, thought Farlow, he really doesn't have a clue about this business. There should be some mileage in this one. He smiled and was about to continue when Lieutenant Eddington's voice sounded throughout the waist, 'Let's go! Let's go! Everybody into cutter!'

'Bloody move!' added the towering Sergeant Burroughs most unnecessarily. Arrogant as the man might appear, one could never misunderstand his intentions.

With a few exceptions the small crew manning the cutter was the same as that which boarded the *Signhild II* and three other ships since stopped and searched. Barrett the navigator, Pincher Martin and even Les Gordy had come a long way. That first foray into this adventure seemed like a lifetime ago now. The rest of the eighteen men of the boarding party crammed into the boat were made up of the usual mix of sailors and marines, all of them standing by with rifles. The remaining few were pulling on the oars for all they were worth.

Farlow was close to the man at the tiller. Clark looked over at him but he would not return the gaze. That fat boy, being the cutter's commander, was the only man allowed to speak during the short journey across to the *Trier Stern* so was concentrating on the task to hand. What that contemptible little stirrer had started would have to wait for another time.

As usual they found that it was no easy matter to climb the side of the ship because the cutter was rising and falling at a height of about six to seven feet at a time. Fortunately the men on the deck above, presumably all German, had decided that they would not put up any more resistance in the presence of the *Burscombe* and so assisted the prize crew by dropping a rope ladder down the side.

Eddington was up first with Burroughs itching to be right behind him. They heaved themselves over the guardrail and looked around at the half dozen miserable looking men who were standing well back from them. Careful not to slip on the fresh layer of snow and with his revolver in hand, Eddington said, 'The game's up. Which of you is the captain?'

A sour looking man with harsh, dirt-filled lines on his face and unshaven chin stepped forward. He was dressed in heavily padded waterproof clothing. From under his black peaked cap he stared hard at Eddington and said, 'I am Captain Halvorson.'

'Don't come the other one with me. I know you're German. What's your real name?'

The grizzled man considered the question for a few more seconds, wondering about his chances of continuing with the charade. He had lost fair and square yet there was something that was making him hesitate still further.

Eddington helped him make up his mind, first by pointing his revolver at him and then by saying, 'We know this ship is the *Trier Stern*, my good fellow. In fact, we could almost be bosom buddies since we almost ran over each other near Denmark four months ago.'

'I remember,' scowled the captain, his English tainted by the strong German accent. 'I recognised you, too.'

'And then you thought you could run from us?'

That was when arrogance appeared on the other man's face. He raised his head slightly and drew his lips closer together.

'Don't worry, sir,' said Eddington. 'There's only one truth that matters now and that is that we're going to take this ship into Kirkwall and you and your crew and passengers are going to be interned for the duration.

Awfully sorry about it but that's the way it is. What did you say your name was?'

'I didn't. My name is Hartman, Emil Hartman.'

'Glad to make your acquaintance, Herr Hartman, even if the circumstances don't favour you,' finished Eddington, suddenly with an empathetic grin.

Clark, who had just clambered up over the side and now stood with the rest of the men, again marvelled at how Eddington had made such short work of the situation. He had perfect command of everything and everyone.

The lieutenant quickly ascertained that there were only forty one people on board. They were all men and seemed to be nothing much more than a skeleton crew. So, if there were no passengers, were they hiding something valuable in the hold? Or was this ship simply trying to make it back home? He signalled across to Captain Dollimore what he had discovered and the reply came back forthwith: "Proceed to Kirkwall. At sunset darken ship. Only light to be shown is one white stern light. *Burscombe* will remain somewhere behind you."

Eddington quickly ordered Farlow and his cutter away to the *Burscombe* then positioned himself, one marine and Barrett on the bridge with Hartman and the helmsman. He ordered Clark to gather the rest of the crew, minus those needed to tend the engines, in the saloon area. With everything else seemingly covered, a few men were set to begin a rudimentary search for any contraband.

'Right,' Clark eventually said to Sergeant Burroughs, after he had managed to acquire a proper list of German names from the bridge. 'Let's find out who we have here. Tell them that I want to see passports or papers; and no fake Norwegian rubbish. Their real papers.'

'Aye aye, sir,' the marine answered and set about terrorising the Germans with relish.

Clark had set himself up at a grand circular table at the fore end of the upper deck saloon and sat comfortably with the crew list in front of him. As he checked names off he sipped at a glass of red wine. He was in no particular rush to get this job done. It was an open and shut case as far as he was concerned. They were just a bunch of Germans who were going to be interned for the rest of the war.

237

Looking about the room he was struck by the fittings, the wood paneling, brass rimmed lamps and white columns. They should have been fine but were looking rather drab. Lining the port and starboard sides of the long room were rows of dark green drapes concealing the great windows, and stretching along the deck was a stylish carpet showing rows of green diamonds. The tables and chairs were of fine mahogany but these too were showing signs of wear and tear. The class of passenger that this saloon was designed for had probably not frequented it during the last few years of the *Strength Through Joy* programme.

He was just checking another passport against the list when he looked up and saw Seaman Gordy staring at one of the detainees who was putting his papers out on the table in front of him. There was a look of intense concentration on the young Irish lad's face. Clark always knew that Gordy was slightly behind the other men in his comprehension of things but something had actually seemed to rattle him.

Clark walked over. 'Are you alright, Gordy?'

'Aye, sir. Sorry, sir.'

'If there's something strange about that man then tell me.'

'No, sir. It's just been a long time since I've seen Ogham, that's all. It... Sorry, sir, sorry.'

Clark looked at Gordy then at the other man. He was a regular dark haired fellow of about twenty five looking as fed up as anybody else here. He was completely unremarkable.

Clark then looked back at Gordy, regarded the black rings around his eyes, and decided that the lad, already acknowledged to be barmy, was going extra barmy through fatigue.

*

The *Trier* Stern's closed bridge had the feeling of being as luxurious as a palace after the experience of the Burscombe's open, windswept arrangements and Eddington sat himself comfortably in one corner while still trying to get information from Captain Hartman. 'So,' he said, 'have you fooled anyone else with your little act?'

Hartman shrugged, 'Perhaps. Some of your ships are not so smart.'

'Yes, well we did have the good fortune of meeting you once before; and to think we were questioning at the time the wisdom of being sent in so close to Germany. What a turnaround this has been. It's truly a pleasure to have bumped into you again. So, you've had a busy month. Where did you set out from?'

'New York,' replied Hartman without a pause.

'Are you sure?'

Hartman's caution began to be strained towards frustration. 'You think I don't know whether I have visited New York or not?'

'Did you dock there as *Trier Stern* or *Hoddøyafjord*?'

Hartman shook his head and looked away.

Eddington smiled. 'We get excellent intelligence from the other side of the Atlantic about which ships are heading in our direction. It wouldn't take much to find out when you docked in New York, if indeed you docked there at all.' He pulled a packet of cigarettes out of his pocket and offered one to the captain. Soon they were both taking in the calming tobacco smoke. 'So, after the last time we saw you, you went back to Wilhelmshaven, offloaded your passengers, coaled and victualled then immediately set out again? Have you been away from home these four months or have you been running back and forth past the blockade the whole time?'

'I have no idea what you're getting at,' said Hartman.

Eddington frowned. 'Don't you think that the FBI would have informed us about a German ship leaving New York, especially attempting to pose as a Norwegian? They're not that gullible, you know.'

Hartman gave another shrug. 'Maybe they did know about us but they did not give us any trouble. I don't know why you always think that the Americans are sympathetic to England just because you happen to share the same language.'

'It's about more than language, Herr Hartman. It's about the difference between democracy and fascism.'

Hartman suddenly became quite agitated. 'For the record, lieutenant, I am no fascist. Even if I have to spend the duration of the war in prison, no one will ever accuse me of being a fascist.'

Although initially taken aback, Eddington suddenly began to feel as though he was addressing the real character of the ship's captain, a man more opinionated, more decisive. 'So, if you're not a fascist, why do you run such risks to supply their war effort?'

Hartman looked at him as though the answer should have been obvious. 'I'm still German. It is possible to hate your government and still love your country. Or are the English above all that?'

'Can't say I've given it much thought. I wasn't old enough to vote back in '35.'

'You're lucky your people are allowed to vote at all,' said Hartman with a short, cynical laugh. 'The führer has banned elections in Germany.'

Eddington smiled and puffed on the cigarette. 'As I said, it's all about the difference between democracy and fascism.'

Shaking his head, Hartman said, 'You know that if England doesn't stand aside and let the führer settle the score with his true enemies then he will put an end to your rights, too? You know that, don't you?'

'Let's not get carried away, old boy. If Adolf ever decides he wants to subjugate us he'll have the devil of a time because he'll have to get through the Royal Navy first and, let's face it, he's not going to do that, is he?' Eddington grinned at his own conviction.

Hartman, not seeing cause for any amusement, said, 'Do not speak too soon, young man. Ships can be sunk.'

'Oh, come off it, Herr Hartman, who has the upper hand right now? It's not you, is it?'

'If you're so powerful then why did you do nothing about Poland? A whole country got swallowed up by us and the Russians and all you did was wave a fist. The Poles never stood a chance and absolutely nobody came to help them. And how was it you allowed our submarine to sink one of your battleships in your own harbour? It doesn't sound like you have the upper hand to me, obstinate boy.'

Eddington stared out of the window at the dark, heaving sea and spared a quick thought for the Poles. Britain and France had given them guarantees of assistance but they turned out to be geographically impossible to get to. In the wake of the *Royal Oak* and other setbacks he had quite forgotten about them. He took a drag on his cigarette and blew out the smoke then looked back at Hartman. 'Touché, old boy, touché. But the game's far from over. We beat you before and we'll beat you again.'

'We'll see.'

It had now been dark for a few of hours and a fresh shower of snow was beginning to build up in the corners of the windows when the portside door opened and Midshipman Clark stepped in, clutching the crew list. He quickly closed the door to ease off the chilled wind which suddenly permeated everywhere, then walked straight over to Eddington. 'Sir,' he said. 'We're missing two people. Herrs Gurtner and Fleischer.'

'Is that so?' He nodded then looked doubtfully at Hartman. 'Evidently there are some who still wish to evade capture. So be it. Clark, you'll have to search through the ship. Find them and bring them to the saloon. They'll probably cause you trouble, though, so make sure you've got some help.'

'Sounds like a job for Burroughs,' smiled Clark.

'Quite.'

As Clark left the bridge, Hartman watched him go in silence. Somehow, thought Eddington, the old captain looks a little more concerned than he was a few moments ago.

*

Having left a decent guard in the saloon, Clark led Burroughs and two other marines in the search, first looking into the cabins, stores and saloons along the upper decks, and not forgetting to poke their noses under the covers of the lifeboats as well. At first it seemed like a daunting task, for there were a hundred and one places where two men intent on concealment could hide themselves away, but their optimism grew because most ships, appearing to be huge at first glance, had a strange way of revealing their true compactness as one became used to them.

With torches they checked through the forepeak, paint stores and cable lockers then on through some basic and poky lower class cabins, which were stacked high with bunks and cluttered with a maze of pipes and flanges. Not much wood panelling was required for cosmetic masking in those particular places.

As they moved along and still found nobody skulking in any of the cabins, the heads, the bathrooms, the crew's quarters, nor any of the numerous store cupboards it became more and more clear to Clark that they would probably end up having to climb through the dingy spaces down below which made up the hold. He apprehensively recalled a story he had heard about one ship where they had Germans hiding in the oil tanks.

After a couple of hours they passed back along the crew's passageway below the saloon area to gain access to the forward hold. The greasy and oily smelling passage was lit by more of those lazy, low-watt bulbs, and Clark saw Corporal Yates standing guard just outside the open doorway which led to the galley. Just inside were a couple of white clothed detainees preparing food on the stoves, the big ugly one disrespectfully smoking a cigarette over the pots. A steady surge of steam rose up into the overhead pipework to disappear against the deckhead.

Yates immediately acknowledged the presence of Clark's team and saluted.

At that point the smaller, sweaty cook saw them too and started talking at speed in his native tongue, waving his hands about. He was very agitated.

'I told you to shut up already!' Yates told him, leveling his rifle threateningly.

Burroughs looked at the gesticulating man with contempt and asked, 'What the bloody hell does he want?'

'No idea, sergeant,' replied Yates.

Clark let out a short laugh. 'He's desperate to get to the heads, gentlemen.'

'This ain't a pleasure cruise,' Burroughs all but spat out. 'Tell him to shit in a bucket.'

'Come, come, sergeant,' said Clark quickly. 'We're not animals. The heads are just back along the passageway there. He's not going anywhere else.' He then gestured for the man to go and be quick about it.

The perspiring man carefully pushed past Yates, shaking his head at him as he went, then glanced back into the galley. Moving to a position where his colleague could not see him, he fearfully raised his finger to his lips to shush them all. It was a solid gesture of secrecy which immediately intrigued Clark. In a heavily German-accented English the man proceeded with a whisper, 'I needed to be away from him. I don't know his thinking but I would help you. The captain, he's not a bad man but there is another on board, I think his name is Fleischer. He was in charge of the job we had to do.'

'What job?' asked Clark, noting but not revealing that Fleischer was one of the two men that they were looking for.

'When we were off the coast of Ireland we picked up two men from a trawler,' the German continued. 'Apparently their steamer was no good, had sunk somewhere in the Atlantic and the trawler had picked them up.'

'So, you rendezvoused with this trawler off Ireland? An *Irish* trawler?'

'Irish, of course.'

Clark considered the information carefully. Was he being told the truth or being spun a yarn? 'Why would you be telling me this?'

'I am a Communist.'

Frowning, Clark said, 'That's hardly a good recommendation right now.'

'You will learn in time which is the greater evil. Hitler will be the destruction of Germany if we are not the destruction of him first.'

Clark decided that there was nothing more he could do at this moment than take the man and his story at face value and sighed. 'Okay, you must come and speak to my commanding officer.'

Again, a more fearful look filled the man's eyes, 'But I don't want the others knowing that I talked to you. I don't know their thinking.'

'Oh, don't worry about that. What's your name?'

'Paul Steidl.'

Clark looked at Burroughs and ordered, 'Give Herr Steidl a bit of whack about the head for me, will you.'

It took the sergeant less than a second to comprehend the order and willingly brought up his fist to crash into the right side of Steidl's head. The left side then connected with a low hanging pipe and the unwitting German let out a great cry of pain and confusion.

Clark suddenly said at the top of his voice, 'Now, you won't be doing that again in a hurry.' With that he took hold of Steidl and bundled him, under protest, up the ladder.

*

Steidl's tale, which was imparted to Clark, Eddington and Burroughs in the privacy of a secure cabin well away from the rest of the crew, had elements both sinister and admirable. The twenty year old chef had been employed by Captain Hartman for nearly two years and in this way knew him to be a decent man, energetic and sociable at sea with his passengers but reclusive in port. The rumour was that his circle of friends once had close links with the trade unions until Nazism had swept away the need for any debate. Since taking over the *Trier Stern* he had kept his head down, worked hard and hoped that one day things were going to get better. Steidl, being younger and angrier and having what he considered to be a keener sense of justice, had decided that he was willing to go out on a limb to help the British.

Since war had broken out, the *Trier Stern* had been moving goods and supplies about the Baltic and that appeared to be what was in store for the foreseeable future until one night at the end of November this Fleischer person turned up and started ordering Hartman around. From then on everything was different. Fleischer possessed the usual arrogant egotism so readily used by the Nazis.

Or by any such bully who relished the power struggle from a position of authority, thought Clark.

Hartman and Fleischer did not agree on many subjects but the captain was soon compelled to become obedient to the Nazi anyway. That was the way of things.

The crew were told very little. They had set out from port as soon as they were provisioned and coaled and headed across the North Sea, pausing once out of sight of land to paint out the name of *Trier Stern* and replace it with that of SS *Hoddøyafjord*. They obviously needed to get through the British blockade so had chosen a very similar Norwegian liner to impersonate. It had worked too, a lot easier than they had expected. They had been intercepted by a British warship near the Shetlands and, with a little swift thinking from Hartman, had easily passed through.

So they then made their way to a position off the west coast of Ireland, sighting only a few merchant vessels along the way, and kept a cautious look out until nightfall. A couple of spare hands, one being Steidl himself, were then called to the starboard side. Once there he could see that some sort of trawler had crept up close to them in the dark and that a boat was being rowed over to the *Trier Stern*. He personally lowered a rope ladder, thus allowing two men to ascend onto the deck. Fleischer welcomed them warmly, particularly the oldest of them, then led them inside.

'So you never went to New York?' asked Eddington.

'New York?' said Steidl in surprise. 'No.'

'And how do you know the trawler was Irish?'

'From the way the man in the boat spoke.'

Steidl, seated in the centre of the cabin surrounded by his small audience, continued, 'There had been some talk about which was the best course back to Wilhelmshaven. I was serving coffee on the bridge when I heard Fleischer put up a plan to slip through the Pentland Firth.' He laughed. 'Crazy Nazi idiot. Nobody in his right mind would ever dare try that. There's not much secrecy in knocking on the front door.'

Eddington and Clark looked at each other, frowned, then looked back at Steidl.

'Could you identify this Fleischer chap for us?' asked Eddington.

'I can't,' Steidl said, again looking fearful. 'But I can tell you that I saw him heading towards the stern about five minutes before you boarded. He had the old man with him.'

'Is that so?' asked Eddington. 'Mm, a tidy mystery. That old gentleman must be someone damned important to risk all this for. Just need to find the silly bugger now. Heading towards the stern, you say? You've been very helpful, Mr Steidl. I'm very sorry you felt the need to play traitor to your country.'

'Not to my country,' answered the German with a look of defiance. 'To Nazism. You would have done the same thing.'

Raising himself up with something that looked a little like righteous indignation, Eddington said, 'No Englishman would ever feel the need to act in such a way.'

Clark barely let his glance at the lieutenant register as a movement. That was not exactly what Steidl had been getting at but this was hardly the time to be distracted anyway. He thought briefly, if a dictator had somehow managed to install himself in Westminster, then there would most certainly be men like Steidl who would do what they could to see him fall. Were there not similar tales throughout English history?

Eddington asked, 'Steidl, is there anything else you can tell us before we put you back with the others?'

'Really, that is all I know,' he replied, looking down in deep thought as though to make sure.

'Thank you,' said Eddington, his previous stance all but disappeared. 'Of course, what you have done for us will be in my report so perhaps the authorities will look upon you with favour. In the meantime, however, you will have to stay with the other chef.'

Steidl nodded, standing as the others did. 'Just one thing. Was this necessary?' he asked, motioning to his cheek that had turned blue and purple and had formed a more accentuated lump.

'Sorry,' said Clark. 'It was the only thing I could think of on the spur of the moment to get you away from your colleague without being suspicious.'

'And my mum always said I didn't know my own strength,' said Burroughs in such a tone that it might have passed for some sort of apology. If that was so then it was as much of an apology as he could expect from the hard headed marine.

After the German had been removed from the cabin, Eddington said, 'Right then. A search in the stern is required, I think.'

'There might be a quicker alternative, someone who might know their whereabouts,' said Clark.

'Captain Hartman,' said Burroughs.

'No,' Clark replied, 'Steidl said that two men came aboard but it's clear that only one of them is with this Fleischer fellow.'

Eddington asked, 'Do you know who the other one is?'

'I think so. I'll get straight on it, though I think it might be beneficial to find out what Ogham is first.'

'Find out what what is?'

Chapter Fourteen

Grappling With the Enemy

Rear-Admiral Clark stood before the mirror shaving the rough white stubble from his chin. Standing with his legs braced to counter the swaying movement of the cabin, he had removed his jacket and pullover and opened the neck of his shirt. This was as far as he was prepared to undress with the temperature as low as it was. He sighed. The way he was feeling was just not good enough, and nor was the fact that his limbs were noticeably thinning. It was as though his muscles were somehow wasting away yet his stomach was becoming fatter. Still, as bad as he was, he was not ready to give in.

He had acknowledged that time was against him but all he needed was just one chance to get a pop at the enemy before he was too unfit to carry on. He had to cement himself a decent reputation as a fighting man before it was all over for him, otherwise how could he happily take his place in the pantheon of the family's greatest?

*

Outside, a new dawn was struggling to bring light to the icy, windswept decks of the *Godham* in her tiresome, lonely journey.

High up in the foretop the lookout also shivered. The young man moaned aloud to himself as he stamped his feet and moved his arms in an attempt to stave off the excesses of exposure to this wind which seemed to bluster in at him from every direction. Icicles hung from the rails and yardarms and every so often another dusting of snow settled upon the shoulders of his duffle coat and the top of his double balaclava. Thankfully the commander had ordered this position to be relieved every hour instead of every four.

It was mind-numbingly tedious work. Neither he nor his shipmates had seen anything out here for the past six days. People were beginning to believe that nothing was going to happen now until next spring. Jerry had caused a bit of trouble and was now sitting back for the winter. Fair enough, so surely there was a chance of some leave over Christmas?

He brought the binoculars back up to his eyes and scanned what he could see of the horizon. The dark grey of the shifting sea merged with the dark grey of the clouds and often the whole scene was completely distorted by fog or a snow squall. This unholy mix had the appearance of moving fast about the Godham's great hulk.

Then suddenly there was something. Had he glimpsed a shadow in a distant gloomy fog bank? He squinted hard, trying to focus his tired eyes on the target. There was nothing there so he paused at raising the alarm. After all, when one of his mates had shouted the alarm a couple of days ago there had turned out to be nothing there and, while the officers did not actually berate him, there had definitely been an underlying hostility.

Everything was just a sheet of grey, so he adjusted his gaze to one side of the position he was looking at, so as to make the most of that strange phenomenon whereby he could always see an object more clearly by not looking directly at it. There it was again! For a couple of seconds he could distinctly make out the bow of a ship with big guns silhouetted all in black. He had already paused long enough. Without any further ado he shouted down the voicepipe, 'Bridge, large warship bearing green zero two five!'

An answer came up from below and within a few seconds the alarm bells were going. The Godham's 714 men sprung into action as one. Men bustled themselves this way or that with purpose, and steel hatches were shut as the reports came in from each section that everybody was closed up and ready. Very suddenly the lookout unknowingly had something new in common with the admiral down below. Neither of them were shivering any longer.

The full attention of the forward main armament was concentrated to the starboard bow with the humming of the powerful electric motors. The guns were not properly aimed as yet since the 'warship' had not been seen again. Clark and Nunn only knew two things at the moment - the general direction where the ship had been seen and that she might possibly be a worthy opponent. Both knew the dispositions of the patrolling ships in the neighbouring sectors so they were reasonably sure that whoever was out there was not friendly.

Then, as Nunn was dictating a message to be sent by wireless, a white squall blew away to the east suddenly revealing not just the large black image of a great German *Deuschland* Class Battlecruiser, but those of two escorting destroyers on her port flank. They could only have been a matter of a mile and a half away. This was spitting distance, but the worst of it was that the main silhouette did not display gun barrels pointed fore and aft. He knew immediately from that smudged image that that vessel's main armament was already trained in their direction. He only hoped that their visibility had been equally as affected by the squall and they had not had time to aim properly. Above his head the Director Control Tower was adjusting to cater for the sudden apparition. Who was going to get their shots out first?

Nunn suddenly realised that the rating he had been dictating to was still standing patiently beside him, waiting for the end of the message that was desperately needing to be sent. Admiral Forbes would not be able to react with the rest of the fleet without this communication. How could he have allowed himself to be put off his stride so easily? He quickly barked out the last of the message and ordered the enemy's position, course and speed to be attached to it, covering up his hesitation with irritated urgency.

Fighting off the understanding that this was their first true action against a much more powerful enemy, the team in the DCT started feeding their target information down to the Transmitting Station. The work was done with automatic professionalism, even when a row of flashes lit up their sights. The German guns were speaking. Quickest into the game, the bastards already had the upper hand.

Nunn, peering through the droplets of water on his glasses, had already visualised this eventuality and was ready to order, 'Steer port zero four five! Give me revolutions for twenty five knots!'

As the *Godham* turned heavily against the rollers, the battlecruiser was suddenly almost square on the beam and the DCT and turrets had to turn to allow for the new course. But fortunately, now the aft turrets could also be brought to bear. 'Now would be a good time to let them have it!' said Nunn, staring hard at his gunnery officer.

'Engage! Shoot!' yelled the young officer.

The eight guns of the broadside thundered out, taking the air from the lungs of the men on the bridge, but the effect of them was almost immediately cancelled out by explosions which made the sea erupt very close astern. It made everybody except Nunn look about momentarily and Clark voiced all their thoughts, 'She has 11-inch guns!'

'No matter,' replied Nunn quite clinically, but he already had other considerations to be concerned with. He knew that another salvo from the German battlecruiser was already in the air and he was pausing only for the few more seconds that it would take for his own gunners to get off another broadside. His fore turrets now trained slightly abaft, he let them fire their shells with another earsplitting roar, then shouted down the voicepipe, 'Port full rudder! Come about, one eight zero!'

Now he needed to evade, open the range and set up another broadside as fast as possible. Once he had done this he would beat a fighting retreat in the direction of the next nearest friendly ship, HMS *Burscombe*, which was presently escorting a prize ship southwards to the Orkney's. Many miles away they may be but as soon as they received the 'enemy sighted' signal they should be steaming towards the fight at about thirty knots. In the meantime things were going to get very tough.

As six great explosions tore open the sea again, mostly on the port quarter, Clark held on as the *Godham* pushed herself into her tight turn to port, opposite to the direction he personally would have wanted. 'Get in closer!' he yelled at Nunn.

Other men around the bridge looked at him.

'She has superior guns,' replied the captain, stepping closer and speaking lower, attempting to exercise a little more discretion. 'We will be destroyed.'

Clark regarded him with a wild look. 'The crew of the *Rawalpindi* closed their target and fought to the last.'

'And that is not what I intend to do here, sir,' said Nunn. 'Your own orders were to tackle surface raiders as a squadron. We've been caught on the hop and that thing over there will pulverise us if we stay here. If we can hook up with Dollimore, we have a chance to win.' He spared Clark a look of embarrassment. It did him no good to have to talk to his superior like this. Hierarchy and respect played too much of a role in his life to let this sit easy with him.

As their own aft turrets fired again, their four relatively small shells soaring away astern, Clark stared at his flag captain with a look of open disgust. The frustrations of these last twelve months permeated his body mercilessly and his head felt fit to burst open with the tension of it all. His family were against him and now his men were against him. After the tragedies of the *Athenia*, the *Courageous*, the *Royal Oak*, the

Mohawk, the *Belfast* and the *Rawalpindi*, where did running away fit into the agenda? 'Dollimore will come to us wherever we are!' he shouted. 'Now close the Hun and cripple him!'

It was fortunate for Nunn that Clark's eyes were so tired and bloodshot, and that his face had taken on such a maniacal expression. It was doubly fortunate that Clark could not keep his voice down, thus displaying to everybody around him that, now that push came to shove, he did not have a good tactical grasp on the situation. For it was then easy for Nunn to say to his navigating officer, 'Pilot, please see the admiral down to his cabin.'

He did not need to add anything like, 'He is not well.' It was plain for all to see.

Nunn reflected sadly that, even if Clark was right, he would not have scored many points for sympathy since he was not very well liked by any of the men right from the highest to the lowest. A lot of these sailors had served on flagships in the past where the admirals, detached and aloof from the day-to-day running of the ship, had had time to be friendly and chatty with all ranks. This had always appeared to be beyond Clark's capabilities.

Flanked by a couple of burly ratings, whose expressionless faces gave no hint as to the bewilderment and joy they were feeling at being part of this tense, unheard-of moment, Clark was led off the bridge. Just before he disappeared he said to Nunn, 'You'll pay for this!'

Yes, he probably would somehow. This was one of those defining moments that would make or break a man. The image of a Court Martial was already flashing through Nunn's mind but it was quickly swept away by a shudder reaching him through the deck below his feet. The sound of a cacophonous detonation came a split second later and fire, wood and jagged steel burst out from Godham's quarterdeck down aft.

A swift glance at the German battlecruiser showed him that she was keeping her starboard side beam on to him in order to keep the full broadside in action, and now she had the range things could only get hotter. It was only fortunate that the destroyers, more aggravated by the increased speed and the height of the waves, could not get into a position to fire their torpedoes.

He waited with gritted teeth as the *Godham* finally completed her manoeuvre. After what seemed like an eternity the ship was steaming her new south westerly course which had already been anticipated by the gunnery officer. He had also just given orders for the two portside 4-inch mountings to join in the fray against the smaller ships, and the information was already being evaluated by the crews.

'Bloody well fire!' shouted Nunn in something that was little more than an angry gesture because he knew full well that the men were working his armament with the greatest possible speed. The 8-inch guns roared out in between the smaller rumblings of the 4-inch secondary armament and after a carefully timed pause on this course, Nunn ordered, 'Make smoke!'

Looking aft at the three high funnels, he waited the couple of seconds for the thick black smoke to begin pouring out before ordering, 'Steer starboard zero nine zero!' The wind was very strong but steering away on this course should keep them concealed behind the smoke screen long enough for them to catch their breath and spoil this formidable opponent's range. Then the *Godham* could come back round on a port tack and present them with another full and sudden broadside.

'Get me a damage report up here on the double,' he said, forcing his tone to be somehow calmer. He cursed Clark for taking his attention away from the game, even for those few seconds.

*

The *Burscombe*, her crew at Defence Stations, was still zig-zagging casually a couple of thousand yards behind the *Trier Stern* when the grey of dawn took over from the black of night. Lieutenant Irwin had kept a careful eye on the liner's stern light for the last few hours and was feeling just about ready to hand over the watch when a petty officer telegraphist rushed onto the bridge and saluted at him whilst trying to force a slip of paper into his gloved hand. The man's very concerned expression and irregular formality immediately set alarm bells ringing in his mind. 'From the *Godham*, sir,' the PO said through his shortness of breath. 'She's under attack by a German battlecruiser.'

'Thank you,' Irwin replied, involuntarily playing up to the urgency and struggling to take in the words as he read the message. 'Erm, after you've acknowledged this maintain radio silence.'

'Aye aye, sir.' The PO left the bridge in the same rush that he had entered with.

Dollimore was next to the lieutenant within thirty seconds of being summoned from his cabin. 'Mr Irwin, set us on an interception course immediately and proceed with all despatch.' Then he turned to Chief Yeoman Ross and said, 'Signal Eddington on the *Trier Stern*. Tell him we're responding to a call to action against a raider. He's only three hours from his rendezvous with another escort. Tell him good luck.'

He did not like breaking away from the liner but he had no other choice. It was not that the heavily armed boarding party should have too much trouble from the crew but the situation during the night had revealed that there was someone very important concealed within the ship. What risks these Germans were prepared to take was unclear but there was nothing better to dampen their resolve than having an array of 6-inch guns pointed at them. Now Eddington would have to make do without them for a while.

Then a thought occurred to him as he matched up the strands of the tactical situation in his head. The raider's course and speed was suggestive. 'Chief, add to the signal, "Suspect the raider engaged was sent to escort *Trier Stern*." Eddington'll have to evaluate the importance of that himself.'

'Aye aye, sir.'

Then Dollimore looked out at the gloomy sea and realised that the *Burscombe* was not turning. Irwin had gone off down to the charthouse quick enough so what was happening now?

Down below, Irwin's brow furrowed as he glanced over the facts and figures, fighting an internal battle with the excitement that threatened to make all before him a jumble of meaningless scribbles. Forcing a dismissal of everything else from his mind, he plotted the relative positions on the chart and approached the voicepipe but just as he did so, the captain's voice came down: 'Mr Irwin, are we steering a course or do you want me to get Mr Peterson to help you?'

'Doing it now, sir,' he called back. 'Quartermaster, steer a course bearing zero seven zero. Maximum revolutions.'

Then he started checking his calculation again because what if he was wrong? He jotted down a couple of numbers on a notepad but, as much as anything else, the lack of Dollimore screaming at him from the bridge told him he had done the right thing. He relaxed. It just remained now to study the chart and make any minor corrections and, yes, Peterson would soon be there to talk to.

A short while later, with a heavy sea crashing every so often over the fo'c'sle, some of the officers met with Dollimore in the shelter of the unused admiral's bridge. The wind and periodic drift of snow made the main bridge unsuitable for this talk. He informed them, 'We should make contact with the *Godham* and her adversary in a little over an hour, though more likely we'll be staring at an empty sea.'

'What do you mean?' Crawshaw enquired, his face blank.

Dollimore looked at him askance, loving every time that the commander could not quite follow his thinking. 'Nunn is up against a *Deuschland* Class Battlecruiser and two destroyers. The *Godham* is not as powerful as all that. She is also the squadron's oldest and slowest ship. Now you do the calculations.'

Crawshaw shook his head. 'I hate it when you talk like this, sir, because you're always bloody well right.'

Suddenly looking very serious, Dollimore said, 'God willing, today I hope I'm very, very wrong.'

Once back in his command position above, Dollimore picked the microphone up from its holder within the bridge casing and tried to shelter himself in such a way that the wind would not run across the mouthpiece. It was time to let the rest of the ship's company know what they were involved in. 'Do you hear there? This is the captain speaking,' his voice resounded throughout the ship. 'By now you will all be aware that we have altered course and increased our speed. We have recently received a signal that the flagship has sighted the enemy and is currently engaged with a heavy surface unit. Our job is to close and support our shipmates as they undoubtedly would do for us. We have all trained together these last months, we all know each other and know that we are strong enough to carry this fight to a successful conclusion. Remember our motto: *Forward without fear or regret*. God be with us all.'

Now, with the *Trier Stern* having dropped out of sight in the grey vastness of this horrible winter, Dollimore thought through the possibilities and continued to pray fervently to God that the Royal Navy would not be short yet another major warship this day.

*

'Keep vigilant please, gentlemen,' said Lieutenant Eddington to young Clark and Sergeant Burroughs after they had digested the signal from the *Burscombe* and watched as she steamed away into the distance at speed. He then made his way back to the bridge where he found everything much as he had left it a couple of hours before. The young marine, watchful and steadfast, was still standing guard by the helmsman while Barrett kept his eye on the compass.

Eddington said to the latter, 'It's about time you got some sleep,' he said.

'I'll be alright 'til the rendezvous, sir,' Barrett replied. 'Ain't been gettin' no f... trouble from this'un either.' He motioned to Captain Hartman who was fast asleep in the corner of the bridge, sitting on a stool and propped up against the bulkhead. What a mess this man had got himself into.

Eddington walked over and shook him awake. He started talking even before the captain had a chance to register where he was. 'Awfully sorry to bother you, old boy, but I'd like to know about the battlecruiser that you were to meet, your little trip round to Ireland, and where the men you picked up are now.'

'What are you talking about?' groaned Hartman, trying to close his eyes again.

'I'm not a particular fan of mysteries and skulduggery. I have to confess I like to put on a uniform and be up front about things. I like to fight the war properly, fairly, by the rules, you know what I mean?'

'Huh,' said Hartman with disdain. 'Prepare to lose then.'

In the meantime, Clark went back to the saloon. It somehow looked less grand with the poor daylight trying to flood it with greyness. The whole scene was now given an extra slovenly look by the German crew who had all bedded down on the carpeted deck using their coats as blankets. Cups and plates were still strewn across the tables just where they had been left after they had eaten their very early morning meal.

He looked around at the guards who still stood hereabouts with their rifles and bayonets. 'Able Seaman Martin,' he said.

'Yes, sir?' Pincher acknowledged.

'Where's Gordy?'

'He's off watch, sir.'

'Get him. I need him.'

Before long the worried boy was standing before Clark. His hair was an untidy mop and he seemed thoroughly bewildered. He quickly came to attention. In fact Clark was quite taken aback by the boy's earnest stance. 'Relax,' he said. 'I'm not telling you off or anything like that.'

'You look like shit,' Burroughs said to Gordy.

'Aye aye, sir,' replied the lad.

Trying to ignore the sergeant's unnecessary remark, Clark asked of Gordy, 'You're an Irishman, aren't you?'

'Yes, sir.'

'And I'm just hazarding a guess that Ogham is Irish?'

'That's right, sir,' answered Les, more confused now than he ever thought to be.

'Just what is Ogham?'

Les, obviously thinking that the world had gone mad and these men were simply taking the micky out of him, looked from one to the other longing to tell them that this bullying was not on.

But Clark's eyes suddenly flashed with impatience. 'Listen, I don't have all day. There is a potentially dangerous situation here and I need you to tell me what Ogham is.'

Suddenly accepting that the midshipman was really not messing about, Les suddenly brightened up and said, 'Oh. It's a really old alphabet what me and my girlfriend used to use to send secret messages to each other because her parents hated my parents and we didn't want people to know what we were saying to each other. Not many people use it anymore so we could avoid having family quarrels because we were the only ones who could read the message. We'd tell each other where to meet and we could say that we loved each other without our parents finding out and giving us a proper hiding. She was a fine lass, my girlfriend, that is.'

Clark stared at him for a couple of seconds, trying to sift out the relevant information from all that he was being told. Such was the flood of words and thoughts from this boy, who rarely spoke or thought, that everything had spilled out in a muddle. 'Right,' said Clark, 'that makes some sense.'

Burroughs stared at him aghast and said, 'It does?'

'The point is,' Clark went on at Les, 'that last night you said that it had been a long time since you'd seen Ogham. So one of these chaps over here has a document with Ogham script on it? An Irish alphabet rarely used that you can read? Have I got that correct?'

'Aye.'

'A code!' blurted out Burroughs, finally catching on.

'Yes,' said Clark. 'It's lucky you're with us, Gordy. This fits perfectly with the other information we have. Who better to figure out what the Irish are up to than an Irishman. Thank you again, Gordy.'

Les smiled just for a moment thinking on that, even if he could not work out what it was all about. He had been on tenterhooks ever since Bonner had left the *Burscombe*. The rough Scotsman had been a complete git but he had been the only person who had shown him how to do anything. Life had been one long mass of confusion since then but now he had got something right, something significant it would seem.

Clark stepped carefully over the mounds of sleeping men on the deck and looked at each one. Eventually he saw one face, pointed, and said, 'Gordy, this was the one, wasn't it?'

'Aye.'

Clark prodded the man's arm and as the form grunted and stirred, he said gently, 'Do you mind, sir, coming with me for a few minutes? Speak any English?'

The young man sat up and muttered a few things in German with an expression somewhere between disorientation and anger.

'Well, in that case, I must compel you,' said Clark, none the wiser to the mutterings. He grabbed the man by the arm and hauled him to his feet. The protests and general scuffle began to disturb other men around him and they began to look up and rise from the deck, wondering what bad tidings had pulled them from their sleep.

As Clark led him towards the door one older man with an impressively large black moustache, carefully combed and pointed upwards at the sides, stood up and began voicing something forcefully in his own tongue, which led Pincher to step forward with the point of his bayonet levelled at his stomach. 'Pipe down, Herman, or it won't go well for yer.'

Burroughs, surprised but satisfied with the way things were progressing, followed Clark and the young German from the saloon, leaving the four guards and Les trying to quieten the remaining detainees down.

After this pacification had been achieved, fortunately by words and implied threats only, Pincher looked at Les with a beaming smile and said, 'You are a gem! Javert woulda been proud of yer! You've actually got a girlfriend?'

'Who's Javert?' asked Les.

'Have you even read *Les Misérables*?'

When Clark and Burroughs appeared in the bridge with their suspect, Hartman tutted and sighed, giving the man an accusing stare. Eddington noted that with interest.

Looking at the name in the passport he had taken, Clark said, 'This is Wolfgang Rodenberger. He is one of the men picked up from the boat off the coast of Ireland but he doesn't seem to speak any English.' With that he gave a look of deference to the lieutenant, not wanting to take over too much.

'I see,' said Eddington. To Hartman he said, 'There, the truth is coming out whether you like it or not. Now you will translate for us. Mr Clark, if you please?'

'Thank you, sir.' Clark then said to the captain, 'Tell him I know about the other document that was with his papers last night and that I want to know what he did with it. Then one of you will tell me where the two missing men are to be found.'

Without bothering to translate a thing, Hartman laughed and said, 'What's the word for this? Fanciful? You do not have a clue what you're talking about.'

Eddington frowned. 'Your story about New York stunk the moment it came out of your mouth. Now we'll have the truth, please.'

'Under the Geneva Convention you have no right to be treating us like this,' said Hartman.

Clark suddenly went on, without any further deference to his commanding officer, 'I would wholeheartedly agree with you if I thought you were a normal civilian crew going about your lawful business. Even if you were carrying reservists or combatants I would accord you all the respect of the Geneva Convention, but there is something much more sinister going on here and, until you produce the two missing men, you will be treated as spies.'

'Not spies!' shouted Hartman, suddenly clenching his fists and shaking with rage. Then he launched into a vengeful diatribe in German against Rodenberger, who said nothing but simply stared back with icy hatred.

Barrett, stunned at what was taking place in front of him, said, 'Sir, I understood one or two words o' what he was sayin'. He seems to be cursin' him for a Nazi scum.'

Hartman glanced at Barrett then back at Clark, saying, 'Yes, I curse him and all his kind.' He looked at the deck and rubbed his dirty forehead in vexation. 'But still I cannot tell you anything. They will kill my parents. There, Mr Eddington, is the real difference between democracy and fascism.'

'Then I cannot vouch for how you will be treated when we land at Kirkwall, captain,' Eddington informed him in a melancholy fashion. 'You or any of your men. We have the whole story except for why the other passenger, Gurtner, is so important and where he is hiding. When the authorities strip the ship out from stem to stern, they will be found and you will all stand trial. Believe me, it doesn't look good, captain.'

Clark immediately took up the proceedings with, 'What is clear is that you've disguised your ship as a Norwegian, taking on an alias for yourself – Mr Halvorson – and have journeyed to the west coast of Ireland where you picked up two passengers, this man Rodenberger here being one of them. Now, he was daft enough to let one of my men see a secret document which was written in an ancient and redundant Irish alphabet. It must be something of some importance to the Nazis as he's now taken such great pains to hide or destroy it. In the meantime, Herr Gurtner has concealed himself somewhere along with the man who is really in charge of this covert little operation – Fleischer, the man you argued with when we stopped you last evening – and still hopes to evade capture and get away somehow.

'All of this would have worked but for a couple of things which went against you. First and foremost was the fact that it was us, the *Burscombe*, which sighted you and, of course, we had already got a good look at you back in August. If you had been stopped by any other ship and even boarded you may have got away with the ruse by use of your fake list of Norwegian names which covered everybody, including the two men you picked up. Admittedly, you kept this corresponding German list to try and cover yourself against accusations of spying but then Fleischer, in his wisdom, decided to break from the plan, thus creating the situation that we have now.

'Lastly, one of the reasons why you thought you could run and get away with it yesterday was because you were due to rendezvous with an escort a few miles from here. Unfortunately for you and the German war machine, that escort – that battlecruiser – is under attack by Royal Navy ships as we speak. Your whole plan has been scuppered.'

Hartman looked to Eddington and motioned at Clark, 'Lieutenant, this is a boy truly to be feared. One should not take him for a fool lightly.'

Clark was quite suddenly struck by those words. Anybody else would have accepted the compliment but his mind just filled with images of his father, mother and sister. They had all taken him for a fool and he was not convinced that they had been wrong. Now Farlow thought he had something on him, too. He needed to put a stop to it, all of it.

*

The *Godham* had received no less than five direct hits so far. Fires raged within her stressed hull and superstructures and an angry, frightened, but resilient crew were trying with all their remaining strength to put aside the fact that many dead and injured comrades were lying all about them immersed in the grizzly smell of burnt flesh and steel.

The high explosives that had burst inside her delicate frame had caused some significant difficulties and the metal splinters from the near misses that had erupted in the water had made things that much worse. Her grey hull which the men had once so carefully painted and treated for rust was now savagely pock-marked by blackened gashes where those splinters had either glanced off or burst through the armour. It seemed that only half the fire hoses were serviceable now thanks to the number of pipes that were cracked. Water from the mains had begun to flow along the inner decks and it was all mixed in with leaking oil. Keeping the boilers and engines running at close to full pelt for nearly an hour had been the only thing keeping the enclosed men from thinking about the hideous fight going on outside the steel walls.

Captain Nunn was sitting in his chair up on the bridge gritting his teeth in pain. One of the shells that had landed in the water in that last straddle had thrown up a splinter that had ripped through the back of his duffle coat from left to right, tearing open his skin. It had very narrowly missed damaging his spine. The strange thing was that he had not felt it at first. Having been so preoccupied with dodging the enemy and trying to throw some weight of shells back at them, it had taken the navigating officer to point out that he had been hurt. But now his attention brought to it, he could feel the pain creeping up on him making his legs become weak so he propped himself up in the seat and continued to give orders. One of the most important he gave was to the rating standing at his right: 'If I lose consciousness it's your job to let the commander know to take over.' As an afterthought he added, 'And you can let the admiral know also.'

There had been two very short lulls in the fight when brief snow showers had passed them by and obscured their vision, but each time the bad weather passed on its way and the protagonists caught sight of each other again, they restarted their uneven match.

From all reports so far one would have thought that it was a completely one-sided contest but the *Godham* had scored some successes too. With the aft turrets used mostly, and consequently running out of ammunition, her 8-inch shells crashed many times about the German superstructure; but unfortunately they could do nothing at all to the machinery within her. To emphasise this point the gunnery officer reported in dismay that he had observed their shells to be bouncing off the enemy's hull.

Nunn had also been informed that his portside torpedo tubes had already been put out of action by one of those direct hits and, with the manoeuvres they were making in order to close the range on the *Burscombe*, they were never in a position to line up the starboard tubes. There was nothing for it but to snake their way at high speed on this general course, getting in a few broadsides when the opportunities presented themselves, laying down a few smoke screens and hoping that they would see the friendly vessel ahead before they died.

Suddenly another plunging shell slammed into the deck on the ravaged portside next to the funnels. This time the explosives found the last pipes which were feeding oil to the furnaces and amidst the aftermath of bent machinery, fire, smoke, blood and bodies, a mortally wounded stoker observed through blurred eyes the needle on the pressure gauge dropping back to zero. Then the lights went out.

His head spinning due to loss of blood, Captain Nunn became aware that the ship was dying underneath him. He did not need the Officer-of-the-Watch to tell him that they had lost all steam and electricity and that, to all intents and purposes, the game was up. There was nothing more to do now but accept the inevitable.

*

Nearly an hour after the first 'enemy sighted' signal had been received on board the *Burscombe* they intercepted another from their beleaguered friend identifying this *Deuschland* class battlecruiser as the *Moltke*.

'Good to know exactly what we're dealing with,' said Crawshaw, rubbing sleep from the corners of his eyes and feeling the ice from his cuffs burn his cheeks. 'Makes the revenge a bit more personal, don't you think?'

'Forget the revenge,' said Dollimore. 'Only professionalism will win the day.'

'Oh, come off it, sir.' Crawshaw had never fully understood the Old Man and he could not help but feel that their relationship was still soured by those memories of the stupidities of their youth. 'You can't tell me that you don't want to make them pay for what they almost did to your son.'

Dollimore's temper snapped. 'I keep my personal feelings quite separate from the task in hand and I advise you to do the same!'

'Yes, sir,' answered Crawshaw in reluctant submission as a couple of lookouts turned to see what was going on.

Then, astonishingly, the captain was suddenly back to his old calm self again, saying, 'Now, when we arrive, if Nunn still lives then my intention is that we should attack the *Moltke* as two separate divisions on opposite beams. That will divide his fire.'

'But Admiral Clark has always favoured the line ahead formation,' said Crawshaw. 'He will be expecting us to conform to him.'

'That would probably be ideal if we had the *Farecombe* with us but we don't. However, now is not the time to comment on the current dispositions of the squadron. Forbes knows my mind on that subject.'

I bet he does, thought Crawshaw.

Dollimore continued, 'All I want is the Moltke's guns divided or trained firmly in one direction while whichever of us is least affected destroys him.'

'Sounds a bit risky to me, sir.'

'The risk is very great,' agreed Dollimore, smiling at the discomfort of the other men around him. 'But the Hun has shown repeatedly that he is prepared to take such risks, so we must be, too.'

'And what of the destroyers, sir?'

'Simple. We give them a hard time too.' As the wind whistled and splashed the flying spray around the pitching deck, Dollimore gave an odd smile of something quite uncharacteristically wicked. From that it was possible to pity the men of the *Moltke*.

Peterson was the first one to match Dollimore's smile and, when Crawshaw and Digby observed this, they smiled too. Only Irwin's face stayed serious. Solid as he was in his aim at what he was trying to do, if not in what he was actually doing, he was the only one who could not see what was so pleasing about all this.

Then Lieutenant Hanwell appeared on the bridge dressed in his flight suit and thick leather coat. His goggles, worn atop his head, already had ice forming on the lenses and his face was an awful picture of seasickness. 'You wanted to see me, sir?'

'Ah, Hanwell,' said Dollimore. 'Now's the time to start earning your pay. The enemy is not too far off now but the co-ordinates we have are only dead reckoning. I need you up there looking for him and, once battle has been joined, I may need you to spot for us if we get blinded by snow squalls and the like. Do you understand?'

'Yes, sir.' Hanwell looked out carefully at the peaks and troughs of the shifting sea and then back down behind the superstructure at the Walrus with its clumsy double wings and ridiculously large tail. Its ailerons and rudder were shaking with the buffeting of the wind and the whole aircraft looked like it was about to topple from its perch on the catapult.

Dollimore instinctively knew the man's fears and said, 'Don't worry about trying to get back to us, Hanwell. I know as well as anyone that the Walrus can't be landed in this weather. Keep an eye on your fuel and make sure you can reach Sullom Voe. Do I make myself clear?'

'Yes, sir,' said Hanwell, saluting with a grin while at the same time trying not to retch. 'Just glad to finally be of use.'

'Godspeed.'

The great thing was that both plane and machinery were stronger than they appeared. Even though the ship rolled heavily with spray and wind lashing the flight deck, the operation was not to be hampered. The catapult was extended over the side, the plane's engines were revved up, and then it was fired off the deck by the small explosive charge contained just below. A strong wind immediately made the port wings rise up almost uncontrollably, making it look as though the plane was about to dive straight into the sea, but then suddenly the machine was climbing, taking Hanwell and his two observers up to look for the fight.

*

Downcast by the way everything had gone wrong and concerned by the tenacious young midshipman's logic, Captain Hartman reluctantly gave up the location of the two men hiding inside the *Trier Stern*, though not before Rodenberger the Nazi was removed from the bridge. They were, he said, hiding in the tiller flat deep in the stern. Then he collapsed on his stool, completely deflated, hoping beyond hope that the Gestapo back home would not equate this failure to anything he had done and punish his parents.

Young Clark, Sergeant Burroughs, Pincher, Les and two marines were now heading towards the tiller flat ready to finish off this sordid little business. They each had rifles or revolvers at the ready, for if these men hiding back there had the least notion that they were going to escape then they might be prepared to behave in quite a desperate manner. From the sound of it this especially applied to Fleischer, the man behind the whole operation, and the only one amongst them whom they suspected was a true thug.

Not wanting to take Hartman along, they obtained from him a copy of the ship's plans so that they could be sure of where the access to the flat was. It was essential that they approach without making too much noise by stomping about the passageways in uncertainty. They reached the stern by walking through the creaking interior of the ship and slowed with caution as they approached the hatch in question.

The dimly-lit passageway ahead was swaying with the ship's gradual roll and they immediately understood why Fleischer would want to hide here. It was so far away from bridge, saloon, engines and hold that secrecy and concealment was a real possibility. They also noted straight away that though the hatch was closed, the locking clips were not in place. It had been opened fairly recently.

'It's a fair bet that Hartman's not fobbing us off again then,' said Clark.

'How would you like to go about getting them out, sir?' asked Burroughs. He had more than one idea about how to do it but after watching the way the midshipman had been handling the whole situation, he was quite happy to defer to him.

'That's why I brought this down with me,' Clark replied, producing a flare gun from the satchel that he had picked up from the bridge. To Pincher he said, 'Just nip along the passage there and unreel the fire hose. Just in case.'

Pincher was gone in a flash.

Clark continued, 'The risk of fire shouldn't be too great, however. The plans show that the tiller machinery is set back a little way from the shaft. It'll be the smoke that drives the buggers out.'

'But if not?' asked Burroughs.

'Then I'll go in and get them out,' Clark replied, as though it was obvious.

'Look, er, begging your pardon on this, sir. Me and *my* boys should be the ones to do that. It's what we do.'

Clark shot Burroughs a look of annoyance. How dare the man question him? But then he noticed the earnest expressions that all three marines had on their faces and it made him soften up. They were right. He realised in that moment that they had complete trust in him, that they respected the way in which he had sorted out this whole affair, and that if harm was to come to anyone then it should not be him. In this way these men would serve their purpose and he would be preserved to see the matter through to the end.

He thought back to when he first joined the ship's company, hardly trusted and under constant scrutiny for his terrible track record. It had all been his own fault, of course. He knew that but being here in this place and having come this far, he understood it all now. He was comfortable commanding these men and they were comfortable being commanded by him. It was just surprising that it should be this simple.

Pincher came trundling back along the passageway in the half-light dragging the hose with him.

Clark said, 'Gordy, get ready to give us some water pressure if we need it.'

Then, with Les standing by the handwheel, Clark ordered, 'Let's do this.'

Burroughs grabbed the handle of the heavy metal hatch and yanked it open with all his strength, then Clark stepped forward and fired a flare into the black shaft which opened out below. All the while the marines stood with their rifles at the ready, the muzzles trained carefully on the new opening. The green flash from inside the hatch made them all wince and Clark felt a brief blast of heat rush across his face as he stepped back and to the side.

As the eerie glow burned into a crescendo of fizzing and gurgling, there came the sound of shouts and coughing from below. That had been the response hoped for. The two Germans just had to come spluttering out of the hatch now for the job to be complete. The seconds ticked by with the coughing and cursing becoming ever more intense down below. The smoke even began to make Clark's eyes water and constrict his throat but still nobody came up. Eventually the flare burned itself out and the opening returned back to its previous blackness, though now permeated with this fouled air.

Still hearing the gasps and foreign chatter of the men within, Clark said to Burroughs, 'Give the smoke a chance to clear a little before you go in. No point in you being asphyxiated, too.'

'Aye, sir.' He took a deep breath and after a reasonable pause, motioned to his men to move forward to the hatch. Putting his rifle through the misty opening first, he then leaned in, shining a torch ahead of him. The smoke swirled in the new light and he saw that the shaft leading downwards was very much a grease-smeared pit with only a single thin ladder with which to negotiate the ten foot descent. Though he could hear the men inside, they were staying out of sight. 'Come on out, you buggers!' he called down. 'This is the only chance you're gonna get!'

Still there was no movement.

'Right then.' With the expiry of patience and full determination, he swung his legs over the hatch lip and planted his boots onto the ladder. He climbed down as swiftly as he was able to with his rifle slung over his shoulder and the torch in the grip of his right hand, careful that he did not slip thanks to the greasy nature of the rungs. Even as he jumped the last four feet the next marine was on the ladder behind him.

Once on the steel deck he swung round and instantly surveyed the scene before him. Two wretched men, one clad in a black overcoat and the other in a beige duffle coat, stood in the shadows to one side of the compartment. They looked pale and sick, no doubt from the effects of the smoke but most surprising was their submissive manner. They had their hands held up, letting Burroughs know that they were going to cause no further trouble.

Though he demonstrated some disappointment that they had given up so easily, the sergeant was actually highly relieved. Climbing into the compartment into an unknown situation had left him in a very compromising position, but fortunately these men had realised that they had stood no chance against whatever retributive force was coming behind him.

He skirted round the side of the machinery, the pipes and gears of the tiller, those which made the turning of the ship's giant rudder manageable, and brought greater illumination onto the two men. The older man stared back at him with no small amount of concern in his expression but the other, he wearing the black overcoat, appeared filled with hate if not resistance. Judging by this and the very neat, short-cropped blond hair, it would be safe to assume that this was the already infamous Fleischer. Well, this was the end of whatever trouble he was getting up to.

By now Burroughs' two colleagues were standing on the deck behind him, their rifles brought to bear. He patted the prisoners' coats in a search for any concealed weapons but there was nothing. Another disappointment. 'Right, come on out,' he commanded them, motioning to the shaft. He stepped ahead of them and called up to Clark, 'I've got two coming out, sir!'

Clark looked closely at them as they emerged from their dirty hole and was immediately struck by the enormity of the result they had achieved here today. The man in the duffle coat had not long ago been in the papers...

With the exception of a defiant gesture shown by Fleischer everything about them was dejection. It struck Clark that they seemed like rats or something just as sinister, but was quickly repulsed by his thoughts. 'Let's get them put into separate cabins under guard,' he said to Pincher and Les.

Almost inaudible with melancholy, Pincher mumbled, 'Aye aye, sir.'

Clark was taken aback. 'Well, what are you so upset about? The plan worked, didn't it?'

'Yes, sir. I just didn't get a chance to hose the bastards down.'

As they bundled their prisoners off down the passageway, Clark secretly grinned, knowing that they had just removed a couple of serious enemies from circulation in this war. Everybody had played their part well, including the strange boy Les. Clark said to him, 'Gordy, you must give my compliments to your girlfriend when you get the chance.'

Les turned back and furrowed his brow, 'Well, she's not my girlfriend anymore, sir. It didn't end well.'

'Oh,' Clark replied, his face turned blank. Then turning back to the matter in hand, he called down to Burroughs, 'Sergeant, search the compartment for any weapons or intelligence before you come up.'

'Already on it, sir,' came the tinny reply.

Chapter Fifteen

Dollimore's Greatest Confrontation

How could Rear-Admiral Clark be anything but furious at the betrayal? He had been prepared to die in action today so that his reputation would be one of inspiration forever. But at the moment of truth it had all been taken away from him. Now he would always be remembered as the admiral who was unable to resist when he was sent off the bridge by his coward of a flag captain and his ship would have the distinction of being destroyed in flight instead of in pitched battle.

As he lay on his bunk with the sound and shuddering of battle going on all around him, his breathing was gradually becoming more and more laboured. The weight of this inglorious end was suffocating him and he found that he had no more fight left in him.

He began to picture David gloating over what had happened here. That misguided boy would probably feel vindicated in the volatile stance he had always taken against his own. This sort of ridicule was what he had aimed for all his life. If there is one thing I should have done, Harper thought, I should have made Dorothy abort that unwanted sprog.

Her lack of appreciation for the sanctity of marriage and the whole life of that damned boy had blemished what had otherwise been a strangely charmed life, but now a new and bitter truth was gnawing away at him. Although the decisions he had made over the years had always been sound, allowing him to hold his head high and lord it over others, those decisions had only carried small risks. The choices put before him had never been a matter of life and death until this new war had come about. But it had come much too late in his life.

His muscles became more tense as his face flushed with the struggle to get enough oxygen through to his brain. The thought that was torturing him now was of that other captain, Charles Dollimore. The man had not put a foot wrong since he had taken command of the *Burscombe*, but how could that be? Was he not the same impetuous fool whose ship had sliced a submarine in half in the calm of the Clyde? Was he not the same man who was distrusted by the Admiralty and kept ashore for six years?

How was it he had got such a prestigious command? How was it that he had sneaked his ship through the Pentland Firth under the nose of the entire fleet? How was it that he had seen straight through the *Hoddøyafjord - Trier Stern* deception when he had not? How was it that David spoke of *him* as though he was a father figure?

As the expiring admiral gasped for another breath, a most alarming possibility entered his mind. It was all my fault. Why did I never have the ability to live up to the Clark family name..?

At first the seamen standing guard outside were glad that he had quietened down, and had stopped shouting threats at them through the door. With that they breathed a sigh of relief because, amused as they were at the situation, they had no particular desire to insult the man any more than they had. As much as anything else the *Godham* had begun taking hits and they had become acutely aware of the fact that they would have preferred to be back where they belonged, on the bridge and helping to fight the ship.

The battle seemed to be going on forever and terrible things were going on down below. Smoke billowed through the passageways and they could hear the shouts of orders and the screams of pain. With every reverberation shimmering through the hull they had the growing sense that each minute might be their last.

Then, following the rumble and shock of a terrific explosion somewhere inside the Godham's battered framework, the old girl seemed to groan and suddenly they were left in darkness. With the sounds of the machinery and generators abruptly absent, the pain of the wounded and the desperation of the damage control parties were magnified tenfold.

As the emergency lamps slowly came to life, one of the guards pointed at the admiral's cabin door and, close to panic, declared, 'Prisoners are supposed to be set free at times like this.'

'He's not a prisoner,' said the other, also unable to hide his growing fear. 'Not really.'

'So let's let him out, then.'

'I'll go with that.'

No officer was coming back to tell them otherwise. All hell had broken loose and they were forgotten, so this was their only course of action. With the ship floating dead in the water they would be destroyed but they would be damned if they would die in here when there was a chance for life just one hatch away. Just to let the admiral out first...,

One of them opened the door and looked in. By the poor light of day which came in through the scuttle they could see him sleeping peacefully on the bunk. He seemed to have laid down on top of the blanket fully clothed and just nodded off. How could that be normal with the whole world exploding just outside the bulkhead?

'Sir,' said the guard, shaking him.

Clark did not stir and his skin was already cool to the touch.

'Snakes alive!

*

It was only a couple of minutes after Dollimore received the radio message that had come down from Hanwell in his tormented Walrus, which had him steer the *Burscombe* onto a slightly new course, that some lazy, mixed-calibre gunfire could be heard above the wind and the crash of the bow wave. His lookouts strained their eyes for every scrap of sight or perception but the patchy fog and snow was enough to blot out what lay more than three miles ahead. Even though the conditions made it impossible to gauge the exact bearing of the sound, Dollimore knew that battle would be joined shortly. The men had long since been called to Action Stations so everybody was committed and ready.

'Sir,' came a voice from below. It was calm, the way Dollimore liked it. 'Another message from our Walrus. "The *Godham* is dead in the water. I have taken fire, no damage."' He then reiterated the position as best as it could be plotted.

'Very good.' Dollimore and the others continued looking through their binoculars at the indistinct horizon. So, the *Godham* was dead in the water, a sitting duck in the middle of a crisis. That eventuality ranked high on the list of any captain's worst nightmares, and one of the reasons why they had made such a fuss when the *Burscombe* had suddenly lost power during her trials.

What was more, Dollimore would not now be able to attack the *Moltke* and her escorts as one of two divisions. He was going it alone. He glanced around the bridge and noticed Peterson and Digby looking at him. They knew that they were in trouble but then their expressions also told him of the complete confidence that they had in him. This venture was now turning into something more reckless than considered but as long as the *Godham* was afloat, how could he leave them? This was going to take all of his skill and judgment.

Sitting, shivering many feet above the Director Control Tower, Smudge might have a chance to spot the enemy first and he would not be mistaken. He had the quality of sureness and self-belief which would prevent him from making something out of nothing so whatever he reported would be accurate. His moment came when he spied a weak flash of light in the gloom to finally compliment the gunfire that they had been hearing. 'Gunfire, green zero one five,' he immediately called down.

Dollimore turned the *Burscombe* onto the new heading.

In the turrets, the men's sweat had already half chilled them as they waited patiently, their first rounds of shells and cordite made ready in the breaches of the big guns. Droplets of condensation, the moisture from the thirty plus men in each turret, started forming and dripping from the white painted deckheads but nobody paid them any mind. Some men looked at their watches and thought on the fact that the moment of truth was too slow in coming.

Down in the machinery spaces it was simpler still. It was nothing more than keeping the engines running at full speed for as long as required, checking the valves and pressures for the oil flows and the throttles for superheated steam being forced onto the turbines. There was a vague worry that the ship was being stressed a little too much by the sea, but closed in behind these sealed hatches underneath the waterline, the men just continued working, checking and monitoring. The world of guns, wind, the salty sea and the agony of the wait to open fire was just a distant idea.

Bretonworth stood in his usual place in the centre of the forward engine room listening to the higher, but by no means insufferable, whine of the spinning turbines. He was happy. The builders had done their job well. He also noted with pleasure that their most experienced petty officer must be at the helm because he could feel the rudder through the deckplates being controlled to work with the sea. Had there been a less experienced man at the wheel things could have got a bit more rough than they were as the hapless fellow fought with it.

'Bridge, foretop!' Smudge called down, 'Enemy sighted green zero five zero! She appears to be damaged and on fire! No sign of the

Godham or enemy destroyers yet.' He glanced down at the snowy deck below him and saw the officers and lookouts training their binoculars in the direction he had called out.

One or two icicles fell from the DCT as it was corrected to the bearing he had given. It would only be a matter of seconds before they all saw the battlecruiser too. Then little white streams of burning tracer bullets went up into the sky and Smudge saw a small black dot circling above which could only be Hanwell in his flimsy machine. Better him than me, he thought.

Great white battle ensigns showing off England's ancient red cross and union flag were hoisted on the fore and mainmasts and from that moment there was no turning back. The last time Dollimore had seen that was on that very different day when the Grand Fleet had met the High Sea Fleet off Jutland twenty three years ago. With difficulty, he tried to banish all memory of the torn steel and fiery wounds inflicted upon the old *Warspite* and suddenly reasoned that he was still the same frightened man who had faced the big guns in 1916. The only difference was that he now wielded all power as captain. This greater responsibility did wonders to soak up the fear.

'Fire as soon as you have the range,' he told Digby. 'Hopefully they won't see us until we've fired but there'll be something very wrong if they're not expecting us. As soon as you're done I'll be turning to starboard to present a full broadside.'

'Very good, sir,' replied the excited officer. He was thrilled to be in the middle of this great adventure. Having studied the navy's big guns for over a decade he felt it was high time that he was able to test them on a live quarry. His views on these matters were always of the most optimistic kind. He was unshakable on this and as a man who was always thinking ahead he had been careful to make sure he had his camera slung around his neck in its waterproof case. Later on he wanted to get some pictures of the damage they were inflicting.

Suddenly the Burscombe's bow was lifted heavily out of the water by a wave slamming into them from ahead and to port, then the whole thing crashed back down into the next trough. It was a one-off, thank God, but it was enough to send a wave coursing along the port waist almost washing the patient torpedo gunners over the side. When the ship recovered and Dollimore managed to dismiss the sudden thought that perhaps he ought to slow down, they continued on their way. He knew that the slower they were going the more steady the ship would be as a gun platform but the time for that was after the first salvo had gone off, not before. Right now surprise was of the essence.

Two minutes passed between Smudge's initial sighting and the Burscombe's guns opening fire. From that moment the AB relaxed. He was happy with the part he had played thus far and now he just needed to continue looking out for those two destroyers and the *Godham*, if she still lived. While watching the battlecruiser coming and going between the drifting mist and snow showers with her rumbling guns flashing out every so often, he relaxed his posture slightly. He had allowed Burscombe's Fire Control to get ready with the saving of valuable seconds.

The team in the DCT had spent the last few seconds before firing assessing the target and passing down a steady stream of instructions to the marines standing around the Fire Control Table. When courses, speeds, wind speeds and air pressure had been entered into the mechanical computer, it calculated the deflection correction – where the *Moltke* was likely to be in a few seconds time – and the aiming instructions were then sent to the layers and trainers in the turrets. Smudge's original information had been so helpful that only slight adjustments were required for the guns. So there was not much of what one could call a pause before Burscombe's forward turrets, comprising of eight 6-inch guns, fired their deafening roar of flame and shell.

'Steer starboard zero six five,' ordered Dollimore as soon as the shells were away, 'and give me revolutions for twenty knots.'

The very second the salvo had gone out the gunlayers pulled the levers which allowed the guns to drop back to the horizontal position. A quick blast of air was sent through the smoky breaches to expel any smouldering residual cordite and the loaders were once again making their guns ready with their well-rehearsed timing.

Warrant Officer Hacklett could feel his turret turning hard to port as the men worked with the trays and rammers. So fast and efficient were they that he felt he could shout, 'Good job! You might finally beat that bunch o' schoolgirls in A-Turret!'

As the officers on the bridge watched from a range of about three thousand five hundred yards, the *Moltke* briefly disappeared amongst a burst of geysers that would hopefully be throwing shell splinters all over her decks. As the water fell back and tried to settle, Digby noted that the shells had either straddled the enemy or had fallen near her bow. That was a good opening and he knew that the observers in the DCT would be reporting the fall of shot directly.

Moltke had been moving quite slowly with all her guns pointing in the opposite direction. Even with the Walrus circling high above giving away the fact that there was another ship in the area, she had still somehow not seen the *Burscombe* racing up on her portside.

Less than a minute later the guns erupted again. The flash, noise and smoke of the full sixteen gun broadside were so powerful to those on the bridge that they found themselves wincing and waggling their fingers in their ears.

Having achieved such surprise and still having the upper hand, the crew's collective demeanour had not changed in the slightest from that of conducting a practice shoot. Some of the men even reflected that they had been more afraid of the Luftwaffe bombers that had surprised them a couple of months ago. Back then the *Burscombe* had not managed to hit a thing and the whole squadron had steamed ignominiously home. Today was going to be very different.

Some of the shells from the next broadside were the exact culmination of the previous corrections and crashed down upon the upper decks of the German warship. Strangely, the explosions and puffs of black smoke appeared insignificant at this distance. However, Dollimore knew of the havoc that had been wreaked upon those decks. The bulkheads would be stripped of their paint and holed where the splinters slashed everything open. There would be injured men screaming, others trying to calm them and still more trying to turn the fire hoses onto the conflagrations. So far it had been a textbook slaying but after a fourth broadside the enemy answered them back.

Having recovered from the surprise at being peppered with hot steel from another direction, the Germans had revolved both their triple turrets towards the *Burscombe* and opened fire with their far superior 11-inch guns.

Here it comes, thought Crawshaw, who had been watching all that had been going on from the aft superstructure. This was the moment he had managed to avoid through the entire duration of the last war. Sure, his reputation for personal bravery was solid enough with the saving of those Indian stokers from that burning oil tanker but beyond that he had never been shot at with the big guns before. He gritted his teeth and waited, reassured that Burscombe's own gunners had managed to fire off yet another broadside before the enemy's shells arrived.

Then came the detonations in the water. The sea burst dramatically into the air with an almighty crash but, Crawshaw noted with great relief, the nearest geyser was at least a hundred yards away. The whole attempt at them had landed well off to starboard and only a few pieces of shrapnel had made it anywhere near them. Some of them clattered against the ship's side or slashed the bulkheads near the torpedo gunners but nobody was hurt.

Since she had slowed, the ship's violent ploughing through the waves had lessened somewhat. The effect of this was that it should make her gunnery, which had already been very good, better on account of the ship becoming more stable.

Up on the bridge, Digby grinned and said, 'We got them again, sir! All about the bridge and just forrard!'

Without seeming to register the other's elation, Dollimore said, 'It won't be long until they have us.' He leaned over the voicepipe and called down the order for a turn of one point to port, adding, 'Make smoke!' to cover their movement. Fingers crossed, it should be perfect because the wind was driving at them quite hard on the starboard quarter so they should just about be concealed.

CPO Vincent was one of the men in the forward boiler room who heard the bell ring on the telegraph and looked over to the large circular dial to see the needle swing to 'Make Smoke'. He knew what to do straight away, hardly sparing it a thought. He reached up and immediately opened the nozzle which allowed a jet of slick, non-atomised oil fuel to be pumped onto the flames in the top of the furnace. As the same operation was carried out for each of the four boilers the burning oil turned into clouds of awful, thick black smoke which inevitably began to pour copiously from the funnels and into the open air.

The helmsman in the steering position then turned his wheel and the ship began its manoeuvre. These men below the waterline in their machine filled caverns had heard the explosions in the water and fully realised that small pieces of hot steel were striking the side of the ship, but there was no point in dwelling upon it. The incessant exercising that had so often made them curse the officers now worked to keep them calm and fill them with a positive sense of interdependency. At the crucial moment all that the captain had hoped for had been achieved.

The smoke that was pouring out of the funnels billowed all around the upper decks, drifting about the stern of the ship, then was pushed further along in an easterly direction in this thirty knot wind. The *Burscombe* was neatly enveloped.

Everyone on the bridge got a heavy dose of the filthy, black cloud as it poured across their position leaving them coughing, spluttering and daring a profanity or two. Still, it was better to be breathing this muck for a couple of short minutes than allowing the gunners opposite to get the exact range and blast them to oblivion.

*

Completely obscured from the Burscombe's lookouts by the inclement weather, the two German destroyers almost casually slipped into their unopposed attack positions against the flaming hulk of the *Godham* and each fired a spread of torpedoes.

Despair filled Captain Nunn's heart. The pain in his back and the loss of blood had finally served to close his mind to the courageous conclusion that he had sought from this fight and fell dead from the splintered chair. The rating standing nearby, half mad with the hopelessness of it all, watched him flop into the red and black snow. Then two giant explosions rocked the deck into impossibly violent spasms and the winter wind suddenly blew hot. Steel, wood and bodies flew in every direction as a result of this man-made hell.

To add to all his other woes, the rating was knocked almost senseless, but even in the midst of this turmoil he remembered the captain's instructions and started on his way to the aft superstructure to inform the commander of his new situation. To deliver the message was the only thing that seemed to give him purpose and the blur of dying men, fire and twisted metal passed by with a bizarre insignificance. Ultimately, it hardly registered with him that the deck was tilting and that the sea was rushing up to meet him in all its churning fury.

The Godham's bow sunk beneath the waves and everything else was dragged down mercilessly as her aging frames split and the sea entered each compromised compartment. The rating hardly comprehended that he was not a victim of the suction, of water trying to enter the wreck. An explosion beneath the surface served to push him clear of the doomed ship, leaving him in the cold greyness, his head half-submerged. He probably would have succumbed there and then had it not been for somebody's strong hand hauling him up onto the relative safety of a Carley Float.

'I've got you, lad,' said a voice. But for the distinctive tones he would have never have recognised the commander, so wretched was he in his oil soaked condition.

'Sir,' said the rating weakly, 'The captain's dead. He wants you to take over.'

'Don't you worry about any of that,' said the commander. 'Everything's fine now.'

*

On the Burscombe's bridge, Dollimore nodded through a short cough. 'Well, we've given the Hun something to think about and now I think it's time we gave him a bit more. Guns, I need swift action as soon as we clear the smoke.'

'Of course, sir,' Digby replied. He had noted the enemy's last position and had briefly conferred with Peterson on where they would likely be next time they saw them. Hopefully their target would be beam on for another broadside. They pointed the DCT and guns to the bearing decided upon and waited.

'Stop smoke!' ordered Dollimore.

Down below the order was rung up on the telegraph. Vincent and his colleagues cut off the relevant oil flows while other stokers peered through the periscopes into the bases of the funnels or the spyholes into the furnaces. Making minor adjustments they quickly achieved the balance of oil and air which converted the exhaust gasses in the uptakes from black to clear.

The smoke swiftly cleared from around the bridge and Fire Control but Digby gave a quick gasp of surprise with a very audible, 'Christ!' The sight that had greeted them was of the *Moltke* racing straight towards them, throwing out a tremendous white bow wave. With her dark grey paint becoming less of a shadow, her wide beam was slanted at an angle to port, making her masts seem to lean right over. At this range of about three thousand yards her huge guns did not require much elevation.

Dollimore had been initially surprised too but Digby's involuntary outburst had instantly made him remember who he was and where he was. He cast the man an annoyed look and said, 'Please do not take the Lord's name in vain!'

'Sorry, sir.'

'And do take the trouble to open fire when ready.' He said that more to demonstrate that the enemy had not put him off his stride than to push his guns along. He knew that everything that could be done was being done, but he also knew that a little show of imperturbability would go down well. He had always been a firm believer that if the captain was alright then the rest of the men would also be alright.

The big guns fired once more with their hot, air-displacing thunder and he noticed that the *Moltke* had fired at exactly the same moment. This was going to be a very hot contest. But let's hope, he thought, that our sixteen shells have more effect than their three. 'Steer port zero six zero!' he called down the voicepipe. Then to Digby, who was looking at him with a worried frown, he said, 'Make ready to fire off the portside torpedoes.'

Digby sent the relevant orders down to Lt-Cdr Gailey in the waist but could not help feeling an inner surge of worry. Fire off the torpedoes they might but it was a notoriously inaccurate weapon and to do this they were presenting the *Burscombe* as a target for the enemy's full broadside.

'Please don't look so worried,' said Dollimore. 'Captain Nunn has softened her up superbly.' But where was Nunn? There had still been no sign of the *Godham*. Also, what about those destroyers? He was uneasy with the implications of his thoughts.

As soon as he had said those words, which incidentally were having a calming effect on those about him, the ship was rocked by a huge explosion. A pillar of fire leapt skyward, forward of the bridge, with such a wave of heat that it made everybody duck behind the casing. They heard the clattering of shell splinters hitting steel somewhere in front of them but fortunately nothing fell amongst them. Dollimore was on his feet, first leaning over the front of the bridge, staring down at the flames and thick smoke which were pouring out of the port side of the ship and whipping up furiously across the guns of A-Turret.

At the same moment those very guns fired, pushing the inferno out across the water for a few brief seconds before the wind pushed them back again. For the first time Dollimore put his hands up to his ears and sighed heavily. Then he straightened his back to retain full control of himself. He gave no orders. The gunners were taking care of themselves. Similarly the torpedo crew was taking care of itself, and the damage control party would report on what had happened below when they were able.

The gunners, sweating in their turrets, continued to load and make ready to fire. It was hard, blind work and there was not even any time to imagine what damage they were inflicting. That was one of the strange things about their lot. They would know nothing unless something actually hit them.

When those last splinters clattered menacingly against the armour of B-Turret, a couple of the men exchanged worried glances, for it sounded like it might be too easy for the steel to open up.

Warrant Officer Hacklett smiled for the first time since he had joined the ship and told them, 'Jerry can't get you. There's none of you knows him like I do. He tried to get me once or twice before and I'm not having none of it.'

No one in the world was more convincing than this frightening man with the scarred, twisted face. He made them believe that they would survive the day, that the *Burscombe* could withstand all that the enemy had in store for them. They fought on confidently even with the knowledge that something terrible must have happened a couple of decks below them.

The armoured plating that the ship was fitted with extended from A-Turret to Y-Turret and was comprised of no more than four and a half inches of steel. It was intended to encompass and protect the ship's vital magazines and machinery and would comfortably absorb the impact of a 6-inch shell, and maybe even an 8-inch, but the assault of an 11-inch shell was just too much for it to bear. This was the only real failing of this otherwise wonderful ship. However, it would be pointless to argue that these cruisers needed extra protection. After considerations of speed, stability, international weight limitations and figuring out just what the government was prepared to pay for, what you saw was what you got.

That was why it was desirable for them to work in squadrons and not alone.

It was at that dark moment that the message reached the bridge that the *Godham* had been torpedoed by the destroyers and sunk. Hanwell, circling far overhead, had borne shocked witness to the disaster. It was with a heavy heart that Dollimore passed on the news to those standing around him. 'There's no reason to keep throwing more ships at the *Moltke* in such a piecemeal fashion,' he added. 'Forbes is hours away yet.' Then he quickly dictated a message for the distant Admiral. '"*Godham* sunk. I am breaking off the action. Will continue to report on *Moltke's* position." And give our present position.'

'Aye aye, sir,' answered his runner, who immediately raced off to the wireless office.

'Gentlemen, we will retire as soon as our torpedoes are away.'

*

Directed from No 1 Damage Control Base, men went forward along 2 Deck discovering fires burning and evidence of serious destruction in sections C and D. These were the messdecks straddling the circular barbette upon which A-Turret sat and those immediately forrard. Another report stated that the fire was equally bad just below.

CPO Doyle had his assembled team don their breathing apparatus and ordered a couple of hoses made ready before venturing through the next hatch. The hoses had already been attached to the hydrants when the ship had been called to Action Stations. It was now just a matter of turning the handwheels and directing the spouts.

Looking other-worldly in their goggles, masks and white anti-flash hoods, the team waited while Doyle unclipped the hatch. His greasy white asbestos-lined gloves prevented his hands from burning on the hot steel as he pushed each clip aside. Before he got to the last two clips Mr Selkirk, the first lieutenant, appeared at his side and shouted, 'Just got word! A-Turret barbette has been pierced and it's getting a little hot in the shell room! They're not out of action yet but they have two casualties down there! We don't have a lot of time!'

'Understood, sir!' answered Doyle.

Just then everything shook with a massive explosive heave and the lights flickered. One of the young men behind him muttered a curse but Doyle said, 'That's just our guns firing, boy! You better start learning to tell the difference!' With that he flung open the hatch and a ball of fire and smoke leapt up to the deckhead.

With Doyle ducking down low, the men behind him already had jets of water trained onto the flames and it was only a matter of seconds before they were stepping into the burning compartment beating the fire back. Benches, tables, lockers, pipes, wood and metal both were splintered and aflame. Parts of them glowed red such was the intense heat. As they moved further in, the room filled up with as much steam as smoke but they made good headway. As a little of the gloomy daylight started to appear through the jagged splinter holes up ahead, Doyle shouted, 'The fire down below is the highest priority! When I open the next hatch I want your hoses right on the mark!'

With that he made the mistake of kneeling down next to the larger of the two hatches and so immediately needed to take his knees straight off the hot deck. 'Christ!' he cursed, but continuing without a pause, saying, 'Here goes!' he lifted the hatch. Fierce flames and smoke belched through the opening as he ducked to the side, then the water started to do its work.

The guns just overhead went off again, shaking everybody to their bones and making the foetid atmosphere shimmer.

*

Dollimore and all those around him were now drenched by the salt water that had been cascading over them from the last couple of straddling detonations. But that was nothing compared to the splinters of varying sizes slicing through the lifeboats, galley and starboard aircraft hangar. News was coming up of minor casualties down below but he necessarily cast them from his mind. There was no choice but for them to take their proper place in the order of things.

He noted with satisfaction that, although the enemy's range was good, the full complement of shells were not being fired at him. With the ships now beam on to each other, he noticed that the Moltke's aft turret was having difficulty in training about in his direction. I wonder, thought Dollimore, we and the *Godham* must have damaged her more than I thought. At a stretch this might just even things up a bit. Thinking hard about the whereabouts of those destroyers, he began toying with the idea of attempting to destroy this beast before him.

It was time to fire the torpedoes.

Amidst the varying sounds of battle and weather they did not hear the firing of the three small explosive charges down in the port waist, but they did see the splashes of the slithery tin fish hitting the water, pushing ahead and leaving behind their subtle wakes. 'Torpedoes away!' reported Gailey from below.

'Steer starboard one eight zero! Put the wheel hard over!' ordered Dollimore.

As the ship began making a violent turn to the right, Peterson noticed that the enemy was also making a turn to their starboard side. So now the protagonists were moving away from each other. He immediately made the captain aware of it.

Dollimore looked through his binoculars for a couple of seconds then stated, 'She's trying to evade our torpedoes.' He felt a surge of hope within him, a true excitement. Although he could no longer see the tracks of those silent weapons because of the swell, he sensed that they were dead on target.

After leaning heavily over to port the ship had come to the opposite course and yet again the DCT and guns worked furiously to realign themselves. The *Moltke* was presently showing them her stern and was almost invisible due to a fresh snowstorm working its way across from the southwest. There was an air of desperation in the speed she was running but she went on without any explosions being recorded about her waterline.

'Missed!' cried Dollimore, thumping his fists on the bridge casing.

As if to assuage his angry disappointment, Burscombe's guns opened up again. It had taken Digby's men less than ten seconds to calculate the angle of the next broadside and just like that, another sixteen shells were on their way through the air. They scored a couple of hits on the Moltke's aft turret, that which was already in trouble, then she was turning to come back at them again.

After Burscombe's next broadside had been fired, Dollimore gave a minor steering correction to the helmsman and waited as patiently as he could to see what would be the effect of the enemy's next effort, for he had just seen the flashes from her good turret. The answer when it came was awful and disparaging for the men down aft.

With a fiery roar and further wrenching of torn steel the quarterdeck disappeared, but when the smoke cleared over the starboard side in the wind, it revealed damage limited to only half the teak decking. Within the hole created by the shell were flames that told of significant damage having been caused in the officer's cabins flat below. Men from No. 3 Damage Control Base, themselves shocked and half concussed, directed their teams into the inferno, already aware that the men at the emergency steering position were dead.

The report telephoned to the bridge was: 'Emergency steering position destroyed, two casualties, approximately ten cabins and stores on fire. Tiller flat reports all okay. Propeller shafts okay.'

'Lucky,' commented Dollimore.

'Sir!' cried one of the lookouts with quite sudden alarm. Everybody's gaze followed the line of sight indicated by his exaggerated pointing. Dollimore shouted, 'Make your report properly, lad!'

'Destroyers bearing green four five!' Even as he followed the procedure everybody could see the two small vessels, one behind the other, bursting out from the blizzard and turning on a course of interception, trying to get into position to fire their remaining torpedoes.

'Steer two points to port and prepare to fire the starboard torpedoes,' ordered Dollimore, his tone finally rising with the tension.

Digby calmly passed the order and also brought the 4-inch guns into play. The higher, sharper crack of those guns rattled the eardrums as they sent their lethal shells towards the destroyers. These smaller guns were not quite so accurate today as the explosions around their fast little enemies erupted wide of the targets.

Dollimore realised that the *Burscombe* was now in a precarious position. It would not take much for her to go the same way as the *Godham*.

The *Moltke* was still coming on, the good half of her main armament still aimed straight at him. The only choice he seemed to have was to pump a superior weight of shells into the enemy's decks in the shortest amount of time possible, and try to get a lucky hit straight down one of the funnels into a boiler room or something. It was unlikely that he could simply outrun them. He still had his three torpedoes but he had just committed them to an attack on the destroyers.

The DCT found the range again and the oft repeated procedures of instructions sent through the Transmitting Station and deciphered for the gunners went on flawlessly. The guns fired once more. The sight of new flashes from the muzzles of the Moltke's guns filled Dollimore with the sense of all initiative passing away. He could not win against that.

Somehow the Burscombe's shells found their mark first. Sixteen terrible explosions erupted around the enemy. Most of it was water being thrown skyward but, for what it was worth, fresh flame and smoke told of more hits. A couple of seconds later three 11-inch shells exploded in the water either side of the *Burscombe* and splinters again peppered the waists and tore a gigantic hole in the front of the forward funnel. With the sea boiling around them, it suddenly became sickening that the battle was devolving into such a barbaric slogging match.

The starboard torpedoes were fired off at the same time and they cut their way through the maelstrom. Too much was going on now. There was great desperation in every action taken. Dollimore, having failed to save the *Godham* and not possessing the power to destroy these three enemy ships, had to find a way of opening the range before the *Burscombe* was also lost.

Time elapsed swiftly and his torpedoes disappeared forever into the depths without even threatening the destroyers. As he watched, his adversaries gradually got into a position to fire their own tin fish making him call down for Bretonworth to push for more speed. It only remained for the *Burscombe* to try and escape and continue feeding information to Forbes so that he might perhaps intercept this enemy and wreak his long overdue havoc.

'Steer a course due south!' Dollimore ordered as more 11-inch shells exploded either side of him. His reluctance and disappointment were apparent to all.

Then came Peterson's cry, 'Sir, the destroyers!'

Even as Dollimore turned to look in the direction indicated, the belated sound of a great explosion came to him across the mile and a half of distance between them. The foremost vessel was spewing fire from her cracked hull and splitting apart amidships. In seconds her bow and stern were raising up in the air as her middle collapsed and was sucked under the waves. It was as quick, lethal and as sickening as the destruction of HMS *Defence* had been all those years ago. 'A torpedo hit?' he asked incredulously.

'Not from us, sir,' Peterson said. 'Ours missed. The explosion came from the other side.'

All binoculars were used to scan the grey horizon but there did not seem to be anything there. 'Bridge, foretop,' eventually came Smudge's voice from the nearby pipe. 'Three British destroyers sighted, bearing green one zero zero!'

'Ah ha!' Dollimore said, which was as close to an exclamation of excitement as he was ever going to let slip in front of the men. Those that witnessed it felt that that moment told them more about his real character than every other moment and mood combined.

Very slowly, three tiny shadows crept out of the gloom with gun flashes erupting from their bows. The small gun of the remaining German destroyer was now trained round to fend off the new threat but her captain was soon breaking off the action and turning hard to port in order to cut away eastwards.

'The Moltke's running too,' reported Digby, who had never taken his eyes off the main enemy. It was barely believable yet true. That superior monster had completely disengaged and was trying to open the range.

'Steer port zero nine zero and continue at this speed,' ordered Dollimore in triumph. 'We must keep after them. Mr Digby, if you want a photograph, right now would be an opportune moment.'

Digby smiled and quickly pulled his camera from the waterproof case. The *Moltke* only appeared as a dark smudge in the lens but he took a couple of pictures anyway. Then he snapped away at the Burscombe's fo'c'sle where the thick smoke was still pouring out of the hole just by A-Turret, but the one that he knew would be the gem was that of Captain Dollimore and Lt-Cdr Peterson glancing grimly in his direction, their faces blackened and wearing battle-weary expressions.

The Burscombe's guns continued to deliver shells onto and around the targets as they ran. Dollimore said, 'Don't let up just yet.' Upon reflection it was incredible how swiftly the tables had turned. The three fast British destroyers eventually fell in on the Burscombe's port quarter about a thousand yards away. The Chief Yeoman of the Signals quickly studied the flags that he could see hoisted on the ships' foremasts and said, 'It's Commander Fulton-Stavely, sir.'

Digby grinned. 'Not a man to be caught with his trousers around his ankles twice, eh.'

Even though he fully understood the reference to the commander's blunder on the night of the Pentland Firth breakthrough, Dollimore still frowned at Digby's choice of imagery. But there was no reproach spoken this time.

The slackened thunder of the British guns went on as the *Moltke* and her little sidekick thrashed their way through the waves. With no working armament facing aft their engines were the only trump card they had left against these odds. The German officer in command had obviously decided that they must run or die.

However, Dollimore's elation had passed quickly and the old sour look was returning to his face.

'Is everything alright, sir?' asked Peterson.

Speaking so that only he could hear, Dollimore said, 'If I've made one mistake during this skirmish it's not allowing for this moment. If he can get one knot on us he might just get away.'

Then Peterson realised the problem. At the moment the *Moltke* broke away she had been in a good position to run for the Baltic without having to get past the *Burscombe*. Dollimore could hardly have done anything about that but he blamed himself nonetheless.

*

CPO Doyle, exhausted but undefeated, was able to report the fires in the fore part of the ship extinguished. Behaving as calmly as though he was just taking tea, though secretly shuddering, he spoke to Lieutenant Selkirk, who listened to the report with discernible horror.

'Thanks, chief,' replied the lieutenant, who immediately picked up the phone, flipped the switch for the exchange and wound the handle to stir the generator. 'Get me the bridge.'

Within seconds the captain was on the other end of the line.

From his tiny Damage Control Base on the fringe of the trouble area, with lingering smoke overpowering the ventilation system and the occasional crash of the guns directly overhead, Selkirk said with a tremor, 'We're making water up forrard, sir. If we don't slow down it'll overwhelm the pumps.'

'I'm busy chasing a German raider, Number One,' came the tinny, aggravated reply. 'Be more specific.'

'We're taking water in through a twelve foot hole in 2 Charlie. Most of the deck has gone in that section so 3 is flooded and water is penetrating to 4 Deck due to a burst hatch.'

'But my magazines are okay?'

'The magazines are okay but we're down a couple of feet by the head, sir. Plus, we don't like the look of the bulkhead between Charlie and Dog. We're doing what we can but the shipwrights say that with this pitching it might give way.'

'Inform me if the situation becomes critical,' finished Dollimore impatiently, then came the click of the receiver being slammed down.

Selkirk turned to Doyle. 'Captain's not stopping for love nor money. Come with me, chief. We'll have to shore it up some more.'

A look of hard concentration appeared on Doyle's face as he immediately began planning how he was going to perform this task. 'Don't see as how we've got a choice, sir.'

*

Dollimore stood at the front of the bridge with the wind and spray in his face, willing his ship to go faster. They were making twenty six knots and that was with every plate and rivet straining against the rush of the angry sea. Now about three thousand yards off the port bow, Fulton-Stavely's destroyers were doing slightly better having overtaken him, keeping pace with the enemy. But the essential and damning truth was that the *Moltke*, better suited to the conditions and powered by first class engines, was making more than that extra knot that he so begrudged them and was getting away.

Very nearly resigned to letting go, he turned and said, 'Chief, send a signal to Fulton-Stavely. "Shadow *Moltke* and report movements to C-in-C Home Fleet. No heroics, please."'

As the range lengthened, the intermittent shots fired from A and B Turrets were more and more scattered and eventually they ceased firing altogether.

He knew what was coming next though he continued to stall for a further ten minutes while he delayed the inevitable and hoped for a miracle. Then, sighing, he picked up the phone and called down to Selkirk. 'How's that bulkhead doing, Number One?'

'Groaning insufferably, sir. There's still a chance it could collapse.'

'Thank you.' With the outcome a certainty, he still watched his escaping quarry for another couple of minutes before leaning over the voicepipe to say, 'Reduce speed to twenty knots. Steer onto a bearing of west-north-west.' Then, 'Pilot, please give me the last known position of the *Godham*. We must go back and see if anyone survived.'

He watched Fulton-Stavely's dashing little destroyers disappearing off to the east until there was nothing but sea and snow to be seen. That convinced him that it was well and truly over.

Chapter Sixteen

Like Father, Like Son

'Please do accept my condolences,' Eddington said. 'Your father was a brave man.'

'Yes, he was,' Young Clark conceded. 'Though God knows our poor relationship was as common knowledge as it was embarrassing. To me he was many bad things but that he was brave I can't deny.' He was seated in the tiny cabin which had been designated as the gunroom while he was on board this sloop, and Eddington was standing in the doorway having popped by to say his piece.

They were aboard HMS *Grey Tor* which was heading down to Rosyth for a refit. Her particular departure from Kirkwall had been timely and Eddington had seen it as the perfect way to get back to the *Burscombe* without any more delay. The officer in command, Lieutenant Watkins, happily made room for the men of the prize crew and enquired eagerly after whatever details they could safely impart of their adventure. Clark spoke happily enough of it all now but he would never forget how glad he had been to see the back of the *Trier Stern* after she and her prisoners had been handed over to the relevant authorities. The whole affair had been exhilarating but exhausting.

Sipping at his steaming cup of hot chocolate, Eddington said, 'Clark, your father's bravery continues with you. I want you to know that that's what I believe. My report includes all that you did out there so the captain should be nothing if not pleased with you.'

'Thanks.'

Thinking back on the very illuminating conversation they had had with the intelligence officer who had come on board the *Trier Stern*, Eddington asked, 'One thing that's been bothering me, though. How was it you managed to guess that that Gurtner chap was actually one of von Ribbentrop's troop from the German Foreign Ministry?'

'Well, firstly he was a bit too old to be a reservist, wouldn't you say? Plus he was important enough to need escorting by a battlecruiser.'

'But the Foreign Ministry? I mean, the captain showed me a communication on German ministers and other officials who might be trying to reach Germany, but that was weeks ago and I'd forgotten all about it.' Eddington was looking a little troubled by his oversight.

Clark decided to mischievously rub his nose in it anyway. 'A couple of months ago there was an article in *The Times* on the subject. They quite coincidentally printed a photograph of him to illustrate their point. When I saw him emerge from the tiller flat I recalled the article to mind. Of course, he was more neatly attired in the picture.'

Eventually, Eddington grinned. 'I see. Well done, Clark. As I said, the captain should be more than happy with you.'

'Thanks,' Clark said again but his mind was already drifting back to the unfinished business he had with Farlow. As a throwaway remark he said, 'It would be great if you could get Commander Crawshaw to feel the same way. I swear I must have shot him dead in a previous life.'

'Ah,' said Eddington, looking a little uncomfortable, 'but surely that's more your father's fault than yours.'

'Excuse me?'

'Oh, come off it...,' Eddington said, realising that he had just put his foot in it.

'Don't stop there,' said Clark, going red in the face as tension built up inside him. He still had in mind how that fat idiot Farlow had sought to antagonise him when they were preparing to launch the cutter with the boarding party. He was nothing but a jealous rabble-rouser but the same could not be said of this man here. 'There's obviously something everybody knows that I don't.'

'Well, there are rumours,' said Eddington, wishing somehow that there were not.

'Go on.'

'Don't you know that Crawshaw and your father were once friends a long time ago?' asked Eddington, hardly believing that he was saying the words. 'They had some big falling out and Crawshaw's been held back in his career ever since. That's how he lost all chance of ever becoming a captain, let alone a flag officer.'

'The Indian Ocean,' Clark mumbled. Stunned, he got up and slowly pushed past Eddington so that he could get out onto the deck for some air.

'Are you alright, old boy?' asked the lieutenant.

After all the powers of perception that Clark had been credited with over this Gurtner business, he had been very slow to see the answer to a mystery twenty years in the making, and which had been affecting his every move these last four months. That gnawed at him as much as the truth itself. 'They were both in the Indian Ocean...'

So, Derek Crawshaw was the man whom his father had thrown from the steps of North Cedars Hall all those years ago? Clark pictured his father's malicious face as he had sat in his sinful retreat and said, 'You will always just be that last unwanted offspring from a dying marriage'. It had always been his intention for this story to come out. Why else would he have assigned him to the same ship as Crawshaw? Had the old bastard hated him that much?

*

Pincher got the round of beers in and pushed his way back through the crowd to the table where Smudge and Les were seated. The jovial atmosphere in the pub had immediately lifted their spirits after twenty minutes of trudging through the snow in the blackout. In that time a car had nearly flattened Les as it skidded this way and that, then an icicle had fallen from a shop sign, nearly clumping him on the head. 'Somebody doesn't want you to make it,' said Smudge.

Now, with the beers set out on the table before them, Pincher and Smudge smiled while Les looked at them suspiciously. Smudge reached into the canvas bag that he had been carrying with him and pulled out a crumpled book, a half-incinerated volume smelling of foul ash. It was Les's *Les Misérables*. The one his dad had given him.

'Hold on before you say anything,' said Smudge, still smiling. 'Now, everybody knows that *Les Misérables* is an impossibly long book so the Germans decided to edit it for you.'

Les, aghast, reached out and touched the book. More ashes flaked from its mangled cover.

'Get to the point,' said Pincher.

Smudge reached back into the bag and pulled out another large volume, another copy of the same book but with a finer, burgundy binding. 'Here, we got this for yer. We know you're only on page two but we don't want yer to give up on it.' After a pause, he straightened up and said, 'Don't cry! Is he gonna cry?'

But then Les pointed at something that had been partially exposed in the bag. It seemed to have colourful pictures on it. 'What's that one?'

'Oh, that's mine,' said Smudge.

'To be honest, I'd much prefer to have that.'

'I told you, it's mine,' protested Smudge.

Pincher laughed and said, 'Go on, let him have it. Didn't we agree that he was the hero of the *Trier Stern*?'

Sighing, Smudge reached into the bag and pulled out his *Beano* comic. 'There you go. But you'll 'ave to lend it to me when I want it.'

Les nodded and, while looking at the bizarre drawings of some sort of ostrich causing everybody trouble, pushed the *Les Misérables* back across the table.

'No, you can keep that an' all,' said Smudge dourly.

*

HMS *Burscombe* was sitting on the huge blocks of one of the dry docks at Rosyth, her flat red keel, rudder and propellers exposed for all to see. It had been deemed necessary to withdraw her from active service for at least a month while repairs were made. Fortunately most of the damage from her inconclusive duel with the *Moltke* was superficial and the time was going to be taken up with strengthening the decks, bulkheads and fittings around the foremost messdecks and the officers' cabins flat underneath the quarterdeck.

Whilst in the dry dock, she was carefully checked for any underwater damage and then the crew set about scraping the barnacles and other marine growth off the keel, not such an inviting prospect with the onset of winter. But with great significance to good morale, the men were given the long leave that they were due – two weeks each to the port and starboard watches.

With a string of temporary lights hanging throughout the length of the hollow, stinking shell that was the wrecked mess down on 3 Deck, Commander Crawshaw listened to the shipwrights' learned opinions on what was necessary to bring this place back to life. Dockyard engineers were already bustling about in between them, measuring, taking notes, studying plans, diagrams and photographs in order to get started on the work.

As they talked they ducked under the jagged steel of the hole in the deckhead that had been left by the 11-inch shell coursing through it. Up above, tarpaulins covered the hole in the side of the ship so that the snow or the rain could not hamper the efforts of the welders.

'We're lucky really, sir,' said one of the shipwrights. 'Once we've reinforced the decks and bulkheads, it's just a matter of fitting out with pipes, electrics and the bits and pieces of the accommodation. We've got more help than we need. After all, the country needs us back out there and not stuck in here.'

Crawshaw nodded in agreement and climbed up the ladder to continue checking on progress further aft. He wanted to get this over and done with as quickly as possible because he was to spend the evening with Anne, the lovely woman that he had been working on these last two months or so. He was quite determined that he was going to take her to bed this time around. What had made up his mind on that fact was that heavy piece of shrapnel which had whirred right past his head at a couple of hundred miles per hour during that awful fight. If it had been travelling an inch or two to the right then he would have been one of those on the list of fatalities. He was not impressed by that and it had made him realise that slowing down his relationship and taking things in their stride was a mistake. He did not want her mind or her favour, he wanted her looks and her body and that was what he was going to get. So getting this inspection out of the way needed to be done quick-smart.

As he walked along the waist past the holed galley he saw Midshipman Clark walking towards him. He felt an inward surge of annoyance the second he saw him. Clark was one of the few people who had the uncanny ability to achieve that and it had been made worse on account of his growing jealousy. Apparently the lad had acquitted himself superbly when they had had a spot of bother on the prize ship. Surely that would only make him more insufferable than before.

Even thinking that, it still took him by surprise when Clark stopped him and said, 'Sir, may I have a talk with you?'

'No, you may not,' answered Crawshaw, his temper almost immediately getting the better of him.

'Well, I'm afraid I'm going to talk with you whether you like it or not.'

Crawshaw, seeing red with the justification of all he had ever thought of this boy, shouted, 'Who the bloody hell do you think you are?'

Men working nearby looked up in surprise. The commander had really lost it over something this time. Ah, it was that midshipman again, the one who always seemed to be at the centre of everything.

'Get back to your work!' Crawshaw shouted at the stunned onlookers. Then to Clark he said, 'And you, lad, are going to find out what trouble really is.'

'Fine,' Clark said, unperturbed, 'but I will still talk with you.'

Crawshaw, full of rage, grabbed hold of Clark's arm and led him to the Sound Reproduction Equipment Room, it being the nearest place that would afford them any privacy. Clark allowed himself to be led.

'Clear out,' Crawshaw said to the electrician, who had stopped tinkering with some exposed wires to turn and discover the manner of the intrusion. Quickly taking up his soldering iron, he scarpered.

'Well?'

Clark started directly with, 'I'd like to talk about the part you played in messing up my life.'

'What?' Now Crawshaw was stunned. 'What claptrap is this?'

'You were my father's friend at the end of the last war,' Clark blurted out on his unstoppable tide of anger. 'You went behind his back and had an affair with my mother.'

Curling his lips in disgust, Crawshaw asked, 'Who told you that?'

'Everybody else seems to be aware of the history between you. How my father has held you back all these years so you'd never reach captain, which would explain your animosity towards me. How you served in the Indian Ocean with him but then had a falling out over my mother, which in turn destroyed any decent family life that I might have expected.'

'Stop right there before you make more of a fool of yourself than you already have,' Crawshaw said. 'People feed you titbits, you add two and two together and get five. That's how it is, isn't it? Rather typical Clark behaviour. Who did you get this rubbish from?'

'It was one of the last things my father told me.'

'And he said it was *me* ?'

'Not in so many words...,' Clark faltered. Crawshaw was very convincing with his look of innocence but then it was probably a well-rehearsed counter-attack made simple by a lifetime of deceit. It made Clark feel that he had perhaps made a mistake but he knew deep down that he had not.

Crawshaw shook his head. 'Boy, you're a hopeless case. It's one thing being indiscreet in front of the men but to accuse your commander of something like this and think to get away with it? God help me, I don't know why the captain thought that a backward snotty like you would settle into a service that you have little understanding or respect for. You're finished, you know that?'

As he said those last words, the door was opening and the imposing figure of Captain Dollimore filled the space with the struggling daylight seeping in behind him. Wiping some grease from his hands with a rag, he looked from one to the other and said, 'Anything I should know about?'

Crawshaw, keeping his composure perfectly, said, 'I've dealt with it, sir.'

'Because just about everybody heard you shouting, Mr Crawshaw.'

Clark, his whole future in the balance, struck out with, 'Sir, I won't be able to serve in the *Burscombe* anymore. I shall need to trans...,'

'I'll deal with you properly, boy!' Crawshaw growled. This midshipman should not have a chance to get the upper hand. 'I'll sort it all out, sir.'

Dollimore looked suspiciously at both men and felt a rising anger over this irresponsible display. He could easily tell that whatever was taking place here was nothing to do with the ship and he could not abide people who would bring their personal problems into his sphere of influence in such a way. 'Perhaps you would like to run it by me now.'

'Sir?'

'By law this is my ship, Mr Crawshaw. Everything and everyone in it is my concern, so one of you will tell me what happened.' Dollimore had rarely been more serious about anything in his life. Good service over these last months or not, Crawshaw's approach to things in general had always fallen short of Dollimore's ideals – and Clark? Exceptionally gifted in certain areas but still possessing the mind of a wayward teenager. Not good enough.

Crawshaw sighed and started cautiously, 'This impudent brat thinks to accuse me that I had an affair with his mother. *Twenty years ago!*'

Dollimore's flabbergasted stare went from one to the other. Even though it finally settled upon Crawshaw, he said, 'Mr Clark, you will leave this ship immediately. Go ashore and await further orders.'

Understanding that his conduct had well and truly ruined everything but still showing no remorse, he silently walked past the captain and made to go ashore for the last time.

When they were alone, Dollimore said to Crawshaw, 'Derek, I was as clear as I could possibly be when I told you what would happen if your private affairs impinged upon our work.'

'But you must see that I have not done anything, sir,' protested Crawshaw.

'This is just like when we were at college. You spent so much energy on dodging the issues...,'

Crawshaw shook his head, knowing real despair. 'I knew you could never put those days from your mind. Have I not served this ship well enough to erase the past?'

'It seems to me that the past has just come back to bite you rather hard,' said Dollimore. After a pause of reflection, he continued, 'As it is, I have no wish to destroy you. Get back to work for now and I'll see about arranging for you a transfer which holds some sort of dignity.'

'Sir, please don't do that. Don't I deserve the benefit of the doubt? The same way you did after you rammed the *Spikefish*?' Crawshaw immediately cursed himself for playing that card.

'That will be all, Mr Crawshaw,' snarled Dollimore.

Then, with the captain gone, Crawshaw could only stand and wonder at how everything had fallen apart so fast. Charles Dollimore had been such a dull boy at college that it had been dubious as to whether he had had enough character to even be noticed. Yet here he was over three decades later, more senior and more powerful than Crawshaw could ever hope to be, toying with his fate over some stuffy morals which hardly anyone ever lived by anymore. This was just one more cruel twist in a long line of intrusions by various officers over the years who had sought to keep him subdued.

He thought of Old Man Clark, the late rear-admiral. The bastard would be laughing at him from his watery grave. How that man had affected his life more than any other was truly remarkable. Even after his death it still went on.

That evening, after he had dispiritedly finished up his reports, he sat in the quiet of a hotel room and decided against meeting Anne. His mind was too preoccupied with the thought of setting David Clark on the right path. He had considered the idea of never speaking to him again so that the little upstart would always know the certain shame of what he thought was the truth, then considered writing him a letter so that he would know how he had unjustly destroyed an innocent man. But writing letters was not really his style. He wanted to see Clark's face when he learned what his family's history was really all about.

An hour later this fifty three year old washout of a commander was handing the nineteen year old failure of a midshipman a glass of brandy. Both had resolved to talk in as civil a fashion as possible and to this end they sat warily opposite each other before the log fire in the room. A high wind had sprung up outside and was rattling the window pane but after knowing the fury of the North Sea, it hardly encroached upon their consciousness at all.

'Why did you do it?' asked Clark, struggling to hold his intense dislike at bay. To add to everything else he was also busy suppressing the hurt that he felt over the discovery that Beatty had been privy to these rumours and had somehow not said anything. 'It's one thing if you want to play about, but why would you try to steal another man's wife, the wife of a good friend?'

Crawshaw said, 'Having drawn the conclusions you have, you're obviously missing some vital facts.'

'So you still deny it?'

'Absolutely I do. However, I do know what really happened. The blame for all this unpleasantness falls upon two people, both of whom are no longer with us. Your father – hold on before you say anything – and my brother, Paul. He was older than me and, although he too had something of a wild character, he had the promise of being a better officer than I will ever be. You were right that a Crawshaw served with your father in the Indian Ocean at the end of the last war but it was Paul, not me. I was there but based in Trincomalee. They were both in Bombay.

'Their friendship was a good one which revolved around a mutual appreciation of drink and women. Does that surprise you that Harper was messing around? I can see that it doesn't. Anyway, my brother was invited on occasion to holiday at North Cedars Hall and was generally accepted as pleasant company. He liked both your parents so much that he even began to try and talk Harper out of his extra-marital affairs so that he might pay more attention to her. But who could tell him anything? I rather think that Paul's advice had the opposite effect. He detected a continual downward shift in the respect that your parents showed each other and eventually Harper managed to decide that what was really going on was an affair between my brother and Dorothy. It was a stupid supposition.'

Clark said, 'Father told me that he found my mother and your brother with their hands upon each other and so he flung him out of the house.'

'Is that all he told you about that night?'

'What more is there to it?' said Clark, his face distinctly showing that he was tiring of the story. 'He said there was an affair and you say there wasn't. Somehow his story rings more true.'

Crawshaw's expression became deadly serious as he leaned slightly forward in his chair. He said, 'Listen to me. Harper Clark was hopelessly drunk that night. Drawing all the wrong conclusions in his filthy haze, he did indeed cast him violently from the house. Harper acted like a madman and could not see reason. So it was that Paul found himself out on the road lacking any sort of transport. It being a late hour, he walked to the inn in the village to secure a room for the rest of the night.'

'Gufford's place?' asked Clark, not at all liking how the facts of the story were slotting together.

'That I couldn't tell you, but I know that it was not far from the hall. In the meantime Harper and Dorothy must have argued further for it ended with your father coming to look for Paul again. Having traced him to the inn, he tried to force his way up to his room but the landlady was blocking his way.' Crawshaw's face took on the pale look of abhorrence as he considered his next words. 'That was when he attacked her with the riding crop he'd taken with him. Paul was the first on the scene and tried to stop it, receiving several blows himself from the madman.'

'Apparently, though, the innkeeper himself was a bit of a handy sort, a demobbed soldier, Paul said. He disarmed your father and expelled him from the building. But not before Harper had seriously hurt both the woman and my brother. Paul had been knocked unconscious against the bar.'

Clark brought his hand up and rubbed his chin in worried contemplation. Now it all came back to him. That day when he had asked his mother just what father had done to the Guffords, she had said, 'Something so awful that it cost us a lot of money to buy their silence...,'

'Christ,' he said, 'no wonder she couldn't talk about it.' And no wonder she went to such pains to separate Maggie from me. But of course he did not voice that bit for the doubtful benefit of this man before him now.

Crawshaw said, 'I see that everything I've said fits whatever facts you already have at your disposal. Now do you believe me?'

Suppressing the pain, Clark asked, 'What happened to your brother? Where is he now?'

'He's dead. He died of a brain haemorrhage about two years after that incident. I believe that it was as a result of what Harper did to him that night, but of course that can't ever be proved.'

'So did my father hold you back in your career because of your name?'

Crawshaw laughed. 'Good lord, no. Even he doesn't go off seeking quarrels unreal, or at least, unperceived. I sought him out and told him I knew him for the lowlife piece of shit that he was and all but accused him of murder. Needless to say I found it very difficult to get on after that and realised far too late that a family with the money and connections that yours has was more than a match for the modesty of the Crawshaws.'

Now knowing all these facts and, through their plausibility, utterly believing them to be the truth, Clark thought about the trouble he had caused this day. Crawshaw himself was soon to be dismissed from the *Burscombe*. That particular eventuality had not even occurred to him when he started up with the issue though it had filled him with satisfaction when he heard it. That satisfaction was now replaced with a deep guilt. 'I'm so sorry, for everything.'

'Don't be,' said Crawshaw with scorn, 'it won't make me like you any better. You're just another Harper Clark in the making, a selfish, horrible little busybody who's going to bring grief everywhere you go. It's who you are.' He studied the boy's aching remorse and smiled. That was what he had set out to achieve when he had summoned him. The boy had been put in his place.

Clark stood up to leave, placing the glass of brandy on the mantelpiece. It was misted by the condensation from his sweaty palm and he had not touched the contents. 'Sir,' he said in some feeble attempt at respect, 'why did you stay silent about my father's behaviour all these years? Yes, he was a powerful opponent but he didn't pay *you* off.'

'What makes you so sure?' smiled Crawshaw. 'I know more than you imagine and I too am capable of anything. Remember that.'

Clark walked the streets with the wind buffeting him all the way though he hardly registered this as he attempted to digest all that he had learned and how his own actions had brought ultimate ruin. To him, his father had been despicable and unstable in his outlook and he had always despised that. The problem was, however, he had now been told more than once of the resemblance that he bore him and at this dark time, he could conjure up no objections to that point of view.

*

HMS *Warspite*, now sitting moored at a quayside up the Clyde, was not quite the same ship that once she was. A few short years ago she had undergone a multi-million pound refit which had seen the removal of her vintage bridge, fighting top and twin smoke-stacks. They had been replaced with a stronger, more streamlined superstructure and a single modern funnel. Complete with faster engines, she gave the impression of being more powerful than ever.

Dollimore, walking these decks for the first time since 1916, thought on those changes and knew beyond the shadow of a doubt that, although you could change her skin, her heart still remained the same as before. Looking at the faces of the young men who had charge of her now, he could see in them those of the past, the Collins and the Hackletts, the same sort of men with the same sort of aspirations. *Warspite* and her crew were as proud as ever they were.

The old girl herself had once been battered and scarred but then she had been rejuvenated and he realised that her life mirrored his own. While ever a ship or a person had people who cared for them they could overcome anything. He wondered what sort of man he would be if he had not had his family to sustain him across the years.

Ah well, enough of the nostalgia and reflection, he thought. There is still business to attend to.

A few minutes later, Admiral Forbes was gesturing for Dollimore to sit in one of the armchairs in his well heated quarters in the stern of the ship. With the winter properly setting in, any extra heat that could be found was welcome. Looking more relaxed than he felt, Forbes perched himself casually on the edge of his desk. 'You have your pipe? Please feel free to smoke.'

Dollimore looked at his superior as he lit a match. The admiral appeared somewhat wearier than the last time he had seen him. It seemed that a lot was being asked of men like him but with the Germans successfully making their lives so difficult it could be argued that they were not being asked enough. The very reason that Forbes was residing here in the *Warspite* was because his own flagship, HMS *Nelson*, one of the prides of the fleet, had been damaged by one of those damned magnetic mines at the entrance of the Loch Ewe anchorage. So she was now added to the growing list of ships that were laid up in dry dock for repairs. If Jerry kept this up then the dockyards were going to have to perform miracles to keep pace.

'My apologies for making this short and sweet,' said Forbes, 'but as you see, we're making ready to sail again. I'm taking the squadron out again in two hours. No rest for the wicked.'

Dollimore puffed on his pipe and waited for the admiral to continue.

'It looks very much like the *Moltke* will be out of action for some months judging by the damage you and Nunn inflicted upon her. However, we're not going to make a huge fuss about it. After all she got clean away after sinking one of our ships, damaging another and killing one of our admirals. I happen to know that Hitler is crowing about it to all and sundry and God knows he deserves to.'

'Sir,' said Dollimore, launching into the diatribe that Forbes had been expecting. 'There were obvious factors which ensured her getting away. Not least of these was the scattering of the squadron to different sectors miles apart from each other...'

Forbes held up his hand to stop him. 'Yes, I've read your report and your recommendations and all will be considered in due course but you must realise the strain we are under. We have many obligations.'

Dollimore wondered if part of Forbes' agitation was down to the fact that he had sortied with the Home Fleet many times now as a result of surface raider action and still had failed to make contact with the enemy. However, with all said and done, there was a part of the wider result that Dollimore was eager to defend. 'I do, however, think it's significant that we prevented the *Moltke* from making her rendezvous, allowing us to capture one of their ships and a valuable prisoner. That should be something worth being thankful for.'

'Of course,' conceded Forbes. 'The single positive part of the action. Winston Churchill has also recognised this and I've received a signal from him to that effect.'

Dollimore felt vindicated at the news until the admiral added, 'I don't know if you knew that the Churchills and the Clarks have been personal acquaintances in the past. Winston has passed on his regrets at the loss of the rear-admiral and has been pleased to note the heroic part that his son played in the *Trier Stern* affair. He and I would be very much obliged if you could pass this on to young David.' At Dollimore's frown, he asked, 'What is it?'

'I've been compelled to put Midshipman Clark ashore, sir. His performance shows no consistency. He's something of an obstinate lad, a bit too individualistic for my taste.'

Forbes shook his head and said sternly, 'Reverse your order and reinstate him.'

'I beg your pardon?'

'*The Times* will shortly be running an article on the late admiral and his son, 'the ancient family upholds the traditions of bravery in the name of Britain and the Empire' and all that rubbish.'

'I don't want him on my ship,' said Dollimore.

'This is important to public morale, captain, and you don't get a choice in the matter. People have got it into their heads that there's nothing going on in this war. Somebody has even started calling it a 'phoney war'. I don't much care for that, so I don't care if you have to put the boy over the capstan and cane him until he can't walk, but reinstate him. The perception is to be that he is a credit to the service as a man of action.'

'Like his father was?' Dollimore said, loathing himself for stooping to sarcasm.

Forbes understood well enough the reason for it. The knowledge that Rear-Admiral Clark had had some sort of nervous breakdown and was taken from the Godham's bridge at the sight of the enemy had only very narrowly been suppressed. The commander and the sole remaining bridge rating were the only two men from that ship who knew it for a certainty. It was just as important not to let the Germans know as to not let the British public know what happened out there.

However, Dollimore in turn did not care for allowing a sick, possibly even a cowardly man being honoured when the real honour belonged to Captain Nunn and the rest of his ship's company. But he was nothing if not farsighted and his practicality easily served to outweigh his emotional instinct. That was why he sent his report on that matter to Forbes in a completely separate package to the official report of the action. The secrecy was essential.

Forbes appreciated his stance and even went so far as to think – but not say – that this man here might one day make something of himself as a flag officer. 'Does anybody else know of this business besides us and those two from the *Godham*?'

'Just Commander Crawshaw and he understands the delicate nature of it.'

'Good.' Forbes stood up from his perch. Dollimore immediately took the cue and rose as well. They shook hands.

The admiral said, 'Don't ever think that I do not appreciate your efforts, Charles. When all's said and done, I thought your Pentland Firth caper was rather good, you were right about Scapa Flow and you did manage to give the *Moltke* a pretty good hiding.' After a pause, he finished up with, 'Anyway, with your ship laid up in dock for repairs, I suppose you'll be having to spend Christmas at home with your wife. I wish you both the compliments of the season.'

Just as Dollimore was about to thank him and return the gesture, there came a hasty knock at the door and a young lieutenant entered without waiting to be invited. His eyes were alive with the excitement of something very positive. All he said was, 'Sir,' and then allowed presenting the admiral with an envelope to suggest the rest.

Forbes opened it and quickly read the signal. He smiled a weary smile but his words were more upbeat than his expression. 'At last. You'll recall, Charles, that another of our squadrons came to blows with an enemy raider in the South Atlantic a few days ago?'

'The *Graf Spee*. Isn't she trapped in Montivideo Harbour?'

'She's scuttled herself. This is the sort of news we need, something to burst the bubble of this 'phoney war' business. People have got to know that the navy's not stopped since this whole thing began.'

It was good news indeed and its timely arrival did serve to bring a warm feeling to Dollimore's heart. It told of a more offensive approach to the conduct of the war. He hoped that once this winter was past and the calmer, brighter days of spring came round such a stronger direction would be taken against the Germans here in the North Sea. Oh, if only he had sunk the *Moltke*!

He left the interview and the *Warspite* with mixed feelings of pride and frustration. Though he was sure that he had put some distance between himself and the shadows that were Jutland and HMS *Spikefish*, he also felt let down by this whole affair with Crawshaw and the Clarks. But he supposed that in time their follies would count for nothing once the war really got underway.

Nineteen thirty-nine had been a turbulent year with as many peaks and troughs as the sea herself. There had been inexcusable failures, fears and terrible losses but there had also been some keen successes. For Dollimore himself, he took comfort from the knowledge that both his family and his ship, though scarred, were not cowed and that Adolf Hitler would never win, no matter who the hell he thought he was.

He walked down the gangway onto the quayside to the shrill whistling of the bosun's call. When it had died away the sounds of commotion and activity, the solemn preparations for another stormy voyage, took precedence again. For once all the bustle had nothing to do with him. He walked away from the Clyde upon the snowy cobbles and did not care to look back at the great battleship as she built up steam. He simply pulled his scarf tighter around his neck, turned his thoughts to home, and walked on.

GLOSSARY

brownhatter - homosexual
bulkhead - wall
deckhead - ceiling
freeboard – the distance from waterline to weatherdeck
leeside - side away from the worst of the weather
marlin spike - tool for tightening shackles and bottle-screws
matelot - sailor
OOD - Officer-of-the-Day
pusser - official gear owned and issued by the navy
scran - food

Made in the USA
Las Vegas, NV
23 August 2023

76470192R00184